Marmee

Also by Sarah Miller

Caroline: Little House, Revisited

Marmee

A Novel

Sarah Miller

WILLIAM MORROW
An Imprint of HarperCollins*Publishers*

MARMEE. Copyright © 2022 by Sarah Miller. All rights reserved. Printed in the United States of America. No part of this book may be used or reproduced in any manner whatsoever without written permission except in the case of brief quotations embodied in critical articles and reviews. For information, address HarperCollins Publishers, 195 Broadway, New York, NY 10007.

HarperCollins books may be purchased for educational, business, or sales promotional use. For information, please email the Special Markets Department at SPsales@harpercollins.com.

A hardcover edition of this book was published in 2022 by William Morrow, an imprint of HarperCollins Publishers.

FIRST WILLIAM MORROW PAPERBACK EDITION PUBLISHED 2023.

Designed by Elina Cohen
Title page illustration © World History Archive/Alamy Stock Photo

Library of Congress Cataloging-in-Publication Data has been applied for.

ISBN 978-0-06-304188-2

23 24 25 26 27 LBC 5 4 3 2 1

To Mom and Dad

❧

You have not lived today until you have done something for someone who can never repay you.

~JOHN BUNYAN

PART FIRST

December 24, 1861

All day long, Amos's letter waited in my pocket—the most perfect of Christmas gifts. If not for Isobel Carter, I might have stolen a peek.

But the Carter boy, missing since the Battle of Ball's Bluff, is reported fallen today. The strands of hope, stretched so bravely across these last eight weeks, are cut. Thin as those threads had become, the severance is no less abrupt than if the news had come the very morning after the battle.

How bravely Mrs. Carter carried on with her duty after the telegram came! It wrung my heart to see the tender way she packed the Christmas boxes, as if each article of comfort was her own boy, being gently laid to sleep.

Nineteen years old. Drowned in retreating across the Potomac, his body swept downstream into an abandoned canal at Goose Creek. How it sickens me to think of that bright boy floating there all this time with the minnows feasting on a mind worthy of Harvard. If not for the engraving on his school ring, his family would never have known his fate.

For myself, I can only be thankful that the families who receive the boxes I filled after the news arrived will not perceive the fury that vibrated in the hands that packed them. It is not the first time my mind has railed at the folly of that battle. One thousand and two men, killed, wounded, or captured, raiding a Confederate camp that did not exist. Noah Carter's was no kind of sacrifice, only a waste. What pride is there for his family in such a death?

We delude ourselves, I suppose, if we imagine all our brave boys dying valiantly on the field. Perhaps their true courage is not in being willing to fight, but in their willingness to face the likelihood of such an ignominious end.

Which is harsher, I wonder—to lose a son this way, in the prime of youth, or as I did, before he ever drew breath? I think of that beautiful stillborn infant, with his blue-gray skin and deep red lips, and wonder, had he lived, would he be fighting now? I doubt if I would possess the strength to endure sending both a husband and a son off to war.

With Mrs. Carter grieving silently beside me I did not dare pull my husband's letter out of my pocket, nor even reach in to touch it. On the way to the relief rooms I had only the time to look at the date, to know when he was last safe, and see the salutation that brought a happy lump to my throat: *My dear sturdy Peg.*

It is more than four months now since I have heard his voice calling me Peg. No one but Amos uses that name. *Always reaching out,* he says, *sturdy as a peg, to help.* It is such a balm, to ease the burdens of a fellow being. That is what I must remember—that, and Amos's fingertip poised at his lips when he sees my anger rising up to overtake me.

For Mrs. Carter's sake, I redoubled my efforts. With her zeal fueled by sorrow, and mine by sympathy, we finished all the boxes in time. Work soothes more than words.

The sound of my girls' merriment reached me before my hand touched the front-door latch. What a wealth I have in daughters! They are a richness and a comfort beyond measure. Sometimes I think it is the way they flutter around me each night that renews my vigor to return to the relief rooms each day. Cold, sickness, hunger, and deprivation, all of it accompanied by some mix of shame and indignity, anger and bitterness, dominate my daylight hours. To be pampered so after being immersed in the misfortunes of others reminds me that the burdens others carry do not belong to me, no matter how heavily they sit upon my mind.

Aside from my time with my diary each evening, the moments that most soothe me are those, like tonight, when I can gather my girls around me and feast on one of Amos's letters. When I read his words aloud it is easy to imagine we are together again. This one affected us all more than usual. Christmas, no doubt. A week of ordinary days without him is easier to bear than a single night and day that happens to be marked December 24 and 25 on the calendar.

Still, there is more to it than that. The urge to do and be our best in the face of Amos's daily sacrifice is irrepressible. I am thankful my girls' burdens are still so light, that they do not have to bear the added weight I do. Vanity, shyness, and selfishness are all worthy dragons to conquer. Only Jo does not recognize her true burden. The fire in her, what she calls being rough and wild, is not what worries me. I would not tame her of that. The way she flares, though, when something ignites her anger, makes me wince. I have singed too many of the people I love with the sparks of my own temper. Sometimes I believe the flames that burned my face and hand as an infant took up permanent residence within me.

The money I had hoped would arrive in time for the girls' Christmas was not enclosed in Amos's letter, but that is of no consequence compared with the gift of his safety. The little books I slipped under the girls' pillows tonight dovetailed so smoothly with their father's words that it is as if he and I had chosen them together. It is a comfort to think that our thoughts remain united even with all these miles between us. Nevertheless, I cannot help wishing I could give Meg, Jo, Beth, and Amy a brighter Christmas, with treats and baubles that have no other purpose but pleasure. Frivolity is such a lovely decadence, but the rag money goes only so far.

Every day I spend helping the destitute reminds me how fortunate our Family is. We have wants, but no needs. It is hard to find contentment in that, though, when you are as young as my girls are and have never known real need. Especially at Christmas, when the shop windows are filled with all manner of delectable things. My own eyes cannot resist the displays of linen handkerchiefs ringed in whole inches of Brussels lace. Someday, perhaps, there will be time and money for pretty things again.

Tonight, I pray Amos is safe, and that the Lord may spare him a little merriment this Christmas.

December 25, 1861

A day of perfect generosity.

A knock came at the back door while the sky was still gray. A big boy of nine or ten years, yet before I could help myself, I was crouched before him with my handkerchief, wiping the yellow trickle from his nose that had half frozen to his upper lip. "Please, ma'am," he said, "have you any milk? Mutti can't get out of bed and the baby is shrieking."

"On Christmas Day, the baby shall have cream," I told him, and poured a little pitcher full. His fingers were so stiff and purple that they fumbled as he threaded them through the handle.

"Have you a fire on the hearth to warm that?" I asked. He bit his lip and shook his head.

I whisked my wrap from its peg and put my woolen mitts on his brittle fingers. "I'd like to wish your Mutti a Merry Christmas," I said, "and bring her some firewood for a present."

Onto a sledge went half a dozen stout logs and two handfuls of kindling. The boy (his name is Karl Hummel) refused to let me pull it, and shouldered the rope with both hands. A child so gaunt ought to have had the luxury of riding the sledge rather than pulling it, but pride is a precious thing when one has little else, and I would not take that from him.

His feet must have been as stiff as his fingers, the way he shuffled through the snow beside me. As we walked he told me how he had found his way to my door. His mother's cousin is Mrs. Vogel, who received a Christmas basket this year after the influenza nearly carried off her husband and left him too weak to work. She had two slices of bread to spare for the children, but no milk for the infant. "And how many brothers and sisters do you have, Karl?" I interrupted.

"Five. No, six now."

Stupid of me not to think to ask while we still stood in my kitchen. Two slices among six children, and what for the mother? His voice drifted almost dreamily as he spoke of the bread, just as Amy's does when she talks of new drawing pencils or hair ribbons. "You gave your share to the little ones, didn't you?"

He looked at me as though I were a prophet. "How did you know?"

"A boy who would not let me pull a sledge of firewood is surely generous in other ways, too."

A little color came into Karl's face at that. "Frau Vogel said to knock at the back door of the house next to the big stone one," he said. "She told me the lady there would help."

"Frau Vogel was wrong to tell you that."

He stopped so fast, the sledge skidded forward and barked his heels. "But you did help. And you didn't even ask why the baby is hungry."

"You are good enough to knock at the front door. Not just mine, but anyone's."

He had nothing to say to that, though I could see it affected him. We walked in silence several paces, until I couldn't help but sing. The sky had turned from gray to silver, with a pale wash of blue spreading upward.

"*Ave Maria, Gratia plena*
Maria, Gratia plena . . ."

And then Karl's voice was alongside mine, reedy and tentative. His German wove in, under, and through the Latin. Together we sere- naded the sky and the snow, until our lungs burned and tingled with cold. He smiled then, for the first time.

When we reached his front door, he sobered. He looked at me with a sort of pity, as though he knew that what waited inside would blot out the beauty we had made of the morning.

The dimness made the room feel every bit as cold as the bright outdoors. For a moment I could perceive nothing but the shrieking of the baby. When my eyes became accustomed to the darkness, I nearly cried out myself at the sight of the place. It was a scene the likes of which I have only encountered within the pages of Mr. Dickens's novels. Everything bare and gray, without so much as an ember in the fireplace. Five children, clustered under coats and blankets in a single bed beneath a broken windowpane. Mrs. Hummel in bed, too weak to do anything but cry, and even that she could barely manage. The tears, so thin they could not roll, drizzled down her cheeks. An unmistakable smell pricked at my nose. A glance toward the hearth revealed the culprit—a basket of diapers, unlaundered for several days by the height of the pile.

I crouched down beside the bed, putting one hand on her fore-head, the other on the newborn. Her face crumpled in on itself at my touch. She is young—at least ten years younger than I, if not more. Her voice was so weak, so punctuated with sobs, I don't know whether I would have understood her if she'd spoken in English. Then and there, I resolved to learn a bit of German. French and Latin served me well enough in the classroom, but they have been of no use whatever in the relief rooms. I knew only that Mrs. Hummel was apologizing. Explaining. Pleading with me not to think badly of her. I have seen all kinds of begging, and this is the sort that most distresses me. Of all the many forms of starvation, the hunger for respect is hardest to cure.

The heat of her forehead raised my alarm. If childbed fever had set in, I would soon have seven orphans on my hands. "How long since the baby has fed?"

Karl translated. "Yesterday," he answered. "She says it hurts too much." Mrs. Hummel indicated the yoke of her nightdress. I asked with lifted eyebrows, and when she nodded, lowered the neck. Both breasts were hard and distended, with pink swollen patches. That eased the worst of my fears. I had the same, though not half so se-verely, after Amy was born. My relief needed no translation. I showed Mrs. Hummel the pitcher of cream, and she wept with gratitude.

"I'll come right back," I promised her. "Tell her, Karl. Please. With food, and enough firewood to see you through the night."

Tears scalded my cheeks as I hurried back home. It is perfectly plain that the Hummels have needed help for days, if not weeks. If I could only teach people not to be ashamed of asking for what they need! Every belly deserves to be filled, no matter what sin or folly or misfortune has caused it to be empty.

The smell of frying buckwheat cakes on Hannah's griddle brought my mind fully out of the Hummels' house and into my own again. I had walked the whole way home without seeing anything but the inside of my mind. My fists and shoulders unclenched, and I inhaled deeply, unlocking the knot in my stomach. With an effort, I funneled my anger into action. The relief rooms are closed until after the new year; anything I could give to the Hummels had to come from our own larder.

There was easily enough in our stores to cobble together a box of mismatched provisions, but what I wanted was to set those hungry children before a tower of Hannah's piping hot buckwheats, to see the melted butter and honey dripping from their chins. I could not hope to enjoy my own portion after what I had seen, but mine alone would not suffice for a family of eight.

My girls were all around the table, their faces nothing but eagerness and merriment. Their dresses, which only yesterday seemed on the verge of shabbiness, had become a veritable kaleidoscope of brightness to my eyes.

As I described the state of the Hummels' home, hope and remorse warred within me. It felt wrong—selfish, almost—to quash my daughters' gaiety when they bear their own small sacrifices with so little complaint. I knew full well that with every pitiful detail I shared I was making it less and less possible for them to enjoy the meal they had waited for so patiently—not just all morning, but all year. At the same time the desire to show Karl and his family that they are as deserving as we fairly scalded my conscience. After all, if the Hummels were guests at our table we would not serve them what would be least missed from the back of the pantry.

I took a breath and finished in a rush, "My girls, will you give them your breakfast as a Christmas present?"

A wordless cyclone of sympathy and disappointment whirled over them. They would not—could not—say no, I knew that. I had lain a trap they could not wriggle free of. I myself had to repress the urge to squirm as their faces clouded. The only question in my mind was whether they would do it cheerfully, or whether they would silently begrudge me for asking this of them, and the Hummels for needing it.

I had expected Beth's tender heart to yield first, or Meg's, but it was Jo who took the lead. Once she did, the others followed as if it were a parade. To see them struggle and overcome it so quickly warmed me through. It warms me still.

To the breakfast basket I added half a dozen jars of broth, the last of the strawberry preserves, a few pounds of potatoes, and a pint of milk. Another load of firewood, heavier this time, was piled upon the sled. My spirits were so buoyed by my girls' sacrifice, I could not help but sing again as we crossed the snowy fields, and their voices joined mine.

Their jollity flagged in the Hummels' doorway, just as mine had. We fancy ourselves poor, but this is the first my daughters have seen of true destitution. Meg gave a gasp. Amy needed a nudge to cross the threshold. Jo set her jaw and advanced like a soldier into battle. Beth, for all her shyness, made right for the bed of shivering children as if they were her cradle full of broken dolls.

Soon the children were scrubbed and the diapers were boiling in a great pot over the fire. The little ones looked every bit as delighted by the breakfast as I had hoped.

"Promise me, Karl," I said as we prepared to go, "that you won't wait so long to ask for help. Come before your stomach roars and your fingers won't bend." He promised. "I will be back every day until the relief rooms open. Come knocking if there is anything you need."

"At the front door," he said, with such a roguish little smile that had he been mine, I would have slapped a kiss onto his cheek. Instead I put out my hand for him to shake. He did so with a solemnity that told me he is far older than his years.

Back home, I went upstairs to see what of our cast-off clothing could be spared for the Hummels while the girls prepared for their

Christmas play. There isn't much. By the time a dress makes its way from Meg to Amy, it's fit only for the ragbag. What I had, left over from better times, would do only for the littlest girls. It tugged at me a bit to take those dainty gowns from the cedar chest, for the ones I had kept back from the ragbag had been my favorites. Nothing at all is suitable for Karl or his brother. They are small enough that perhaps I may be able to patch together a few shirts and pairs of drawers from the set of threadbare sheets I have not made time to tear into scraps.

As I came down the stairs there was a flurry of whispers and shushings, then the piano sang out and four voices cried, "Three cheers for Marmee!"

Their glee came at me so unexpectedly and with such force that I staggered back a step. Meg linked her arm through mine and escorted me to the armchair before I had found my voice. On the table stood a vase of red and white flowers, encircled by green vines and a pile of bundles wrapped in colored tissue paper and bound with hair ribbons. Such a bounty found its way into my lap as I undid the little packages! My speechlessness, which grew with the unveiling of each gift, delighted all four of them. Handkerchiefs, gloves, slippers, and cologne, and not one thing for themselves.

What a roil of emotions came over me then. Amy said it best, clapping her hands victoriously: "Marmee is positively stupified!" I had not realized all my girls had already given when I prevailed upon them to give up their breakfast. Any one of these presents would have left me stunned with gratitude.

Such generosity gives me hope that they would not begrudge me for all that I have caused them to do without these last ten years. Perhaps they are old enough now to know the truth. If they understood what their small daily sacrifices truly meant, it might be easier for them to bear. My courage always fails me, though. I want so much to be the kind of woman they believe me to be!

Just when I had found a moment to sit by myself and try to absorb the day's unexpected happenings, another knock came to the back door. I groaned before I could help myself. Another distress call on Christmas Day? All at once it seemed to me that I had done so much and felt so much already today, I could not possibly make room for anything more.

Instead, Hannah brought me a note on stationery so thick and fine, my fingers might have mistaken it for cloth rather than paper. Mr. Laurence next door had sent it. "Why, he must have seen us carrying our breakfast out of the house," I said to Hannah as I read his praise of our goodwill toward the Hummels. *I hope you will allow me to express my friendly feeling toward your children by sending them a few trifles in honor of the day.*

I felt a snap inside me, quick—surprise and indignation striking like flint and steel, but thankfully no sparks flew. If I am to give charity, I, too, must learn to accept it with grace. Had I not wished for this very thing for my girls last night?

Hannah saw, though. After all these years, she knows me too well. "I bragged a bit, Mrs. March. Told Mr. Laurence's kitchen maid what your girls did for the Hummels. She must have gone and blabbed to her master. Did I do wrong?" Hannah asked.

"No, of course not. I only wish I could be the one to treat them so." She smiled and patted my arm as though she were my mother. She is only two years older than I, though to look at us one might gauge the difference at six or eight years instead.

For the next half hour a regular parade of servants processed from Mr. Laurence's house into our dining room. Hannah guarded the parlor door, but the girls were so taken up in assembling the stage and costumes for their Christmas theatricals that there was hardly any chance of them ruining the surprise. And what a surprise it was! Fruit and cake and sweets piled up on the table. Two big covered dishes of ice cream were nestled in the snow by the back door, ready to be whisked in at the last moment.

Last of all came a black-haired young man about Jo's age, with his arms so full of hothouse flowers it seemed as if he were blooming out of them. He looked, in his way, as hungry as Karl Hummel, though I daresay he was starving for something not found on any dinner table. He placed the two bouquets on the table and said, "I'll go fetch the rest."

"The rest?"

His black eyes sparkled. "Oh, yes! There's two more, of course—one for each of the young ladies."

Hannah and I could do nothing but stand, gape-mouthed, before it all. "This is what he calls a few trifles?" I said. The flowers alone would have done justice to a wedding banquet even before the Laurence boy returned and doubled the bounty.

He took a step back from the table, plunging his empty hands into his pockets, clearly loathe to leave. "May I . . . May I help you arrange everything?" he ventured.

"If you would like to."

"Oh, I would!"

He went to work as though he had already painted a picture in his mind of how it all should look. Watching him, I began to understand that it was not vanity that drove him, but delight—and that of his unsuspecting audience rather than his own. Again and again he returned to the doorway to see that each item on the table was placed in such a way as to cause the greatest pleasure upon its discovery. Each time, he turned his back and then spun around, trying to see the arrangement as if for the first time.

"Wouldn't you like to stay and enjoy all of this with them?" I asked. "There is certainly more than enough, and the girls will surely be eager to meet their benefactor."

He refused, adamantly. Everything was for them and their guests, he insisted. "If I stayed, then they should have to thank me for bringing it all, when it's their generosity that brought it here in the first place. I only carried it. Do you see?"

I did see, and suddenly wished that I might have the chance to know him better.

"Would it be selfish of me to ask one favor?" he asked.

I laughed without meaning to, and told him I could hardly think so, after bringing more to our table than St. Nicholas himself.

"It's only that—" He broke off, and looked for all the world as though he were gathering his courage. "Will you leave the curtains open?"

Having braced myself for something as weighty as a marriage proposal, I had no reply. It seemed a queer thing to ask, and all the more so when he blushed. I followed his gaze to the window, and understood even as he stammered out an explanation. He wanted to go home and watch through his own window, as if at a stereoscopic slide of a perfectly posed Christmas party.

I considered him more carefully this time, and his ears darkened from pink to red under my scrutiny. The possibility that he thought of us as no more than a doll's house that he could arrange according to his whim crossed my mind and nearly settled there. And yet the fact that he had asked, and had been so self-conscious about doing so, shooed the notion away again. The hungry expression that I could not define at first sight at last came into focus, and I could not deny him what was mine to share any more than I could have denied Karl Hummel.

Oh, their faces when they saw that table! I have not seen such wonder, such perfectly round eyes and mouths since they were little girls delving into their Christmas stockings. Their first thought was of magic, though only Beth and Amy are still young enough to say so.

As for myself, I was nearly overcome by the way the day had wound itself full circle. "Angel-kinder," the Hummel children had said when Meg, Jo, Beth, and Amy unveiled their breakfast. It seemed so sweet, so childishly lavish. But tonight on my daughters' faces I saw the same awe and gratitude reflected back.

More than once I peered toward the Laurence house, wondering if the glow of their happiness was bright enough to reach the boy's hopeful eyes, and whether his grandfather was watching, too.

I must find some way to thank them. Both of them.

December 26, 1861

Mrs. King has promised to personally see to it that the Hummel family is provisioned until the relief rooms open. It cost me only a pinch of pride to ask her, and that is currency well spent. Once, I could have fed a family of eight for a week without enlisting help. What a luxury it was, though I did not realize it fully at the time.

Meantime, I busy myself with tending to Mrs. Hummel and the baby. The infant has a terrible rash from want of clean diapers. A bath in apple cider vinegar, followed by generous applications of lard and browned flour with each change, ought to set things to right. I've shown Karl and the biggest girl, Lottchen, how to apply both—one to soothe and the other to take up the moisture. As for Mrs. Hummel, the only way out of her pain is through it. I have shown her the least disagreeable way of draining her milk. We collect what we can on a clean rag, and give it to the baby to suck. It is not enough to fill her belly, but it placates her so the rest of the family is not tormented by her squalling. Her name is Greta.

December 28, 1861

Mrs. Hummel has begun to improve. Her fever is down, and the swelling has decreased so that she can tolerate the pain enough to begin suckling Greta a few minutes at a time. Each morning I stop by Mrs. King's house to collect a quart of fresh milk for the children. Karl comes for a second quart in the afternoon. Cow's milk makes the baby fretful, but that can't be helped. Often I bring something extra—a pocket full of hickory nuts, or a half dozen of apples. Today it was a little jar of pickled beets. That house could use a bit of color, as well as a bit of flavor. The flour, lard, potatoes, oats, and rice Mrs. King has sent provide ample nourishment, but little relish.

Hannah shakes her head each time I pull something else from the pantry. "You'd share your last bite of bread if you were starving," she said yesterday. Hannah is right. If I no longer needed them, I would rather someone boil my bones for broth than bury them and starve. It pains me that I cannot put the Hummel baby to my own breast, to save her the windy colic that comes with cow's milk.

Bit by bit, I am learning how the Hummels' circumstances became so diminished. Karl and I talk while I fix oatmeal for the children, peel potatoes, or knead bread. Mrs. Hummel's name is Birte, and the children are Karl, Lottchen, Ada, Monika, Minna, Heinrich, and Greta, the baby. They moved here only a few months ago, from Pennsylvania, after Mr. Hummel died in the smallpox outbreak. Three of the children had it as well; Minna and Heinrich both bear the scars. The oldest boy, Bertram Jr., died five days after his father. That day, Karl turned from a nine-year-old boy into a nine-year-old man.

Mrs. Hummel's only family in this country is her cousin, Mrs. Vogel. That is how Karl and his family came to live in Massachusetts. But the Vogels have little more to offer than companionship, for they are just as poor; Mr. Vogel has not been well enough to work since October. He forced himself from bed late in November, and his impatience cost him another six weeks in relapse.

Mrs. Hummel was taking in laundry, but the further her pregnancy progressed, the less she could manage. Between that and the birth and the fever, it has been close to a month since she has had steady work.

This accumulation of hardships is so often the way. A family with money bounces back up from misfortune like an India rubber ball, while a poor one topples like a block tower if only one carefully balanced piece is nudged out of place.

Only today I learned that Greta, the baby, is a twin. Her brother lived just twelve days. Why is a mystery. One morning a week before Christmas they woke up, Karl said, and only one baby was crying for breakfast. The other had simply stopped living sometime in the night.

December 30, 1861

The Hummels' laundry, diapers and all, has been caught up for two days now, and yet a stink pervades. There is no other word for it. Today the scent was so unambiguously reminiscent of a barnyard, I summoned the nerve to have Karl ask his mother if the bed's ticking had been soiled during Greta's birth.

"The room smells a bit like . . . dirty straw," I ventured.

Karl did not bother to translate. "Ach, that never goes away," he said. "It's the cellar. There used to be pigs."

Pigs. Someone in the town of Concord has had the temerity to rent a room over a former pigsty to a widow and seven children, without bothering to clear out the animals' leavings. As though the broken windows and buckling chimney stones were not disgraceful enough. I turned so white with rage, Mrs. Hummel mistook it for illness and begged me to sit down. Karl ran for a mug of water. I could not explain; had I tried to speak, I might have sheared off my tongue. This kind of abuse shall not be tolerated.

December 31, 1861

The house is half full of stillness, and I have a rare hour or two both to write and reflect. Meg and Jo are off at the Gardiners', dancing away the last hours of 1861. (The scent of Meg's singed hair is at last beginning to fade. Why she ever entrusted Jo with the curling tongs is beyond my comprehension.) Through the gentle patter of rain, I can hear the thin whine of Amy's snores squeezing in and out past her clothespin. No doubt she is dancing in her dreams, the belle of an imaginary ball with a perfect Grecian nose held high in the air. Beth, though—what does my contented little cricket dream of? Sometimes I wonder if her mind strays back to the happy past rather than toward a make-believe future.

There is no more fitting night of the year for reflection. Leafing backward through my diary has the feel of revisiting an old friend. Here in these pages is a woman I know more intimately than any other, and yet in the space of a year I am apt to forget some of the intricacies of her heart and mind if I do not make time to sit with her now and then. Margaret March is a valuable counsel, steering me back to course when I stray from my convictions, or prompting me to break a fresh path when I see that my thoughts have matured in some way.

I lingered most over August 21, the day Amos went to war. It wasn't wise. My fear for his safety has dimmed with time into a dull, constant anxiety. I have become so used to it after all these months that it hardly cuts into my consciousness. Immersing myself in his departure once again revived its rawness, honing it into something sharp and bright.

The morning Amos departed, I could not bring myself to sing. I had forgotten that. *There are no melodies but silence for such moments,* I wrote. *I have no doubt that I am capable of piloting the small vessel of our Family through calm seas, but what of the storms that are sure to come?* Thanks be to God, there have been no storms yet. Only the girls' small domestic squalls. How I wept that night, with his pillow clutched in my arms. I hate to think that our girls were doing the same, too proud or too ashamed to ask for comfort.

I want to miss him bravely—we all do—but it proves to be a far more delicate line to walk than I could have foreseen. Amos is worthy of being missed; we cannot simply go about our lives as if his absence means nothing. The quandary is how to feel the sorrow without giving way to it, yet hold it at bay without denying it entirely. It is a feat that consumes the majority of my strength each and every day.

That day is the pivot upon which the whole of the year has turned. Everything lies before it or beyond it. I pray that it will not be the day our lives pivot upon. The war—any war—is always to be over by Christmas. Now, on the brink of a new year we are no nearer victory.

Here I turned the page, and the sight of Amos's handwriting startled me:

My good sturdy Peg,
   My hand <u>was</u> on this page as I wrote these words. The sound of my voice <u>is</u> in your ears as you read it. I <u>will</u> be in your mind each time you return to it.
           Love reaches through all times, touches all places.
                                         Amos

It is true. His voice—I can hear no other when I see the familiar shapes of the letters formed in his favorite red ink. The simple awkwardness with which he expresses a sentiment we both know so well is Amos, through and through. I have no doubt that he spoke these words aloud as he wrote them, as though he were indeed speaking to me. The most elegant of his thoughts never fail to disintegrate into their component parts when he voices them—as if in trying to convey the full savor of a banquet, his tongue can do no more than recite the recipes.

At this moment I cannot be sure whether he is dead or alive. And yet his presence is suddenly here with me. Not in the manner of ghost stories or spiritual visitations. No brush of air at the back of my neck, no rise of gooseflesh. It is all within me; I simply feel the way that I always feel when Amos is here. Calmed. Bolstered.

My left hand rests curled around the blank space surrounding his words as I write. I want to preserve this companionable feeling as long as I can, to experience it fully without consuming it. Every day I touch any number of things he has touched. Chairs and bowls, doorknobs and carpets, the very sheets I sleep upon. His own diaries are lined up on the shelves in his study, should I care to read them. But these few lines transcend all of that. Our own hands have worn away his presence from everyday things, while this, hidden in the clean white pages, is somehow new and fresh.

If only I had thought to do something similar for him. If I could do one impossible thing, it would be to transmit my gratitude to him without translating it into words and sealing it into an envelope to grow stale before it reaches him.

All I could think to do was to creep past Beth and Amy's bedroom door, down to Amos's study, and settle myself in his chair. With its wings and arms curved around me, I closed my eyes and cradled my open diary to my breast, so that the beating of my heart pulsed against the page.

Love reaches through all times, touches all places. I would like to have those words inscribed upon my palm, that they might touch all that I touch.

January 1, 1862

I have sent a letter to the Hummels' landlord in the morning mail, threatening legal action if the refuse is not cleaned out of the cellar. It is a bluff, to be sure—I have no more money for lawyers than the Hummels have for firewood—but I am hopeful that the tenor of my threat will have more force than the futile pleadings Karl has already dictated on his mother's behalf. The chance to unleash a righteous tirade is rare, and I am not too proud to admit that I savored it. My studies with Miss Robbins and Miss Allyn furnished me with a formidable vocabulary, and I made certain to wield its full weight. Little intimidates a man more than a learned woman.

Between the girls' clamor and the rattle of my own indignation, it took three attempts before I managed to produce a clean copy. As a final barb, I concluded with Matthew 25:40. *Inasmuch as ye have done it unto one of the least of these my brethren, ye have done it unto me.* Under any other circumstances, I would cringe at the use of scripture as means of shaming another, but this man has earned himself a healthy dose of shame. Words, aimed properly, are often the sharpest of weapons.

Meg and Jo made the acquaintance of the Laurence boy last night. His name is Theodore, though Jo insists he is to be called Laurie. He came to Meg's rescue with his carriage after she turned her ankle pirouetting in the high-heeled slippers she refuses to admit that she has outgrown. His kindness reminds me that I must pay a call on the elder Mr. Laurence. I have yet to properly thank him for his generosity.

As for Meg, an invitation to visit the Moffats in the spring made her all but oblivious to the pain in her ankle. I managed not to blanch at the idea, which I cannot find good reason to refuse. There is nothing wrong with the Moffats, except perhaps that their heads are as empty as their purses are full. And well do I know how that can end.

January 3, 1862

A letter from Meg in the Family post:

> *Dearest Marmee, please be extra sweet to Amy tonight. She came home from school today with her feelings all bruised again. Your Meg*

It had to do with Amos, no doubt. If the taunts were about anything but her father, Amy would have told me herself.

While we all sat knitting before the fire this evening, I let my own needles lie idle and chose two of Amy's favorite stories to read aloud: *The Snow Queen* and *The Princess and the Pea*. She delights in them, without realizing how perfectly apt they are. The hobgoblin's mirror poisoning the hearts of all who are pierced by its falling shards on one hand, and the exquisitely sensitive princess on the other. Snip the two stories each in half, sew those two pieces together, and there you have Miss Amy March. If tears could truly melt the shards of cruelty embedded in the hearts of her schoolmates, Amy might by now be the happiest child on earth.

January 5, 1862

Beth has spent this Sabbath coaxing another stray kitten in from the cold. This one is gray as a Confederate uniform, with a tail and hindquarters that look as if it has been dunked in milk. The poor creature was more bedraggled even than Karl Hummel was, and simply hopping with fleas; Hannah wouldn't let it into the kitchen until Beth had bathed it in hot vinegar. It fought and yowled the whole time, then promptly fell asleep, bundled into a towel on Beth's lap before the fire. I don't know which glowed the brighter—the triumph on her face, or the crosshatching of scratches on her hands.

This makes an even half dozen cats in Beth's menagerie. I don't know how to tell her how near we are to being unable to feed ourselves, much less yet another animal. There aren't mice enough in this house to keep such a clowder of felines on this side of eternity. (Sometimes I think eternity would be hip-deep in cats by now if not for Beth.) If I did confess the precariousness of our finances to her, she would only offer to give her milk and porridge to her pets every morning, just as I persist in taking pint jars of preserves to the Hummels whenever Hannah's back is turned. In light of that, I suppose I have no business protesting her ministrations.

"Takes after her mother, that one does," Hannah said later as Beth fed the creature nibbles from her dinner, and I confess I was proud to hear it said.

January 6, 1862

Anxiety for Amos never abates. No sooner have I read his latest letter and assured myself of his safety than I begin to wonder when the next will come. *If* the next will come. The date of his last letter— December 17—is ingrained upon my thoughts. There is a malevolent part of my mind that persists in imagining that Amos has fallen in the time it takes the mail to reach us, and that we have read and rejoiced in and been comforted by the words of a dead man. The knowledge that he is not in combat is no comfort, either. Disease takes so many more than cannon fire, and a chaplain is ever present at the bedside of the sick.

January 7, 1862

I arrived at the Hummels' this morning to find the building's cellar doors flung open and two men with shovels laboring below. They carted away three wheelbarrows full of dung and fouled straw. I stood by, watching them with my sternest expression, all the while trying not to whoop aloud at my success. And that is not the whole of it. A glazier had come yesterday afternoon to replace the broken window-panes. Before today, I did not know there was such a thing as bright brown and bright gray, but the light coming in through those new sheets of glass seemed to wash the room clean of half its dullness. If only it were spring, we could give the place a good airing and fill the windowsills with mugs of snowdrops and crocuses to sweeten the air.

January 9, 1862

A long day today of cutting out blue flannel for jackets. Necessary work, but it is difficult for me to sit still and attend to such a static task. Moreover, my scarred right hand will not allow the scissors to open fully. Every piece required twice the number of snips. I would do better filling orders for those who have come for help. Mrs. King knows that, but today she was not present. Her absence left us all at loose ends, taking up whatever task was nearest, or simplest, or most coveted. The result was confusion and inefficiency. If Olive Kirke were still in Concord, she would have taken matters in hand. (I must remember to write to her—it has been almost three months since she and little Minnie moved to her parents' home in New York to await her confinement and I have not sent a single letter. Her baby will likely arrive any day, if it has not already.)

Of course it had to be a Thursday. Mrs. Weddleton came sweeping through as usual, scrutinizing the efforts we have made all week long without her help. Everything we've done, she could have done better, yet never has she deigned to sit down among us and work her needle and scissors for an hour. She regards us as if we are her servants, not sisters united under a common cause.

I have no doubt that she would like us to endow the collar and waistband of each soldier's garment with a tag reading, *Donated through the munificence of Mrs. Henry T. Weddleton, Jr.* If the funds for the yards of flannel on the table before me had not come straight from her purse I would tell her just what I think of her magnanimity. Her presence puts me in as foul a temper as Aunt March. Fouler. If I have anything like a human nemesis, it is she.

Perhaps if she were a sour old matron I would not be so rankled by her noblesse oblige. But she is young, with two small children, and nearly as pretty as my Meg. Decked out in all her costly finery, she might fool some into believing she is prettier. Her voice has a certain lilting sweetness in it—the sort most often reserved for speaking to nursery school children, or kittens—that wrenches my lips into a scowl if I do not sit with my jaw clenched tight as Aunt March's. Does she truly believe we will not perceive her criticisms as such if they are dredged in sugar? By the time she sailed back out the door again, I had my usual Thursday-morning headache, thanks to the munificence of Mrs. Henry T. Weddleton, Jr.

Amos would remind me that my disdain of this well-meaning woman is a form of pride. I cannot say that he is wrong. Criticizing others is so often a circuitous way of praising ourselves. Each time my temper flares, I think of Amos, and how his finger would reach up to touch his lips if he saw me fuming. When we are beside each other, he sees it before I feel it. Perhaps because his temperament is naturally so much more tranquil than mine, the change in equanimity is more apparent to him, whereas I am long accustomed to the steep peaks and valleys of my disposition.

How often would his letters have to come to snuff out my worries for his safety? Daily, perhaps, or even hourly. Days like today it seems that my anger and fear meld themselves into something entirely new—a caustic emotion I have no name for. We have lived without Amos for almost half a year, and all five of us have borne up so well that it brings me pride. Yet all the while it is plain that what makes it bearable is the knowledge that he is alive. If that solace were taken from us, the fortifications we have built up in our minds to protect us would crumble. Each day that passes without word from him opens another tiny fissure in my own foundation.

Amos loves nothing more than to write, to parse his thoughts on paper like specimens from the natural world, neatly pinned and labeled. Of all the many reasons that might explain why we've had no letter this month, my mind insists on clutching tight to the worst. The fear sits like a magnet in the center of my brain, drawing my thoughts back every time they stray toward something less distressing.

Sorrow, large as it looms, constitutes only half of my fretfulness. Amos has sent no money since November. In addition to his rations, he receives one hundred dollars per month for his services. Knowing Amos, I had hopes that we could expect eighty dollars after his expenses. The reality is more often nearer to seventy than eighty. Thankfully there are no bookshops on the battlefields, or we should likely receive no money at all.

How long could we subsist without him before beginning to skid down the same steep slope that plunged the Hummel family into destitution? Aunt March was so adamantly opposed to Amos going to war that I cannot imagine her becoming our benefactress; the most she is likely to share with us is remonstration. Any means Aunt March did bestow upon us would be encumbered by an unspoken demand for penitence, which I will never give.

To gain employment as a nurse, I might have to go as far south as Washington, leaving the children behind. Hannah would care for the girls, of that I am sure, but I could not ask her to do that. Not after all she has already done for so little. Knowing Hannah, she would not let me ask at all; she would simply do it.

Hannah's loyalty has been a gift like few others I have known in my life. It defies reason. As it is, she is working for barely more than her board. Twice, now, when the money from Amos has been slimmer than I planned for, the envelope with her wages has remained on the kitchen shelf where I leave it each Friday. "What right have I to put that into my pocket," she says, "when I know the table will be twice as bare without it? We all eat from the same larder, Mrs. March, and I'll not shrink it further."

Once, she considered herself in our debt. Now, I regard myself in hers, though I shall never convince her of that fact. In Hannah's mind, the scales between us will never fully balance. It is true that years ago she would not have found work outside of our home, but the days when her name might be recognized and whispered of have long since passed. The only thing tying her to us now is that imponderable ironclad fidelity. Should the worst happen, it would not surprise me if she were to insist upon staying for no pay at all. That is a mercy, for I cannot bear the thought of letting her go. It is altogether possible that she would be as lost without us as we would be without her. If any of her own family remains, she has not spoken to them in nearly twenty years. For that matter, I cannot recall her ever speaking _of_ them. Whatever may become of our Family in the months ahead, I must be sure to hold a place for Hannah, too.

How it galls me to think that the education I fought and pleaded for is of so little practical use, simply because of my sex. No school will hire a woman with children as a teacher, no matter how much Latin I can conjugate or how many theorems I can prove. Only if I were to crop my hair, bind my breasts, and cinch a pair of trousers around my waist could I find a position that would keep the six of us as comfortably fed and clothed as we are now. Instead I suppose I would find myself washing or sewing or cooking for a woman like Mrs. Weddleton, who has had no more learning than Amy.

Before noon, I'd wound myself into quite a state. My heart ached, my head ached, and my hand ached. It was finally the pain in my hand that forced my mind away from Amos. I'd been slashing away at those jacket pieces with a perfect vengeance from the time Mrs. Weddleton darkened our door. When I looked up, I was surprised to realize that the entire world was not composed of Union blue flannel. In fact, an old man stood quite near me. He had a paper in his hand, and looked from it to one table after another with a defeated expression. I asked him if he had an order, and he showed me the paper. "Mrs. Emerson and Mrs. King are seeing to that today," I told him, and pointed them out. At the sight of the queue lined up before their table, he exhaled heavily and sat down on the edge of the crate where I had stacked my bolts of flannel.

"Have you sons in the army?"

I have asked that question so many times that I spoke in the same tone one might use to inquire of the weather. His answer stilled my scissors mid-snip. My own complaints withered so quickly, I could feel the newly opened space they had occupied in my mind. Four sons—two of them dead, another captured, and the fourth lying sick in Washington. Few have paid a steeper price.

"You have done a great deal for your country, sir," I said, all meekness.

"Not a mite more than I ought, ma'am," he said, brightening. "I'd go myself, if I was any use; as I ain't, I give my boys, and give 'em free." Four of them. That is a number guaranteed to jab at my heart. For all that women are denied in this world, I thank God each night that the army can make no claim to my daughters. Jo would have marched off at the first bugle call.

I considered him again, this time without my troubles fogging my sight. I took him for an old man, but in truth I do not know whether it was age or sorrow that stooped his shoulders and lined his face. He was as towheaded as a child, making it impossible to guess whether time had faded his hair. (Sometimes I fancy that gray hair comes from suffering, while white signifies a life of cheer. It sounds more like one of Amos's philosophical notions.) A man need not be much older than I to have sons old enough to fight. His smile was bright, yet brittle, and that brittleness made his anxiety plain to me.

I could give him everything I own, and it would not ease his pain. Still, I wanted to relieve what I could, for a man whose heart is aching should not have to endure the aches of hunger or cold as well. I tied up my lunch in my napkin, tucking a few dollar bills into the bottom. Had he seen the greenbacks, I have no doubt he would have refused the lumpy bundle. Yet a glance at his rusty-looking black coat, cut in a style I have not seen displayed in a shop window since Franklin Pierce was in office, betrayed his need.

"God bless you," I said. "And your boys."

January 10, 1862

The only envelope in the letterbox today came from Olive Kirke, as though the very thought of her had conjured it. (If I could perform that feat with Amos, I should be flooded in correspondence.) She has given birth to a girl and named her Katherine Adelaide. Minnie—and hence the whole family—calls her Kitty. George is stationed in Maryland, his regiment being assigned to picket duty at Indian Head. A relief for her, after the anxiety of Manassas.

I find that the old gentleman at the relief room is much on my mind. If I were to lose Amos, could I go on with such cheer? I know myself better than that; my pride and sorrow would be more apt to smolder than to shine. Perhaps what I took for cheer was a simple brightening at the memory of his boys—the chance to make them live again in words. Without his sons, there is little else left for him to cherish but their sacrifice.

Give 'em free, he said of his boys. He gave of his own flesh and blood as openhandedly as I give from my pantry. His example shames me, for in my heart, I have not given my husband at all—only loaned him. I cannot pretend to give Amos cheerfully. His service, yes. Not his life. That truth vexes me to no end. How can I call myself an abolitionist, if I value one man's life over the freedom of millions?

None of these questions torment Amos, of that I am sure. He is the most selfless man I have ever met, in every sense of the word. So much so that he is prone to forgetting himself. Sometimes I half believe he does not even know he possesses a body, he lives so much within his mind. That is what worries me most—that he will put himself in harm's way without consciously choosing to do so. With his eyes fixed ever upward as they are, he might step off a precipice and remain unaware of his peril until the moment he struck the ground.

Were he to enter blindly into mortal danger, I could not hope to reconcile myself to such a death. If I am to be widowed, I will crave the comfort of knowing that he laid himself willingly upon the altar of freedom. That he is capable of that, I have no doubt. My Amos has the faith of an Abraham. I do not.

January 11, 1862

The Kings' son is in disgrace. Drunkenness and gambling and forgery. How the gossip squirmed its way out of the King home and into the ears of Concord, I cannot begin to guess. Even Meg, who overheard the family's distress on Thursday while she helped the children with their arithmetic, did not know its cause. Now everyone is so familiar with the story, one might think it had appeared in all the papers this morning.

My heart goes out to them. The debts, they can smother quickly enough, but the shame cannot be buried. I am sure Mrs. King is aware that word has spread. All day long, the entire room was filled with the most awkward of silences. Every one of us behaved as though <u>we</u> were ashamed, and in a sense, we were—ashamed of knowing. It was a mercy to scurry out the door when the day's work was done.

When I returned home this evening, there was no flurry of welcome. "Where is everyone?" I asked Hannah as she took my cloak and basket. She nodded toward the parlor with a finger over her lips.

I crept to the doorway and peeked in. The scene that greeted me was fit for a vignette on the frontispiece of a novel.

Sprawled before the hearth were Jo and the Laurence boy. Jo was reading a poem aloud from a book with a finely tooled leather spine and gilt-edged pages, while Meg sewed and Amy sketched their guest in profile. Beth sat in her corner, trying to convince her newest kitten—the gray one with the white rump—that caressing is beloved by every feline on this round earth. The glow of the fire bathed all of them in a rosy-orange tint.

Theodore's (Laurie's, I should say, for he hates his Christian name most passionately) attention was fixed firmly to Jo's back, which seemed quite queer to me until a log in the fireplace popped and he sprang to brush the sparks from her skirt before it could scorch. Jo thanked him for saving her second-best wool and scolded him for interrupting her all in one breath, then returned to the final couplet of the poem—Marlowe's *Hero and Leander*.

Where both deliberate, the love is slight:
Who ever lov'd, that lov'd not at first sight.

"And here is a scene to love at first sight," I broke in. Up they flew in a four-part chorus of "Marmee's home!"

The Laurence boy looked bereft, standing there before the fire by himself, and a bit sheepish with nothing to say but "Good evening, ma'am." He truly does suffer for want of affection. The girls' momentary abandonment seemed to have pushed him back into a hole he had just climbed out of.

I reached for the book, which Laurie handed over. Just the texture of the leather was a joy to my palms. The title proclaimed itself, proudly and simply, *English Verse*. I scanned the contents and found each of the names I had hoped for: Addison, Pope, Shakespeare. "It's most kind of you to lend such a fine volume, Mr. Laurence. Now, if you will permit me to join your cozy circle, perhaps I may choose a few poems for us all to enjoy together?"

I have never heard a young man utter a heartier "Yes, ma'am!" in all my life.

All scattered to their usual places: Beth with her cats, Jo on the sofa with the pillow known as "the sausage," Meg in the rocker, and Amy at the desk with her paper and colored pencils. When I motioned to Hannah to come in and take her place at the opposite end of the sofa, it left only Amos's chair. Laurie hesitated, seeming to sense the sacredness of that place. I scooted my footstool between my chair and the fire and bade him sit beside me. And there he perched, arms folded upon his knees to pillow his chin. I did not need the book at all; the poems I chose have been embedded in my mind since my youth, which gave me ample opportunity to observe the young man at my feet. I could not help imagining that he saw not my face, but his own mother's as he listened. Perhaps tonight settled half my debt to the Laurences for their Christmas kindness. Now there is only Laurie's grandfather to thank.

January 13, 1862

Not one letter, but two! Praise be to God for Amos's safety. The latest of them is dated Epiphany.

One hundred thirty-three dollars of his salary were enclosed, along with apologies for its tardiness. *There were men in my regiment who received no comforts from home for Christmas,* he wrote, and so he spent the bulk of his December pay to brighten their lonely holiday. *I knew you least of all would begrudge what we can so easily spare.*

Easily is not the word I might have chosen, though Amos is correct in sum. I cannot very well resent his generosity when I have been ministering to the Hummels straight from our pantry for nearly three weeks.

January 16, 1862

Mrs. Hummel is well now, and the children begin to look less spindly, too.

I feel something toward the Hummels that has been absent from my work at the relief rooms. It is one thing to fight poverty, oppose slavery, or bolster our troops, quite another to enter another fellow-being's home, to feed her children and slacken her fever. Something that may prove to be friendship is taking root, I think. The children come scampering when I arrive, competing as much for a space in my lap as for the contents of my basket. I have quickly come to know each of Karl's younger siblings by name, face, voice, and attitude, and they are as different from one another as my own girls.

Lottchen is a regular little woman. She fusses over baby Greta and bosses all of her siblings, including Karl, in a stream of German so swift it sounds like one everlasting word. The only one exempt from her vehemence is Ada, and no wonder. I have never seen a more solemn child than she. Looking at Ada's wide dark eyes, I cannot help thinking that she is the repository of all the family's saddest memories. She is wholly devoted to Monika; I do believe she could sit all day long on the bed with her sister in her arms. Ada holds her as if she is afraid Monika will be stolen, and nothing anyone says will convince her otherwise—her father and two brothers have already been taken from her. Fortunately Monika is docile as a kitten and happy to be petted from sunrise to sunset. Monika, in fact, is happy to do anything that will make anyone else happy. Minna, on the other hand, is pure trouble of the most bewitching kind, a four-year-old imp eager to prod at anything and everything to see if it will bite back. Heinrich toddles along after her. They are a well-matched pair, for he is as impervious to harm as a potato bug and can curl himself up into a neat little ball just as quickly. Minna's favorite game is to pile all the laundry beside the bed and roll her little brother from the mattress to the floor.

Mrs. Hummel has been tormenting herself over her inability to repay my kindness, and so today I asked her to pay her "debt" with German lessons. The way her face changed when Karl relayed my proposition to her made me believe I was seeing the woman she truly is for the first time. "Ja!" she exclaimed, and added "Jawohl!" for good measure. *Jawohl*, I immediately learned, is a fine word. A dictionary might define it as *yes, of course* or *yes, indeed*, but that does not begin to convey the hearty enthusiasm with which the Hummels imbue it. My first lesson began immediately, as she pointed from one object to another: Stuhl, Kind, Teller. Chair, child, plate. And so on.

By the time I left, all of the usual Thursday irritations had been scrubbed from my mind. I chirped like a bird all the way home, singing half a dozen of my father's favorite songs.

How many hundreds of boxes, bundles, and baskets of provisions have I dispensed without ever forging such a connection?

We are fooling ourselves if we think our work in the relief rooms places us in among the poor. In fact, we have separated ourselves—forcing them to come to us on neutral ground, that we may not be sullied by entering their homes. If no one asks for help, we presume no one is hungry, neglecting those like Mrs. Hummel who are too sick or ashamed to come and stand before us, proclaiming by their very presence their status as paupers.

When Karl came to our door, he asked only for milk. Not firewood or bread or blankets, all of which were needed just as desperately. We cannot assess anyone's true needs without becoming acquainted with them.

January 17, 1862

I must call on Aunt March. What with my devotion to the Hummels, it has been since before Christmas. If I avoid her any longer, Jo is sure to suffer for it. Already she reports that Aunt March has been sighing and dropping sorrowful hints about her loneliness for the last week. Soon the grumbling about ungrateful relatives will begin. As it is, I do not know how Jo keeps her temper with the old lady day after day.

How it is that Aunt March fails to understand why visitors are so infrequent baffles me. The mere fact that she must hire someone to keep her company all day long ought to be a hint. Has she truly no awareness of how unpleasant she is, when all she does is point out flaws and foibles? An hour with her is like being bathed in acid.

I shall go on Saturday, so that Jo need not witness my dressing down. I do not know which of us is the flint and which the steel, but sparks are sure to fly.

January 18, 1862

The call on Aunt March is over, and I am nearly unscathed. I began by gushing out an apology so lavish, Estelle likely had to mop it up off the floor after I left. It is hard to say who was the more impressed, Aunt March or her parrot, who exclaimed, "Bless my boots!," obliging us both to laugh. Before Aunt March could steer the conversation in whatever direction she pleased, I had commenced explaining my absence by telling her all about Birte Hummel and her family.

"Well," said she, "I am gratified to know that you were looking after someone while you were neglecting me." That was surprise enough. Then she asked, "How old is the infant?"

"Greta," I said. "Six weeks yesterday."

"It is a precarious age."

We paused in mute acknowledgment of Aunt March's own loss. I do not know her daughter's name—if she lived long enough to receive a name at all—nor how old she was when the diphtheria snatched her away. The stone in the churchyard reads only *Beloved Daughter & Lamb of God, 1823*. Had Amos not pointed it out to me, I would never have known its significance to our Family.

"These Germans must explain why I've seen you hurrying past my gate every morning with your basket full, and coming back again with it empty," she said.

"I only wish I could give them more. The children are no longer hungry, but the grocery orders allocated by the poor board are more adequate than plentiful."

For the first time in my memory, Aunt March did not remark that our financial straits are no fault but our own. I thought I detected a softening. Maybe it was cruel of me, but I told her about Greta, with her tuft of hair the color of corn silk and her deep-set, gray-blue eyes, hoping that Aunt March might be gently cajoled into opening her purse for the Hummels' sake. She is not a stingy woman, so long as she believes you are worthy of her generosity, and none can be worthier than a little child.

Before we fell from her good graces, she lavished our girls with treats. Those first few Christmases, her parlor held a tiny spangled tree, hardly more than a sapling, for each of them, the table beneath it stacked with gifts. I don't know if Meg and Jo remember—they were only four and five the year the tradition abruptly ceased. Aunt March had likely already begun shopping that December; I have always wondered what she did with the children's presents. It has rankled me ever since that she would deprive the girls of those joyful moments because of something they had no part in.

Aunt March must have seen something brewing, for she turned the conversation abruptly in a direction she knew I would be helpless to follow. "I had a letter from my nephew yesterday, the first in two months." Unable to curb myself, I interrupted her to ask for its date. The answer I received was well worth the glare of censure: January ninth. Three days more in which I may count him safe.

"It seems he is faring well enough, though I am surprised he finds time to write," she said. The slant of her eyebrow conveyed a whole paragraph of meaning. A man at war hundreds of miles away found time to post a letter, while I have not managed to cross the street and knock at her door.

The depth of my relief was plain to her, though she did not make mention of it. I have been on the receiving end of the look she sent me over the rim of her teacup often enough to know what she was thinking: If Amos had listened to her advice and not put himself in peril by enlisting, I would be spared this worry. But neither Amos nor I could have been at ease with ourselves knowing there were soldiers in need of the spiritual guidance he can provide.

And that is the difference between Aunt March and me. She prizes her own comfort above all else, while I cannot enjoy a moment's rest so long as I am plagued by the knowledge of anyone in need. I envy her that, sometimes. What would it be like to sit with my mind at peace and allow myself to luxuriate in what I have? But I could not do that. Amos teases that he shall engrave nothing but James 4:17 on my gravestone: *Anyone who knows the right thing to do and doesn't do so—to that person it is sin.*

The conversation turned dry after that. The weather. The recurring scarcity of pork. I don't know why she craves these conversations that always devolve into self-conscious banalities. There is nothing of any significance that we may talk about, for we are always at cross-purposes or in danger of rekindling old arguments. If she takes any real pleasure in my presence I cannot detect it, and she is certainly not fool enough to be taken in by any pretense of affection I concede to put forth.

The fact is that each of us fancies herself above the other. In Aunt March's eyes, Amos and I are foolhardy wastrels, while in mine she represents the epitome of selfishness. She resents my unwillingness to come calling. I resent the obligation of doing so. Her frustration comes out in pointed remarks, mine in the long gaps between visits. I enter Plumfield full of dread, which I exchange for irritation. What pleasure she derives from my calls, I cannot imagine, unless it is simply to gloat.

Anyway, it is over for another month. I can take pleasure in that, at least.

January 20, 1862

What a bittersweet joy it is to have a boy about the house, to see five children capering together instead of four. It is as if Laurie is a peg whittled to fit the gap in our Family, down to the cleft in his chin that allows me to pretend a resemblance between him and Amos. Even the girls, who have grown up wholly unconscious of any absence among themselves, have taken to him like a brother. Somehow I also feel Amos's absence the slightest bit less. Though the space where Amos should be remains unfillable, Laurie's presence renders its emptiness less apparent.

I do wonder, though, if Laurie's grandfather is vexed by the boy's regular departures. (Or by the absence of the orchid and rose blooms Laurie has twice brought me from the conservatory.) Despite all the glories that the Laurence mansion has to offer, his grandson is to be found here far more often than there. Laurie eats our squash pie and pea soup with the sort of relish usually reserved for beefsteak, champagne, and ice cream. This house, it seems, has something that the larger one lacks.

Today he presented me with a great long swag for the mantel, made of fresh evergreen boughs set here and there with three different kinds of pine cones. The scent of cedar and pine fills the whole parlor and wafts into rooms beyond. "What is the occasion?" I asked.

Laurie simply smiled and shrugged. "Winter," he answered.

January 22, 1862

I am at sixes and sevens over the Hummels, and in my preoccupation I fear I have bruised Hannah's feelings.

We sat together before the kitchen fire as we so often do on a Wednesday evening, sharing out the mending between us. Without a thought of where my words were headed, I spread out my full breadth of worries at once:

Mrs. Hummel must have work, and the baby must be nursed half a dozen times throughout the day, so there is nothing she can do but take in the usual drudgery—sewing and laundry. Their future is as predictable as a line of arithmetic. The labor will render Mrs. Hummel an old woman before she turns forty, and her family will live forever on the edge of hunger. That will drive the boys out to work as soon as they can lift, pull, or take orders, forcing them to choose food over schooling. The girls will marry, or go into service.

"Service is not such a terrible fate," Hannah said quietly.

I felt as if I had trod on my own tongue. Here I am, forty years old, and still unable to see anything beyond my own frustration before it is too late.

One thing I will say on my own behalf: I am capable of begging pardon as quickly as I am capable of embarrassing myself. Hannah accepted my apology without hesitation, as she always does when my tongue outpaces my thoughts. Whether she accepts out of loyalty or sincerity, I am rarely sure. I have yet to utter an insincere apology, but the fact remains that I am her employer, meager though her wages may be—what choice does she have?

I silenced my tongue, but my mind would not be quieted. How can it be that I am less willing to accept Mrs. Hummel's circumstances than she is? How can she not want more for her children?

"It isn't the same when you're born poor," Hannah answered as if I had spoken aloud. "You don't expect things. The sooner a poor child learns that, the better."

"I was born a girl in a boy's world," I insisted. "Surely that is not so different."

"A wealthy girl." She did not argue further with me. She only looked down at her work with a knowing smile for herself that says I will never understand.

Hannah is the only person alive who can hold a match so near my temper without setting it alight. She seems to know, perhaps from watching my husband and children parry with me, just how much she can say before my indignation throws sparks. In part it is Hannah's esteem for me that holds me at bay. She persists in thinking so well of me that I want to be the person she sees, the person worthy of the admiration and respect she insists on bestowing upon me.

We talked amiably enough of other things until it was time to douse the lamps and go to bed. But I cannot begin to sleep. I wonder if Hannah is also awake, running the lines of our exchange through her mind, as I am?

I was four years old when I began to realize that the world had been fashioned for my brother's benefit and not for mine. My great good fortune was to have a brother who saw it, too. It was Samuel who taught me to desire more than what was allotted to me. The moment I saw how much there was to learn, I wanted it all. In that, I was unique among my three sisters. They were content with what was laid before them, never looking to see whether other paths existed. All of them married young and died young, seemingly without regret.

Perhaps Hannah is right. Poverty, true poverty, is something I merely comprehend, without fully understanding. For the first thirty years of my life I hardly gave a thought to where my food, clothing, and shelter came from. They simply existed. I had been married nearly a decade before I grasped how much work and worry were necessary to keep the cold and the hunger pangs at bay. If all seven of the children I conceived had taken firm hold in my womb, our straits might by now be as dire as Birte Hummel's.

For all that I have complained through the years of Amos's tendency to live in his mind rather than his body, I have in truth been fortunate in this regard. So many women's lives are consumed by the effects of their husbands' carnal appetites. Not I. My Amos can hardly bring himself to take honey from a bee without the insect's consent. Even when we had the means to bring up a dozen children if we cared to, Amos was mindful of the toll childbearing exacted from me. After I miscarried in 1851, Amos and I agreed to moderate our passions. Both of us were as much relieved as we were grieved by that loss, though we were too repulsed by our relief to express it in words, even to one another. We simply could not afford to feed another child. We had known that, of course, during the heat of our coupling, but after six months during which we could only touch one another through iron bars, even Amos did not possess the force of will to restrain his ardor.

There is so much I have never asked Hannah. Did she want children, a family of her own? Employment rather than education? I have always assumed she desired more than what Providence saw fit to grant her, as every woman who has less must assuredly want more. Could it be that I have had it backward all these years? That I have spent my life imposing my own aspirations upon every member of my sex?

The possibility forces me to contemplate whether contentment is not so elusive for other women as it is for me. Before my own hearth, surrounded by my Family, I am entirely satisfied with what I have. These walls contain riches beyond measure. But the moment I consider the world outside, and what is denied to me and others due to the accident of their race or sex, I can hardly sit still for wanting to remedy all that ails our society.

January 23, 1862

Another Thursday, another headache.

Mrs. Weddleton is not here for the sake of the poor. She is here for the adulation that comes from tending to "those less fortunate," as she so grandly puts it. Each time that phrase leaves her lips it seems to me that she is reminding herself—and all of us—that she is more fortunate.

Her mother-in-law is among the finest women I have known, tireless in philanthropy and generosity for the last thirty years. Now that her health is failing, the great mantle of Adelaide Weddleton's charitable reputation has fallen on the daughter-in-law, whose shoulders are not sufficiently broad to fill it. If she were a less exasperating woman, I should feel sorry for Harriet Weddleton. Instead, I sit back and watch her struggle. It is satisfying in the moment, but leaves me brooding over my selfishness later. A minister's wife ought to be more charitable. Then again, perhaps a minister ought to have better sense than to choose such a volatile wife.

January 24, 1862

Hannah confessed to me this evening that Amy came home from school crying. That makes the second time this month, so far as I am aware. If not for Hannah and Meg, I would likely be oblivious to the worst of Amy's schoolyard woes.

She has never told me what her classmates say about Amos. No doubt she knows how it would inflame me to hear of it. The words themselves—*radical, abolitionist, Unitarian, liberal*—are not so troubling as the way they are said, and the sneers that accompany them. I pray that she has been spared the worst of the jeers. *Blasphemer. Charlatan.* And the one I dread most of all: *n—-lover.* As if showing kindness to a fellow human being is shameful. There are Copperheads enough in Massachusetts that such hateful anti-Union taunts are well within the realm of possibility.

Children know how to hurt one another, no matter whether they mean what they say. In the schoolyard, it is the hurt that is most important. While Jo was still in school, no one would dare besmirch Amos's name. Now that Amy is left to fend for herself, she has become easy prey.

I cannot pretend to be ignorant of what causes Amy to be the target of such cruelty. Anyone who has been in Amy's presence for more than an afternoon has, at the very least, sighed inwardly at her conceit. For all the effort Amos and I put into teaching our children that they are no better than anyone else upon this earth, Amy managed to absorb the lesson in reverse, and ever since has remained intent upon teaching everyone else that they are no better than she.

The task of showing Amy the part she plays in her own misfortunes is one far better suited to Amos than to me. He has the patience to enlighten her gently, crafting a series of conversations in such a way so as to let her arrive at the discovery herself. Where my affinity is for learning, his is for teaching. I must write and ask his advice before taking Amy in hand, else risk making a hash of the whole affair.

January 27, 1862

To hear the girls talk of their visits to the Laurence house, you might think they'd been to Europe for the afternoon. The flowers! The books! The paintings!

I confess: I envy them. How lovely it would be to have such leisure, to leave my own world behind for an hour or two at a time and revel in beauty and abundance! More than a decade has passed since I have been inside the place. I cannot say I recall being overawed, but of course things were different then.

Even after all these years it pains me to think of the books and portraits we once had. It is a foolish thing to mourn; the money they fetched prevented us from having to sell this house to pay the fines required of us. I refused to part with the Shakespeare and the herbal therapies. Amos clung to his philosophies. The rest went under the auction block. Over the years we have managed to rebuild the library somewhat with cheaper volumes. The shelves do not look so comely as they once did, but the words within the cloth and pasteboard covers are no different than those in the leather-bound ones were.

Meg, Jo, and Amy visit as freely as though the mansion were their own, without so much as a knock. Only Beth has not entered the Laurence house. She cannot bring herself to raise the latch on that big front door, though her mouth fairly waters every time one of her sisters mentions the grand piano. I believe she pities it, standing unplayed in a room that Jo reports is big enough to make whispers echo. Beth's reluctance bedevils me. It is one thing to be fearful of an unpleasant prospect, quite another when timidity stands in the way of something that can only bring pleasure. I have half a mind to take her by the hand, like a four-year-old child, and march her straight up to that piano. But I shall not. She is old enough now to take her own fears in hand.

None but Jo has reported seeing the elder Mr. Laurence, and I see no evidence of other callers. Is it possible that it has already been over a month since Christmas? Time has not been the same since Amos left—either it crawls or it leaps. What with my preoccupation over the Hummels, I yet to properly thank Mr. Laurence for his kindness. This must be rectified. Immediately.

January 29, 1862

Tonight Jo treated us all to a reading of her latest fairy tale. It is most aptly titled *Little Bud*. Her stories are so unlike her—so full of delicate whimsy with their elves and dewdrops and glittering gossamer butterfly wings—they sound as though they were written by someone who dresses solely in sparkling white silks trimmed with pink satin sashes.

What a puzzlement that in her work, where it is least necessary, Jo is more conventional than in any other facet of her life. If ever she uses her pen to mark down her own thoughts in her own voice, I suspect that Jo will leave us all gape-mouthed with wonder. Still, as I sat before the fire with my own brood, I could not help but smile at the cozy bird's nest with four blue eggs in it at the beginning of the story. There are, after all, tiny fragments of herself embedded in these frolicsome fantasies.

January 30, 1862

Laurie's birthday. Sixteen years old. As of this day he could legally enlist in the army as a musician, had he a mind to. I am thankful beyond words that he does not. And anyhow, grand pianos are not to be found upon the battlefields.

The sort of gift I should like to give him is far beyond the reach of my pocketbook, so I have knitted him a pair of stout wool socks. Union blue, of course. All the yarn and fabric in Massachusetts is Union blue, these days. The best I could do to smarten them up with a bit of trimming was to knit the heels and toes in black, and add a set of cables up the sides. It is such a terribly practical gift, I almost did not want to give it. In a fit of cowardice, I decided to put the package in the little mailbox Laurie and the girls have contrived. There was also the unexpectedly complicated matter of putting my name to the tag. My pen hovered for a whole minute above that blank fold of paper. How to sign it? Mrs. March, Margaret, Marmee—each of them did not quite fit. In the end I settled for simplicity: *M.M.*

January 31, 1862

Mr. Laurence is a thoroughly unexpected delight. I ought to have called upon him long ago. Tending to the poor, it is too easy for me to forget that all of us, even the richest of us, need more than food and shelter to thrive.

The last time I was in his house, it was draped with mourning for his wife. When his granddaughter died, he saw no one. It has been my mistake to regard the house as though it remains in perpetual mourning. The man is stern in appearance, yet quite affable.

The conversation quickly turned to his grandson, and soon he was confiding that the reports from the boy's tutor are not good. No doubt as I am a woman, he deems me an expert in all matters regarding bringing up children, forgetting that he has spent far longer raising a family than I.

"Theodore has no appetite for his studies," Mr. Laurence said in a tone of disgust.

It is a foreign notion to me—I hungered for knowledge and could not lap it up quickly enough. Still, a portion of that desire was common envy. I wanted the same education my brother was entitled to, and could not understand why I was not entitled to it as well. I still cannot, for that matter. The mere fact that mathematics, Latin, history, botany, and all the rest dangled beyond my fingertips made them all the more desirable. (The yearning was not nearly so intense when my mother deemed it time for me to learn to sew. Only when my father demonstrated his surprising skill with needle and thread did I consent to be taught without protest; the further fact that as a boy Father had been compelled to learn to sew as a form of punishment seemed to justify my own suffering.)

"Perhaps he has been overfilled, and needs time to digest it," I countered. "It may be that he is starved for other things."

That took him aback, and I feared for a moment it had caused him offense. "Starved?" he said. His hand made an involuntary gesture toward the plenty that surrounded us. "For what?"

"Amusement. Exercise." He began to scoff, but I would not be interrupted. "Companionship," I insisted.

He fixed me with a look that would have shriveled Beth on the spot. "Your father provided you an ample education."

"A feast of knowledge."

"Yet you tell me to let Theodore forsake his studies and run wild?"

It was my turn to scoff. "Mr. Laurence," I said, daring to use a tone I reserve for scolding the children. "A bright mind will not be content with idleness for long. We all reach toward what we do not have. When all that he needs is within his grasp, he will realize it need not be feast or famine."

"And what do you reach toward, Mrs. March?"

"Emancipation for slaves. Education for women. Relief for the poor."

His eyebrows lifted. "Nothing for yourself?"

"What could bring me greater satisfaction or pleasure than justice for all?"

He thought me too good to be true. Anyone who has not seen me rage inside does. They see only half the scale, not understanding how much good it takes to balance the weight of my most leaden fault on the other side.

"Nothing for yourself alone?"

I could not say it at first. My throat shut until I had taken a second breath. "My husband's safety."

He sat back with a sigh and nodded. The room fell quiet. It was a soothing silence—a silence that recognized Amos's absence, and praised it. Mr. Laurence was the first to speak. "You learned generosity at your father's knee. I daresay he would be prouder of your good work now than he might have been ten years ago."

"You're very kind. I only wish I had as much to give now as I did then."

"Surely you learned better mathematics than that. You give a greater proportion of your means than I."

"That is a comfort only to me, but I thank you anyhow. I'm sure the men and women who come to the relief rooms would prefer to see the benefit from a thousand of your dollars than ten of mine."

His laugh could not be said to boom; instead, it seemed to crackle through the air. "You are your father's daughter," he said with a slap to the arm of his chair. "And so is that feisty girl of yours."

"Jo. Josephine."

"Named for her grandfather, I suppose?"

"Indeed."

He chuckled to himself, rubbing the arms of the chair with both palms. "Never one to mince words, was he? Or to prance about with niceties when he could get right to the point."

"That is a fact."

"I wish he could have been in this room when Josephine judged me less handsome than her own grandfather."

I had to clap a hand over my mouth to stop my laugh, which made my apology considerably less convincing. "Please tell me she didn't say so—not to your face. Oh, that Jo! I'm so sorry, Mr. Laurence."

"She did. And I'm not sorry. She's right, and I know it as well as

she does. Fifty years ago, every debutante in Boston saved a place for
Joseph May on her dance card. I made it my duty to cheer up the ones
he disappointed, and I assure you, I had no shortage of work to do.
Had I been distracted by the belle of every ball, I might not have met
my Tabitha."

It was good to laugh that way, and it must have showed.

"If I may say so, you weather your trials with a great deal of grace,
Mrs. March," he said. I don't know whether he is kinder than most,
or whether his gruff veneer makes his kindness seem all the greater.
I only know that I could not thank him that time. It was all I could
do to wink away the tears before they dropped. "Your family's fall has
been a most honorable one."

"That is what makes it bearable. Maybe it is prideful of me, but if
it had been for nothing . . ."

"The man escaped then, did he?" He spoke in a confidential tone,
though no one was there to hear.

"So far as we know." No more was said.

He has lost so much more than we have in the last ten years. Ours
are easily measurable: two thousand dollars. His—a son and daughter-
in-law, a wife, a granddaughter—cannot be quantified. Nor have I
seen Mr. Laurence's daughter visit since her little girl died. Why, I do
not know. But the child's death occurred here, and so I sense that it is
better not to ask; that wound may well be double-edged.

"I hope you will do me the honor of paying a call someday, so that
I may return your hospitality," I told him as I took my leave.

"And when might I find you at home, Mrs. March? It seems I see
you striding off toward town six days of every seven."

In a flash of brilliance, I told him Thursday morning, happy to
trade his company for that of Mrs. Weddleton. My expression must
have betrayed my sudden jollity, for he asked me if I was up to some
mischief. I assured him I was not, and we made our goodbyes. Or
rather, we voiced them. There was something in his manner that kept
me from stepping past the threshold.

"Is there something else, Mr. Laurence?"

He fidgeted and stammered so, I could not guess what it might be. When he spoke, it was a perfect non sequitur: "One of your younger girls does not go to school." The statement carried a prong of censure—my own, not Mr. Laurence's. That fact still smarts each and every time I think of it.

"Beth," I answered, too puzzled to say more.

"I see her in the garden many a forenoon, tending to her sweet peas and heart's-ease. And I often hear the piano when the windows are open and no one else is home. Is it she who plays?" I told him it was, and apologized for the jangling of the poor battered piano. He waved that away. "She plays quite well, except for E flat and C, which is obviously no fault of hers but of the instrument itself. Will she be at home on Thursday?"

"She will. But she is not likely to join us. Beth is rather bashful, I'm afraid."

"Pity. I should like to meet her. She reminds me somehow of Lyddie." He cleared his throat so severely I nearly jumped. "Lydia. My granddaughter." I had not expected that. The child I recall had a riot of blond corkscrew curls, and cheeks spattered with freckles.

I could not promise. But nor could I bear to disappoint him. "We shall look forward to seeing you on Thursday," I said. Even that, I fear, may have lent him more hope than is fair.

Back home, I opened my desk drawer and took out the lock of my father's hair. How I used to love to comb that hair for him before scampering off to bed at night. It is one of my fondest childhood memories, and yet I cannot recall the last time it passed through my mind. I have not spoken of him in so very long. Not from avoidance, but simply a lack of anyone who shares my memory of him. Amos knew him only briefly. To my girls, he is both as familiar and as distant as a character in a fairy tale. With Mr. Laurence, I can remember the real man once again. His recollections have added new color to the graying portrait in my mind. It is a favor I should very much like to repay, and I fear Beth is the only one with the power to do so. I have less than a week to convince her to meet him.

Postscript: I nearly forgot—when I slipped my hands into my muff on the way home from the Laurence house, there was a little packet of Jordan almonds inside. Who could have put them there but Laurie? Part of his birthday gifts, no doubt. He is very like a crow, with his inky hair and eyes and his offerings.

February 1, 1862

Ninety-nine days of one hundred, Beth is by far the least troublesome of all my daughters. Then comes the hundredth day. She fairly quivers at the mere mention of Mr. Laurence's visit.

I should not have told Beth how keen he is to meet her. I'd thought to reassure her; instead the notion has put her in a flutter of anxiety. No matter how I cajole her with assurances that he was Grandfather May's great friend, it does no good. "He told me stories that made me laugh, Beth," I pleaded, "stories I'd never heard before." She only shakes her head, too fearful of the prospect even to answer me in words.

What she fears is invisible to me. I have spent most of my life wishing for more ways to make my presence felt in the world, to make my voice heard. For Beth, the prospect of being seen, looked at, watched, is paralyzing. I could better sympathize if it were only strangers that unnerve her so, but any kind of attention makes her curl up within herself. Even on her birthday, with none but those she loves best orbiting her like planets around a cherished sun, she always looks as though she'd like to bolt under the table at the first chance.

There is no one I can turn to for counsel. Hannah is too fond of Beth to be impartial. I would rather drink a quart of vinegar than ask Aunt March's advice. If only I knew enough German to talk this over with Birte Hummel. But with little more than nouns currently at our disposal, we cannot begin to discuss anything as intangible as fear or frustration.

As I was not aggrieved enough with the state of things, I foolishly glanced through the auction notices in the *Advertiser* this evening. Two large private libraries are to be auctioned this month—one the theological collection of the late Reverend Maltby of Bangor, and the other a veritable treasure chest of illustrated volumes on art, architecture, and botany. Oh, how Amos and I used to savor the chance to peruse the auction houses and lug home books by the crateful. Adopting an orphaned library gave a particular gratification not to be found elsewhere. I thought I had learned not to miss the old days, but now that Amos is away, I find myself drifting further backward. Reaching, I suppose, for untroubled times.

February 3, 1862

A perfect compromise occurred to me this morning: Beth could simply play the piano in the hall while Mr. Laurence and I visit in the parlor. "He would not even see you, Beth."

She would not consider it—not for a single second. "But he would hear me," she said before it seemed to me that she'd had time enough to take in the words. "Oh, I couldn't. I'd be so ashamed of the wrong notes."

I curbed myself from telling her that he has been listening to her play for months now, and already knows every note her piano cannot produce in tune. She might never lay a finger on the instrument again.

How Amos and I managed to produce a child of such innate shyness utterly eludes me. Amos is tranquil, yes, but not timid in the least. He relishes his Sundays in the pulpit, and never refuses a chance to address a schoolroom, opera house, or town hall filled with prospective abolitionists. Had I a platform to stand upon, I would lecture to anything with ears about the deplorable conditions of the enslaved, the ills of the poor, and privations of women. Beth must muster her courage for two days and two nights before she dares ask a shopkeeper for a sheet of music.

The tender way she ministers to her nursery full of castoff dolls plainly shows the depth of her heart, the compassion she is capable of. All that love, lavished on cotton, wood, and porcelain that will never return it. I cannot make up my mind whether it is the epitome of selflessness, or the most pitiful of tragedies. How much of herself can she give without replenishment?

I have always hated the frills and pretenses of society—I cannot blame Beth for that—but people? Simply people. To see her cringe like a little kicked dog at the prospect of mixing with others, when not a soul has done her harm in all her life, sometimes drives me beyond the brink of sympathy and straight into a quiet whirl of fury. When it takes hold of me, I can imagine swooping up all those broken and battered dolls in a single armload and dropping them into the stove, so that she would have no choice but to associate with people who are made of something other than cotton and wood. It is a vicious thought. But that fault is mine, not Beth's. It is not Beth herself who vexes me, but my own inability to either help her, or let her be as she is.

I could end this impasse easily enough with a demand. It is an unfair advantage, for Beth's serenity prevents her from indulging in any kind of disobedience. And so I have not demanded—only requested. I pray I have the strength to continue as gently.

February 4, 1862

Another attempt has failed. I had thought that perhaps if Beth visited the Laurence house, taking Jo as her armor, it might somehow render her less frightened of Mr. Laurence himself. Surely the sight of that grand piano—broader and longer than our own dining table—would convince her to become acquainted with its owner.

That is what I thought. I could not have been more mistaken.

They were hardly gone ten minutes before Beth came skittering back and flew into my arms.

"Mr. Laurence saw us."

"And?"

There was no *and*. Not if you ask Jo, that is. Mr. Laurence simply came round the corner and saw them at the piano. He said a single word—"Hey"—and Beth bolted for home.

"My feet chattered on the floor," Beth said, in such a tone that I found myself rocking her like a baby. I understood a little better then. It is not only that she is afraid—it is that she is ashamed of being afraid. That is surely in part my doing. I am not as patient with her as Jo is, and it must show despite my best efforts. My best efforts are likely what makes it show. My frustration vibrates at such a pitch, it must feel like an earthquake to one as tranquil as Beth.

"He wasn't angry, Marmee," Jo told me after Beth had gone up to console herself with her dolls, "only surprised. You know how Beth is."

I know too well. Which is not to say that I comprehend it. Quite the contrary.

Later

It is well after midnight now. My mind will not be still. *Beth, Beth, Beth*, it chants at me. My body followed, tossing me from side to side until I gave up any pretext of sleep and left my bed in hopes that pinning my restless thoughts to paper will arrest their ceaseless motion.

It is the oddest feeling, like a dream in which everything is mismatched. Jo and Amy have given me abundant cause to toss and turn over the years, and even Meg from time to time has rumpled my thoughts, but Beth? Even in her infancy, she rarely needed me to walk the floor with her. She has not kept me awake like this but once, while Amos and I contended with the dilemma of whether to withdraw her from school.

It was a decision Amos ultimately left to me. I knew his position on the matter—it was he who had suggested that she could study at home—and he knew what it would be like to live with me if I were compelled to capitulate.

Allowing Beth to abandon the schoolroom was among the most

difficult decisions I have ever grappled with. Had we the means to hire a tutor for private study, the decision would have been an uncomplicated one. Those days were long past, though. Beth could never have done as I did, and leave home for months to study at the side of a learned woman like Abigail Allyn. How much I learned from her! Not only languages, mathematics, science, history, philosophy, and theology, but how to comport myself to my own satisfaction. Her character was so admirable, her intellect so keenly honed, that you could not sit in a room with her and feel anything but aspiration. At the end of ten months with Miss Allyn, I felt as though my mind had given birth to a new version of myself. That is an experience I wish I could bequeath to all my girls, but especially to Beth, who seems not to know that the world is made less rich when she hides herself from it.

For the first week of school, I was proud of her for doing something so difficult, and doing so without complaint. Beth never refused to go, never voiced a wish to remain at home. Every afternoon when she returned home I congratulated her for prevailing yet again, promising her that the more often she faced her fear, the more quickly it would diminish. "Soon," I remember saying, "it will be the size of a housefly instead of a dragon." But neither my praise nor her bravery was enough to keep her anxieties at bay.

Her misery simply never abated. Meg had cried on her first day of school, then came gamboling through the kitchen door that same afternoon, reciting in a singsong the names of all the girls she had skipped rope with in the schoolyard, and the color of their hair ribbons. There was never a hint of apprehension afterward.

With Beth, I could not detect even the smallest increment of improvement. She cried the first week, and the second. By the third, she had run out of tears, but her misery was so plain that I thought at first she had taken sick. Seeing Beth's stricken face morning after morning as she struggled to eat the oatmeal Hannah put before her without vomiting—a battle she too often lost—was more compelling than any philosophical arguments Amos might have proposed. It was more pitiful, somehow, to watch her struggle to eat than it was to see her come home so wearied that she could hardly play with her kittens or tend to her dolls.

In the end, simple practicality won out. If her mind was so crowded with apprehensions that there was no room for learning, I asked myself, what was the good of schooling? A mind must have space to expand.

But what was the good of keeping Beth sheltered if now she cannot endure even the prospect of a social call from a neighbor? Have I in effect cultivated what I had hoped to gradually choke out with other growth? I do not want her to choose home and hearth because it is the place she dreads least, but because it is the place she loves most. Home should indeed be a refuge, not the metaphorical bed she cowers under.

February 5, 1862

The *Herald* reports this morning that sickness is on the rise among our troops. And why? Simply because the officers and surgeons are not requisitioning proper amounts of shoes and clothing. Whether this is through negligence or ignorance is not known; in either case, it is unconscionable. The reports from Washington state that the depot of the Sanitary Commission is amply supplied, and yet the necessary articles lie unused. It is disturbing enough to know that our men are wanting such basic necessities. But when the suffering is needless, it whips me into a hurricane of frustration. What are we working for six days a week if not to keep our soldiers—our husbands, sons, and brothers—warm and healthy?

Between the war news and Beth, my mind was so preoccupied that I was the next best thing to useless in the relief rooms today. Clumsy and snappish to such a degree that I could not tolerate my own company, much less justify inflicting my bad humor upon anyone else.

By three o'clock I admitted defeat and left early. To my surprise, I found myself on the doorstep of the Laurence house instead of my own.

Mr. Laurence himself answered the door. He looked abashed and distressed, as though I had come to scold him. "I'd hoped you'd come, Mrs. March. I didn't dare chance startling the poor girl all over again by knocking at your door to make my apologies. I was so astonished to see her here after what you had said about her bashfulness that I suppose I rather barked."

"It isn't simply that she is shy. It is more akin to an infirmity with her." My conscience pricked at me. "I shouldn't say *akin to*. Understating it does no good, as yesterday amply proved."

"Should I not call on Thursday?"

"No. The less attention drawn to it, the better. Beth will only be more miserable if she believes she has ruined a call for me."

"This troubles you a great deal, doesn't it, Mrs. March?" Mr. Laurence asked with such concern that I dropped all pretense.

"It does. I confess I haven't any idea how to help her overcome it. There seems to be no cause for it."

"Perhaps every symptom does not have a cause."

My mind jolted as though he had thrown open the curtains of a dark room. *Intelligence is not always sufficient*, as Miss Allyn used to say. I have turned my head inside out and back again in search of a reason for Beth's shyness, when there may be none at all.

Again and again during those first miserable weeks of schooling I asked her, "What's wrong, Beth? What has happened to make you dread it so?" And every time the answer was "Nothing." I presumed then and ever after that she was keeping something terrible from me. I could not understand why she would not tell me, why she would not allow me to vanquish whatever was causing her such suffering.

All these years later, it has at last become clear. There was no reason. No spark or provocation. That itself was the terrible thing that she could not confess. Beth knew my wishes for her. How could she not? Amos may be the minister in this Family, but I have given more than my share of sermons on the importance of education for women. All along she knew she could not achieve what I wanted most for her, and that, she could not bear to tell me.

Mr. Laurence and I talked for a good while about how we might proceed tomorrow, during which he was most understanding. And yet he never did rescind his hope that Beth might be present.

Armed with fresh insight, I resolved to make one last attempt with Beth. I had to do so with great care, for at their age I do not want any of my daughters to obey out of blind compulsion, or without measuring the cost to themselves of another's request. If there is a price to be paid, it ought to be relinquished in full knowledge of its value.

Nor did I want to loom over Beth as I made my final entreaty. Even if I brought her onto the sofa beside me, she would have to look up at my face. So instead I sat her in my own chair and took the stool before her.

"Mr. Laurence expects nothing from you tomorrow," I assured her. "You need not speak a word; he will not think you rude if you remain utterly silent."

I could not bring myself to ask again. Not in words. I simply looked at her and took her hands in mine. Her chin trembled.

"But why, Marmee?" she whispered.

The words were given to me. That is all I can say. In one moment I had nothing to say, and in the next, they had arrived. The thought itself had not come to me earlier—only the feeling, perhaps.

"Do you know how it is when we all sit here together, happy and cozy before the fire with our songs and sewing, and suddenly look up to see Father's empty chair?"

Her eyes—I am at a loss to describe how they change when she is taken with sadness. Sometimes I think the look of them could reduce a sheet of iron to a puddle.

"That is how Mr. Laurence feels in that great hollow house, without his granddaughter. Laurie cannot fill her place, just as no other man can fill Father's place among us. He has not expressed it in so many words, but I think Mr. Laurence would like to remember how it feels to sit in a parlor with a young lady sewing quietly in the corner. Can you give him that small comfort, Beth, as a favor for the kindnesses he has bestowed?"

She looked again to Amos's armchair. As she thought it through,

I could fairly feel the courage mounting up in her. Her chin steadied, her chest lifted with a brave breath.

"Yes," she said.

February 6, 1862

Just as Mr. Laurence had promised, he paid no mind to Beth as we entered the parlor this afternoon. Instead, he spotted the chessboard immediately and wanted to know if I played. When I told him it has been one of the rarest of my rare delights since Amos went to war, he gave the floor a mighty thump with his cane that made Beth jump. "Capital! Shall we have a match, Mrs. March?"

Of course I was agreeable. It has been months since I played.

"You mustn't let me win because I am old," he admonished.

"And you mustn't let me win because I am a lady," I countered.

His crackling laugh rumpled the air and he sat down on the black side of the board—the side that put his back to Beth.

"Your skill is considerable, Mrs. March," he said after we had taken half a dozen turns between us. "I have not had so worthy an opponent since I played opposite your father."

"I could say the very same of you, Mr. Laurence."

"If you learned the game at your father's knee, I might as well give up now. Joseph May never shared his strategy with me; he only trounced me with it."

"Surely you have learned some tactics of your own in the years since?"

"I have. And I believe you have as well."

"Indeed," I replied as I checkmated him.

He sat back, dumbfounded, then leaned forward with one fist upon his knee. "Where did you learn to play like that?" he demanded.

I told him then of the nightly matches Miss Allyn challenged me with during my studies in Duxbury. I knew most of Father's maneuvers by then, and still it took six weeks before I won a game—six weeks during which I endeavored not to knock every piece from the board in paroxysms of sheer frustration. My clenched jaw ached worse than my pride by the time I climbed the stairs to bed after every one of those defeats. (The memory of it remains so vivid, I still have to remind myself not to grind my teeth each time I play.) But in the end I learned to checkmate both my temper and Miss Allyn, and when I returned home I could best my father six times out of seven.

"Will you play another match?" Mr. Laurence asked.

His eagerness made me saucy as a child. "If you are willing to be bested."

I had expected him to concentrate all the harder, but instead he began to chat most amiably. "I hear you singing quite often on your way to work, Mrs. March. Many of the songs are familiar to me, though I have not heard them in many years."

"My father's favorites are mine as well. He did so love to sing."

"One of my life's great disappointments is having not been favored with the gift of musicality. Each time I try to raise my voice in song, nothing but a shout emerges. My grandson would likely tell you that a shout emerges any time I open my mouth," he added as a wry aside. "Musical notes on paper are as indecipherable to my eyes as ink splatters. My only talent in that vast sphere is appreciation, and so I have made it my duty, you might say, to exercise that talent as widely as possible in the concert halls of Boston, New York, and Europe."

He proceeded to reminisce about a staggering number of performances. Those I can recall included Louis Gottschalk, the great pianist; *I Lombardi alla prima crociata*, the first of Verdi's operas to be performed in the United States; the Boston premier of Beethoven's *Symphony No. 1*; Elizabeth Taylor Greenfield, the so-called Black Swan; and the Swedish Nightingale herself, Jenny Lind.

"I would have loved to see Miss Lind," I told him, "but the tickets were advertised at such exorbitant prices that I could not justify it—not even in support of her fine charities."

"It was a vanity, buying those tickets. I told everyone it was Tabitha who had set her heart upon it," he added in a confiding tone, "for a man is sooner excused for indulging his wife's extravagant fancies than his own. But I have never regretted the expense—it was the last concert Tabitha and I attended together."

He paused then, bestowing a fond and wistful look at the queen on his side of the board. Before I could offer my sympathies, he took up the thread of conversation as though it had never dropped.

"Miss Lind produced notes of such exquisite purity, you hardly dared breathe for fear of disturbing the air they floated upon. And yet I would be hard-pressed to say whether I most enjoyed the Swedish Nightingale or the Black Swan. Have you heard of Elizabeth Taylor Greenfield?" he asked. I have indeed, and would surely have pressed Amos for tickets to hear her sing if we had not been in financial disgrace by then.

"I was fortunate enough to see Miss Greenfield's premier at the Metropolitan Hall in New York before she departed for London," he went on. "I daresay that had you been there, you might have relished watching the audience's reaction to Miss Greenfield's artistry more than the performance itself. The absolute shock of that refined voice coming from a Negro throat was impossible for much of the audience to conceal. I had considered myself a man of very little prejudice, but I confess that I felt my own eyes widen when the program shifted from Stephen Foster's parlor songs to Bellini's arias. It was she who made me understand that I, too, had underestimated the humanity and potential of the Negro race."

His talk was so invigorating, his perspective so singular, that I found it impossible to concentrate fully on the chessboard. Where usually I am able to plot four and five moves ahead, I could only keep track of two or three. The thought crossed my mind that he was using distraction in place of strategy. And yet I could not bring myself to challenge him and risk hearing no more of Elizabeth Taylor Greenfield.

"Perhaps it was all in my mind, but I must say that it was easier to believe that Miss Greenfield understood the role of Bellini's Norma than it was to imagine Miss Lind comprehending the full tragedy of the character. A woman born into slavery almost certainly has a greater emotional range to draw upon than a pampered Swedish prodigy. The latter delighted the ears and the eyes, while the former altered the heart and mind."

I agreed. Having seen her newspaper portraits, it is difficult to picture the angelic Miss Lind as a convincing Norma, holding a knife over her sleeping sons in contemplation of their murder. But I have heard more than one story of an enslaved woman murdering her children to save them from the degradations of bondage. "It is not merely the perfection of the notes," I said, "that render music beautiful."

"I knew we would be of a mind on this topic!" he exclaimed, punctuating the thought with the soft thud of a rook upon the chessboard. "Given the choice between an indifferent musician playing a perfect instrument, or a true lover of music playing a flawed one, I will take the flaws without complaint. That is not at all to suggest that Miss Greenfield gave a flawed performance, mind you. Quite the contrary. Those who had greeted her appearance onstage with laughter were faced with a banquet of humble pie by the concert's end. Her remarks at the close of the performance, apologizing to the Negro people for their exclusion from the concert hall, were most affecting, and drew a roar of applause."

When next I looked up, there was Beth, poised behind Mr. Laurence's chair with palms pressed together before her heart as though she were praying. I had forgotten her entirely. I cannot say whether Mr. Laurence noticed her presence until she was beside him. If he did, he gave no indication of it. That is what I thought in the moment, at least. Now, when I recall how artfully he swung the conversation in the direction of Laurie and the grand piano, I can only conclude that he had maneuvered the entire visit with as much strategy as I moved my pawns and knights across the chessboard.

"All this talk of music reminds me," he said, and launched into a lament about the poor grand piano, suffering from want of use. "Wouldn't some of your girls like to run over and practice on it now and then, just to keep it in tune?"

The effort of not looking at Beth was so great, I could not reply. She was moving so slowly forward, it made me think of the way she coaxes the most reluctant of cats into the house—stretching a length of yarn across the yard and patiently tugging it nearer a quarter inch at a time without so much as tilting her head toward the creature. Except this time Beth herself was the kitten, and Mr. Laurence's words the yarn.

Then he gave what amounted to the final tug: "They needn't see or speak to any one, but run in at any time, for I'm shut up in my study at the other end of the house. Laurie is out a great deal, and the servants are never near the drawing room after nine o'clock." Just as Beth reached the arm of the chair, Mr. Laurence stood as if to go. "If they don't care to come, well, never mind."

As Beth slid her hand into his, my own hand flew silently to my throat. "Oh, sir!" she said. "They do care, very, very much!"

"Are you the musical girl?" he asked gently.

"I'm Beth; I love it dearly, and I'll come if you are quite sure nobody will hear me—and be disturbed."

How her voice trembled! How I trembled to see this girl who looked like Beth, sounded like Beth, approach a virtual stranger and speak without prodding.

Mr. Laurence looked at her in much the same way as he had gazed at the queen upon the chessboard when he spoke of his wife. With a single finger, he brushed a tendril of hair from Beth's forehead. "I had a little girl once with eyes like these," he said, his voice the furthest thing possible from a shout. "God bless you, my dear; good-day, madam."

Beth and I stood blinking in the parlor, neither of us sure that what had happened was real, until the bang of the front door shutting behind him startled us both. Then Beth threw her arms around my waist and squeezed the very breath from me. It was then that my gaze fell upon the chessboard. The black queen—Mr. Laurence's queen—stood one move away from checkmating my king. He had been on the verge of besting me, and said not a word of it.

The rest of the day seemed not to exist; no matter what placed itself before my eyes, all my mind could see was that scene in the parlor.

On my way up to bed, I noticed an envelope on the hall table, with my name upon it in an elegant script. Inside was twenty dollars, and a note from Mr. Laurence. For the relief rooms, the note explained, which had been twice deprived of my labors at his behest. I am beginning to think James Laurence is a man whose kindness cannot be equaled.

February 7, 1862

My attempt to evade Mrs. Weddleton failed. It seems there was some uproar at the Weddleton house yesterday that delayed her weekly visit until today. A maid has been dismissed in disgrace. The offense is too horrid to be spoken of, as she made sure to tell each and every one of us. Consequently, no one can fail to guess what the precise nature of the crime must be. I sincerely hope the young woman has family to take her in, for she will be unable to find employment until her child is born and will surely not dare appeal at the relief rooms for help.

To hear Mrs. Weddleton tell it, the woman's name is simply That Bridget, which gives me no chance of locating her myself. Concord and Boston are fairly swarming with Bridgets, many of them, I'm sorry to say, in a similar predicament.

Hannah had held a plate of supper for me, as always. Potato soup and biscuits. She seems to have a sixth sense for the days when I am likely to be late, and rarely fails to cook something that will keep warm easily.

I did not notice the change in her straightaway as I related the doings of my day. It was stupid of me. Hannah has been with us so long and is so thoroughly integrated into our lives that I failed to see how closely the uproar at the Weddletons' paralleled the circumstances that brought her to our doorstep.

"Is she Irish?" Hannah asked. "The maid that was dismissed?"

"I presume so. Her name is Bridget. 'That Bridget,' Mrs. Weddle-ton calls her now."

"The girl always bears the brunt of the blame, doesn't she? Especially an Irish girl."

I made some sound of assent as I split open a biscuit and reached for the butter. "Your biscuits are lighter than ever tonight," I said. "I'm sorry I wasn't home sooner to enjoy them fresh from the oven." I could pillory myself now for being so oblivious.

It was the sound of my knife striking the butter dish that at last made me conscious of the fact that I was not just the only one speaking, but the only one moving. Hannah had stilled. Completely. Her back was to me, her arms at her sides. Her breath sounded sharp, like that of someone in pain. "It was the master of the house that did it to me," she said quietly, "before I came here."

Never have I felt such a chill in the pit of my belly. Her words lodged there, their weight like that of a cannon ball. "Hannah," I said. It was all I could say. In nineteen years I have had my suspicions, certainly. When a tearful woman comes begging for work with her apron beginning to bulge at the front, there are questions you need not ask—as well as questions you do not ask. The strongest indication was the simple fact that from the start Hannah stoutly refused to tell us the name of her previous employer. But the confirmation of my suspicions left me sickened beyond nausea.

She turned and took hold of the back of a chair with both hands. Her eyes fixed themselves to the opposite wall. "Always at me he was, with his words or his eyes, and then one night . . ." She averted her gaze entirely, speaking as if to the stove. "He'd leave a coin on the mantelpiece after, as if I were—as if it were part of my job. A silver dollar. By the time the missus turned me out, I had seventeen silver dollars knotted into an old stocking."

Every one of them went into the poor box, she said. She could not abide the sight of anything bought with that money. "I'll never forget the clash and clatter they made, falling into that box. I wish now I'd saved the whole lot for Mr. March's church."

Afterward, she said she was glad I knew at last. "All these years, and I never could tell you truly what it meant to be in a house like this. A house where a woman is safe. I wouldn't trade that for a mountain of silver dollars." She wept then, and I with her.

I am sorry now for every silver dollar I ever put into her hand, and I told her so. "I would rather have paid you in pennies than to yank that memory out of its grave."

She pushed the tears from her cheeks with both palms at once. "Ah, Mrs. March. We haven't seen a silver dollar in this house for a good many years." Mischief twinkled extra brightly in her wet eyes and we erupted into such a gale of laughter as would rattle the china in the cupboards.

"You could have told us, Hannah," I said when we had recovered ourselves. "You needn't have carried this alone."

She smiled in that way she has, with the corners of her mouth turned down. "You could have heard it, but I couldn't have said it."

"We wouldn't have turned you out."

"That I knew, and that in itself was enough. Anyway, telling it doesn't set it down. I'll always carry it, like as if it's sewn up in between my skin and my bones. The burden isn't so much in the load itself anymore, but in trying to pretend it isn't there."

After she had gone to bed, I opened my cedar chest and retrieved my diary of 1843 from its depths. It was that January we hired Hannah. It is as I remembered; she told us she had sinned, not that she had been sinned against. Too ashamed to appeal to her own church for aid, she found her way to Amos's. Had we been anything but Unitarian, she might never have come to us. Judging herself to be in a state of ruin, she had little else to lose by appealing to such radicals. As it turned out, all of us had much to gain. The leap of faith she took in joining our household must have been frightening—to live among people who reject the Trinity, the divinity of Christ, and original sin.

Hiring Hannah marked the first deep fissure that would widen into our breach with Aunt March. I have never regretted that decision. It is dreadful to say so, but given a choice between Hannah and

Aunt March, I would choose Hannah a thousand times over again. Rereading the words I wrote after Aunt March and Amos argued, my fury is plainly visible in the slashes of my handwriting:

"You know where she'll end up if we turn her out now," Amos said.

"Indeed! Out in some back alley, trying to sell what she's already given away. What concern is that of yours?"

I could not keep still and watch Amos bear the brunt of her browbeating. "And what concern is it of yours if we keep her out of that back alley?" I retorted.

"There are plenty enough poor, <u>virtuous</u> women who need work." Aunt March can underline a word with her voice like no one else I have encountered. "Yet you're determined to settle for the dregs."

I still remember how she pointed at my own belly. I was more than six months gone with our first child by then.

"And that is the kind of woman you want bringing up your own children?" she said, while the parrot, agitated by her mistress's distress, screeched, "Phoebe! Oh, no, Phoeeebe!"

Polly's shrieks seemed to snatch Aunt March's breath away, and I leapt to Amos's defense. "Better they come to understand the perils of wantonness under our roof than collide with them in the street," I said.

That was one time Amos made no attempt to quell my temper. I feared a dressing down afterward; I ought to have known my husband better than that. He was just as furious as I, and had not the temerity to express it fully.

Once started, I continued reading well into February of 1843, the days coming back to me with renewed clarity. Hannah had not been here but three weeks when she miscarried. I had forgotten how soon it happened—my own loss two months later would render my memory of her ordeal less distinct. I have never forgotten the quantity of blood, though. I still believe it would have filled a bucket; we ended up burning the mattress. Hannah would not permit the doctor to see her, and was back on her feet within two days despite my protests and Amos's, both.

She grieved that infant, though society permitted her no space to do so. It was a grief shaded with guilt. Because she had not wanted the child, she deemed herself responsible for its death. I suspected an entirely different cause. In the frenzy of her gratitude, she'd worked at a furious pace until the pain pinned her to her bed.

Aunt March would have had us turn Hannah out as soon as she'd finished tearing up the bloodied linens for the ragbag. There was no reason to keep Hannah on, she said. No reason except that neither Hannah's family nor her church would have her, and that we had made Hannah a promise.

Life without Hannah in the years that followed would have been different beyond imagining. When I think of all I owe to her, ample pay is the least of my debts. It is because of Hannah that I am able to attend to my work at the relief rooms. Because of Hannah, I could spare Beth the torment of going to school, much as her absence there pained me, knowing that she would be looked after. Meg, Jo, Beth, and Amy have been as sheltered in her arms, on her lap, and nestled against her breasts as they have been in mine. Meg, especially. Meg was a welcome balm for both our wounds.

Hannah was there when our son was born. She is one of but three human beings who saw his face and have a memory of his existence. I believe she saw that day that if I could not will my child to live, she had not willed hers to die.

When I miscarried the infant that would have come between Jo and Beth, Hannah was my greatest comfort. She recognized the signals before I understood them myself. At my first complaint of the ache in the depth of my back, she appointed herself my watchman, and ordered me to bed the moment she found me at the laundry sink, rinsing the first telltale specks of blood from my underthings. Four years she'd been with us then, and never had she spoken sharply to me before. "I hope to God I'm wrong, Mrs. March," she said, "but if I'm right about what's coming, you'll not want to be standing up when it hits." She was right, of course. She nearly always is. During those days when my heart and my body throbbed with pain in equal measure, she sat beside me as my mother would have, or my sisters, had they still been living.

Loyalty is not a fine enough word for the devotion Hannah has shown to us. It is fidelity. Her confession has left me in a state I cannot put a name to—both sickened and gladdened. All this time, I have not known how to thank her, and all this time our Family has been giving her what she most needed without knowing it.

It was a long time that I sat with both diaries open before me, contemplating the distance between that year and this. There are things, perhaps, that should go unwritten—things that belong only to the lips that speak them and the ears that hear them. It did not occur to me to ask Hannah's consent to record what she had told me until I was looking at the words themselves. And yet I want our stories to exist somewhere, even if it is only for ourselves. There are still so few places in this world for a woman's voice to be heard.

Let me be fully honest as well as lofty: I am reluctant to deny myself the remembrance of this day. Memories are so apt to fade and brighten with time, until they metamorphose into something that may bear little resemblance to the reality that forged them. I find such comfort and satisfaction in revisiting my life as it occurred, to lay my former self and my current self side by side and see how their perspectives have merged or diverged.

Now that it is written down, there is little choice but to keep this diary locked in my cedar chest, alongside the 1843 volume that holds the other half of this story. I ought to burn the two beneath them, dated 1850 and 1851, or at least tear out the pages from December to February, but I cannot bear to do so. Perhaps when the war is won and the words they contain can no longer bring harm to anyone, I may return those two volumes to their rightful place on the study shelf.

February 8, 1862

I did not fully understand what Hannah meant until this morning. I could see the difference in her, and it was the opposite of what I had expected. She is not lighter, not fluttering about on a breeze of relief the way the girls do after confessing a fib. Instead Hannah seems more substantial. All these years, she has been living as if on tiptoe. Now her feet are flat upon the earth once more.

The change in her jarred me at first. To me, her wound is raw and open, yet in reality, it has knitted and scarred over years ago. I must have looked at her differently. After the girls had gone—Meg and Jo to work, Amy to school, and Beth to the Laurence house with a whole sheaf of music—Hannah said to me, "You won't tell now, will you?"

"Not if you don't wish it."

She shook her head. "The way people look at you when they know, it's hard to pick which is worse, the pity or the blame."

"Am I doing it now?"

She gave a great *pshaw*. "The farthest thing from it. Look at me like that and I feel ten feet high. I'll break the ceiling open if you don't turn away."

I lifted my chin and looked her full in the face then. "I want you always to feel ten feet high," I said, "for you have been a bastion of strength to me ever since the day—" I could not finish.

She offered her hand, and I clasped it gladly. "I know the one well enough," she said. "Leastwise, I think I do. We've had our share of fine days and foul, haven't we, Mrs. March?"

We have indeed. And I pray we will be together for all that remain.

February 9, 1862

Beside my diary tonight lays the latest installment of Jo's flower fairy book—a story in rhyme of a clover blossom who shelters a lowly worm under her leaves until he becomes a butterfly. Beneath that lay a note:

Dear Marmee—You are Clover-Blossom, of course. With love from a grateful little worm named Jo

The rhyme and meter are as clumsy as Jo herself in places, but the sentiment is so unalloyed, my heart swelled until it seemed the size of a pumpkin. With a pang, I noticed the time—well past midnight. Poor child! How long might she have lain awake, waiting to hear some sign that I had received her gift, before dropping into a troubled sleep? I crept into Meg and Jo's room and sat down on Jo's side of the bed. Her loose hair rippled over the covers like a yard of chestnut silk. I ran my hand down the length of it twice before she stirred with a little murmur. Not a word passed between us. She looked up at my face, smiled dreamily at what she saw there, and nuzzled herself back down into her pillow. I kissed her forehead in gratitude and returned to my room.

February 12, 1862

Beth has taken a notion to make Mr. Laurence a pair of slippers, as thanks for her privileges with the grand piano. Every day but Sunday has found her at the Laurence house, and her rapture over the music she can produce on that superb instrument is such that it cannot be contained. When she comes home from an afternoon of practice, she is as bright-faced and breathless as Jo is after one of her runs through the orchards. It is a joy to see. So little but fear has ever exhilarated her.

Handwork is a fine idea, as there is nothing in a shop Mr. Laurence does not have the means to purchase for himself. Nor is there anything within our meager budget that is worthy of the sentiment Beth wishes to express. So, slippers. Purple has been deemed the proper shade for a gentleman, with pansies embroidered on the toes.

Of course there was nothing remotely suitable in the ragbag, so I extracted a few coins from my own money box for a quarter yard of claret-colored velvet and glossy embroidery floss of violet, black, and yellow. It is a trifling thing to pray for, but I pray Beth makes no mistakes in the cutting and sewing, for we can ill afford this small length of velvet, much less a replacement.

It was fortunate indeed that I had coins enough for this purchase. Paper currency is much in disgrace these days, as the newspapers report that the treasury is nearly empty. Gold and specie hold their value, while treasury notes provoke sighs and frowns from shopkeepers. If the situation is not remedied, I fear Amos's pay will not stretch far enough in the coming months, even if he were to send every cent of it.

February 13, 1862

Each Thursday afternoon I reward myself with a German lesson at the Hummels'. Mrs. Hummel has proven as eager to learn English as I am to master her language. She calls me missus and I call her Frau, for we have both challenged ourselves to speak as little of our respective native languages as possible when we are in one another's presence. With the help of a tattered primer, we are making steady progress, though we cannot be said to converse. At first, we sat across the table and traded nouns, passing Karl's slate back and forth to write the pairs of words.

There is not much in her house, and so we have each already memorized the name of every object. It makes both of us feel terribly accomplished. Today Mrs. Hummel made a joke, summoning Karl to translate: "It is quicker to learn German in one room than in a mansion, ja?"

"Jawohl!" I laughed, savoring the perfect fit of the word.

Hers is the type of good cheer I most admire. She neither laments, nor pretends the hardships do not exist, but dares to mock them with a humor so unexpected, it seems to come from nowhere. (I should not say it is unexpected. I make the mistake, over and over again, of presuming she is not intelligent simply because she cannot express herself fully in English.)

In the last two weeks we have made attempts with less tangible parts of speech. Red, rot. Sit, sitzen. Heavy, schwer. The little ones have yet to tire of helping us act out prepositions—on the chair, in the bed, under the table. In exchange for their good behavior, I've begun to teach them the alphabet by posing their arms and legs in the forms of the letters, just as Amos taught our girls. Mrs. Hummel and I have had to learn each other's alphabets as well, for the German Gothic script differs from English in several particulars. Her handwriting is a thing of beauty, each bend and loop formed with practiced precision. This she can do with Greta nursing and Minna and Heinrich trying to see who can climb highest on the rungs on the back of her chair. My writing looks as though the words are racing one another to plunge over the edge of the slate.

German is a marvelous language. I confess my tongue, or rather my throat, is not well suited to replicating its sounds, but Mrs. Hummel today declared that I have Sprachgefühl. Dissected into its parts, the word means language-feeling. As nearly as I can determine, it describes a natural instinct for languages. It is words just such as this which make German such a delight. The Hummels can describe nearly anything with a single word, it seems.

Mrs. Hummel is eager for her children to learn English as well. Only Karl and Lottchen can be said to be bilingual; the little ones know nothing but German, though the middle two seem to understand snatches of what I say. If I ask Karl to borrow his slate, for instance, Monika wriggles free of Ada to fetch it for me. (I must remember to buy him a new slate pencil. Mrs. Hummel and I have already worn a quarter inch from his with our lessons.)

This indulgence means trading away an hour or more of time I would otherwise devote to my girls. It seems as if I have not seen Jo in particular since January. She is so often in her garret when I return.

The only evidence of her existence is the depleting store of apples, and the creak of footsteps on the attic floorboards as she paces. Likely she is caught up in another of her vortexes. When I do see her, her fingers are stained with ink. Her little book of fairy tales will soon be finished, no doubt.

Today I also missed a visit from Laurie, who left as his calling card a spray of forsythia cuttings on the verge of blooming. He must have tended them for a week or more, to have them ready to burst by now. I shall have to find time to make it up to him. And perhaps an extra piece of squash pie, as thanks.

But what a treat it is to be a student again, to feel my mind widening itself with each new word. It seems to me that the way we speak of the world around us colors the way we see it. With each new language I learn, the hues of meaning at my disposal only increase—like looking through a prism rather than a simple lens.

February 15, 1862

Another visit with Mr. Laurence, replete with fine reminiscences of my father. We laughed together over the fact that for as brilliant and handsome as he was, his stockings almost never matched. Already I have forgotten what caused us to recall such a trivial thing, but quick on its heels another pair of long-lost details rose up in my mind: Father's fondness for bright red gaiters, and the little bow he wore in his cravat.

How I wish there was someone who could help me remember my mother in the same way. My memories of her are so pale, they are almost transparent. I was sixteen years old when she died, and yet my recollections are so few, I might have been a little child. Perhaps because her health faded so early in my life, she began to dim even before she had gone. She had the power to calm my rages, but like Amos, it was not a power that came from force. It was she who taught me how to turn my anger into something of use, to harness its power and reroute its flow.

"Make of it an oven rather than a conflagration," she would say. "Fire consumes, but an oven transforms." I do not see her face as I recall these words, but her hands, kneading the dough that would become bread. It was a task she loved, and too soon had to relinquish to Cook when the sickness warped her joints and sapped her strength, sending her from the breadboard to her bed. I can remember quite clearly how she made me feel, if not the shade of blue in her eyes or the musical pattern of laughter that was hers alone. Sometimes, when I was nursing my daughters, a tendril of a scent that reminded me of her seemed to rise out of nowhere.

February 22, 1862

There has been little time to write this week, as we hurry to meet the needs caused by the losses at Fort Donelson, Tennessee. Even a victory for the Union exacts a steep price, and the fact that none of our Massachusetts regiments played a role in the campaign makes no difference to our work. The stores of supplies must be kept high, lest any who suffer be forced to wait in pain for relief.

But today something occurred that I could not bear to risk forgetting, however unlikely that may be.

The sound that greeted me when I arrived home this evening made me wonder if I had happened into the wrong house. Music poured from the windows, the notes so sweet and nimble, I simply had to sing along with them. And there, in my own parlor, was the source: Beth, playing a cabinet piano lovelier than any I have seen since my own childhood. A brass medallion above the keyboard proclaimed it the work of one Thomas Tomkison, Manufacturer to His Royal Highness, the Prince of Wales. The rosewood cabinet gleamed bright as satin in the lamplight, yet it was dim compared to the glow of Beth's face.

Mr. Laurence had sent it. When I read the note that had accompanied it, I had to wink back tears. The instrument had belonged to his

Lydia, the granddaughter he so cherished. This, in exchange for a pair of homemade slippers. By a stroke of serendipity, the pansies Beth had chosen to embroider turned out to be his favorite posy. Heart's-ease, he calls them. Perhaps that single word explains everything.

When I told her she must thank Mr. Laurence, she said she already had.

"He is the kindest man, Marmee."

I sat there in pure awe. The two of them have somehow bewitched one another.

To my utter joy, not even Amy is envious of Beth's good fortune. The enormity of the gift is staggering, and yet somehow the sentiment expressed in Mr. Laurence's note renders the trade an even one. The cost of the instrument itself is but a trifle to him. He could just as readily have ordered a brand-new piano to be delivered to Beth. Instead, he has sent one of his dearest possessions to her. She has barely lifted a finger, and yet she has managed to touch a heart that, from all outward appearances, has lain dormant for most of her life. Oh, my Beth. Her world may be narrow, but those of us fortunate enough to exist within its boundaries have been uncommonly blessed.

February 24, 1862

A letter from Amos today, with the leavings from his salary enclosed. Seventy-two dollars this month—less than he has ever sent before. With the state of paper currency as it is, this will buy what thirty-five or forty dollars would have purchased last year. There is no explanation for the shortage this month, unless his postscript quotation of Acts 20:35 is a hint. Surely he has not been dispensing paper valentines to cheer his regiment. This is war, not a schoolroom.

Amos counsels patience with Amy's conceit. That I know well enough, just as I am aware that gold or silver specie is the solution to our debts. The difficulty with both problems is how I am to obtain such elusive commodities.

My complaints are petty, for the *Traveler* today contains a notice that little Willie Lincoln succumbed to typhoid fever four days ago. Attended night and day by a pair of the nation's most eminent doctors and still the boy could not be saved. Four children born, and two of them buried. God has asked a great deal of Mr. and Mrs. Lincoln.

February 25, 1862

Amy has been whipped—whipped!—by her schoolmaster.

I should not be as furious as I am. She broke a rule, and was duly punished for it. Not only broke a rule, but willfully evaded it, simply for the sake of a popular fad. Pickled limes, for heaven's sake.

Never before has anyone raised a hand to any of my children. My temper may be quick as gunpowder, but I myself have struck a human being but once in the whole of my life. It is a mistake I shall never repeat.

There was little I dared to say while Amy sobbed out her woes. If I opened my mouth, the dam would have burst, and all manner of umbrage flooded the room. I merely held her and petted her and gritted my teeth, though the sight of the welts on that small palm stung me like the strike of the blows themselves. My voice was silent, but my mind? Never.

What sense is there in punishing the body for the shortcomings of the character? Amos never thrashed a student. On the contrary, he compelled those who transgressed to whip <u>him</u> instead. All repented most pitifully, and behaved not from fear of punishment, but to recoil from causing pain to others.

This Mr. Davis lays down rules like planks and nails himself to them. No eating of pickled limes in school, he has decreed. For all the difference it will make. Anything that siphons attention away from him, he summarily bans, only to see the problem crop up in fresh guise. Chewing gum, novels, newspapers, nicknames, limes. It seems to me his difficulty is not with citrus fruits or newsprint or anything else, but in maintaining order. Were he to teach more captivating lessons, perhaps he could keep better hold of his students' attention.

Just as galling is the thought of the quarter Meg so generously gave to her sister to purchase them. Her pocket money is to do with as she pleases, but I cannot help thinking—we might have had a pound of fresh pork and a half dozen eggs for that twenty-five cents. How could Mr. Davis be so wasteful in times such as this? Two dozen limes, pitched out the window! Though perhaps they were better appreciated by the Irish children who picked them from the snow than by the pretentious girls Amy longs to impress. She, of course, is more distressed by the injury to her dignity than to her flesh.

Amy does not want to return to school, and I shall not force her. It will do her good to spend her days apart from those schoolmates of hers. Had she not felt beholden to them, she might never have flouted the pickled lime doctrine. I don't know how to make her see that her schoolmates are not her superiors, no matter how fashionable their dresses and hair ribbons.

Later

Tomorrow I shall task Jo with collecting Amy's things and giving notice to Mr. Davis that Amy will not be returning to school. I don't know whether it is an act of cowardice or mercy to send her in my place. Were I to go, I would set upon him like a hurricane. Jo, I have no doubt, will treat him to all the glares and silent reproach she is capable of.

It is well after midnight. Before me lies a stack of pages addressed to Mr. Davis, one diatribe after another, crammed by turns with philosophy, theology, and psychology. I wrote until the pads of my forefinger and thumb were indented by the shaft of the pen. As I sat back to massage my aching hand, it became evident that I had thrown a pen and ink tantrum. Several, in fact.

In the end, the version that is giving me most satisfaction is the one that says almost nothing at all:

> *Mr. Davis,*
>   *Effective immediately, I am withdrawing my daughter, Miss Amy March, from your tutelage until further notice.*
>
> > *I remain,*
> > *Margaret A. March*

There is a queer pleasure in such curtness. By paring away every outward indication of fury, I am left with its unmistakable pith—that pith which whispers to the recipient, *You are unworthy of the effort it requires to express my displeasure.* And all of it will be heightened by the fact that no one expects anything but cordiality and deference from a minister's wife.

All of this is wildly uncharitable of me. A grown woman, sitting here like a petulant child, savoring the thought of the discomfort my words will cause to another. At this moment, I do not care. Anger cannot be damped out like a candle. *A flame not only burns, but illuminates,* my mother used to counsel me. Well, Mr. Davis shall find himself amply illuminated.

The rest of the pages have just gone into the fireplace in two great fistfuls, where they blazed up into the most satisfying conflagration, like the roar I will not permit myself to bellow.

Now that the fire has dwindled down again, I sit blinking at the room, surprised to find walls and furniture around me—surprised that the world consists of more than my pen and paper and the inside of my mind. I wonder if this is what it is like for Jo when she falls into one of her vortexes up in the garret? How lovely it would be to be swept up by a benign whirlwind of creation rather than a cyclone of outrage, to have something to be proud of at the end of all the bluster. Instead, I feel like a steam locomotive overstuffed with coal. There is no choice for me but to plunge ahead, regardless of the peril, until the fuel has burned itself out. And there I sit at the end of the track, empty and puffing from the exertion.

This time, though, I am not eager to let go of my anger. As soon as it subsides, I will have to contend with my disappointment in myself. Never in my life would I have dreamed that all four of my daughters would leave school before graduating. One need not enter a school building to learn, thank heaven. Nevertheless, it is difficult not to view this as my greatest failing. I would rather they grow up with corsets cinched permanently around their waists than around their minds.

February 26, 1862

Amy is the smuggest thing in the world when she is wronged. It would take less strength for me to haul a fifty-pound sack of flour home from town than it did to keep my eyes from rolling heavenward when she flounced to the breakfast table with her injured hand cradled like a kitten in the crook of her arm this morning. She has forgotten entirely that the fault was hers for breaking the rule, however inane that rule might have been.

This evening when I returned from the relief rooms, Amy was still sweeping about the house as though she were St. Agnes, martyred for the cause of limes. "I wish all the girls would leave, and spoil his old school. It's perfectly maddening to think of those lovely limes," she pronounced. I had been thinking much the same thing about the school itself, but Amy's mourning over her contraband limes as though they were a flock of slaughtered lambs jerked me straight to my wits' end. "I am not sorry you lost them," I snapped, "for you broke the rules, and deserved some punishment for disobedience."

I cannot say that I take any pleasure in speaking sharply to my children, but there is a certain satisfaction in at last being <u>heard</u> that occasionally makes me willing to endure the wounded look I receive in return. Judging by her shock, the thought of her disobedience might never have occurred to Amy had I not spoken up.

None of us, not even Meg, can deny any longer that Amy's conceit is getting out of hand, and I told Amy so, with all of her sisters and Laurie there to hear it. The fact that Laurie witnessed her dressing down gave Amy pause at last. (I confess that I, too, shrank a bit from the idea of Laurie seeing my faults exposed. He looks at me—at all of us—as such a familial ideal that I hate to topple from my pedestal.)

Did we coddle and pet her too much, to make her crave adulation so? Or is it just the opposite? I wonder, too, if she had grown up with no end of frills and furbelows, whether they would mean so much to her as they do now. Amy takes such pleasure in the physical world, it is harder to make her see the value of intangible things. Perhaps that comes of her artist's eye.

Her art itself is telling; even Amy's drawings evoke admiration rather than emotion. There is nothing in them yet that marks them as her own. She prizes accuracy above all else, as if she means her hand to act as a camera.

She, more than any of my daughters, has yet to learn that the true defense against the petty insults life forever thrusts at us is to be morally invulnerable. It is how Amos and I bore the punishment for breaking an unjust law. We weathered the loss of two thousand dollars and endured six months apart without ever feeling an iota of the humiliation Amy experienced over the loss of two dozen pickled limes. When you can say with utter confidence that you have done right, there is nothing anyone can do or say that is any more vexing than a mosquito's sting.

February 28, 1862

Jo came down the garret steps this morning all in a daze, looking, quite frankly, like a bride on the first morning of her honeymoon.

"It's done!" she proclaimed, and flopped into her chair.

Her book, of course. One might call it a bouquet of fairy stories, every one of them told against a backdrop of garden and woodland delights.

Hannah proposed a special breakfast to celebrate, and asked Jo what she wanted most.

"Anything but apples," Jo said, and let go the hem of her black pinafore. A dozen and more withered apple cores spilled onto the floor. Poor thing, she was asleep before Hannah could put a plate of fried potatoes and buckwheats with jam on the table.

After supper we all gathered round the hearth and listened to the last two stories. Jo does not read them so much as perform them, stopping on nearly every page to reach for a pen and scratch out or add something.

Meg cannot wait to read the book to the King children, but Jo insists each story must be neatly recopied and corrected first.

It is not high literature by any means, but I am just as proud as if it were. Fifteen years old, and she has written a book—a book!—fit to grace any nursery shelf in Concord. What did I have to show for myself at her age but a bevy of haphazardly embroidered samplers, soon to be relegated to the bottom of a trunk?

March 1, 1862

Meg's pay came in coins this week rather than bills. A kindness from Mrs. King. I can only deduce that she has read the news about the treasury, and surmised its effect upon us. When she senses a need, she fills it, and that is that. No remarks or knowing glances. Concord's poor are fortunate indeed that she has been given charge over the relief rooms.

March 2, 1862

When, precisely, did we all decide to love Theodore Laurence? As we arranged ourselves before the hearth this evening, it became apparent that this Family has opened itself and absorbed Laurie without any sort of ceremony or announcement. He has his own place at our table and in our parlor, places no one would dream of sitting any more than they would take Beth's corner or Amos's wingback.

It is as if he has always been here, as if the petit point stool beside my armchair has been patiently awaiting him. From that stool he is equally able to pose for Amy's sketches, help Beth wind a ball of yarn, or slap away the sparks that dare alight on Jo's skirt. Tonight as he read aloud to us from *Pilgrim's Progress*, he leaned his black curly head so sweetly upon the arm of my chair that I found myself transported to one of the most secluded corners of my imagination.

Were he and Jo to marry, I mused to myself, I could rightfully call him son. And the next thought, flowing so naturally that the improbability did not so much as brush against my better judgment: Were he and Jo to marry, what a varied crop of grandchildren they might create! A boy like Jo, a girl like Laurie, or any of a thousand-thousand amalgamations thereof. Chestnut curls, raven waves, gray eyes, black eyes, minds sharper than pins, and hearts softer than velvet.

It was Amy's voice that pulled me back to the parlor. "Marmee, where have you gone?" she asked. Five faces—six, when Hannah straightened up from her mending—were fixed upon me, their quizzical expressions like owls'.

I blushed so deeply, they gaped all the harder. Oh, what a face Jo would have made at me if she knew what fancies I had been entertaining. The memory warms my cheeks even now. It warms my heart, too, if I am to commit nothing but honesty to these pages.

March 4, 1862

For the first time in my memory, the poor are grateful to receive grocery orders in lieu of cash. The orders, which specify the quantities of each item to be dispensed, are holding their value while paper currency fluctuates most alarmingly.

Those who rely on treasury notes for their pay are in a panic. Employers are in a moral bind, though only some of them see it that way. Too many are content to hand over the usual amount of bills, reasoning that the numbers printed on them have not changed. It is leaving scores of families scrambling—families who have not had cause to scramble before.

As a consequence, we are beginning to see bewildered, unfamiliar faces in the relief rooms, people unsure of which lines to stand in, or where to present their orders. Soldiers' wives, many of them. Women of twenty should not look so worn and haggard—particularly not those who have sent their husbands to defend the Union.

There is one good thing to say for Mrs. Hummel's pay: a laundress's wages are so meager, she has little cause to worry about the devaluation of treasury notes. Just now, with a quarter nearly as valuable as a dollar bill, it is possible to feel richer with a handful of coins than with a sheaf of cash.

March 6, 1862

A note from Laurie in the Family post today. Always, he addresses my letters to "The Lady of the House," as if he is as unsure of what to call me as I was of what name to sign to his birthday present. When we are in each other's presence, he calls me ma'am. Brightly, eagerly, even tenderly. But *ma'am*, nonetheless.

How I would relish the sight of *Mother* on those envelopes, or the sound of it on his lips. But he had a mother, and I have no right to usurp her memory. I wonder if the Germans have yet contrived a word that captures the nature of the tie I feel toward Laurie? It is something to inquire of Birte, when I have learned the right words to ask the question.

March 8, 1862

The faces that greeted me when I returned home this evening were so sober and stricken, I feared news had come of Amos. Meg and Beth sat at the table, holding hands. They rose together as I stepped inside, and Hannah emerged from the kitchen to stand behind them, hands folded solemnly before her apron. The sound of wailing seemed to come at me from two different directions at once.

Meg gulped before she spoke. "Something dreadful has happened, Marmee," she said with a tremor, and Beth's great eyes were so sorrowful that I gathered my strength to bear the blow I have dreaded all these months.

But it was not what I feared at all—Amy has burned Jo's manuscript. My relief was so great, my knees nearly buckled. For the first time in my life, I was too dumbfounded to be angry. Jo and Meg would not take Amy to the theater (an excursion paid for by Laurie, to which Amy had not been invited) and so Amy fed every last page of Jo's work to the fire in retribution.

"Jo boxed Amy's ears," Beth confessed, as contrite as though she had done the deed herself. "She shrieked just like a cat and shook Amy so awfully hard, I was afraid Amy might bite her tongue off."

Jo was in the garret, fuming with grief, while Amy whimpered in the parlor.

What a woeful inheritance I have bequeathed to my two girls: to Jo, the flare, and to Amy, the smolder, of my unquenchable temper. What a mercy that Meg and Beth take after their father, or the whole house should go up in flames.

I shall not tell Jo, lest the knowledge feed her outrage, but Amy's transgression is the one that troubles me most. Jo lashed out in a blind fury, while Amy took the time to seek out the revenge that would wound her sister most deeply. Amy's sense of proportion, so keen in her drawings, fails her entirely elsewhere in life. I believe if Jo had not struck her, Amy would have seen her crime for what it was sooner. The physical blow only brought to stinging life her conviction that she had been most grievously injured. It is the pickled limes all over again, with Amy willfully ignoring her own misdeed.

Again and again, I told her the same thing, rearranging the words so that they might penetrate her indignation: "Jo denied you an evening's enjoyment, yet you robbed her of years of patient work." Still, Amy refused to hear them.

"She was so <u>mean</u>, Marmee. You didn't hear. Jo never would have said such things if you'd been here. She wouldn't have dared. And she wouldn't have hit me, either."

I drew in the deepest breath my lungs could contain, and held it until the need for air became greater than the desire to shout. I should not have to explain to a child of twelve that there are people with more pressing needs than her own right now. That when I stay home, poor families must be hungry longer, while soldiers bleed for want of bandages.

"Amy," I finally said, nearly gritting my teeth to hold in my frustration, "this is the <u>ugliest</u> thing you have ever done."

The emphasis I placed on that dreaded word pierced her indignation at last. "Marmee?" she said, aghast.

"So much that it is hard for me to look at you right now."

It felt cruel to slice at her that way, yet there seemed no other way to make an opening for the words I needed her to hear. They did their work at last, and when Amy begged Jo's forgiveness, I was as proud of her as I have ever been in my life.

Jo, though. I do believe I sank a good six inches at her refusal of Amy's apology. Nothing will satisfy Jo until Amy's pain equals her own. The heat of it radiated from her forehead as I kissed her good night; to douse it, I would have to plunge her into the Atlantic. Knowing Jo, she will feed its flames until every scrap of fuel she can lay her hands on has turned to ash. She is hellbent on ignoring my pleas to forgive her sister, and would not so much as look at me as she refused.

I cannot tell her how rapidly anger festers overnight—no one can tell her anything at all when she is like this, not even Beth.

And now Amy is doubly miffed. Instead of taking solace in the earnestness of her apology, she is affronted by Jo for rebuffing it. No doubt she will flounce from one end of the house to the other until she feels her precious dignity is restored. Their ends are at such cross-purposes, this could go on until they are sixty.

I am exhausted.

These children ought to be old enough to govern themselves by now. Dealing properly with Amy and Jo while holding my temper at bay requires more endurance than an entire week in the relief rooms.

My anger aches like a muscle that begs to be used. When I give way to it, there is a blinding instant of utter satisfaction, a white explosion too beautiful to resist. That explosiveness is part of what makes me the woman I am, no matter how troublesome and destructive. Reining it forever backward has the feel of a lie.

If there were a way to express it without causing pain, I might be the most contented woman alive. Work is a great help. Nothing makes me fume as much as injustice, and in the relief rooms I can refine my rage into a fearsome weapon against iniquity. There is great satisfaction in that. But I wish—oh, I do wish—that there was some use for the pure, untempered fire I possess. The sheer scale of the energy I devote to keeping it in check could be more profitably spent on so many other worthier causes.

March 9, 1862

Jo still will not forgive Amy, and I cannot summon the fortitude to address either of them sensibly. I'd like to remind the both of them that there is an authentic war on, that this is no time for indulging in domestic skirmishes. My tongue feels like a fireplace poker when I even think of speaking my mind.

Jo is insufferable; the smoke of her fury clouds the whole house. She is not content simply to grieve her novel, but must display her grief for all of us, as if performing the role of tragic heroine in a play she has written. When I am at my most uncharitable, I suspect that part of her is enjoying watching us all scatter at her approach. I know better, though. The same black cloud that is choking us all is thick enough to obscure Jo's sight of anything but her own misery. I know too well how it feels to be enveloped in that awful haze.

March 10, 1862

I have not cried as I cried today since the night Amos went to war.

The quantity of the tears is the same, but the quality is different. That night was plain sorrow. Today has made such a sea of my emotions, it is not possible to contain all of them simultaneously: tides of relief and pride warring with terror and shame, swirled together with eddies of gratitude and humility. In the midst of it, I managed to keep my head. Surprise likely blunted my reactions. Now that everything is put to rights, I have no choice but to feel it all at once.

All is mended between Amy and Jo, though nearly at a cost too steep to pay.

When I arrived home, Amy lay before the fire, swaddled tighter than the infant in the manger. She had taken up her ice skates to tag along behind Jo and Laurie, and in her effort to catch up, plunged through a patch of rotten ice at the center of the river. Jo and Laurie managed to fish her out before the cold had fully penetrated her, I think, for Amy was warm as a sausage fresh from the griddle by the time I kissed her forehead and squeezed her hands. The numbness in her expression was purely shock.

Jo was in a state. Torn dress, bloodied hands, scuttling about with such a frenetic energy that it seemed as if she might break into pieces if she stopped for an instant. It was she, not Laurie, who wrenched a fence rail loose so that they could reach the center of the river.

After Amy was tucked into bed, I took up a roll of cotton gauze from the medicine box and called Jo to me. Her hands were such a sight, crusted with blood and swelling up purple but she seemed not to feel them at all. With reluctance she approached Amy's bedside. "Are you sure she is safe?" Jo whispered. Such a queer question—Amy was as snug as one of Beth's dolls. When I praised Jo for getting Amy home to the fireside so quickly, Jo broke. Cracked in half down the middle, as if my arms were the only thing holding her together.

Never in my life have I witnessed Jo like this. I have not seen her cry with such passion since she was a child. Not angry tears, this time, but frightened ones. A bolt of fear shot through me as though Jo's distress was made of electricity. What but a telegram from the War Department could cause such grief?

The truth, when she told it, flabbergasted me.

Jo had <u>known</u> the ice could not be trusted. Her anger at Amy over her lost manuscript prevented her from relaying Laurie's warning to keep away from the thin center of the river. When Jo heard Amy's cry and the gulp of the river as it tried to swallow her sister, she feared herself a murderer.

For the first time since last August, I was glad Amos was not here. What I heard in Jo's voice made it impossible for me to rebuke her: self-contempt. If Amos is capable of being unkind it is in the way he employs shame to discipline the children. Though he would never humiliate another living soul outright, he has a decided knack for making others aware of the shamefulness of their wrongdoing. A deftly placed question, spoken with the utmost gentleness, and the tears bubble up from their very depths. Without meaning to, Amos would only make Jo believe that she is right in despising this part of herself.

I think she nearly coveted punishment, and the way it brings a transgression to a neat and tidy end. As if anyone could censure her any more severely than she has already censured herself. The throbbing of her hands was of no consequence by comparison. There are times when there is no task greater than forgiving yourself. Penance is so much simpler.

Instead I gave her the thing I have wished for my whole life long: someone who shares the very same temper. My mother helped me, and Amos helps me, but earnestness is not the same as true understanding. Truth be told, it did me a kind of good to let Jo soak my shoulder with her tears. How many times since I was sixteen have I wished I could cry on my own dear marmee's shoulder? That I could be a comfort to Jo was in turn a comfort to me. I feel as though I have thrown off the hood of a heavy cloak. A burden shared is easier for the both of us to bear. And truth be told, being seen as faultless is another albatross I am glad to unwind from my own neck.

In one way I am proud of Jo. She might have cast herself as heroine in Amy's rescue, but her conscience would not permit it. My Jo is nothing if not honest. Nor will she bend easily to defeat. The pertinacity that is all too often trained out of girls runs marrow-deep in her. As I held her in my arms, I could feel her mustering that resolve. Determination thrummed through her. She will fail. Again and again, she will fail. I did not tell her that. *Never get tired of trying*, I said instead.

I did not have to tell Jo how dire the consequences can be. She still does not know the full weight of the guilt my temper has saddled me with these last eleven years. For all my assurance that she may tell me anything without fear, I have not been fully honest with her myself. Her disbelief at the idea that I had any temper at all was so genuine, I could not summon the courage to confess the true extent of it. She and Meg were so little when it happened, it was easy enough to keep the full truth from them. They were old enough to remember John's presence at breakfast, yet they have never asked what happened. Perhaps they were young enough simply to take the happenings of that winter for granted without wondering over details.

Now that I am alone with myself, with no one to soothe me as I soothed Jo, guilt pierces me anew. My daughter's anguish is greater punishment than any disgrace my temper has brought upon me. There is no doubt that Jo's misery is all my doing; my husband utterly lacks the volatile tinder that plagues Jo and Amy and me.

Jo and I, we have more than just tinder to combat. Both of us are stacked to the brim with kindling, stove-lengths, and limb-sized logs enough to fuel a blaze for days on end. If I had any doubt of that, today has proven it. It was not the flare, but the smolder that overtook Jo this afternoon.

I have been wrong to hide my temper so completely. All this time I have been inadvertently teaching my girls that goodness is the absence of faults. An unattainable goal that can only lead to a lifetime of discouragement. Effortless virtue is a fairy tale, so far as I can tell. The honor is in the struggle.

March 11, 1862

While Jo and Amy were occupied with clashing in the parlor and on the ice, federal troops at Pea Ridge in northern Arkansas managed to drive the rebels back from the Missouri line. Ten thousand five hundred Federals prevailed over sixteen thousand Confederates. It is an exhilarating victory, securing a critical border state from invasion.

Victory. That is the word for it, though after nearly a year of bloodshed my emotions snarl each time the Union triumphs. Even as I record this good news, three or four thousand families are mourning. I cannot help pitying the southern women in particular, whose losses must seem so futile without a victory to accompany their sacrifice. One might argue that these casualties are the South's just reward for committing the sin of slavery. But if that is so, the North has a debt to pay as well—for permitting it.

What kind of arrogance is it that makes men more willing to settle such feuds with blood than to lay aside pride and privilege? The men of the South would rather die than admit that Negroes are their equals. Perhaps after generations of subjugating their fellow human beings, it is easier to die in pertinacious defense of those wrongs than to live under the weight of them.

The small triumphs of the March Family give me more unalloyed cause for celebration than news from the battlefields. What a revelation it is to see Beth setting off for the Laurence house with an armful of music. Now that she has her own piano, she need not do so, and yet she persists. The grandness of the instrument surely draws her, but I think more than that, she has come to understand that the sound of her music wafting through those hollow halls is a gift to Mr. Laurence. Watching the boundaries of Beth's small universe expand brightens my spirits each time the door swings shut behind her.

March 17, 1862

Oh, I could turn somersaults, cartwheels—the Act Prohibiting the Return of Slaves has passed through Congress four days ago! No more will our commanders be permitted to send runaways back to the Confederacy! Whatever possessed them to do such a thing when the South needs every pair of hands to work against us, I cannot fathom.

It seems as if the world should look different, that the snow should be brighter, the air clearer. The Fugitive Slave Act, though it still exists on paper, has been eviscerated at last! Not since the morning he left have I wanted to embrace Amos more than I do this day. My buoyancy baffled the girls as much as it delighted them as one by one I swept them into great crushing hugs at breakfast. The joy I feel merely bounces off them, as if they were mirrors. Only Hannah's hand, when she offered it for me to clasp, responded with some measure of the understanding I craved.

"Eleven years," she said. "I'll wager Mr. March is smiling broadly as you are this morning."

I could not reply. Not in words, anyhow. A squeeze of the hand and a winking away of tears said all that I could not. This evening, standing alongside Beth's piano, I conveyed my thankfulness to heaven the best way I know how—in song. The hymns thrummed through me as they have not in many a month as I sang not only with my voice, but my heart.

Now, if the federal army could only be convinced to treat these runaways like free men instead of "contraband" fit only for ditchdigging, perhaps freedom would live up to its name.

March 20, 1862

Beth came with me to the Hummels' today, bringing her newest kitten for the children to play with. Minna and Heinrich are not gentle, but that savage little puss didn't mind a bit.

"Blitz!" they shrieked each time his white tail flicked and his claws shot out. "Blitz-Katze!"

"It means lightning-cat," Karl told us when he came in from school. Lightning indeed. They made a fearful racket together, hissing and snarling and squealing so that as we bent over our slates Mrs. Hummel and I could hardly tell which sounds came from the children and which from the cat. Minna and Heinrich fought duels with him, offering him twigs to pounce on and snap between his wicked little teeth.

"He likes it," Beth marveled. Gentle as she is, she cannot imagine the exhilaration of such tussles. I should like to have one myself now and then, if it meant I could turn my furies loose without harm to anyone.

On the way home, Beth asked if she might give the kitten to the Hummels. She'd had to pry Blitz loose from Minna's shoulder while they both yowled in dismay. "He liked it there so much but I'd hate for him to go hungry, the way the children were on Christmas."

"There ought to be mice enough in that house to keep him fatter and feistier than Aunt March," I said without thinking.

"Marmee!" Beth exclaimed, aghast and giggling all at once.

"Truth and kindness are not always one and the same," I said with a conspiratorial smile.

She stood a minute, thinking, while Blitz tried to claw his way out of her basket. Then she turned and scurried back to the Hummels'.

When she returned, the basket was still and Beth's face was bright. Times like this, she is the most beautiful of all my girls.

March 25, 1862

The front page of the *Traveler* this morning contains several accounts of grievous injuries done to men by cannon balls in the battle of Pea Ridge. I had to put the paper down and breathe slowly and deliberately for a full minute before I could continue. Of all the ways we have devised to do harm to one another, this warfare is among the most barbarous. What good is knitting socks for soldiers when a single twelve-pound ball can shear off both a man's legs in less time than it takes to cast on a single stitch?

I might have remained shrouded in my dusting of gloom all day had Laurie not left me a bunch of daffodils. Hannah had put them in a vase on my desk to await my return. Last week it was a little nosegay of purple crocus. With all the rare and exotic flowers at his disposal in Mr. Laurence's conservatory, Laurie lately chooses to tramp through the fields, seeking out the freshest flowers of spring for me. The charm of it encircles my heart like a ribbon.

March 28, 1862

Mrs. Carter returned to the relief rooms today, much to our surprise. It has been only three months since she donned her mourning dress, though, in fact, her son has been dead since October. As she put it, she could not bear to stay home and knit socks when there was so much more she could do here for the men and boys in the field. That is a sentiment I find myself in absolute accord with. What good is it to her son for Mrs. Carter to sit in her parlor draped in black, when soldiers just like him have need of every scrap of help we can give?

She is changed, in subtle ways. Isobel Carter has always had an almost childlike eagerness to be of use; seeing her standing quietly to one side, awaiting an assignment from Mrs. King, made her seem almost a stranger. Of course I expected her mood to be subdued, but it is more than that. There was an odd sort of clumsiness about her, as though her hands have been numb all these months and have only half thawed.

It was not courteous of me to watch, but I could not help myself. Each time she dropped something, the sound commanded my attention. Before long the entire room was feigning deafness on her behalf, which to me felt more deceitful than kind. Surely she knew we were all willfully ignoring her difficulties, and that in itself is an uncomfortable sort of scrutiny to bear. When she fumbled with a box for the third time, she did not pick it up. Nor the spilled bandages which silently unrolled themselves across the floor. On the periphery of my vision I saw her brace her two palms against the table and rest her chin upon her chest, plainly trying to collect herself.

I did not know what to do—whether to let her grapple alone or to offer my help. When we are not in pain ourselves, we shrink from drawing attention to the discomfort of others. I felt it myself, that pulling back for fear of opening a wound that might have begun finally to knit. And yet when I am suffering, nothing exhausts me more than pretending, for the sake of others, that I am not.

Everyone seemed to become further engrossed in their own work as I approached her table, repeating a single sentence in my mind as if I were a schoolgirl rehearsing a troublesome recitation: "May I work with you today, Mrs. Carter?"

Her head lifted, and her face bore the look of a woman hearing the opening chords of a cherished hymn. "Certainly, Mrs. March," she said. "I shall be glad for another pair of hands."

We said almost nothing to one another after that, but our silence as we rerolled and repacked the bandages was not cumbersome. I cannot say what solace my presence gave. In the past we have been merely cordial, without any real ties between us. Yet the effects were as plain as though I were a trusted friend. Mrs. Carter's hands steadied, and an earnest determination emerged to take the place of her usual enthusiasm.

Whatever strength it was that I loaned to her did not deplete my own stores. On the contrary, I left the relief rooms feeling deeply renewed.

April 3, 1862

The King children have come down with measles, and so there is nothing to keep Meg from packing her trunk for a fortnight with the Moffats. I do not know if this is a wise visit for her to make. It is difficult enough for her to go to the Kings every day, watching other girls enjoy the same fine things that she can recall from her own childhood. At the Moffats' she will bask in luxury for a solid two weeks and return as if bereft, with any empty space in her head inflated with envy and vanity. I do know that to deny her the chance would only double her envy. And now she needs an umbrella for her trip. A black one, with a white handle, to be precise.

Just now I can imagine no greater luxury than the feeling of paying all our debts. They are not insurmountable—twelve dollars here, seventeen dollars there—yet each one tugs at me like a stone in my pocket, stone after stone until it seems the whole garment will be torn asunder. With Christmas behind me and no birthdays until June, I had hoped to whittle the sums down before adding to them again.

There is no dodging the fact that it is easier to manage our finances, paltry as they are, without Amos. Long ago I learned never to send him to town with money for necessities. Amos is more apt to buy nourishment for his mind than his stomach. When there was cash to spare it was only a bemusing inconvenience if he came home with a volume of Plato rather than a cut of beef. Now, though, such a lapse would leave us hungry. Hannah hardly knows which of us is worse—me for my habit of giving away necessities, or Amos for his perplexing indulgences.

I ought to be accustomed to sacrifice by now. From the beginning, Amos's ideals have meant doing without certain luxuries. We have always been sparing with coffee and sugar, knowing what it costs in human toil and misery to produce. They have been easy enough to renounce, though there are still certain days in each month when I crave the sweetness of my mother's iced sugar cookies. Cotton, too, produced under the lash, troubles his conscience and mine mightily. Were we still able to afford it, we would dress solely in linen. (Amos would even leave the wool to the sheep, but there I stand my ground. Shearing does no harm, and I will not watch my children shiver through New England's winters to spare a sheep the indignity of a haircut.)

There is a righteous satisfaction in denying yourself such splendors when you are rich. It was not until we had no other material pleasures to enjoy that I understood how sanctimonious our stance had been, what a privilege it is to be in a position to make such choices at all. Only then did I realize the true meaning of sacrifice. Now, I would happily go ten thousand days without a grain of sugar if it meant I could still provide my children with the small comforts and indulgences they deserve. Never when I was in my twenties did I imagine I would ever lose sleep over an umbrella. An umbrella, for pity's sake!

No doubt Meg is envisioning a silk umbrella, which puts me in a double bind. Amos, who cannot swat a fly, can hardly stomach the thought of how many worms must die for a yard of silk. Meg further has her heart set on a silk dress when she turns eighteen, and no matter how I gently try to discourage her with "may" and "perhaps," I know she shall spend the next two years imagining yards of fine silk piled up on the table on her birthday. It is one thing to put cost and convenience aside for the sake of men, women, and children in bondage. It is quite another to ask a young lady to renounce fashion for the sake of worms in China.

But here I am, borrowing trouble when there is trouble aplenty sitting right before me. Tomorrow I shall buy the umbrella, and worry about the dress when the time comes.

April 4, 1862

I could not buy the one Meg wanted, not with that credit looming over me. If the black and white umbrella had been the only one in the shop, yes. But with the two lying side by side, and seventy-five cents difference between them, I could not justify the additional cost—not to myself, nor to Mr. Brown. I cannot ask him to do without seventy-five cents (though he most assuredly can) simply because my daughter has an eye for fashion. The fact that Mr. Brown is not only proprietor of the dry goods shop, but also the eldest son of the selfsame Mr. James P. Brown, Sr., who sits on the committee overseeing the poor, makes it doubly difficult.

For a little while, among a certain set, we were heroes. Those first several months, I wore my paucity like a medal. Credit was extended to our Family like a red carpet before a monarch. But memories fade after ten years and more, and the bravery loses its shine. A decade of perpetual insolvency tries the patience of even the most sympathetic of shopkeepers.

The girls know well enough that the shops extend us credit, but they do not know the extent of it. So I lied. I feigned forgetfulness and told Meg I had forgotten the colors she wanted. Sweet thing that she is, she pretended not to be disappointed. I gave her more than I intended from the cedar chest, to make up for it—a pair of silk stockings, my carved fan, and the blue satin sash that I wore to my first ball.

April 6, 1862

The house is a strange place with Meg and Amos both gone. It seems the hole left by one is widened by the departure of the other. Everything feels off-balance with both of them away, like a ship whose cargo is loaded all to one side.

My mind is inclined toward gloom this week. Sometimes I believe that I could be locked into a room devoid of calendars for a year, and my mood would still plunge into a mire during the first week of April.

No matter how often I remind myself that Meg's absence is temporary, I cannot hope to ignore the gap in our Family this week any more than my tongue can resist prodding the cavity left by a missing tooth.

Even the relief rooms are off-kilter, for Mrs. King was not present yesterday. So far as I can recall, this is only her second absence since the war began. I am anxious for her two youngest. They must be ill indeed to keep Mrs. King from her duties. They shall have the best doctoring money can buy, but as Willie Lincoln has lately proved, that is no assurance of a safe recovery. Measles is a cunning disease, cunning enough to whisk away a child's sight or hearing just as it seems their life has been spared. There is not a thing I can do for her but pray.

April 7, 1862

Today it is nineteen years and one day since my firstborn entered and left this world in a single moment. It is strangely, perhaps shamefully, soothing to find my own somberness reflected in every face I see. Over 13,000 Federals have been killed, wounded, captured, or gone missing at Shiloh, Tennessee, since Monday. The rebels are likely to count nearly 10,000 casualties.

The staggering losses compound my mood. Each April, I have struggled not to let my sorrow show, to go about my work as usual. It is what the world requires of me. Margaret March does not take to her bed—the selfsame bed where he was born and died—to grieve an invisible wound that refuses to stop throbbing. And every year, my sorrow turns to anger as I pretend that he never existed. Even my girls do not know of their brother. The most selfish part of me envies the mothers who are grieving today. They had their sons for fifteen, twenty years and more. They lost their boys not only for a reason, but for a cause. Mine simply failed to live.

April 10, 1862

The Laurences have clipped half a dozen of their choicest rose blooms from the conservatory to send to Meg at the Moffats' tonight. Ivory, with the most delicate peach centers—as chaste in their beauty as Meg herself. Laurie brought them by to see if I would like to enclose a note in the box. Indeed, I did.

> *Meg, my dear,*
> *Remember, when the other girls bedeck themselves with frills and ornaments, that nothing but a simple dewdrop can render a rose any lovelier than God's own hand has already made it.*
> *Your loving Marmee*

How fortunate we are to have such friends. Their generosity, yes, but their absolute accord with what I hold most dear. They might as easily have fortified Meg's vanity with the loan of any number of jewels from the late Mrs. Laurence's fine collection. Instead, they chose the perfect complement to Meg's character.

As I gave Laurie the envelope, I clasped his hand in both of mine for a moment. He took it to be thanks, I suppose, though it was more than that. A wish. A moment's imagining. There are times, such as when I arrive home to find myself greeted by five bright young faces instead of four, that I believe he is indulging in a matching daydream.

There is no substitute for what either of us is missing, yet I should like to think that I am as much a solace to Theodore Laurence as he is to me.

April 11, 1862

As I was already downcast, I called on Aunt March to round out a thoroughly disagreeable week. I succeeded marvelously.

There has been so much discord between us in the last twenty years that Aunt March need not even open her mouth before I feel chastised. I do not know if she is calculating enough to do so deliberately, or if in reality I am the only one filling our silence with the echoes of past arguments.

I could not take my eyes from Aunt March's pearls, which are as large as peas. Meg had looked so longingly at my mother's pearl set when I opened the cedar chest to fetch her the sash and fan.

I don't know what I was thinking, telling Aunt March that Meg was away visiting the Moffats. Off she went about the Moffats, conflating their good fortune with good sense, which is so ludicrous that I could not be bothered to find words to contradict her. In fact, there was no reason to bother; I did not particularly care to talk, and Aunt March never wants to listen.

All I could think of as I sat in that fine room as she sang the Moffats' praises was the day Aunt March offered to adopt one of our daughters.

We had been sitting in the selfsame parlor. (Could that memory be part of why I resist visiting her as often as I should?) I cannot remember now how she phrased her proposal. When I recall that moment, it is as if the entire scene is sealed between two thick panes of glass. That is how I felt then, too—immobile, as if the air that carried her inconceivable words had hardened around me.

My shock must have shown; Aunt March had vowed in no uncertain terms that she would not come to our aid if we defied the law, no matter how inhumane that law might be. "There is no reason for the children to suffer because of your foolhardiness," she pronounced. But there was a starved look far back in her eyes that belied the scolding tone of her voice, and I did experience a strange prickling of pity. That lasted only as long as it took for her to specify Meg.

Of course she wanted Meg. The prettiest, the most docile. That woman must always have the best of everything. Jo, she considered in need of housebreaking. Beth and Amy were mere babies—likely they terrified her. To this day, I don't know which infuriated me more, that she wanted to skim the cream from our Family, or that she was blind to Jo, Beth, and Amy's worth.

As I sat there, my mind gazing inward and outward simultaneously, it seemed to me that perhaps Meg would have been happier in Aunt March's house, with all of her fine things.

And that is when one of the most brutal thoughts I have ever had in my life thrust itself into my mind like a red-hot fireplace poker: *All four of my daughters are alive, and yours, for all your money, is dead.*

I must have blanched. Aunt March asked if I were ill. I shook my head, but I <u>was</u> ill.

"You are, Margaret," she insisted, and shooed the poodle out of her lap to heave herself from her chair and come to me. The parrot squawked, "Phoebe! Oh, no, Phoeeebe!" Aunt March froze at the sound of that name, just as she did so many years ago when we argued over Hannah, and suddenly I understood—Phoebe can only be Aunt March's daughter's name. Polly, who is older than I am, must have witnessed that baby's death, and her mistress's wails of grief.

I made it through Aunt March's gate and to my own garden wall before I vomited. Hannah saw me through the kitchen window and was at my side with a rag and a glass of water by the time I'd finished retching.

I held up a hand when she asked me what was wrong. "If I explain, it will only make me sicker," I said.

I am sick still. The thought may be purged, but not the mind that created it.

April 13, 1862

Today after services I paused a moment longer than usual in that section of the churchyard where the smallest gravestones are scattered. The melted snow had exposed a bunch of delicate white hothouse violets tied with black satin ribbon lying wilted before the white stone cross that reads *Beloved Daughter & Lamb of God, 1823.* When Amos and I were married, that patch of earth had fresh flowers on it two and three times a week. Now that Aunt March is lame, the plot is more often bare.

Does she envy me my daughters, I wonder? My mind refuses to fully imagine the horror she experienced, watching her baby girl struggle for air as the diphtheria slowly closed its grip on the child's throat. Standing in front of that grave, I can summon sympathy, and even something like affection for Aunt March, widowed and childless as she is. Sitting in her own parlor, however, is another matter.

I am wealthier than she will ever be—in love, in Family, in charity both given and received. Ten thousand dollars from Aunt March could not equal the value of the piano Mr. Laurence gave to Beth.

I am sorry for her. Truly.

April 14, 1862

Jo informs me that Laurie has received an invitation to the Moffats' this Thursday. Meg is surely the cause. What this portends, I can only imagine. At least I can take comfort in the knowledge that Meg and Laurie have more sense between them than a whole houseful of Moffats.

This is the seventh day without Mrs. King. It has been nearly two weeks since her children became ill. One would hope that their symptoms had abated by now. Each day as I pass the house, I am relieved to see that no black crepe has been hung over the doorway. Please, Lord, have mercy upon those children.

April 16, 1862

Mrs. King is back at the helm of the relief rooms today. Both of the little ones are on the mend at last, and show no signs of permanent harm from the measles. She is exhausted but almost exultant. I remember that feeling—Hannah and I both had it after we nursed Meg and Jo through scarlet fever.

April 19, 1862

Meg has returned. She looked at everything with a forlorn expression, as if she pities even the furniture for having to live in a house where the latest fashions date from the Taylor administration. Even I was the target of some furtive glances, which further ruffled my own state of mind. I tried to tell myself that it is my own guilt that magnifies Meg's discontent, turning her smallest sighs into great heaves of discontent.

Meg herself appeared quite worn out, though she put on the gayest of faces to regale us with all the happenings with the Moffats. I should have thought that a fortnight of leisure and luxury would be more restorative.

All became clear after I had kissed Beth and Amy good night. Meg had something to confess. A waver in her voice as she said so prompted Jo to offer to excuse herself, though Meg refused. And then the way she came to me, leaning her elbows upon my lap and asking to "'fess" as though she were not much more than five years old made me wonder what transgressions she was trying to soften. I ought to have known my Meg better than that.

At first her confession charmed me. Dressed up like a living paper doll by her friends, she acted the part of a coquette at Thursday's party. As if our Meg could be expected to resist the seduction of silk and silver bracelets and coralline salve. (I would have hoped that she'd at least have the sense to refuse the champagne, but that is a matter for another discussion.) Though I'm sure Annie Moffat's set did more to obscure Meg's beauty than to augment it, I still should like to have had a glimpse of my daughter turned out in the finery Amos and I might have afforded her if things had unfolded differently. But all the compliments meant nothing, directed as they were at a faux Meg

March in borrowed plumage. It is a fine thing for her to realize that she is satisfied with herself as she is.

After admitting all of that, Meg still looked as though she had a spoonful of vinegar in her mouth and nowhere to spit it out. "There is something more, I think," I said with a caress of her cheek, and her skin turned the color of a plum beneath my fingers.

What she told me next was not so much a confession as, well, to put it in schoolyard terms, tattletale-ing. Gossip Mrs. Moffat had told her guests, unaware that Meg was within earshot. The very idea that I would scheme to make a match between Meg and Laurie, simply for the sake of his wealth! She has not the slightest conception of that young man's true worth to this Family. My teeth might have cracked from the effort of holding my tongue caged behind my lips.

That Moffat woman! Thank goodness Jo let her thoughts fly, for everything that came from her mouth was careening through my mind like hail smacking a windowpane. Laying plans and playing cards, indeed! If money were all I cared about, we would still have $2,000 in the bank and Meg would not be borrowing silks from anyone. Only a woman capable of such conniving would suggest it in another. And only a woman who has never seen Laurie with Jo could think of him having eyes for Meg.

There was a measure of uncertainty in Meg's expression, though, and I knew part of her feared that such a thing might be true. That pained me enough to stifle the flame that was on the verge of roaring out of control. I should hope my children know me better than that. Then again, fear does not always yield to logic, and by then the Moffats and all their vacuous nonsense had turned Meg's head thoroughly inside out.

So I told Meg and Jo my plans for them, such as they are. Wishes, really. What more could I hope for them in the way of marriage but that they be cherished as I have been these last nineteen years? It is no mere platitude when I tell my daughters I would rather see them happily married to poor men than to sit on thrones. Meg and Jo know it best, for they have seen that our loss of fortunes has not diminished the happiness in this house.

As true as that is, I was not wholly honest with them. Money cannot buy genuine contentedness, but there is no question that it can buy a great deal in the way of peace of mind. I do not know <u>what</u> I used to fill my head with before I had to spend half of every hour thinking about how to keep the pantry full and the girls from wearing out their woolens before the snow thaws. Since 1851 I have spent more time fretting over the longevity of shoe leather than it took to master the teachings of Euclid, Plato, and Erasmus.

Where Meg was visibly soothed by my reassurances, Jo looked as though she'd have liked to dash outside and bound through the woods like a deer at the very thought of marriage. Only when I approved her notion of being happy old maids rather than unhappy wives did she breathe freely again.

One would think, from her relief, that she has never been in the vicinity of a <u>happy</u> wife, much less been brought up by one. How oddly it stings to see her instinctively recoil from a life like my own. Such a conviction should make me proud, after all the care I have taken to inculcate my daughters with the knowledge that they are equal to any man. And yet the sting persists.

Jo has never wanted what other girls want, and does not yet want what other women want. All her life I have been unable to decide whether or not to worry myself over it. It is like having a marble rolling about in my brain. Not sharp or painful, but forever bumping here and there.

I cannot help but wonder sometimes if some wisp of the spirit of that stillborn boy inhabits my Jo. There is something in her that most girls—indeed, most women—lack. If not for my other three I would think all girls are born with it, only to have it tamed out of them. It is not solely ambition; Amy has that and is as prim and feminine as a fashion plate. It is the brash sort of confidence that men have, though being female, Jo is not permitted to feel it as such. She feels only the uncomfortable way she scrapes against the world's expectations. Life would be smoother for her if we sanded away the edges that do not fit neatly. But then Jo would not be Jo at all.

Aside from her temper she is not discontent with herself, only with what others expect of her. Then again, she is young still—in some ways younger than Meg was at fifteen. All things come in their due time, I suppose, and no sooner. In the meanwhile, I should like to help her see that pledging herself to another need not be synonymous with stepping into a cage and handing your husband the key. The cords which bind two hearts are not fetters. Perhaps Laurie may open her eyes to that fact, should their friendship continue to deepen. It is not Amos, after all, who keeps me from making my voice heard and my presence felt. It is a world deaf to the voices of women.

April 21, 1862 ∽

The house has returned to a more even keel, now that Meg is in it again. We are still lopsided without Amos, but it no longer feels like the water is creeping too close to the gunwales.

Talk in town is that Mr. Davis's contract has not been renewed for the spring school term. I mentioned this fact at supper as casually as I could manage. Amy's face bloomed into a wicked little smile that perfectly mirrored my own satisfaction at the news. I wish I could say I am ashamed of myself for taking such gratification in his departure, but that would only stack a lie on top of my uncharitable thoughts toward the man. Perhaps we are not the only family who found his discipline as ineffective as it was rigid.

April 24, 1862 ∽

Three months of German lessons and Mrs. Hummel and I are both progressing admirably. Our sentences may be short and halting, but they are sentences nonetheless.

Blitz has become the king of that house, and the hero of the alley. Though he is little more than half grown, there is hardly a rat in the Hummels' corner of town that can best him. He deposits his kills on doorsteps up and down the street and is rewarded handsomely for keeping the rodents at bay. I do believe Blitz is the best-fed member of the household. He will take food from anyone, but accepts affection only if it is Minna who offers. No one else can so much as point at him without coming back bloodied. Even Karl is wary of Blitz, and poor Monika has a scratch across her nose—her reward for foolishly attempting a kiss. Ada scowls and calls him Dämon-Katze (Demon-cat) for daring to sink a claw into her beloved Monika.

Yet Mrs. Hummel is pleased with him. "We have not so many fleas now," she told me. No droppings on the table in the morning, either, and no hollows nibbled into the potatoes. Fewer vermin should mean less disease as well.

All in all, my instructions were quite clear: Beth is to be told danke schoen no less than eight times in a row—one for each grateful Hummel.

May 1, 1862

Wonder of wonders, Amy has asked to return to school at the opening of the spring term this next Monday. It would seem that she craves the society of others, as I do when I am left too long with naught but my own thoughts for company. I am pleased, even if she is likely thirsting more for gossip than learning.

An abundance of lilacs from Laurie today. The bunch of blooms just barely fit into our largest vase. He is endlessly attentive, my thoughtful crow, always so eager to please. He does not know that among his greatest gifts to me is his friendship with Jo.

To see her enjoying the company of another, of someone outside this Family? I had all but despaired of her finding a boon companion.

Jo is so insular in her own way, the very mirror of Beth—eager to devour every inch of the world, but almost scornful of the people who walk upon its surface. The young ladies of Concord she regards as though they are another breed of humanity, and the young men? They might well be blades of grass for all that Jo pays them mind. Laurie is such a fine complement to her that watching them together is a pleasure like no other.

May 5, 1862

The rebels have fled Yorktown; General McClellan has pledged to "push the enemy to the wall." With this gain in territory comes abandoned artillery, ammunition, camp equipage, medical stores, and some of the officers' personal effects. Also an abundance of flour and a good quantity of meat. As many as one hundred thousand Confederate troops evacuated west to Chickahominy Creek, much disheartened, if the reports are to be believed.

Others may rejoice over the captured territory; I shall reserve my most fervent thanks for the food and medicine now in federal hands. The prospect of any of our men and boys battling hunger and sickness on top of all that we are asking them to endure is indefensible.

May 6, 1862

Amos's dear friend Mr. Thoreau has died. A mere forty-four years old. The loss of this kindest man of letters shall be felt far beyond Concord. I fear Amos will learn it from the newspapers before my letter can reach him. How cruel that not only life, but death, must continue at home while our men are fighting. Amos deserves to be comforted by those he loves most, and who share his grief—not informed by a headline while surrounded by young men who never knew the privilege of sitting in Mr. Thoreau's serene presence. It should not be so, but at this moment the thought of Amos's pain grieves me more than the loss itself.

As for myself, Mr. Thoreau's death has left me with the feeling that the ghost of a bullet has struck Amos. It defies logic. Our friend succumbed to the ravages of tuberculosis, safe in his own bed. His death portends nothing for my husband. And yet I am shaken. I feel as if the calamity I am braced against day and night is stealthily testing my strength in preparation for the moment that it will strike in earnest.

The girls attribute my red-rimmed eyes and trembling hands to grief, and they are not mistaken; they do not know it is a grief displaced. This evening as we sang, my voice broke. In an instant all four of them were around me, ready to absorb my sorrow. Dear, sweet children. Up to my room I fled, for the tableau we formed bears too keen a resemblance to the scene I so dread to imagine.

May 7, 1862

Yesterday's dispatch from Washington reports that fighting at Williamsburg was "extremely obstinate on both sides and the loss is heavy." The battle is said to be a victory. I wonder what the southern papers are telling their readers. I wonder, too, how to measure loss and gain accurately anymore. How many men did it cost to gain this territory? The Confederate killed and wounded were abandoned on the field when the rebels retreated. General Hooker's division is reporting considerable losses. A number of Massachusetts regiments are under his command, including Amos's.

I cannot sleep. That Virginia field stretches out before my closed eyes: mud, and blood, and tatters of gray. I know my Amos. He will not reserve his ministrations for men clothed only in blue. He will not rest, much less write, so long as there is a man in need of solace. It is no cause for alarm if I do not hear from him for a time. That is what

I will tell the children if they ask. Our girls are so trusting, they will believe what I tell them, no matter whether I believe it myself.

May 8, 1862

I am overwhelmed with gratitude. Not in the way I should like to be, for there have been no envelopes in the mailbox. Instead I am battered by the grateful tears of the poor.

Gratitude without deference is as scarce as beefsteak in the relief rooms. Hand a woman two pounds of potatoes and she weeps. Give a man a pair of boots and he gazes at me as though I have just leaned down from heaven.

I do not want to be venerated. I do not deserve adulation any more than those I assist deserve to live in squalor. At times the depths of their gratitude leave me silently raging. Compassion should not be so scarce a commodity that it brings people to tears.

The deeper their gratitude, the more conscious I am of my own selfish reasons for helping. Without this work, idleness would fill my hands and my mind with worries. Without this work, the outrage that bubbles up in me at the slightest provocation would boil over and set my own house ablaze.

May 9, 1862

Not one of the girls has said a word about the battle at Williamsburg. Only Amy has come close. Today she came home from school announcing that Susie Perkins has been absent two days, for her brother is terribly wounded. When Jo asked where, Amy said, "In Will—" and then halted. "In the belly," she amended.

If the others noticed the slip, they did not show it. A belly wound is so certainly mortal that the news is almost more sobering than a death. The end will be the same; only the suffering is prolonged, for the family and the soldier alike. Amy asked to remember the Perkins family in our nightly prayers. Perhaps she is beginning to grow up after all.

May 12, 1862

A letter has come from Amos. My eyes flew to the date—May 3—two days before the fighting at Williamsburg commenced. I folded it back up again and placed the envelope between the pages of my diary. I cannot bring myself to read it until I know which side of eternity the words have come from.

May 18, 1862

How I wish Hannah would call me Margaret instead of Mrs. March, but nothing I do or say will induce her to change. I despair of finding a way to tell her, without injuring her feelings, that familiarity would be a greater gift to me now than deference.

If Amos were to be lost, I fear I might never hear anyone call me by my Christian name again. (That is not entirely true—there is always Aunt March, but she will no more soothe me than a horse's whinny. She has the most uncanny way of pronouncing the three syllables of Mar-ga-ret as though they are an admonition.) That *missus* in the relief rooms and in my own kitchen holds me at arm's length. My own initials nearly spell out *ma'am*. When I am at my lowest, even the girls calling me Marmee, as I called my own mother from the time I was a lisping child, reminds me of all that I am responsible for rather than warming my heart as it always has, and always should.

Mrs. March, Mrs. March, Mrs. March, all day long, makes me feel as if I am in charge of the whole world. It's an absurd notion, and one I'm sure Aunt March or Mrs. Weddleton or a score of others would be happy to disabuse me of. Knowing it is only in my mind does not cause it to disappear any more quickly, though. On the contrary, the knowledge that I am plagued by something of my own invention heightens my unhappiness.

How strange it is to be surrounded by people who love and care for me, and yet be lonely. Worse, the absences loom larger when my mood strays this way. My sisters are long gone, and Marmee and Father. It has been close to two—no, three years since I have seen my brother. Samuel's letters are rarer even than Amos's. Little makes me prouder than the work he and William Lloyd Garrison are doing for the Negro people, but that pride does not prevent me from missing my youth's companion. Samuel has been my champion since I was four years old, the one who first took me to school and opened my mind to learning. He fought as fiercely as I did for my education, and together, we prevailed upon our parents. It was through him and his work that I met Amos. How it would strengthen me to see him again.

It is not that I crave coddling. A single look of shared understanding would be enough to soothe me, the wordless exchange between two people who see their own struggles mirrored in another.

In all the world, the person I feel the greatest affinity with just now is Birte Hummel. I would not have to explain to her what it is like to be alone with her children, wondering how things can ever be as they once were. If only I had the words to do so. That is not an exchange I can ask Karl to translate. Even with all of English at my disposal, I am not sure I could adequately convey to her what her companionship has meant to me. Nor am I sure she would believe it.

May 23, 1862

Today marks twenty years since Amos and I were married. I had never thought to spend this day apart from him. How many more days will there be? Six hundred and seventy-two? One thousand eighty-one? I could bear three times that many, if I only knew the number to be finite.

I do not know how to observe this anniversary. Am I, in fact, a widow on this day?

Longing for his presence, I went to the bookshelf in the study where his journals are lined up and took down the 1841 volume, in search not of our wedding day, but those that followed our first meeting. Those were the entries Amos showed me on the day we became engaged.

Had I waited for him to voice a proposal of marriage, I would quite possibly still be sitting on the edge of that sofa in my father's house. Amos's thoughts have always flowed straight to his pen. Give him ink, and he will unspool one idea after another as smoothly as a length of ribbon. Make him speak them aloud instead, and the words bunch together like so many burrs. The more fervently he feels a thing, the more stubbornly it tangles. And so all Amos could do was hand me his journals, indicating the days that he had written of me. What I saw in those pages was a perfect echo of my own hopes.

I was, his diary said, the selfsame interesting woman he had so often portrayed in his imagination. He had been most taken by that which I hold dearest in myself: my intellect. And he saw beyond it, to the tender, sympathetic recesses of my character that those outside my family circle (and even some within it) could so rarely find.

When I lifted my eyes to his, his lips were trembling like a palsied old man's as he tried to make the shape of just one word. No more than one letter—*W*—would form. Oh, that eager, pleading look in his eyes, asking me to ask the question he could not speak aloud. And so I did. "Yes!" he answered, loud and sudden as a sneeze.

Dear God, let me live to hear that voice once more.

May 26, 1862

A letter. The mercy of God is surely upon us.

It was as I thought—Amos pushed himself to the brink of exhaustion seeing to the wounded and dying of Williamsburg. When there is need, he seems able to tap into the energy of the Lord Himself, but Amos forgets that God's strength is only borrowed. Not until the connection is withdrawn does he realize the true extent of his fatigue. It is visible in his handwriting. From one letter to the next, the words might have been formed by two different men: one composed in measured and graceful ink, the other scratched out in hurried pencil. Which of these men might return home to me, I wonder?

Now that Amos has time to be still, he will have time to think, to recall what he witnessed in those field hospitals and on the muddy fields themselves. I know how the everyday woes of his parishioners trouble him. He takes such care at a deathbed to ease the passing, both for the dying and those left behind. Among all his duties, this is the most sacred to him. There are times I think it brings Amos as much peace as it imparts to the grieving. How will he cope with a field of broken men and boys who have no one else to bring solace to their last moments, far from his own beloved Family? None but I know that on the evening following a funeral, the Reverend March sometimes weeps in his wife's arms. Gentle tears, tears of grace and renewal, but tears nonetheless. Who shall comfort Chaplain March after he has smoothed the path into the next world for scores upon scores of soldiers? No one but God, whose own arms must be full to overflowing with the sorrows of this war.

The magnitude of this weight Amos must bear alone frightens me to contemplate.

May 28, 1862

Now that I am assured my husband has been spared in the latest round of carnage, I can indulge in the luxury of being cross with him.

Amos sent but $47 this month. Less than half of his pay, with no explanation or apology. I don't know what kind of magic he imagines me capable of, to get by on so little. We have been scraping along as it is, and now this.

I cannot fathom where his money goes. The army feeds and clothes him. Even the cost of his stamps are borne by the federal government. At this rate, he must be bestowing gold-tooled calfskin Bibles upon every man in his regiment.

I cannot pay Hannah, and she is woefully underpaid as it is. The grocery bills are outpacing me by a greater and greater margin each month. If it weren't for Meg and Jo, I would be standing before the poor board myself by now. I am so grateful that they want to help, and so angry that they must do so, all I can do is pace the floor of my bedroom, alternately giving thanks and fuming.

The days when I could count on my children's minds being as full as their bellies are so far behind me, they have the feel of a half-forgotten dream. Meg must teach the King children to chant their ABCs and count by fives, when she ought to be mastering the likes of Latin, geometry, and botany. Jo, at least, has Aunt March's library, and Mr. Laurence's, to keep her brain fueled. She is better versed in literature than I by now, and reasonably well-read in any history that includes adventure and romance, but woefully ignorant of sciences and mathematics. Amy ought to have drawing lessons to cultivate her talent, and Beth? Well, Beth's education is a conundrum for another day.

Forty-seven dollars. Not one of the algebraic equations I learned to master will multiply these banknotes into anything more plentiful. I shall have to do without. So long as the girls are not in need, no lasting harm can come to me; their well-being forms a cloak thick enough to protect me from suffering.

May 29, 1862

A letter from Samuel today, the first in months. He enclosed $45, thanks be to God. My brother is as cognizant of Amos's faults as of his virtues, and, as always, knows what I need before I have mustered the courage to ask. I cannot help but wonder sometimes if there is an invisible telegraph line between our minds.

What a joy it would be to sit down with him, to hear his voice and see his face. His columns in Mr. Garrison's *Liberator* are earnest yet formal, like the difference between Amos's Sunday sermons and his weekday conversations before our own hearth. It is my whole brother I wish to see, rather than a single facet of him. And it is only in person that he will acknowledge, even obliquely, the most dangerous part of his work. Never in words. But I know my brother. A phrase spoken with a certain upward slope, perhaps accompanied by a particular angle of his brow, and I know that the "robins" he has seen migrating north are not animals at all—no more than the doe and her two fawns pausing in his dooryard in the moonlight.

He denies it, but I know Samuel harbors some guilt for the financial straits we've found ourselves in these last ten years. I count him among the best men I know, but he is still a man with a man's ego, and therefore cannot be made to believe that I might have found my way to the cause of abolition if he had not been there to break the path for me, or, for that matter, that Amos and I would have taken the risk we took if he had not suggested it. I could write Samuel ten letters a day to remind him that it was Amos and I who decided to assume that responsibility, and it still would not assuage his conscience.

I have made a rule for myself, knowing as I do that every dollar my brother spares for me means that a Negro family in greater need than we are is doing without, that Samuel's money may be put only toward necessities.

The temptation to break that rule is greater today than it has ever been. Three of the girls' birthdays loom ahead: Beth in June, Amy in July, and Meg in August. All four of them were so selfless with their Christmas money that I will not be able to bear it if I cannot give each of my daughters proper birthday celebrations.

June 1, 1862

The girls have all four resolved to treat themselves to a week of vacation. Mischief got the better of me, and I goaded them into abandoning even their small household duties until Saturday, in hopes that by week's end they will better understand that idleness and refreshment are not one and the same.

The prospect of lazing about for a week does not appeal to me in the least, but I must say I am curious to see how it suits my daughters. Amy, I imagine, shall outlast the lot of them.

June 3, 1862

This experiment is not unfolding as I had foreseen. All it has meant thus far is more work for Hannah and me as we pick up the slack the girls have left behind. The two of us have made a pact to leave the girls' chores undone for the rest of the week. *Cahoots* is not a word I have much occasion to use, but there is no other word for this scheme Hannah and I have hatched. The two of us are winking at one another as though we were a pair of mutinous schoolgirls.

June 4, 1862

Am I wrong to shield my girls from the realities of the fighting? Is it fair that they gad about oblivious to the misery that has been wrought by bayonets and cowardice at Seven Pines, Virginia, these last few days? It is a lie of omission, for the newspapers are just as much within reach as they have ever been. To them the progress of this war is not much more than a geography lesson, for they have the implicit faith of the young that right will prevail. As long as the battles do not come too near their father, war does not intrude on their lives. Yet not one of us chooses to read those bloodstained columns aloud as we sit before the fire each night, knitting and sewing for "our" soldiers as though they are no more imperiled than a troop of neighborhood boys who set off on a camping trip without packing enough socks. Perhaps we are all trying to protect one another.

Jo, I suspect, reads some of the war reports on the sly before Hannah claims the papers for kindling, though she discusses them no more than I do. Meg and Amy would have no desire for such details, and Beth—our gentle Beth would be distraught day and night if she knew the extent of the bloodshed. Like me, she cannot find peace if she is conscious of suffering. Surely it is best to guard her from the savage pictures the mind cannot help but conjure while reading these dispatches.

Yet is it fair that their lives go on so blithely, with worries no greater than pickled limes and singed skirts? They could be doing a great deal of good by my side in the relief rooms instead of lounging about this week. But if the worst were to befall us, I should hate to have denied them these carefree days.

I should like some carefree days myself. Or rather, carefree nights. Each night as I climb into bed and each morning when my eyes open, Amos's blank side of the bed pains me like an open wound. Before this war I would often wake in the night—or even in the morning—and smile sleepily at the empty space beside me, knowing that he was reading or writing by candlelight in his study below, his mind too busy whirling with philosophies to register the passage of time. Then, it was an oddly contradictory reminder of his presence. Now each time I see it I am confronted with the fear that this is the sight that will greet me morning and night for the rest of my life.

It is a problem I might solve easily enough by lying in the center of the bed, but I cannot bring myself to sleep anywhere but my own half of the mattress. To do otherwise seems a potential concession to fate—a signal that I do not expect him to return. Every day, I feel an obligation to hold his spaces open, so that his absence cannot take root.

June 5, 1862

Oh, didn't Hannah and I think we were clever when we conspired to leave the girls' housework undone! Instead we have been outwitted by indolence. If Meg, Jo, Beth, or Amy has taken any notice of our dereliction, there is not the slightest indication.

The house has rapidly devolved into a state of utter disarray. Hulls of birdseeds crunch beneath my feet if I walk within three paces of Pip's cage. Meg's abandoned sewing is strewn all over one end of the kitchen table. Jelly jars half full of paintbrushes and muddy water clutter the sink, and books and shriveled brown apple cores turn up everywhere I look.

It is not the messes that vex me, but the apathy that seems to eddy in the air around them. I had not realized how much the disorderly bustling within these walls has helped to keep my spirits afloat all these months. Hope and keep busy, I have always said. Now that I come home to find everything dulled with dust and everyone bored to exasperation yet unwilling to admit to it and call this nonsense to a stop, I feel as though the dust is piling up on <u>me</u> and there is nothing I can do to shake it off. No matter how busily I work all the day long, the inertia that has overtaken this house swallows me whole the moment I walk through the door.

June 6, 1862

Amos's latest letter troubles me. This is the second in succession that has not closed with a verse of scripture. The first time, after the battle of Williamsburg, I hardly noticed, I was so relieved to hear from him at all. It ought to be a trifling thing—as trifling as the temporary state of housekeeping that has nettled me all week. But it is so unlike him.

The two things taken together have left me feeling as though the nails in the boards beneath my feet are quietly wiggling loose. How many more can slip free before the floor gives way? I cannot rid my mind of that question. Nor do I understand how anything so small has managed to erode my self-assurance so quickly. The more I remind myself that the depth of this unease is unwarranted, the more uneasy I become. What would happen to us all if a true disaster struck?

I am much in need of a steadying influence. For the first time in months, I find myself thinking of Miss Allyn. Though she was not a teacher, I learned lessons from her that are not to be found in any schoolroom.

Miss Allyn took such care to cultivate my mind, planting seeds of thoughts she knew would take root. *The soil is not bad,* she would say to me with a wry smile. Even now, I continue to model myself after her. Her example was so perfect, so impossible, that I strove every minute to follow it. Studying with her was like a vacation both <u>from</u> myself and <u>within</u> myself. My temper has never been unprovoked for so long, before or since. In Miss Allyn's presence, there was simply nothing to incite it. Without its relentless stamping and galloping through my thoughts, I came to know more of myself than I had previously been acquainted with.

If I could go anywhere in the world tomorrow, it would be to her home in Duxbury. Instead, I shall pack my journal and pen into a picnic basket and take myself out of this house. To the woods, the library, anywhere that I can be alone with myself. It isn't idleness I crave, but stability. I want only to feel capable of the task that has been set before me. I will tell the girls I am tired, which is true, so far as it goes. They haven't any idea <u>how</u> tired, or why, and I shall see that it remains that way.

June 7, 1862

Beth's canary is dead. Starved.

When I came down the stairs, my basket packed with pen and ink and paper and a book I have been meaning to read since before Amos left, there was Beth, sobbing quietly over Jo's domino box. Pip lay inside on a tuft of cotton batting, his black eyes dull and his sunny feathers flattened tight to his body.

My head reeled so with guilt, I do not know what I said to Beth. An embrace, a murmur of sympathy, a dab of my handkerchief upon her cheeks, and out the door I went before I succumbed to tears myself. The moment I turned the corner, I scurried down to the Mill Brook as fast as I could fly without drawing undue attention. The curtain of a willow tree gave me shelter. There, I pressed my forehead against its trunk until the roughness of the bark began to sting.

She who needed the lesson least has learned it the most harshly. And Pip, who needed it not at all, forfeited his life. How did I miss his morning chirps? It was I who told Hannah to ignore the girls' undone chores, without even a thought of what it would mean for Pip. I am so angry with myself, I'd like to climb out of my skin and set it ablaze.

By the time I summoned the courage to return, Pip's funeral was done. That was a mercy I did not deserve, and one I thanked God for, nonetheless. Beth bears me no ill will. Not even a flicker of blame shadows her great blue eyes. That, somehow, is the worst punishment of all.

June 9, 1862

A new canary chirps in Pip's cage, but I believe it brings Beth more pain than pleasure.

This has been a costly mistake in more ways than one. In my self-reproach, I spent more than I ought for the brightest bird that could be had in the town of Concord. A few dollars for a new canary will not send us before the poor board, but it may well pinch Christmas tighter yet than last year. The money I have endeavored to put aside seems always to dwindle instead of grow. This is the second month in a row that Amos has sent less than fifty dollars. His own expenses, I expect, have been affected by the fluctuations of prices and currency. At any rate, I <u>hope</u> that is the cause. If Amos has been indulging his mind while I scrimp to fill our stomachs, my temper and I shall have a battle royale before he is forgiven.

June 11, 1862

After a week's pursuit, General Fremont's division has engaged with General Jackson eight miles from Harrisonburg, Virginia. Jackson has used the woods and ravines of the Shenandoah Valley to his advantage once again. Only as our troops ascended did they realize that the full extent of Jackson's forces had been masked by the woods. The line of battle stretched for two miles. It is deemed a Confederate victory, though the notorious Colonel Ashby is believed to be among those lost.

All is quiet in the March household with the exception of Meg and Jo. The two of them went out shopping today and came back all a-twitter after running into Ned Moffat on the way home. He bowed at Meg. Jo's laughter when they'd shut the front door behind them sounded like a small explosion. All evening Meg and Jo bowed at each other each time they crossed paths in doorways and halls.

Their childishness reassures me. I should hope Meg had her fill of the Moffats in April, and has sense enough not to bother with such a frivolous young man as Ned Moffat.

June 12, 1862

Another of the Weddleton servants has been dismissed. Stealing, this time. Caught in the act of filling a satchel with flour and potatoes from the larder. I should like to know why a young woman employed by one of the richest families in this city should find it necessary to steal food, of all things, when she had ample access to the china and silver plate. Not only that, but in a pantry where she might have helped herself to anything from beefsteak to port wine, she confined herself to the cheapest, plainest provisions on hand. But it seems a potato is worth as much as a diamond to Mrs. Weddleton, so out the girl went.

"I shall not hire another Irish girl so long as I live," she vowed. "Good help is so rare these days."

I managed not to wonder aloud if it is the finding, or the <u>keeping,</u> of good help that eludes Mrs. Weddleton. Her mother-in-law never faced this dilemma once, much less twice in succession.

"I don't know how you get along with one servant, Mrs. March, let alone an Irish one," she said.

It never fails to take me aback when someone mentions that. I don't think of Hannah as Irish. I do not even hear her brogue as such anymore. The lilt in her speech is simply Hannah's voice to me. She certainly bears no resemblance to the Irishwomen I see in the streets, with their black shawls and dour faces. Her temper is ten times more docile than mine, and she regards hard liquor with the same disdain Amos and I do. To look at her now, you might never guess she was brought up a Catholic. I cannot even recall the last time I saw her cross herself.

"If I didn't have Frieda, I don't know what I would do," Mrs. Weddleton went on. "Germans are so much more orderly and methodical. I've hardly finished telling Frieda what to do before it's done."

My brain came alight as though it had been touched by lightning. Birte Hummel! "Mrs. Weddleton," I said, "what would you think of hiring another German servant?"

"Does she speak English?"

Oh, was I pleased with myself then. "I can say with perfect confidence that she knows the name of everything a kitchen can hold," I replied with only a little exaggeration. I did not specify what <u>size</u> kitchen I referred to. "And with Frieda there to translate, you will be sure of understanding one another."

"You may bring her to see me on Tuesday next. If she makes a satisfactory impression, I shall consider taking her on. Ten dollars a month with board, or eighteen without."

I wanted to run through the streets the way Jo does, with her hair streaking backward behind her. Kitchen work is another kind of drudgery, but the labor should be lighter and steadier than taking in washing. I did not even knock, but burst in as I sang out like a Wagner soprano, "Frau Hummel, Ich habe dir einen Job gefunden!"

When I told her the monthly wage, English failed her. "Mein Gott!" she cried. "But the children?"

I had anticipated that very dilemma as I walked. "Greta is old enough to eat porridge now, and with school nearly out of session, Karl and Lottchen can mind the little ones."

In my excitement, I was speaking too quickly. She blinked at the battery of words as they flew at her. I explained again, more sedately.

Mrs. Hummel looked at the children. Karl puffed himself up like an eagle. Lottchen, to my surprise, looked a little frightened at the prospect of truly being in charge of her siblings. "I will look in on them on my way to and from the relief rooms every day," I promised. That eased Lottchen and her mother, both.

By the time I arrived home, I was positively gloating. The girls all cheered and applauded my good news. Hannah alone seemed uneasy. Just as I was poised to go up the stairs to bed, she asked me, "Will it be a good place for Mrs. Hummel?"

"I'd rather see her with a less trying mistress, that's sure," I admitted. "Then again, although Mrs. Weddleton may be one of the most obtuse and tactless of women, I cannot say that I have ever known her to be the least bit cruel, or even unfair. The woman she just dismissed was clearly in the wrong, regardless of how much I wish it were otherwise. No matter what, it will be better than bending over her washpot and ironing board sixteen hours a day, filling her house with the stink of other families' sheets and diapers."

"It's not the missus I was thinking of," Hannah said. "What with that girl Bridget who was dismissed this winter." One of her eyebrows lifted meaningfully.

Bridget. I had forgotten that.

"I can't imagine that Mrs. Weddleton would have flounced all over the relief rooms talking about it, had her husband been responsible," I protested.

Hannah snorted. Actually snorted. "You'd be surprised what some wives can contrive not to see."

"She won't stay there. She can't, not with the children. She'll sleep every night in her own bed."

"It doesn't always happen at night, Mrs. March."

That sobered me. I am sober still. Hannah is right. I cannot offer up Mrs. Hummel to the Weddleton household until I know she will be safe there. And already I have gone and lifted her hopes higher than a church steeple.

June 13, 1862

As usual, Hannah may be my salvation. No one knows a household better than its servants, she reminded me this morning, and most of them speak more freely with one another in the streets and shops than with anyone else. "The women of this town know where it is safe to send their daughters and sisters to work. Leave it to me, Mrs. March," she said with a solemn nod.

June 14, 1862

Hannah came back from the market and plopped her basket down on the table with such a look of satisfaction that I knew at once that our worries about Bridget and Mr. Weddleton were unfounded.

"Frieda told me Bridget married her man straightaway and had a red-haired little boy just last week," Hannah said. Red hair! Praise be. There hasn't been a redheaded Weddleton in the last three generations. Gossip has never made me so happy as it did today.

It seems Frieda takes a peculiar pride in working for one of the most exasperating mistresses in the county. Anyone with eyes to see what needs to be done and hands ready to do it without hesitation will get along well in that household, Hannah relayed back to me. "Do what you're told before you're told" is her motto. I have no doubt Birte Hummel is capable of just that.

Laurie came calling this evening, for the weekly meeting of the Pickwick Club. I can hear the five of them overhead now, laughing and prancing about together. Perhaps their antics will cheer Beth. The loss of Pip still pains her, which pains me in turn. Before Laurie hustled up to the garret, he presented me with a bouquet of peonies large enough to bury my whole face in. All white but for one, the center one, which is the color of claret. I don't know where he found it. The only place I have ever seen such a peony is in Aunt March's gardens. Surely he wouldn't dare? And yet the image of him pilfering such a glorious bloom from the gardens at Plumfield made me grin shamelessly.

June 17, 1862

I awoke this morning buzzing like a telegraph wire. Only Beth's new canary was awake and twittering merrily. The two of us roused the whole house with our singing.

I presented myself at Birte Hummel's door a full half hour earlier than necessary, for I simply could not keep still. I only half recognized the woman who answered my eager knock. She wore a dress I had never seen, no doubt from the painted chest at the foot of the bed—a smart blue and brown plaid, with a somewhat old-fashioned fan front. Her hair was parted in the center and plaited into two glossy brown braids that swept from her temples to the knot in back. I'll wager she had been up as early as I, plagued by nervousness as insistent as my excitement.

"This dress is correct?" she asked. "It is not too fancy? Or too plain?"

I stood back to look, perhaps truly seeing her for the first time. She is thinner than she ought to be, and more plain than pretty, which makes her appear earnest and dependable—two qualities I hoped would hold her in good stead with Mrs. Weddleton.

As we walked to Barretts Mill Road, her questions came ceaselessly.

Would her English be good enough? Was I sure? I confess, I was not wholly sure. Her nerves made her suddenly mismatch prepositions, stilting her speech so that she sounded like a rudimentary student rather than a woman who has been studying diligently for five months.

At the front gate, she stopped short. "Me, on that fine house?" I could not blame her for hesitating. The Weddletons' is one of the most gracious brick homes in Concord. The front door alone, framed by two white pilasters and crowned with a triangular pediment, is sufficient to make anyone stand up straighter before ringing the bell. Each of the nine front windows has no less than twenty-four panes, and a pair of chimneys ascends from either side of the roof. Two dormer windows are perched above the roofline like raised eyebrows. I laced my arm through hers and pulled her through the gate and up onto the portico. With her free hand she patted anxiously at her hair and tugged the pleats on her bodice.

"You look neat as a pin," I assured her as we awaited an answer to my ring. The unfamiliar idiom distracted her.

"Das ist gut? Mrs. Weddleton will like it?"

"Es ist perfekt," I said.

"Das ist perfekt," she corrected, and we were both smiling when the door opened.

I had thought I was not nervous. And even as we were ushered into the foyer and then the parlor itself, I felt not a quiver. Yet when Mrs. Weddleton began to look Birte Hummel up and down like a bolt of cloth, my confidence quailed. She sat behind her maple writing desk, radiating the feel of a schoolmarm. I might have been standing before her with my slate, waiting for her to correct my long division. I half expected her to speak only to me, as if Mrs. Hummel were a child or a puppy in need of training. To my relief she addressed Birte directly.

"Mrs. March informs me you speak English?"

"Yes, ma'am, I am. I do."

I held my breath, wincing inwardly at the simplicity of her error and knowing that Birte was doing the same. Mrs. Weddleton took no outward notice of it.

"And you can cook?"

"Yes, ma'am."

"American food? Not only German dishes?"

Mrs. Hummel gave a small shrug of genuine perplexity. "American potato or German potato—what is the difference?"

To my astonishment, Mrs. Weddleton's lips slowly curled upward, showing unmistakable signs of amusement. "That is a fact, Birte." She sat back in her chair then with an air of satisfaction, as though she had achieved something that pleased her. "I think you'll do just fine. Please return Monday morning. The kitchen door is at the north side of the house. Mr. Weddleton expects his breakfast at six-fifteen."

And that was that. Hardly ten minutes after we had rung the bell we were back on the pavement outside the gate.

"That is all?" Birte said. "I have this job?"

"That is all," I assured her, and tugged her home to tell the children.

This is the most satisfying thing I have done since the night I opened the kitchen door and beckoned a Negro man named John in from the shadows.

June 19, 1862

Today when I arrived at the Hummels', no one came to the door. Mrs. Hummel's voice called out, "Willkommen, Frau March!" That gave me half an instant's pause, for she always speaks as much English with me as she is able, and I taught her how to say *Welcome* months ago. Nevertheless, I turned the knob and found the entire family ranged in a line before the table from biggest to smallest with Mrs. Hummel on the left and little Heinrich on the right.

"Danke schoen!" seven of them chorused, while Greta burbled and clapped in her mother's arms. Then Mrs. Hummel counted "Eins, zwei, drei!" and they parted like a curtain—four of them one way and four the other.

The table behind them was laid with the most exquisite cloth of

Battenburg lace. I have seen fine linen tablecloths with Battenburg insets and lush edgings six inches deep. This was crafted <u>entirely</u> of lace. A star-shaped center medallion, ringed with loops and whorls of flowered garlands, then edged in latticework.

"Es ist—Das ist schön," I said. *This is beautiful.*

"It is for you," Mrs. Hummel said in English. "With many thanks for all you have done."

A thrill ran through me. Over my scalp and down my arms it went. True beauty rarely fails to affect me thus, as if I am seeing with my entire body. And what a sight! All of those faces gazing at me with perfect delight and satisfaction while my mind instantaneously painted a picture of how splendid that cloth would look on my table with Beth's birthday presents arranged atop it, crowned with a vase of summer flowers. I have not been so surprised since Christmas Day.

"My oma made it," Karl said.

Oma. His grandmother. The beautifully laden table in my mind was swept clean and bare.

"Das ist zu viel," I protested. I could not go on in German. The few hundred words I know are too paltry to express what I meant. "It's much too much. This is an heirloom. It belongs with your family. Please tell her, Karl."

Yet even as I refused, I took the hem of the cloth in both hands, lifting it to admire the way the strands intersected—not quite like spider webbing, nor quite like honeycomb. This type of lace is both sturdy and delicate. I remember when I had time to attempt fancy-work, in the days before patching and darning dominated my sewing, when everything that came from my work basket was largely unnecessary. Knitting, and the requisite samplers I mastered well enough to spare my mother from dejection. But with the exception of broomstick lace, the intricacies of finer needlework elude me.

Mrs. Hummel's face clouded as Karl explained. Or tried to. I feared I had not adequately expressed my misgivings to him. I know well enough the sense of feeling yourself on unequal footing with a benefactor. It is very like being the smaller child on a seesaw, dangling helplessly in the air with no power to return yourself to solid ground. To offer something in return helps to bring the ground back within reach. But accepting something as precious as that cloth would have catapulted me from my end of that same seesaw straight into the heavens.

Karl spoke quickly enough to his mother that I could catch hold of only the simplest words: *can't, doesn't want.* The younger children sobered as they listened, and I tried not to grimace. My protest had whisked their glee out from under them. When Karl finished, Mrs. Hummel pursed her lips and looked at me so intently, I feared I had offended. Then she suddenly delved into the painted chest at the end of the bed and brought out a small stack of linens.

"Servietten," she said, as if it were a new word in one of our lessons, and held them out to me.

"Napkins," I replied, and ran a finger around each scrolling, lacy border. Though smaller, they were no less breathtaking in their own way. Each one might have served as a tablecloth in a doll's mansion.

"My own." Mrs. Hummel's brow crinkled. "That is, of my own sewing."

"You made these?"

Her head dipped up and down in one quick bob of pride.

"They are perfectly sumptuous." Mrs. Hummel cocked her head at the unfamiliar word. I looked to Karl for help, but he only shrugged. I lifted a loose fist to either side of my face and turned my eyes heavenward. "Schön!" I proclaimed, pronouncing the word like a note of music as my fingers blossomed open.

"Ach!" Mrs. Hummel said, clasping her hands in delight. "Exquisit."

"Exquisite, indeed!"

"You will take these," she insisted. There was no arguing with her. Her face was so sincere, it put a little twist in my chest. Truth be told, I did not want to refuse. I wanted the napkins themselves as much as I wanted to oblige her, and this was a much fairer trade. No matter that I did not need to be thanked; Birte Hummel needed to thank me.

How I wish I could call her Birte. But women like Birte Hummel hear their Christian names only from their so-called superiors, and I will not have her thinking that I consider myself above her. But for the grace of God, our positions might very well be reversed.

June 26, 1862

Meg, Jo, Laurie, and Amy have put on a fine play for Beth's birthday. I don't know why we didn't think to celebrate this way years ago; Beth was infinitely more content to let her sisters take center stage in her honor than she has ever been to assume her place upon the birthday throne and let us fuss over her. Today may be the first time I have seen her joyful since poor Pip.

Jo's script was pure comedy—a satire of Beth herself, trying to coax a lion in from the cold despite Hannah's vehement protests. Laurie took the part of Beth, Meg played Hannah, Amy pantomimed as a frightened kitten, and Jo, of course, was the lion. All five of Beth's own cats had supporting roles. My peeks at the script had led me to believe that Jo or Laurie must certainly steal the show, but in fact it was Meg who absolutely shone. With her talent for mimicry, she could cause a great deal of hurt if she were inclined toward cruelty instead of kindness.

Everyone laughed until their sides ached—Beth, Mr. Laurence, all the Hummel children, Laurie's tutor Mr. Brooke, and even Hannah herself chuckled until tears leaked from the corners of her eyes.

July 3, 1862

Meg has somehow managed to lose one of her good gray gloves. Only one—Laurie found the other, after Beth's party, I suppose, and dropped it in the Family post this morning. I expect such things from Jo, but Meg? There is no use scolding her. She shall have to wait until her birthday for another pair; there is simply not enough to spare in the meantime.

It seems I am not the only one in this house who has taken an interest in German. Meg received a translation of a German song in the post from Laurie's tutor.

July 7, 1862

In a single week, the south's General Lee has wiped the battlefront clean of federal troops, as if sweeping his arm across a chessboard. Only a month ago it seemed as if the scent of victory might waft into our troops' nostrils at any moment. Federals had penetrated to within ten miles of Richmond when Confederate commander Johnston was wounded at Seven Pines. Now we are driven back to Harrison's Landing on the James River, twenty-five miles from the Confederate capital.

These last seven days have been nothing less than a slaughter. Fifteen thousand to twenty thousand men killed, wounded, or missing. A year's steady progress, gone.

This is the most sobering defeat yet. In the relief rooms, people shuffle and murmur as if numbed. It is not only the staggering losses. There is a feeling that the whole tenor of the war is changing under Lee's command. The shadow of the destruction this man will wreak has chilled us all in midsummer.

It would be easier if we had not begun to hope. The nearer our troops drew to Richmond, the easier it was to imagine Amos back in his chair before the hearth. Now, I hardly want to look toward that corner of the room.

July 9, 1862

A discomfiting note from Meg in the Family post:

Dearest Marmee,
 Did you enjoy my part in Beth's birthday play? No applause means

more to me than yours. Don't you think I ought to be an actress? I do
hate teaching, and acting would pay so many more bills, Marmee.
It isn't anything like a whim, I've thought about it ever since Jo's
Christmas play, when everyone said I did so well. I love it as much as
Jo loves writing, and Amy loves drawing.

Dear girl! Does she fancy she could walk onto a stage and find a position as easily as one inquires of a shopkeeper for employment? Or that she could expect an offer of more than the $5 she receives from the Kings each week?

My sweet, simple Meg at last has managed to tie herself a knot I must untangle. And what a tangle it is. My daughter has talent, I cannot deny that. She would not believe me if I did; I've always encouraged her theatrics. Here among her sisters, amidst pasteboard sets, bedsheet curtains, and tin spangles, her knack for drama shines like a polished gem. But talent is not genius. The same hands that applaud her acting in our parlor would lift to muffle yawns if they saw her on the great stages of Boston and New York.

All of this is true, but it is not everything.

I must own that my distaste for the idea weighs as heavy as all the practical reasons put together. Premature pride does not swell my chest at the thought of Meg center stage, even if she rivaled the likes of Lotta Crabtree or Fanny Brown. Instead, my heart squirms backward at the idea. How do I discourage her from this, without simultaneously discouraging her from aspiring at all? She is so conventional, my Meg, that I fear limiting her view further. I've always thought her path a straight one, somewhat to my dismay. It seemed I could have placed her upon that deeply rutted path nearly every woman follows, and she would have crawled, then toddled, then walked from the cradle to the edge of her grave without ever straying more than an inch or two. Sometimes it seemed that had I tried to place her on a less trodden path, she would have found her way to the rutted one. At last she is aspiring to something, and it is something I cannot abide.

I've backed myself into quite a tight little corner—a scrape, Jo would call it. How can I implore my daughters to make the world feel their presence, and then refuse Meg this desire?

July 12, 1862

Every day Meg looks at me so hopefully, I can hardly bear to meet her gaze; her eyes are like those of a beggar, telling me I have the power to change her life with a pittance.

I have hesitated so long, she surely must know that I am less than enthusiastic. But which is the worse—to crush a dream while it is small, or to let Meg nurture a fancy that has no viable chance to become a reality?

Ned Moffat was among those at Laurie's party today, along with a pair of British twins, Fred and Frank Vaughn. Making eyes at Meg, no doubt. I would rather see her on the stage than attached to one of those foolish Moffats. I've told Hannah to send him politely away if he attempts to come calling.

July 15, 1862

I am a coward. I have placated Meg with a temporary excuse.

"Acting is an uncertain profession, and so long as Father is away, we cannot risk diminishing our income," I told her. It borders on cruel, to saddle a girl so young with that responsibility. I don't know if she cried when she went to her room; I only know I did.

She and Jo both begged to leave school to help with the bills, and against my better judgment I allowed it. I reasoned with myself that working and earning would be a good lesson for them, and one they could not learn in school. Now both of them detest their jobs, and we cannot afford to do without them.

~~What would I give to free them both to pursue their own desires?~~ Oh, why do I vex myself with such questions, when there is nothing left of any value to trade? I can only pray that Meg's attachment to this idea will fade with time, that other joys may loom larger.

No doubt my father said a version of the same prayer over me during the winter of my nineteenth year, when I refused to return home from Duxbury unless I could be excused from all social encumbrances, so that I might continue my studies uninterrupted. My passion was for learning, not for visits and dances and suitors. What did he think of a daughter who found more pleasure in translating the Gospel of John from Latin Vulgate to English than in the gaiety of waltzes and parlor games?

To me it felt as though my life were just beginning. The wide world opened before me each time I opened a new book. How could Father expect me to be mollified by the same old people, the same old rooms, the same old dance steps? The thought of it made me want to scream. I was not permitted to shout, but I could sing. And sing I did, again and again, until I gained the courage to commit my desires to paper and send them home in my place:

> No, no, I'll take no less,
> Than all in full excess!
> Your oath it may alarm you.
> Yet haste and prepare,
> For I'll know what you are,
> With all your powers arm you.

The words and melody are Handel's. The highest notes nearly exceed my reach, for of course when a man composes the melody to express a woman's anger, he turns to the flittering tones of a harpsichord. Never the thunder of cymbals and drums, or the blaring of brass.

Singing those notes would do me some good now, I should think. The strain of stretching to such heights is precisely what used to scour my brain so that I might think clearly again. And there is satisfaction in refining a tumult of frustration into something as lithe and pure as that music. The words themselves, though, they would burn my throat tonight.

> *No, no, I'll take no less,*
> *Than all in full excess!*

And yet that is just what I expect from Meg. My parents did all they could to put everything I reached for within my grasp, and here am I, telling my own daughter to keep her hands firmly in her pockets. I should like to tear this whole page from my diary, that I might never have to revive this memory.

July 17, 1862

Congress has finally realized that permitting black men to enlist is to the Union's advantage. Negro soldiers are to be paid $10 a month, with $3 deducted for clothing. (Whereas white recruits receive $13, and keep every cent.) But they are not to fight. Heavens, no! For this, they have the honor of digging entrenchments, "performing camp service"—a lofty phrase that smacks of servitude—and whatever other labor that white officers are willing to admit black men are capable of.

A fine message we are sending to men willing to risk their lives for the Union cause: "You are worth fifty cents more than half a white man."

In addition, any man whose master is bearing arms against the United States is now free, according to Congress, along with his mother, wife, and children. I ought to be pleased that this step toward emancipation has been taken. But as usual, the law must be constructed with a man at its center. The Congress cannot simply state that any <u>person</u> currently enslaved by a member of the Confederate army has been emancipated. What of orphans, I wonder, and widows? Unmarried women kept as white men's concubines? What of families who have been splintered and sold to different masters? Do any of those men who sit in the Senate chamber or the House of Representatives have the slightest understanding that the rules of our society have no currency among those kept in bondage?

Of course not! Any mother, wife, or children of a freed Negro whose master is <u>not</u> engaged in the rebellion is not made free by the Militia Act. How perfectly sickening. I must shut this book before I am forced to vomit upon the page.

July 24, 1862

I had hardly arrived at the relief rooms this morning when Mrs. Weddleton made her way straight toward me. I tried not to cringe and did not fully succeed. That woman does not advance upon anyone with such velocity unless she is about to ruin their day.

"My mother-in-law wishes to see you," she announced. One might have thought her a messenger for a queen, she spoke with such formality. "Will you come calling this Saturday?"

My shoulders fell a good two inches as my apprehensions vanished. "I would be honored," I said with absolute sincerity. The invitation is for luncheon. What this portends, I cannot guess. No one in the relief rooms has seen Adelaide since the spring of '61.

July 26, 1862

Precisely at half past twelve this afternoon I presented myself at the Weddleton house. Mrs. Weddleton took me by surprise straightaway with her nervousness. Her hands fluttered, and she spoke in such a hurried whisper that anyone within earshot might have thought we were discussing something indecent. "She is much changed outwardly, you understand," my hostess explained as she led me up the stairs to her mother-in-law's bedchamber. "The surgery."

"Of course." I know enough of anatomy to understand the consequences of the operation. It ought to be called disfigurement rather than surgery.

I thought myself well braced for the shock of Adelaide's decline. It has been since before the war, after all, that she was last in the relief rooms, and even then the effect of the cancer was becoming evident. Nevertheless, it was with an effort that I curbed my reaction.

It might have been easier if she had not been so much herself. Adelaide Weddleton's eyes are such a dark midnight blue, they make the whites look like skimmed milk. They have dulled somewhat in the last year (no doubt by pain) but the spark remains, too deeply embedded to be pried loose by anything but death itself.

Her hands held a fragment of lace and a tatting shuttle. A double row of pillows beneath her upper arms propped them at a comfortable angle.

"Mrs. March!" she exclaimed with such warmth that her voice had the feel of an embrace. One hand lifted to clasp mine. "I am so pleased that you accepted Harriet's invitation."

Her body has always seemed too small to contain her. Now it is smaller yet, consumed as much by the ravages of the cure as of the disease itself. She has endured the carving away not only of both breasts, but a great swathe of the pectoralis muscles beneath. With so little flesh to level the plane of her chest, her sternum bows outward like the prow of a ship. That was not the worst of it, though—for me, that is. In her face I recognized the first shadings of a color I have not seen since my own mother lay on her deathbed, a yellow-gray cast that portends the worst. She is not much more than fifty, and she is dying.

A chair and small side table with a single luncheon place setting were positioned beside the bed. There I took my seat. And then who should come bearing a bed tray of chicken salad and lemonade but Mrs. Hummel. She betrayed not a hint of our acquaintance, acting every inch the ideal servant. I wanted so much to wink at her, but I resisted, as she seemed to be taking great pride in her formality as she set my plate before me.

I daresay the salad alone would have been worth the visit—chicken, with pineapple and almonds and a dash of Worcestershire sauce if I am not mistaken, laid out on curling fans of leaf lettuce.

Harriet Weddleton's devotion was a marvel to see. That simpering which I find beyond endurance was entirely absent from our conversation, for in her mother-in-law's presence, she evinced the sincerest humility and respect. Every bite Adelaide ate was first spooned onto her fork by her daughter-in-law. (Though her hands still function ably enough to tat and crochet, Adelaide has not the musculature to move her arms in any direction but up and down.) From time to time, Harriet paused to divide a larger bit of meat into two or even three pieces.

"I have not been able to cut meat since the operation," Adelaide explained. "Once you have felt the knife saw against the grain of your own flesh, the sensation of slicing through the tenderest fowl or brawn becomes intolerable."

Thank goodness I had swallowed my latest bite before she spoke. I had to coax my throat open again with several sips of lemonade before I could think of chewing another forkful of chicken.

There is no sign of a nurse. Only Harriet, who must be assisting Adelaide with everything from eating and dressing to bathing and toileting. No wonder she visits the relief rooms just once a week. I have sorely misjudged her, and must ask God's forgiveness for doing so.

Our talk was of no consequence. Each time Adelaide inquired of the goings-on in the relief rooms, Harriet twittered out a cheery reply before I could speak, ending with *Isn't that right, Mrs. March?* or *Don't you think so, Mrs. March?* so that I had no choice but to agree. Nothing she said was untruthful, but I quickly began to prickle at being talked over like a child.

I don't know whether Adelaide sensed my displeasure, but in the midst of one of Harriet's answers she interrupted. "My dear, would you fetch us all a plate of those fine Pfeffernüsse cookies Birte made yesterday?" she asked her daughter-in-law. "I seem to recall that Mrs. March has a weakness for sweets second only to my own." Adelaide turned to me with a devilish grin. "When I learned that Harriet had hired a German woman in the kitchen, I prevailed upon her to make a batch. My grandparents on my mother's side were German, did you know that? It has been years since I have had Pfeffernüsse, and I see very little wisdom in presuming I will be here to enjoy any at Christmas."

Harriet grimaced as though a pin had been stuck in her side and hurried from the room.

"Now then, how are things truly getting on in the relief rooms?" Adelaide asked when the sound of Harriet's footsteps had faded. "My son and daughter-in-law are determined to strain the bad news from the good before it reaches this room. Perhaps they fancy that a steady diet of glad tidings will feed my health and starve the cancer. If Harriet had her way, I would not even know there is a war on."

"I can say with perfect honesty that we are getting along very well, indeed," I told her. "When the hostilities broke out I was worried that the soldiers' needs might overtake those of the poor, but volunteers and donations have both increased since the war commenced. Your daughter-in-law never neglects us for a single week, as I'm sure you know."

"You are being tactful, Mrs. March."

I opened my mouth and closed it just as quickly. There was not one more thing I could say on Harriet Weddleton's behalf that either of us would believe. Adelaide chuckled softly and gave the bedcover a playful slap, plainly enjoying my chagrin. "I know as well as you do that Harriet has a great deal yet to learn about dispensing charity," she said with a conspiratorial glint in her eye that might have made me smirk if she had not gone on. "And I am afraid my opportunity to teach her has passed."

What could I say to comfort her? Adelaide Weddleton is no fool. Whether or not the tumors recur, the surgery that has granted her this extra time has left her too diminished physically to ever return to the work she so loved. In lieu of words, I moved from my chair to the edge of her bed.

"Birte has been a welcome addition to our household," she said. "Harriet has nothing but praise for her."

I told her how glad I was to hear it.

"Knowing you, I can assume that this position represents a great reversal in her family's fortunes."

"A widow with seven children living," I replied, "and two lately buried." What more was there to explain?

Adelaide nodded, giving me a long and thoughtful look. Her hand lifted. It hovered above the bedclothes before I realized she meant to place it over mine but could not direct her arm the few inches to the left to do so. I slid my hand within her reach and her warm palm blanketed it. Her thin skin had the feel of satin. "You see? You have a rare affinity for your brothers and sisters in humanity. Where Harriet perceives only a mass of poverty that must be obliterated, you recognize individuals and strive to find for them what they most need. That is a far more valuable service than showering them with whatever commodity happens to lately be in abundance."

Before I could take hold of words with which to thank Adelaide, Harriet appeared with the cookies and offered the plate to me. Two little girls came scampering in behind their mother, their dark ringlets as glossy as the ribbons that adorned them. They bounded up onto the bed beside Adelaide, each lifting one of their grandmother's arms as though it were a gate latch in order to settle themselves into her embrace.

"Addie, Julia!" Harriet scolded. "Your manners! Granny has company."

They looked abashedly at me. "There almost is nothing I like better than a room full of boisterous girls," I said, passing them the plate of spicy brown cookies. "And it looks as though they do their grandmother a great deal of good." The younger of the pair—funnily enough the one who does not share her grandmother's name—has a face so like Adelaide's it might have been chiseled by a master sculptor. She helped herself to two cookies and proceeded to hold one up for her granny to nibble. My heart beat as if it were being squeezed by those fat little fists. Oh, how my mother would have reveled in her granddaughters.

The elder girl, Addie, shyly passed the plate back to me. I hesitated only an instant.

That Pfeffernüsse! It has been an age since I tasted molasses and sugar all in the same mouthful. These are flavors Amos is unable to enjoy. I, on the other hand, despite uniting with him wholeheartedly to boycott products of bondage in our household, have never been able to convince my tongue to be as noble as my principles. I persist in craving sweets like a child, and have been known to placate myself with a spoonful of honey straight from the jar. (Even honey is theft, according to Amos, though thanks to Hannah's persistent laments from the kitchen he has been persuaded to concede that stealing the work of bees is less corrupt than purchasing goods that fund the institution of slavery.)

If my husband had been in the room I might have steeled myself to politely refuse the plate of cookies, though I have not had a taste of confectionary since Laurie's gift of Jordan almonds. But in the sweetness of that moment with Adelaide and her family, how could I refuse? Perhaps even Amos would have bent his rules, for it was in truth a kind of communion.

By the time we had all indulged ourselves in Mrs. Hummel's sweets, an hour had passed, and I could see that the length of the visit was taxing Adelaide's strength. With reluctance I made my excuses, offered my thanks to both of my hostesses, and rose to take my leave.

I paused a moment in the doorway, taking in the sight of Adelaide, bolstered by her granddaughters, and wondering if I should ever see her again. Her visitors may be few, but I am far from the first to look at her this way; she knew my thoughts as clearly as though I had spoken them aloud.

"If love alone were enough to sustain a life, Mrs. March, you and I could be assured of immortality," she said.

My heart swelled so that my breath could not move past it. Winking back tears, I nodded and ducked out of the room.

At the front door, I paused again. "Your devotion to her is a truly beautiful thing," I told Harriet Weddleton, "and I feel privileged to have witnessed it."

The praise dumbfounded her. Gauging by her reaction, I can only conclude that my past disdain of her has not been so well hidden as I believed, and for that I am ashamed.

By the time I reached home, I knew what I might have truthfully said to Adelaide about her daughter-in-law. I took out a sheet of note-paper and wrote,

> *Dear Mrs. Weddleton,*
>   *Rest assured that Harriet strives daily to follow your fine example,*
> *as do each and every one of us who have had the great good fortune of*
> *knowing you.*
>
>> *With fondness and gratitude,*
>> *Margaret March*

August 5, 1862

A letter from Olive Kirke. Her husband has been missing since the Seven Days Battles last month. She asks for prayers for his safe return. Surely it is best for her to be among her family now, but I cannot help wishing she were here so that I might offer the comfort that only a sympathetic face or hand can give. All along I have prayed for him, as Olive well knows. Now I shall do so with especial fervor.

August 11, 1862

A Confederate victory at Cedar Mountain, Virginia, two days ago. The report in today's *Traveler* is short, but vivid. The woods and ra-vines hid a crescent of rebel batteries three miles long from General Pope. The 46th Pennsylvania Infantry led the charge and were mown

down by a burst of fire from a thicket where the Confederate infantry had concealed themselves. The Federals had no choice but to
retreat—or "retire," as the *Traveler* so daintily puts it—from the range
of rebel guns.

A year ago such news horrified me. I felt as though I had not done
my duty until I had conjured up every retreating man's terror in my
own mind. Now I can manage nothing but dismay, as if I have set
one of my girls to a task only to find she has left it undone. That itself
should trouble me, but it seems I have been driven beyond the reach
of such sensitivities.

August 15, 1862

Amos's salary is late again, and there is not enough in the money box
for a new pair of gloves for Meg's birthday. Every time I look into that
box, I fancy a mouse must creep in each night and nibble the pennies
away. Of course, the child to whom worldly things mean the most
must come at the end of the summer succession of birthdays, when
so much has already been spent on her sisters. Meg's dreams are all
lined with silk and ribbons, and I fear I am at a loss to make even the
slightest of them come true.

I would sooner give Meg a pair of gloves fashioned of leather cut
from my own skin than appeal to Aunt March for such a trifling sum.
The only thing to do is to purchase them on credit.

It is one thing to buy necessities on credit. But the very thought
of walking up to that sales counter with a pair of pretty white gloves
and less than fifty cents in my reticule makes me feel as small and
irritating as a flea.

I can wait no longer. Hannah has pledged to trim the wrists with
the finest tatting she can manage, and she must have time enough to
do it. I can be of no help in that regard. My knitting is sufficient for
socks and scarves and mittens, but even Hannah lacks the patience
to help me gain mastery over a tatting shuttle. The instant the thread

tangles—usually within forty seconds of my touching the shuttle—
the back of my throat starts to burn and all is lost.

August 16, 1862

Who should walk up to the counter just as I was laying down the
gloves I had chosen for Meg, but Mrs. King? I should have liked to
have sunk into the floor. At least I can be thankful it wasn't Mrs.
Weddleton. Of course Mrs. King knows we are much reduced. How
can she not, when it is my Meg who is teaching her children how to
count and recite their alphabet? Worst of all was the middling quality
of the poor little gloves. I wish I'd had the audacity to choose the best
pair in the shop.

It is one thing for others to know; another thing entirely for them
to stand beside you as Mr. Brown adds yet another figure to the bottom of the long column under your name in his books. I shall never
regret the decision that put me in that position, but on occasions such
as this I cannot help missing the days when I could treat my daughters
to any item in any shop I pleased without feeling pinched.

Mrs. King, of course, was gracious and tactful. Mrs. King is made
of grace and tact, so far as I can determine. "Meg's birthday, is it? She
must take the day off as our gift to her, with best wishes for many
happy returns." She even remarked on how well the gloves would look
on Meg's dainty hands, and it is true—simplicity is best for a girl as
pretty as Meg. One always leaves Mrs. King's presence feeling lighter.

August 21, 1862

Today marks one year since Amos was mustered into service. A year.
I know now what it is like to be without him on any given day. From
Christmas Eve to any arbitrary morning, afternoon, or evening in
April, February, or October. What can be endured for minutes can be

endured for an hour. What can be endured for an hour can be endured for a day. And so on. Until here I sit, a year later.

And yet the days, the weeks, the months without him are only tolerable thanks to the implicit promise of his return. If he should not come home—

Those words have the look of sacrilege, but I must write them. Otherwise the thought will bore a hole straight through my skull in its insistence to get out.

If he should not come home, I have a framework now for how to live without him. It is a bare framework, though—the flimsiest of scaffolds. I don't know if it would bear my weight, much less that of our children.

My prayer never varies: *Dear God, in your infinite mercy, protect thy servant Amos March.*

Day and night. Before I close my eyes, and the moment I open them. Chanted in the rhythm of every footstep between here and the relief rooms. Silently wailed each time I read the casualty lists. *Carry him back to those who cherish him.*

He has granted our Family so many small mercies in these last years, and I would sacrifice every one of them and beg in the streets in exchange for Amos's safe return.

How can He hear me, I wonder, through the cacophony of voices that must be imploring the very same thing at all hours of the day and night? How can He possibly decide whose plea to grant, and whose to deny? I should not like to be God on any day, and least of all in the midst of a war.

August 24, 1862

Olive Kirke's husband is dead. The letter arrived yesterday and I did not open it, for the black-bordered envelope spoke for itself. I had hoped (though *hope* is not the right word for it at all) that the envelope would contain news of one of her elderly parents' passing instead. But it was George, wounded in the field and dead of exposure before he could be found and attended to. In his last hours he managed to scrawl a note to his family on the back of the carte de visite he carried of Olive and Minnie. Every time I picture that scene, my own composure deserts me.

Olive is fortunate to be so well off, and surrounded by her own kin in the city. None of that will ease her grief, of course—only give her the luxury of devoting herself entirely to learning how to assimilate George's absence into her life. It is a wretched thing to say, but should the worst befall my Family, I will envy her that liberty.

August 27, 1862

Meg's birthday.

If not for Amos's absence, it might have been a party worthy of old times. Laurie came bearing a great silver salver topped with a bowl of pink and white roses. Jo, Beth, and Amy had pooled their rag money for a lovely little snood trimmed in bright glass beads and ringed with a velvet ribbon. The King children sent cookies and sweets. Hannah brought out a cake three layers high, smothered in buttercream and wreathed with rosebuds. When she saw my face, Hannah nodded in the direction of the Laurence house. And a note from Amos, just in time. That made Meg smile more brightly than anything. She has written him as faithfully as I, this last year.

Pleasure makes Meg blush as much as modesty, and so she remained pink as a rosebud all the day through. It is a picture I should like to hold in my mind for years to come: Meg, clapping her white-gloved hands with delight as the beads in her snood winked in the tremors from every gale of laughter.

Seventeen years old, my Meg. What a day it was, the day she was born. I was so hopeless and hopeful, so fearful of bringing forth another lifeless child that I did not want to bear down at all. So long as the babe remained within me, I reasoned in my terror, I could count it as living. But my body would not permit such cowardice. The pain pulled at me, refusing to relent until I had no choice but to push it back.

And then Meg did not cry. She yawned. She inhaled a great taste of the world, and, finding it satisfactory, settled down to sleep. Mere seconds old, she was as pretty and content then as she was today.

August 29, 1862

The news is as dark as these summer days are bright.

General Stonewall Jackson has burned the federal supply depot at Manassas Junction. Somewhere between $300,000 and half a million dollars' worth of stores are now in Confederate hands. Every building in the vicinity has been torched, as well as the railway bridge over Bull Run. All lines of communication between the army and the capital are severed, and the rebels are but thirty-five miles from Washington.

The loss of those supplies touches me in a way the abstract numbers of human casualties has not. It is a portion of my effort that has gone up in flames. Bandages, uniforms, socks, mittens, scarves, and blankets stockpiled against the coming winter, gone. I do not value things over people. I should not have to remind myself; one look around this house is enough to prove that. But never in sixteen months of war have I felt a sting like this. Waste offends me nearly as much as injustice, and what is war but waste personified?

There is already so little I can do. That is forever the way of it for women. I had to beg for the kind of schooling my mind was capable of, and then once attained I discovered there was no outlet for my learning. For ten straight years I was either carrying a child or nursing one, or both. I can count the number of abolitionist meetings I was able to attend during those years on one hand. On those scarce occasions I did manage to attend, men held the floor. Always. You would think women had no throats, no tongues, no lips with which to form words, much less brains capable of forming thoughts. Now, in this conflict over the nation's soul, all that is permitted me is to knit and sew.

Tomorrow this fulminating shall likely sound as foolish to me as Amy's mourning over her pickled limes. Tonight, though, I can feel only what I feel. No more, and certainly no less.

September 2, 1862

How arrogant of me to imagine that I had begun to propagate some kind of immunity to the death tolls. Losses at Manassas are mounting into the tens of thousands. Tens of thousands, in three days' time. I cannot comprehend that many men's lives, much less their deaths. It is like trying to grasp the breadth of the sky. Not until this war is over shall we see the holes it has scooped out of us; the face of the nation will be pocked with scars.

It is rumored that General Pope's correspondence has been captured. If it is true, the rebels are now in possession of all his plans, reports, and orders for this campaign. Even his letters from his wife were ripped apart and strewn over the ground. That is an act of pure savagery. Every soldier knows the solace that only the letters of his beloved can bring. As for myself, I would rather go without food for a week than miss a letter from Amos.

September 5, 1862

What a predicament I have created for Birte Hummel. And how blazingly stupid of me not to have thought of it before now. Mrs. Hummel's willingness to take a position outside of her home was predicated on the fact that Karl and Lottchen could look after their younger brother and sisters while she was away. That was June. Now the autumn school term is upon us, and it appears that the Hummel children may be fed, or educated, but not both. Ada and Monika are old enough to attend lessons, but that still leaves Minna, Heinrich, and Greta in need of minding all day long. Karl or Lottchen will have to stay at home. Of course it is Lottchen who will be deprived. It is always the girl who bears the brunt of these duties. A boy's schooling trumps, for an educated boy can always earn more for his family than a sister who is every bit as smart, if not smarter. Eight years old, and she must take her mother's place in this house instead of learning to read and write words of more than a single syllable.

What Lottchen herself thinks of this I cannot divine. She is as insular as Beth and as fervid as Jo, a combination that befuddles me. I only have the feeling that her temperament sits perpetually on the narrow border between a simmer and a boil. One degree too many, and small as she is, she froths up and scorches the whole room.

September 7, 1862

A solution woke me out of a sound sleep. Were it any more obvious, it might have snatched the hair from my head. If Beth can learn at home, so can Lottchen. We have the girls' old primers and readers on our shelves. Only a little scrimping on my part would buy her a slate and pencil. I will tell Hannah to buy five fewer pounds of potatoes this week and do without my share. That will free up enough pennies to see that Lottchen has what she needs to learn.

September 8, 1862

Oh, that child's face when I presented her with her own slate and a stack of worn readers! She held them to her chest the way Ada cradles Monika. "Whatever lessons you can work while the little ones are napping, I will check for you when I return in the afternoon. Point out what you do not understand, and I will explain it to you. All right?"

What a fierce nod she gave. I do not sense the same hunger for knowledge in her that has stirred ceaselessly within me since I was a child of four. Rather, it seems to me that Lottchen is most gratified to be singled out from her siblings for something besides responsibility. All her short life she has been expected to give without receiving anything in return. Such an arrangement within a family may cultivate an admirable sense of selflessness, but left unchecked it all too often proliferates into worthlessness instead. Every day in the relief rooms I encounter women who have never learned the difference between giving, and being taken from. If Lottchen learns nothing else, the lesson that she, too, is worth investing in will be of great service to her.

September 11, 1862

Lottchen proves to be a dedicated student, if not a particularly patient one. Arithmetic troubles her not at all, for numbers are the same in any language. Reading is another matter. Already exasperation pervades her time with the inane little sentences of the primer: *A cat and a rat. A rat and a cat. A fat hen.* Lines that make a five-year-old child delight at their newfound proficiency leave an eight-year-old indignant at such meager rewards.

If only I could free enough time to teach her myself. Until she reads fluently, she can learn nothing of history, the sciences, or any of a thousand other subjects that might touch a spark to her mind.

September 18, 1862

What is there to write? I cannot imagine there could possibly come a time when I wish to recall the appalling sameness of these days.

Everlasting fighting. How many wounds can a single nation bleed from at once? Harpers Ferry, South Mountain, Mundfordville, Antietam, all in a single week.

Everlasting loneliness. The empty pillow beside me night after night. I am half tempted to invite Hannah to sleep alongside me, solely for the comfort of having the breaths of a fellow-creature lull me to sleep.

And the everlasting pull of the purse strings, cinching tighter than a debutante's corset. Worse than a corset. So many bills and figures run through my mind at all hours of the day and night, it seems they spill out and encircle my neck like a noose.

September 19, 1862

A bouquet of asters awaited me on the parlor table when I returned from the relief rooms today. A gift from Laurie, the girls informed me. My clever crow. How he learned that they are my favorite, I do not know.

September 23, 1862

Mr. Lincoln has issued a threat to the states in rebellion: lay down your arms within the next hundred days, or your slaves shall be emancipated on January the first.

I am torn between jubilation and exasperation. The prospect of millions being made "thenceforth and forever free" in a few months' time is enough to make my heart flutter and my eyes prickle with tears. A decade of work, on the brink of fulfillment! But what of the enslaved people of Delaware, Maryland, Kentucky, and Missouri? This proclamation is of no use to them. Once again our commander in chief is capitulating to the border states at the expense of tens of thousands of human beings. He himself said that this government cannot endure half slave and half free. Are we now to suppose that he believes it can endure one-quarter slave and three-quarters free?

I do not envy the president his task of trying to keep this nation balanced on a ridgepole while it is cracking down the center. Still, it is made abundantly clear yet again that Mr. Lincoln will never run if he can crawl instead.

September 26, 1862

Amos's last letter contained $39. Thirty-nine dollars, and winter around the corner. Has he forgotten that we must have fuel for the stove and the fireplace? At this rate I must choose between cold and hunger.

I can only imagine where his pay is going. If the men in his company required woolens, Amos would likely buy them a flock of sheep. Hannah never tires of echoing my lament, "Send him for a pail of milk and he will come home with a cow!" There are times when I half believe the only hunger he feels is for knowledge. So long as his brain is satiated, his stomach is never heard to grumble.

My mind returns over and over to the time he returned from a winter-long lecture tour of western New York with a dollar in profit. One single dollar. "Promises were not kept," he explained sheepishly, "and traveling is costly, but another year I shall do better." How I lavished him with praise for his noble efforts! No price could be put on the knowledge he had disseminated, I loftily proclaimed. It is a lesson he learned too well. I dread to think of how he may be applying that same financial logic on the battlefield. At the time, I meant every word of it. To this day I still believe that each and every mind Amos swayed to the cause of abolition is an asset to freedom beyond measure. But money meant so little to us then. Had I foreseen the circumstances that would shortly befall us, however, I would have tempered my praise.

We thanked God that night and for many weeks thereafter that we could afford to take no worldly profit from Amos's good work. Our prayers were both sincere and arrogant, for I do not believe either of us managed to imagine the extent to which our words would be tested in the years to come.

October 1, 1862

The maples are turning scarlet. If I had to choose but a single fragment of nature to enjoy for the rest of my life, it would be a bouquet of flaming red maple leaves. Even my beloved blue asters pale in comparison to the glory of a vase brimming with autumn foliage.

My birthday fast approaches. I shall be forty-one this year. If I were to live as long as my mother, this would be the last year of my life.

Already I have fared better than she. I have my health, something my own marmee had begun to surrender by the time she was thirty. I have so few memories of her that are not framed in my mind with bedposts and pillows. The clink of medicine bottles on her nightstand remain more vivid to me than her voice. Always Father was bringing home some new tonic for her to try. He never lost hope, and she never took it away from him, no matter how useless each concoction proved to be. Her joints persisted in warping and swelling despite the draughts and liniments. Perched on the edge of her bed with a bit of embroidery, I marveled time and again at how she had learned to let the pain wash over her without possessing her. Ever since, I have endeavored to do the same with my anger. It was not until the last, when she became insensible, that the agony won out.

How eerie to think that Meg is now a year older than I was when Marmee died. I felt so much older than Meg when I was sixteen. Infirmity is a slow, quiet tyrant, not content until it has devoured not only the body of its intended victim, but also nibbled away a portion of the heart and spirit of every member of the household. Marmee taught me that death is not to be feared—for her, it was the key turning in a lock that had bound her to a decade of ever-increasing pain. A valuable lesson, to be sure, though one I would have been grateful not to learn so young.

October 3, 1862

Hunger is sweeping the town at a more fearful rate than is to be expected so early in the season. It is as if every pantry has been scraped bare all at once. The relief rooms were jammed with cases today, many of them seeking assistance for the first time in their lives. I could scarcely make my way to the table I had been assigned to manage without being bumped or entreated for instructions. Halfway across the room a small boy scampered so close, my elbow knocked the cap from his head. He was moving too fast to notice, so I ducked down to scoop it from the floor before some lady's skirt could sweep it away forever.

That's when I heard it: "It's a wonder Margaret March isn't among them, what with that husband of hers."

I am thankful the little brown cap in my hand did not blacken to ash at the sound of those words. Whose voice it was, I do not know. The bustle and confusion of the room obscured its source. In that, God showed the speaker mercy.

Down to the Mill Brook I strode the moment I could excuse myself without suspicion, my feet seeking out every bit of stone and gravel big enough to kick. With each impact I wondered which of these women, all of whom I consider compatriots in the cause of aiding the Union and the poor, would malign my Amos. No name stood out as more likely than any of the others, which made it all the worse.

No doubt whoever made that remark would hasten to assure me it was intended to reflect well upon me, rather than poorly upon him. I am not so easily fooled. It is a simple enough thing to compliment one person without disparaging another.

At the shore I stood panting, wishing I might jump in and douse myself. Instead I took up one stone after another and hurled them into the water—the heavier the better. The crash and splash, the ripples as each one shattered the placid surface, gradually soothed me, though not before my skirt was splattered halfway to the knees with cold water.

Splash by splash, my thoughts became rational once more. I cannot expect the women of the relief rooms to understand my husband. Even Amos's dearest friends struggle at times to comprehend the workings of his mind. No man this side of heaven holds to his principles more firmly than he. No man is less selfish in adhering to those principles than he. And no man is more compassionate toward those who do not aspire to the same impossible ideals than he. That is the man I fell in love with. If others cannot apprehend his worth, it is <u>they</u> who are the poorer for it, not I.

Hours later, my thoughts have not fully cooled. At the back of my throat is a burn so slight, it feels like an itch begging to be scratched. Never have I murmured a word of discontent in the relief rooms about our Family's situation, and yet someone had the audacity to—

Oh, I do not want to feed one more stick of kindling onto these dwindling coals. All it amounts to is this: Amos is <u>mine</u> to complain of, and no one else's.

October 6, 1862

Reports of a great slaughter in Corinth, Mississippi. The only thing the papers are sure of is victory.

October 8, 1862

An afternoon picnic beneath the maples. I cannot think of a more pleasant way to inaugurate my forty-second year. Hannah baked an apple pie this morning and somehow managed to drive its scent from the house by the time I returned from the relief rooms. Its emergence from the hamper took me completely by surprise. Mr. Laurence and

Laurie joined us. I should like to have asked the Hummels, too, but we cannot afford to more than double our party.

The girls and Hannah had conspired to hold back Amos's latest letter as an extra treat. His gift to me is a quote from the book of Isaiah: *And if thou draw out thy soul to the hungry, and satisfy the afflicted soul; then shall thy light rise in obscurity, and thy darkness be as the noon day.*

Two words followed: *None brighter.*

October 9, 1862

This morning, in the crook where the gate meets the post, sat a tissue-wrapped package hardly bigger than a calling card. I nearly passed it by, for Laurie and the girls are forever swapping trinkets and notes in their mailbox. And then a speck of crimson and silver snatched at my eye—the smallest red maple leaf I have ever seen, pinned carefully to the tissue.

For me. From Laurie, I knew, though there was no tag to tell me so. My crow does not sign his name, but I recognize his call nonetheless. But why had he not presented it yesterday, among my other birthday gifts?

Carefully I turned back the paper to preserve the miniature leaf, and there in my palm lay a handkerchief. The linen was so fine, it was almost translucent. Raised Swiss white-work lace of the likes I have never seen, all patterned in flowers and vines with leaves and petals as beautiful to the fingertips as to the eyes. And in the center, three letters embroidered in white satin.

The initials are not mine. I looked and wondered and puzzled. And then my mouth fell open. I made a sound like a bird. His mother's initials. They can only be Laurie's mother's initials. Thank heaven I was alone, for my throat shrank to the size of a needle and the tears sped down my cheeks as though they had been waiting all day to fall.

His mother's handkerchief.

"Dear, dear boy," I said aloud. Laurie must hear me shouting out to Meg and Jo every morning, "Girls, girls! Have you both got nice pocket-handkerchiefs?" like some kind of addlepated ninny. What could I do but laugh and cry, embarrassed and touched to the core by the simple sweetness of the gesture. He has called me mother in all but name.

Could he see me, I wondered? Was he watching? He had to be, to have placed the package on the gate when he did, so that only I would find it. I spun to face his window, to find the maple tree itself shadowing my view. Without knowing if Laurie could see, I dabbed each cheek and then pressed the handkerchief to my heart, holding it there a moment. I should like to keep it there, always.

October 10, 1862

Two thousand Federals reported killed or wounded at Perryville, Kentucky. The fight began while we sat beneath the trees, eating apple pie. No word yet as to which side is victorious.

October 12, 1862

Jo is troublesome as a mosquito this last week, buzzing and whining and darting about until we'd all like to slap her away. She seems simultaneously thrilled and dismayed, exultant and vexed, and I can make neither heads nor tails of it.

October 15, 1862

My hand is almost too sore to hold the pen. An entire day of scraping linen into lint soft enough for wound dressings left my mind feeling as cramped as my fingers. Lint-scraping never fails to do so.

Fortunately, I returned home to find a fine article by Frederick

Douglass on the president's forthcoming emancipation proclamation in *Douglass' Monthly*. He scoffs at the notion that loyal Union officers will tear up their commissions and throw down their arms if forced to fight for Negro freedom. Better that the army be purged of "pro-slavery vermin," he says. Now the European countries that the rebels have been courting in hopes of securing intervention will have no cause to prevaricate over the troubling reality that the federal government has given no more consideration to the abolition of slavery than the Confederates.

Mr. Douglass also prevails upon all who oppose slavery to make their convictions felt, be it through writing, speaking, charitable contributions, or simply through example. Only this last is available to me. I have a pen and a voice, but no platform from which my thoughts can emanate. I never have, and I begin to wonder if I ever shall. The last twenty years have wrought many changes for the better in this nation, but a willingness to give equal weight to a woman's ideas is not among them. When the abolitionists were at their most fiery, where was I but at home with a baby at my breast or a belly too large to be seen in public? Now that I have the time to be of use, I have not the means. My contributions to the cause have been all but invisible, and barring some cataclysmic change, will almost certainly continue to be so.

October 18, 1862

Jo is published.

The newspaper lies spread out neatly on the desk beside me. I cannot write more than one line without my eyes drifting over to look at it. There is her name, *Miss Josephine March*. Our Jo, an author.

Tomorrow I shall buy two more copies of the *Spread Eagle*—one for myself, to lay away in my cedar chest, and another so that I may clip out Jo's story and send it to Amos.

It is a trifling, frivolous tale, as nearly everything printed in the

Spread Eagle is, and brimming with the sort of happenings and coincidences that can only exist in the imagination. Her characters, though, they feel as real as anyone you might pass on the streets of Boston, even if they do soliloquize like Shakespeareans. But my word, if she can capture this success at fifteen, imagine what awaits her when her abilities bloom fully! I thank God that she already has mettle enough to hold tight to that talent. When she has something to say that matters, she will know where and how to do it.

October 25, 1862

What would I give to be touched again? To be held?

My daughters are always willing to fill my arms. Amy is yet young enough to perch in my lap and let herself be petted like a little peacock. But it is not the same. No matter how grown-up my girls are becoming, they are still reaching up to me. Not only for comfort, but for protection. They comfort me and bolster me; I would be lost without them. But always I must be their shield.

Amos and I are their foundation, and with him away, my daughters rely doubly on me to keep their footing stable. I cannot confess to them my worries and fears. Hannah helps me bear some of the weight, but she, too, depends upon me for her shelter and livelihood and cannot truly shoulder half the burden, no matter how sincerely she wishes to.

Together Amos and I are the ship's wheel and rudder for our Family. Without him, it does not matter how deftly I steer—the craft cannot keep a steady course. Without him, there is nothing between me and the rocks and shoals that loom nearer with every day this war drags on.

That is all I want. The gentle weight of a sheltering embrace. I can lay my hands where only Amos's so often rest: my hips and thighs, even the warm and satiny recesses between them. It is not the same. For it is not the physical sensations of coupling that I miss. Those pleasures I can reproduce well enough for myself, should I so choose. There is no satisfaction in it—not of the kind I crave. The body alone can be gratified. The heart knows better.

The intimacy I yearn for is of the heart and mind.

There is God's embrace, of course. *The eternal God is thy refuge, and underneath are the everlasting arms,* says the thirty-third chapter of Deuteronomy. Without those arms to retreat into, I should be lost entirely. It shames me to confess even here, where no one else may see, that they are not always sufficient.

I speak aloud to the empty room: "Increase my faith."

What more can I do but ask?

November 5, 1862

I have at last fitted up a German word of my own. It is made of more than one piece, as all the best German words are.

First, Herz. That is the word for heart. Then, Mutti. Birte's children do not call her Mutter, the proper word for mother, but Mutti. You might say it is their family's way of saying Marmee.

And so, Herz-Mutti.

That is who I should like to be to Laurie.

And so it follows that he may be a Herz-Junge to me. Heart-boy.

November 14, 1862

I cannot begin to sleep. Tonight, we are all six of us upon this earth. What the next days and nights will bring, I dread to imagine.

The telegram sits on the desk before me. The yellow paper is already smudged with the print of my thumb.

When Hannah handed me the envelope, for that instant, I was a widow. And then, before there was time to breathe, Amos was alive again. Alive, but ill. *Very ill. Come at once.* My heart plunged and soared and plummeted all over again. A telegram can mean only that the doctors have no hope. "It may be too late," I blurted aloud without meaning to. "Oh, children, children," I cried, "help me to bear it!"

They are such a balm to me, my girls.

What happened next was akin to an explosion of assistance. I had hardly begun to founder in the depths of that awful thought before Hannah reached in and fished me out again, declaring that she wouldn't waste time on tears. Her warm hand and determined face returned me to myself.

A telegram to the hospital, a note to Aunt March asking for train fare, a message to Mrs. King at the relief rooms, my black trunk from the attic—I hardly remember who I sent where. The telegram gave no indication of the nature of Amos's illness, leaving me no choice but to prepare for every possibility I could think of: camp fever, dysentery, malaria, typhus, pneumonia, grippe, cholera. Anodynes, blue mass, paregoric, and quinine all had to be procured before the shops closed.

Aunt March, of course, could not resist a scolding. The envelope she sent contained twice the amount I had requested, folded into a note I ought not have bothered to read before I flung it into the fire. She might just as easily have stuck out her tongue and chanted, "I told you so!" That woman gives nothing without lifting her nose higher into the air, so that she may look down upon the recipient. How much richer all of us would be if she would make herself a comfort rather than a scourge.

I ought to be thinking of other things—of Amos—not brooding on one old woman's faults, but my brain spins round her like a hurricane. Anger is so much more tolerable than fear, though neither fury nor fright does any measurable good in this situation. It infuriates me that one small act of spite can outweigh the absolute flood of goodwill that engulfed me today.

Laurie's tutor, of all people, is to escort me to Washington! I have never done a thing to warrant such kindness from a near perfect stranger. No doubt he comes at the behest of Laurie and Mr. Laurence, yet the concern in Mr. Brooke's face when he presented himself was so genuine, I could see that to refuse would be a kind of disappointment to him, he so wanted to help. Mr. Laurence, bless him, had already volunteered to be my escort. He is not in the least like my father, but his offer reminded me of how it feels to have that same sheltering presence that I had thought only a father could give. That in itself was contribution enough, though he would not be satisfied until he had done <u>something</u>. The two bottles of wine he brought to relieve Amos's suffering is more fit for a banquet table than an invalid.

And my Jo. When she tossed that roll of bills down on the table my mind went in seven directions at once. Twenty-five dollars! I hardly had time to wonder before off came her bonnet and there she stood, shorn. All her beautiful, beautiful hair, sold! In that instant, I saw her as the boy she has always wished to be. So straight and proud and defiant. And beneath all that, the tender girl she keeps hidden from all of us but Beth, with the quiver of her chin begging me not to cry. I set my jaw and did not cry, though I thought the pride I felt would split my skin. I should like to take the chestnut ringlet she saved for me on the train to lend me strength, but it shall be safer here, laid reverently alongside the lock of Father's hair in my desk drawer.

Thank God—again and again—for Hannah. Meg and Jo are old enough to look after the household if I were to go on an everyday visit, but I fear the anxiety will leave them too distracted to cope alone. With Hannah here for the girls and Mr. Laurence ready to leap to her aid should any difficulties arise, I have no apprehensions about leaving the children behind.

Nevertheless I almost wish some trifling detail remained for me to fret over. Now that everything is so perfectly arranged, what can I do but brood over Amos? There may be nothing I can do for him but ease his passage from this world to the next. If the doctors and nurses knew me, they might have hesitated to summon Margaret March for such a task. I am far better suited for action than to waiting and watching. Amos himself would counsel that no one can do better than to give freely of whatever is theirs to share. I, too, would have said the same, before I understood how much easier it is to say than to do.

In the pragmatic sense, at least, I am well provisioned. With $50 from Aunt March and $25 from Jo, I can surely see to it that Amos receives all the comforts he deserves. I have kept this entire Family afloat for a month with less. But my God, how is it that I have come to the place where I must beg, and my children chop off pieces of themselves?

The children are my one true comfort now. All day long, Meg never left my side, just as Amy was Hannah's shadow, seeing that everything that must be done was done. How Beth sang tonight, when the rest of us could not manage the words of Amos's favorite hymn:

The earth, the ocean, and the sky
To form one world agree;
Where all that walk, or swim or fly,
Compose one family.

Lord, may our union form a part
Of that thrice happy whole;
Derive its pulse from thee, the heart,
Its life from thee, the soul.

There is an atom of pure strength buried within Beth that none of us is sturdy enough to contain.

And Jo's sacrifice. It could only have been greater if she had sold her heart or her brain. She is both son and daughter to me, with her gallantry and her grace in equal measure. She would deny the latter, but Jo's is not the sort of grace that shows itself in a ballroom.

No matter what may come to pass in Washington, I have the assurance of knowing my girls will be here waiting for me when I return.

November 15, 1862

My hope feels so thin, and my hands so idle. Only my mind keeps busy, and it produces nothing of use. From Boston to New London and all the way across the sound on the ferry I managed to keep my-self in hand. Outwardly, at any rate. But by the time we boarded the train at Jersey City I could no longer bear the clatter of my thoughts.

"Teach me something, Mr. Brooke," I demanded.

"Ma'am?" he asked, rather startled at my outburst.

"I cannot sit idle. Please, teach me something. There is too much space in my mind for worry. Give me something to fill it with."

One thing after another he suggested: Latin, French, geometry, chemistry, astronomy, botany, history, philosophy, and theology. In every topic, I had been ably instructed by Miss Allyn and Miss Rob-bins. Even the German I have learned from Birte Hummel earned his praise.

"Perhaps, if you were to teach _me_?" he asked timidly.

"What might I teach you? It seems we are well matched in educa-tion."

He glanced at the scarf tassels my nervous fingers had woven themselves through. "Could you teach me a bit of knitting?" he asked, with a quirk in his lips. Not teasing at all, but earnest. "We are not so well matched as you say. My education was wholly lacking in the domestic arts, and I should like to be able to make scarves and socks for myself. A man without mother or sisters is apt to find himself poorly supplied, you see, and store-bought woolens can't hold a candle to homemade."

A little pang of sympathy worked its way between the claws that gripped my heart. "Of course. But I haven't my work basket."

Hardly a moment's consternation passed before he unlaced one of his boots and pulled two pencils from his breast pocket. "Will these do as yarn and needles? For practice?"

Such ingenuity coaxed a smile to my lips. The bootlace was only long enough to produce a few narrow rows at a time, but that was enough to show him how the stitches are formed. The mechanics and mathematics he grasped immediately, though his fingers proved slower than his mind. A child learns to knit on pure faith, nimbly copying the movements and trusting that the unfathomable loops and tangles will amount to something. That, it turns out, is something of a mercy. Once I had demonstrated the fundamentals, Mr. Brooke's mind could chart the construction of anything from cuffs to cables, yet he struggled with his large hands to form the basic stitches. I watched the way he bore his frustration, channeling it into determination, and found it thoroughly admirable.

After an hour his fingers began to obey more readily, and the rhythm of the stitches and the rhythm of the train interwove in such a way as to soothe my thoughts, ordering them into neat columns and rows.

From Jersey City to Philadelphia, he knitted his bootlace over and over, working with such diligence that I taught him not only to knit and purl, but a simple increase and decrease as well. "You are an able student, Mr. Brooke!" I exclaimed. "With two real needles and a ball of good worsted, you will have yourself a scarf in a week's time."

By the time he ceased his labors his hands had grown fatigued. He squeezed his fists and stretched his fingers open and shut several times, just as my mother used to do when her joints pained her. Perhaps he had kept on with such rigor to keep my thoughts focused on his efforts instead of what awaits us in Washington.

With the knitting set aside there was nothing to do but sit with our heads tipped back against the seats, eyes roving the ceiling. For a while my mind settled into a blank spot within itself where I could feel a curious absence of fear. The sensation proved more unnerving than comforting, as if I had come unattached from myself. How long could it last? How long could I float in this way before my worries found cracks wide enough to seep through? The question to Mr. Brooke rose out of nothing but a desire to prevent something unpleasant from dropping into that void uninvited.

"May I ask, why you are not fighting?"

The question ruffled him. I heard him bite at the air as his breath quickened. He perceived an accusation where there was none. No doubt he has been asked before.

I touched a hand to his sleeve. "I ask this without judgment, Mr. Brooke. My husband is serving, but he, too, has chosen not to fight."

"It is a question I wrestle with, Mrs. March," he said, looking at the back of the seats in front of us rather than at me. I did the same and in a moment he continued, slowly. "Whatever it is that spurs men and boys to take up arms, I do not seem to possess it. Is it my duty to do so nonetheless? Or is there another duty I can better perform?"

"War is in many ways a sausage grinder," I replied after letting his words settle. "Sometimes it seems to me that despite all the strategy, the side that will win is the side with the greater stock of meat. I confess that the thought of educated minds such as yours going into that grinder sickens me. But that is not to say that an uneducated man should be regarded as cannon fodder," I amended quickly.

He nodded. "Other men with much more to lose have enlisted willingly, and I, who have so little, cannot bring myself to take up arms," he said. "Not out of cowardice, you understand. There is something in me that rebels against this slaughter." Frustration limned his features, pulling down his brow so that I perceived his dissatisfaction lay within himself rather than with the fighting.

"There is no better answer than an honest one, Mr. Brooke," I told him. He said nothing in return. The train whistle sounded its mournful note, returning both of us to contemplation of the upholstery. "My husband, if he were able, would willingly and wisely counsel you," I said after a few miles had passed in continued silence. "But if I may, I believe I know what he would advise."

"Please."

"Your loyalty is first to your own conscience, for that is the voice of God within you. If you can stand before a mirror and meet your own eye squarely, then you are doing right. That is something only you can know."

His expression eased so considerably at that, his face almost seemed to belong to another man. He has betrayed no trace of this gnawing discontentment in the time I have known him. Perhaps I simply do not know him well enough. Or perhaps he has carried this so long, it has become embedded in his countenance.

He is asleep now, and I have borrowed one of his mock knitting needles to write. Was it mere coincidence that he dropped off to sleep not long after we spoke of war and conscience? He has already pacified my anxiety enough that I should be pleased to have done the same for him.

I envy him his slumber. The train rocks like a cradle and yet my brain will not be lulled into relinquishing consciousness. Only writing soothes me now; forming the words with my hand as well as my mind keeps less welcome thoughts from intruding. But Mr. Brooke's pencil grows dull, and even if I cannot sleep I must at least rest—in body if not in mind—and save my physical strength for whatever ordeal awaits me.

November 16, 1862

1:15 p.m.—103.5 degrees
4:30 p.m.—103.7 degrees
8:00 p.m.—104.2 degrees
10:25 p.m.—103.9 degrees

November 17, 1862

Midnight—104 degrees
3:50 a.m.—104.9 degrees
8:37 a.m.—104.8 degrees
Noon—105.2 degrees
4:15 p.m.—105 degrees
7:50 p.m.—105.3 degrees

November 18, 1862

Midnight—103.5 degrees
2:30 a.m.—103.6 degrees
6:45 a.m.—102.9 degrees
Noon—101.7 degrees

Amos lives. In the last six hours his temperature has dropped enough that I may take my eyes from him for more than a moment at a time. I cannot be sure yet that his life will be spared, but I feel myself at last tilting more toward hope than despair. Each time I touch his forehead I cannot help marveling at its coolness despite the fact that the fever has not fully abated.

The cot next to Amos's holds a different soldier today. A man died or was released and I never saw it happen. It is astonishing what the mind can become used to in so short a time. When I arrived two days ago, this place overwhelmed my senses entirely.

The smell of effluvia thickened the air half a block away. Even the lofty sound of Latin cannot disguise that scent.

The suspense of being led through the ward, past bed after bed of broken and battered men, nearly felled me. Every man with long, light-colored hair was, for an instant, my husband. Men with arms or legs absent. Men bandaged and splinted. Worst of all, the cots with sheets pulled up over the occupant, leaving me to guess whether the lifeless silhouette beneath belonged to Amos.

At last we stopped at a corner cot at the far end of the ward. At first I did not know him; never in my life have I seen Amos unshaven. That peculiar pucker in his chin was obscured by a scraggy beard flecked with lice. As one feature after another began slowly to co-alesce into a familiar whole, my mind went black. Mr. Brooke's steady arm brought me back to myself. Amos's skin looked like clay. His breath came shallow and fast, each inhale a quick stab to the chest.

Pneumonia.

At the sight of me, a fear I have never seen before blazed up in his eyes. An army chaplain knows far too well what it means when a man's wife is summoned to his bedside. "Peg," he panted. "Peg." He clutched at my sleeve like a man plummeting backward. "Don't." He could hardly catch enough breath for more than a syllable. "Don't . . . let go."

I clapped my hand over his as he rattled and coughed. "I won't, Amos."

This was not what I had expected. I had steeled myself to do just that—to let him go, to see him peacefully off. This was not my tranquil Amos, whose calm penetrated and steadied my impetuous heart the first time I heard his voice. "Not . . . yet." He had the look of a cornered animal, the desire to live so fierce it could have been mistaken for rage.

"No," I promised him. "Not before you are ready." With those words said, he seemed to truly see <u>me</u> and not what my presence portended. The fear relaxed. I cannot describe it any other way. It did not shrink, but its clutch upon him eased.

With that, my own fear began to retreat, and my consciousness opened like an aperture to take in Amos's surroundings. The entire hospital has the feel of a strained pocketbook. The sheets on Amos's cot were lately laundered, yet they are permanently stained with hues that bring to mind all manner of unpleasant happenings. His blanket is good wool, if threadbare. He is fortunate to have a corner bed, for the cot beside him is so near that I could feel the air stir each time his neighbor coughed. The nurses are on the verge of exhaustion, moving from bed to bed with a methodical determination. The food is plainer and thinner than what we have at home. Nothing but dysentery can account for the number of buckets I saw being carried out.

From all this I concluded that a shortage of nurses and supplies threatened his life nearly as much as the disease itself. Amos needed warmth and nourishment. And steam.

"Mr. Brooke, I will need a basin, a towel, and a kettle." I fished in my pocket with one hand and gave him Jo's roll of bills. "Find a shop and buy them if you have to. And pillows. No less than three of them. And will you uncork a bottle of Mr. Laurence's wine, please?"

Mr. Brooke did as he was bid, and so quickly that I did not believe he'd had time to accomplish it. All I had managed to do in his absence was coax a bit of wine down Amos's throat and use my handkerchief to mop his forehead with the tepid water from the pitcher on the table beside his cot.

When I moved to release Amos's hand from mine, the panic flared up again so brightly that his eyes seemed not to see at all. "Amos," I said, putting my face directly in front of his. "Amos, listen to me. I must have two hands to care for you. I cannot bring you back with just one." He blinked, shivering with a chill, then let go.

With Mr. Brooke's help, I lifted Amos forward and arranged the pillows into a gentle slope behind him. The ease this position brought him was evident immediately. The cadence of his breath did not change, but his face softened with relief. "I," he said between breaths. "I have . . . been running . . . for days. Days . . . and nights." He panted a moment more. "And now . . . the race . . . has ended." My heart leapt up in fear before I understood his meaning. Even in direst sickness, my husband speaks in metaphors. All this time lying flat on his back, he has been fighting to draw air past the fluid in his lungs. Now he can simply breathe. Not more than a mouthful at once, but without straining.

I, too, felt as though I could breathe once again. Learning to do without him has been as easy as learning to live without breath. I do not know what has filled my lungs up to this time. "Save your breath for your body," I told him. "It is hungry for air." I placed the basin of steaming water on his lap and tented the towel over his head. With one hand I steadied the basin while the other stroked his back— slowly, that he might ease the frantic pace of his breaths. "Slowly, Amos. Use each breath, however shallow."

Mr. Laurence's good wine made him woozy, but he fought against succumbing to its effects. "You must rest," I told him. "Your body demands it." He shook his head frantically, gripping at me once again, and I realized that he was afraid to sleep, afraid to drown in the sea rising within his own lungs. I promised him I would not leave his side until he woke, and he acquiesced. Hardly two minutes passed before he was asleep, and he remained so until his fever breached 105 degrees the next day. That day was a horror I do not care to recount. It is enough to thank God for bringing Amos through it. There is no other way to account for how he found the strength to continue breathing.

Now, after two days of constant steam, wine, and elevation, he can truly rest. There is nothing he needs more than that. Fighting for each inhale has exhausted him. That and the constant terror of losing the battle. His breaths are not deep—he can no more than sip at the air—but the relative ease of them is nothing short of a luxury of the purest kind.

Sitting here as he sleeps is the hardest thing I have done. Men are suffering all around, their nurses run so ragged they are a hair's breadth from falling ill themselves. But I have promised Amos. I write as I sit, so that some part of me can feel a sense of movement and purpose.

3:45 p.m.—100.8 degrees
8:15 p.m.—100.9 degrees

November 19, 1862

Midnight—100.5 degrees
8:45 a.m.—100.4 degrees
Noon—100.4 degrees

Praise be to God, Amos's fever has eased—his temperature has not risen above 101 degrees since yesterday noon—and his lungs no longer sound engulfed with fluid. He can speak a few words at a time, now, though I rarely permit him to do so. He smiles when I put <u>my</u> finger to my lips.

When the nurses come by I wave them on to the next cot. There are soldiers here without family, and we have no right to consume precious minutes of the staff's time when others need it more.

Besides, there is little else to do but rub Amos's hair and whiskers with kerosene, and comb out the dead lice and nits. It soothes us both beyond reasoning. Such a distasteful thing on the face of it, and yet the methodical movements, the bare intimacy, imparts a most unexpected solace. From time to time he awakens and looks at me in such a way that I feel utterly joined to him. He has always been my anchor. And now I am his.

I am thankful that there is no mortification in his eyes when he wakens to find me tending to him in this and other ways. To accept, without shame or apology, the necessary indignities of sickness is a rare grace. Were we not willing to perform these duties for one another, we should not have become husband and wife.

To be permitted to help without being asked is a gift to me. The need is acknowledged and addressed simultaneously without all the fuss and bother that the relief rooms require.

4:05 p.m.—100.2 degrees
8:20 p.m.—100.6 degrees

November 20, 1862

For four days and three nights I kept vigil at Amos's side. Yesterday, Mr. Brooke protested.

"Mrs. March, you must sleep, for Mr. March's sake if not your own. Please allow me to relieve you for a few hours, at least." He held up two bright new steel knitting needles and a ball of Union blue worsted. "I have work to do, you see."

He was right, and I had no hope of denying it. I felt as exhausted as the nurses looked.

I turned to Amos. "Is my trust in him enough?"

Amos nodded. "Of course."

Mr. Brooke listened most attentively as I gave my instructions: Record his temperature every four hours. Steam at the slightest rasp or rattle. Wine for restlessness, regardless of whether Amos suddenly finds breath enough to lecture against the effects of intoxication. Ask simple questions to conserve his breath. Never under any circumstances let his head fall level with his chest. When I had finished, Mr. Brooke handed me a slip of paper with an address just two blocks away. He had already procured me a bed at a boardinghouse—not only a bed to myself, but the entire room, I discovered upon arrival. Mr. Laurence's funds, no doubt. I cannot begin to repay such thoughtful generosity.

I did not truly comprehend how exhausted I was until I woke this afternoon. Nineteen hours, I had slept. My head and limbs lay exactly as they had been when I climbed into bed and pulled up the quilt. When I arrived at the hospital, Mr. Brooke looked as though I had left only minutes before. A good foot and a half of scarf dangled from his lap.

"I hope I haven't kept you from your business," I said.

He bade me good afternoon and offered the chair. "Not at all. Mr. March and I have had a very pleasant morning, discussing the Sixth Commandment, as it applies to war."

My first instinct was to chastise him for sapping even a drop of Amos's strength, but I had not said more than "Mr. Brooke," before Amos lifted one finger and pressed his lips together. I understood, and managed to curb myself.

"It does me good . . . to be of some . . . little use again," Amos said.

When I paused long enough to look, I saw that it was so. A hint of brightness had returned to his eyes. My lips unfolded themselves. His mind is so prone to exercise that to hold it still is an exertion. I hate to think how his thoughts, without something to orbit, must have been ricocheting through his fevered mind. Mr. Brooke has steadied him in a way I had not perceived was necessary.

I reached for levity. "You haven't been spending your breath preaching sermons, I hope?"

"Oh, no," Mr. Brooke assured me. "I have done most of the talking. Mr. March asks the most canny questions. Each one leads my mind farther forward, until it seems he has drawn me a map and handed me a lantern to illuminate my own conclusions."

Those words were the medicine I needed. That is my Amos. The hope that welled up in me then eclipsed my fears for the first time since I set foot in this hospital.

"This one has . . . a sharp mind," Amos said with a nod toward Mr. Brooke.

"You've been shaved," I replied, suddenly struck by the sight of his bare chin and its familiar pucker. Had his lungs their proper depth, my non sequitur would have snatched a laugh out of Amos. Instead he ended up only gasping. He gestured toward our companion.

"I did it last night. You don't mind, I hope," Mr. Brooke said. "I thought it would help relieve the itching."

"Of course not. It was most kind of you." Mr. Brooke must have a steady hand with a razor, for there was not even a nick in the uneven terrain of Amos's countenance. Ever thoughtful, Amos's impromptu barber made a little bow and excused himself, that my husband and I might be alone together now that he can speak.

Amos opened his hand so that I could slip mine into it. "You look thin," he said.

"Worry," I said, but he sensed the lie, as well as its cause, and held my gaze until I conceded, "It has been a leaner year than most."

He sighed. "There were men . . . boys, really . . . in my regiment . . . without shoes or blankets. I did my best . . . to provide . . . what the army could not. I knew . . . you wouldn't mind . . . so long as you had . . . enough."

"Of course not," I said, though my throat ached with a knot of sympathy and frustration. After all these years, Amos still hasn't any idea of how many dollars it takes to make "enough."

To Amos, money has always been for obtaining comforts. He trusts solely to God for necessities, and as he sees it, God never fails to provide. What Amos seems not to see is how often God has provided those necessities through the work and worry of his wife.

I have lived alongside him for twenty years, and still failed to understand: All these long, lean months, he has had absolute faith that the Lord would feed and shelter his Family. And it is true that over the years God has indeed obliged him in ways that would not be believed outside of a parable. I well remember how he gave away our last stick of firewood one bleak winter morning. Not only gave it away, but carted it to the needy family in our own wheelbarrow. Never would I begrudge a neighbor warmth, but it seemed to me overgenerous of Amos not to leave enough wood in the pile to keep his own children from shivering. Beth was just a babe in arms that winter. And did he go straight to town to order more fuel when I pointed toward the heaviness of the clouds at the western horizon? Of course not. Into his study he burrowed to commune with his books instead.

"Trust in Providence, my dear," he said. "Wood will come or the weather will moderate."

I managed not to wonder aloud whether he thought the wood would drop from the sky. Or why anyone should trouble Providence with a task he could accomplish just as well himself—and sooner, too.

My husband must have faith enough for two, for I have never yet been able to sweep my mind clear of doubts when he does such things. How I fretted and grumbled to myself all that long after-noon! Of course I could have gone to procure the wood myself, but Amos seemed to me long overdue for a lesson in abdicating his re-sponsibility to a higher power. So I resisted, all the while scolding myself for holding my daughters' warmth hostage to my husband's eccentricities.

And didn't a man stop at our very door even as the storm clouds began to spit hard little flecks of ice at our windowpanes, asking if we would buy his load of wood so that he might lighten his wagon enough to reach his home before the snow. That was the day I learned what it means to be purely and truly stupefied.

What money Amos has sent was therefore meant for enjoyment and indulgences. No wonder he thought I could make do on so little. My eyes welled, and I lifted his hand to my lips.

How can I begrudge his generosity, when God has been so generous to us?

The afternoon passed in a serenity so unexpected, it hardly seemed real. Letters arrived from the girls—each in its own envelope, so that Amos and I had the pleasure of opening one after another. We had no choice but to savor them, for the sound of my voice reading our daughters' words aloud never failed to lull Amos to sleep before I could reach the bottom of a page. There I sat, in a mirror image, it seemed, of all the times Meg, Jo, Beth, Amy, and I gathered before the hearth to read Amos's letters. The sight of all those pages with their familiar handwriting spread across Amos's blanket brought tears to my eyes, and I could not help but think that despite the miles between us, we were all of us held together in God's arms today.

November 21, 1862

Amos has relapsed. I dozed off in the night and when I woke, bright beads of perspiration glinted on his brow in the lamplight. I touched his sheets and found them clammy.

Now when he coughs, it comes up rusty-looking. The spasms wrack him so fiercely, I expect to see fragments of bone in his handkerchief. Not since Meg and Jo had scarlet fever have I felt a forehead so fiery. I do not like to contemplate what it is using for fuel.

Mr. Brooke sits with me when he can, though there is not much for him to do but knit.

November 24 or 25, 1862

I no longer know what day it is, only that Amos is neither better nor worse.

November 27, 1862

Yesterday Mr. Brooke persuaded me to leave the hospital for the night, to sleep in a bed. Amos's condition had steadied enough that I could contemplate leaving him in Mr. Brooke's care.

I arrived this morning to find Amos asleep and Mr. Brooke beside him, reading. The cadence of Amos's breath reassured me at once. Not deep by any means, but easier than I have seen it since the fever returned. Two deep pink splotches still flushed his cheeks, but his skin felt merely warm rather than scorching to my palm.

"Have you finished your scarf, Mr. Brooke?" I asked.

"I have."

"And where is it?"

He laid his book aside and led me to where a man lay covered by a sheet. Only his feet were visible, and the tasseled end of a scarf hanging out from the white hem. No more.

"He came in last night. Hopeless case, shot through the back. He couldn't feel a thing below his shoulders, but the cold was a torment to him. Mr. March gave his quilt, and that did no good. Finally I wrapped my scarf around his neck, and the feel of the wool soothed him so he could rest. He never woke."

The kindness of his gesture awoke a bit of feeling in me. Or, I should say, <u>out</u>side of me. With Amos so ill, it has been days since

I have been aware of others, much less had the reserves to register anything happening beyond the boundary of Amos's bed. Suddenly my body and my emotions felt familiar again. It is strange to realize that I am not fully myself without the ability to take stock of others. "It seems I am not the only one who finds this hospital more bearable thanks to your presence, Mr. Brooke," I said.

He contemplated his shoes for a moment, with the posture of a small boy gathering his courage. "Will you call me John?" he asked.

"I would be delighted to. And will you do me a favor, John?"

He simply beamed at the prospect. "If it is within my power."

"Will you call me Margaret?"

Never have I seen anyone so categorically nonplussed. He could not produce a syllable, much less an answer. The request had flustered him so, I could only be gentle in spite of my disappointment. "It is not within your power, then?"

He flushed and shook his head. "I've disappointed you." I did not acknowledge it; I did not have to. We sat, each regretful of the other's unhappiness, until an idea struck me. An absurdity, perhaps, yet one I was willing to risk. "Will you—will you try to imagine calling me Margaret? Until perhaps one day you can do it?"

He seemed unable to discern whether I was serious. "This means a great deal to you," he finally said.

"It does."

"Then I will try."

"Thank you, John. I will tell Amos of our arrangement when he awakens. I'm sure he will be agreeable as well."

What a journey this has been! These last two weeks have not borne the slightest resemblance to any of the worries that filled my mind on the train.

November 28, 1862

Today is the first day I have found no lice or nits in Amos's hair.

November 29, 1862

Amos's birthday. To think that I was able to spend it sitting beside him.

Passing by the window of a bookshop this morning, I could not resist purchasing a copy of Young's Literal Translation of the Bible for him. My husband certainly could not have passed that shop without stopping. An extravagance, to be sure, but it seemed the most appropriate—the most Amos-like—way to celebrate his existence. Besides, I reasoned, there was still some of Jo's money rolled up in my pocket. But when I unrolled the bills to pay the shopkeeper, I had to count them twice before I believed what lay before me. Twenty-five dollars. Mr. Brooke had not used a single one for Amos's needs, or my room at the boardinghouse. Mr. Laurence's generosity, it seems, is bottomless.

How I sailed along the streets to the hospital with that book, light-hearted for the first time in months. I could not think of one thing our Family lacks. More riches awaited at the hospital. On the table beside Amos's cot lay another stack of envelopes from home—birthday greetings from everyone but Beth. No doubt her letter has been held up by some quirk of the post.

All morning long I paged back and forth through Young's Literal Translation, reading out Amos's favorite passages. You can fairly hear his mind whir when he encounters something as fresh and new as this. Young's use of the present tense is remarkable. *God saith, "Let light be"; and light is,* he writes in the book of Genesis. The change to such well-worn words is jarring, and yet it also feels as if that simple alteration has scooped the ancient stories up and set them down alongside us.

When Mr. Brooke—John—arrived we invited him to sit with us, and all took turns choosing passages to read aloud. John remarked that he thought we ought to be reading from the Book of Amos, in honor of the day. Amos rarely quotes from the book of the Bible for which he is named. So rarely that I might truthfully say never. There is too much fire and brimstone to suit his docile nature. And yet I can think of no better personification of the message contained in the book of Amos than my husband. His love of justice and righteousness. His utter intolerance for those who indulge themselves at the expense of the poor.

But Amos, like Beth, would always rather turn attention away from himself. "I have never shed my childhood fascination with Noah and the ark," he said. "Imagine, all of God's creatures side by side on one vessel, weathering the storm in accord without preying upon one another. The literal image enthralled the child, just as its figurative counterpart inspires the man." He paused a moment to regain his breath before asking, "What passage first captured your imagination, John?"

John confessed that as a child he had always thrilled at the story of Samson. Amos nodded, and I turned to the sixteenth chapter of Judges. As we reached the shearing of Samson's hair, suddenly I remembered—neither of us had told Amos of Jo's sacrifice.

"The most gallant of young ladies"—that's what Amos called her. A perfect compliment for our boyish girl. I told them how laid I that lock of her beautiful hair away among the most precious of my mementos. "But now I have half a mind to press it between the pages of this Bible," I said. "Right in the middle of the story of Samson, where it will remind me of her strength." On impulse I turned to John. "What is your most cherished possession?" I asked.

What a knack I seem to have for asking questions that penetrate this man. The fluster that came over him then! He gave a weak cough that was not a cough and leaned forward, resting his elbows on his knees. Twice he tried to look up at us and failed. "I have never wanted so much to lie and to tell the truth at the same time," he finally said, flummoxing both of us.

Then he reached into his waistcoat pocket and drew out a small gray glove. Meg's. He held it in his two hands, stroking its palm before he dared meet our eyes.

"Why, John," I breathed.

Amos was puzzled. Of course he did not recognize it, or its significance.

"I . . . I love her," John confessed. "Meg," he added, when he saw Amos's confusion. "Or at least I believe I do. It isn't like in the poems, where men's minds go somersaulting through the heavens at the sight of the woman they love. When I look at Meg, everything steadies. In all my life I've never known where I belong in this world, but when I imagine myself beside her, I feel like . . ." He hesitated there, scoffing at himself. ". . . like nothing so much as a button being sewn into place."

What a dear, dear man he is. I blinked and blinked to keep the tears from coming. I could not choose a man of finer character for Meg in all of Concord. Adroit in his thoughts, clever in his hands, tender in his heart. I have grown so fond of him so very quickly. But would Meg choose <u>him</u> in return? I cannot say if her daydreams of romance have yet begun to be peopled with faces, much less John Brooke's in particular.

"She is very young yet, John," I said gently.

He nodded. "And I am too poor a man to ask any woman to be my wife. I would ask, though, that you allow me to—" And there he paused, searching for the word he wanted so that I was reminded of how Amy sometimes surveys her paints for just the right shade before realizing that she must mix it herself. "To aspire to her," he finished. "To work for her. Both to earn her love, and for the honor of being worthy of her."

Amos and I said nothing, but my husband fixed his gaze on John in that way he has that silently welcomes you to say more. "For as long as I can remember I have wandered as if without a destination," John went on. "It is a hard thing to feel at home in the world when you are an orphan. Now at last it seems as if a compass has sprung alive within me, pointing the way. Meg may not want me for her husband. But there is no other path I would rather tread, regardless of whether I reach that destination."

John's revelation left me as breathless as Amos. We simply looked at each other. How many emotions is it possible to experience at once? Jubilant, trepidatious, overwhelmed, grateful. And those were only the handful I could name. John rose to leave us alone to consider it, but with a confirming nod from Amos I stopped him.

"There is no harm to anyone in what you ask," I told him, "provided that you pledge to rely on <u>Meg's</u> heart, and not your own, as your lodestone." He thought of that a moment, taking in my emphasis, before he nodded. "In return, we ask only for patience. Meg is more than a child, though not quite a woman. Give her time not only to learn to fully know and perhaps to love <u>you</u>, John Brooke, but to grow into herself, to ensure that she becomes the woman you envision as your wife. I should hate to see either one of you set your heart on an imaginary version of the other." He nodded gravely, absorbing the possibility of Meg transforming into someone other than the woman in his mind. I turned to my husband. "How long, Amos, until we might place our trust fully in Meg's judgment?"

He was quiet. Picturing the girl he left behind just days before her sixteenth birthday, I'd wager, and measuring her against the young woman whose growing maturity he can trace through each of the weekly letters she has written in his absence—sixty-four in all. "Three years?" he proposed.

I smiled. In three years Meg will be twenty. I was twenty when I pledged myself to Amos. I nodded my assent.

"Three years," John agreed.

Amos and I both reached to clasp John's hand at once, forming a happy knot. Now it is all in Meg's hands. Perhaps when I return I shall suggest to her that she school him in the art of sock-knitting.

November 30, 1862

Once more I am on a train with a rumpled telegram in my pocket. When John handed the envelope to me, the sight of that yellow-brown paper made me feel as if I were plummeting backward two weeks.

"A telegram?" I said as though I had never seen one before.

A telegram can mean only bad news. Aunt March, or Mr. Laurence, I thought. I could not make sense of the words printed there instead.

Amos saw my face. "Margaret?" he asked. I could not speak. Dumbly I handed it to him. Beth, it said. Scarlet fever. Laurie sent it.

"Go, Peg," Amos said at once. "John is here."

If only he were here now. I would not have thought of asking him to leave Amos's side, but I must own that to be alone with my fears on this train as it trudges through the muddy night is torturous. I had not realized the difference it made to sit next to someone whose mind is not a whirling cloud of dread.

Again and again, I pause to rub the wobbly embroidered letters on my handkerchief. *Mother.* The floss is smooth as Beth's hair. She picked a beautiful shade, exactly the color of the asters I love so well. I have vowed not to cry. Not on that sacred little handkerchief. Not while she still lives.

The velocity of my fear is greater than that of the train. What if she should be blinded? Eager to wall out thoughts of greater tragedies, I have allowed that possibility to gallop all over my brain. Timid Beth, locked in perpetual darkness. Her world is already so narrow. If she could not read music, or sew, or read, what would be left to her?

The Perkins Institution is a mere twenty miles from Concord, I remind myself. No school in the world boasts greater success with blind pupils. And yet as far as Beth is concerned, it may as well be in Egypt.

December 1, 1862

The intricacies of that one thought occupied my mind all the way to Jersey City. Consumed it, I ought to say, for my head felt strangely hollow by the time I had exhausted every dire prediction. Still, trying to fix a problem that did not yet exist was easier than wondering if I would arrive in time. I might have traveled faster in a wagon in that storm.

By the time the train reached Jersey City the weather had whipped up Long Island Sound, delaying the ferry. I should have liked to swim, even if the weight of my fears would have dragged me straight to the bottom. I have moved faster in nightmares than the trains, boats, and horses between Boston and Washington did last night.

The sun was rising when at last my feet touched the flagstone path to our own front door. Laurie must have been standing with his hand on the knob to open the door so quickly. His expression jarred me for an instant, like a laugh at a funeral. I was halfway up the stairs before I realized that what I had seen glinting in his eyes were not tears, but hope. The fever had broken in the smallest hours of the night.

Beth's face when she opened her eyes and saw me beside her was almost worth the terror. She possesses the trust of an infant. I parroted her own thoughts back to her as I spoke: "Everything is all right, Beth. Marmee is here." Though those two facts were entirely coincidental, in Beth's mind, they were bound inextricably. Naught but luck and the grace of God have brought her through.

I sit by her now, to write. I cannot leave her side. Had Dr. Bangs not already assured me she was through the crisis, I should be terrified by both her condition and her expression. She looks like nothing so much as a little twist of white tissue paper. One hand lies palm up upon her pillow, cradling Joanna's scuffed wooden head.

All her suffering has been my doing. The scarlet fever was caught from the Hummels, and it was I who insisted that the girls remember to look in on them. Worse yet, Greta Hummel is dead, a week short of her first birthday. Beth was there when she died. Holding her. Meg and Jo whispered it all to me as I clung to Beth's hand and they spooned bites of Hannah's chicken pie into my mouth, for it was several hours before I was willing to let go of my Beth, even to eat.

When I think of Beth holding that baby in her arms, watching the life drain out of her, I am sick with guilt. Of all my girls, that tender Beth should have experienced such a trauma!

A single white rose sits in a vase on her bed table. From Mr. Laurence's hothouse, I thought, but no. Meg found it trying to bloom on Amy's bush. Imagine, a rose in December. Now and then when Beth rouses she looks at it in the way she looks at us, or Joanna. Though its presence this time of year is completely incongruous, it reassures her in some way.

I have yet to lay eyes on Amy. Hannah and the elder girls wisely quarantined her with Aunt March. Someday when I have the ability to devote my attention to anything but Beth, I must hear how the three of them managed that feat.

Meg and Jo are haggard. I have never seen them like this. When the telegram came about their father they were brave as soldiers for my sake. But with the weight of Beth's illness added to their worries, their fortifications crumbled. Their courage has exhausted them. If only they had sent for me sooner. It was Hannah who made them wait so long, when it was plain that they needed me as much as Beth did. More, even. My presence would have soothed them.

Poor Hannah. When I rushed upstairs last night, I saw genuine fear in her that stung past my own panic. How fearsome must I be when I am angry, that she would dread my reaction? In twenty years, I have never lost my temper with her. After my trip I hardly had the energy to be relieved, much less upset. "I cannot speak of this now," I told her when she began to apologize.

My words left her frantic, and in my exhaustion I failed to notice. It was nearly noon today before I took notice of the fact that I hadn't heard her voice all morning.

"Hannah, are you all right? You haven't said a word today."

"Nor you to me, Mrs. March," she said, and burst into tears. Down on her knees before me she went in a torrent of apology. It was like watching Gibraltar tumble into the sea. All that time, she had thought me too furious to speak.

I took hold of her by both her forearms, pulling her up to put her face level with mine.

"I'd seen Meg and Jo through it," she sobbed, "both at the same time. You remember how it was." I did. We were worried then, and run ragged from tending the two of them at once, but never truly frightened. "I should have known Beth would take it harder. She hasn't ever been strong like they are. Mr. Laurence was so upset, I think he would have fired me if he could," Hannah said.

"And I would have hired you right back again," I told her. That gave her a jolt.

"I was working so hard to keep Meg and Jo from being afraid, I got myself believing there wasn't anything to be scared about."

"You needed me, Hannah," I said, realizing it as I heard myself say the words. "As much as Meg and Jo and Beth did."

She looked aghast. "I would never put myself before your family."

"And that is why I left my children in your care. I trust you, Hannah, mistakes and all."

"But Mr. March—"

"You know Mr. March well enough to know that he would never keep for himself what another needs more." The tiniest chirp of laughter broke through her tears at that.

"That's so," she said through sniffles and hiccups. "Mr. March can't enjoy a drop of honey if there's a bee within fifteen miles."

I have every right to be angry with her for the suffering she caused to Meg and Jo, but I cannot summon even a pinch of ire. There is simply no space in me for it. I am too full of gratitude that my Family remains intact. And Hannah is part of that Family. Her loyalty runs even deeper than I understood. Her only error was in putting me before the children.

"Hannah," I said at last, "I shall only be angry with you if you keep crying."

Her chin squared up and she looked right back at me. "Well, Mrs. March," she said, "you'll just have to fume, because I've been storing up these tears for a good many days and they won't quit until they've drained."

She may never know the good that did me, hearing her speak up for herself instead of coddling or deferring to me. "Thank you, Hannah," I said. "For everything."

December 2, 1862

Minna Hummel is dead. Her mother knocked at the door late last night—so late I had unpinned my hair and settled into my dressing gown.

"I am so sorry to wake you," Mrs. Hummel said. "I have come to ask for a sheet. For Minna. She must be buried."

"Oh, Birte!" I reached for her and she stepped back, throwing up both hands between us. For an instant I feared I had offended her. I have never called her anything but Mrs. Hummel.

"No. I do not want to share more of the fever." She would not come inside, either, but stood in the dark, numb with cold and grief as I searched for something worthy of impish little Minna. My mind was such a roil of horror, I could hardly see what I was looking for. Four children dead in fifteen months. And her husband. That is equivalent to my entire Family. I cannot comprehend how she is able to stand up, much less walk half a mile to ask for a shroud for her child. I am so fortunate, it nearly sickens me. I could not bear to trade my daughter for hers, but my God, when will it stop?

Nothing in my linen closet would do. I gave her a sheet from my cedar chest, edged in tatted lace. That was when she cried. Standing on my doorstep in a swirl of snow, clutching that sheet to her breast. When I reached for her the second time, she did not resist. Nor did she return my embrace, instead remaining just as she was but for the circle of my arms.

"Soll ich mit dir zurückkommen? Dir zu helfen?" I asked when her sobs ebbed. *Shall I come back with you? To help?*

"Nein," she said, and drew herself away. "But thank you. Thank you, Margaret March."

How I managed not to break in half at the sound of my Christian name, I do not know. For most of a year I have wondered, and now I know: Birte Hummel is my friend, and I am hers.

December 3, 1862

Beth is well enough to speak now. The delirium that so frightened everyone has turned out to be a mercy, for she has no memory of the days when she hovered so near the threshold of death. It turns out she has memories enough to torment her without those.

"Mrs. Hummel's baby died, Marmee," she told me today, her voice so small it stole between the narrowest cracks of the armor I have been wearing since the telegrams came. I could have lifted a barrel of flour with less effort than it took to make my own voice steady and soothing.

"I know, darling."

"She went so quietly, I didn't know it was happening. I didn't try to stop it."

I climbed right onto the bed beside her then. "Oh, Beth. Beth, you couldn't have stopped Greta from dying any more than you could have held back a train. Poverty took that child. It's a mercy you've been spared, and you have spent your whole life warm and well-fed." I don't know why I chose then to tell her. Perhaps I thought that she should recover from everything all at once, rather than regain her strength only to have a new sorrow knock her backward again. "Little Minna has gone, too. Hannah and the girls didn't want to tell you."

For the longest time she did not speak. Then she said the last thing I expected to hear. "Is . . . is Father going to die now, without you?"

A whirlwind of—of what? I do not even know what to call it. As if I were a cyclone of protection, trying to wrap myself around her. "Gracious, no! Oh, Beth. Mr. Brooke is there. He will see that Father gets all that he needs." For the first time since I returned, her face lost some of its pinched look. Here we all thought it was sickness, and it was worry. Until today I did not understand the weight she bears, how much she takes onto herself. None of us does.

December 6, 1862

How odd it is without Amy in the house. Like a cake without rose-water or vanilla, some essential flavor is missing from our days. I have visited her only once at Aunt March's.

Such a solemn little creature I found there. She looked like my Amy—pretty, pert, and proud—and yet her pride was of an entirely different character. It would appear that Amy has grown up more in these last two weeks than in the two years preceding them. Her craving for superiority has vanished, and in its place, an earnest desire for the virtues I had come close to despairing of her ever learning: humility and altruism.

A turquoise ring glinted on her plump little hand, and to my surprise she did not wriggle it beneath my nose to demonstrate its luster. Instead of showing off, my youngest daughter informed me that she had made a will.

A will. Once, I could have laughed at the notion. Not now, though. It is not only her own solemnity, or how close the scarlet fever came to claiming Beth. I have always believed I would rejoice if Amy's eyes were ever opened to her vexing ways, but these last weeks she has been so much grieved by the thought that she would not be missed half so much as Beth that it hurt me to hear it. And what could I tell her? She is both wrong and right, for who would say *Oh no—not Amy!* the way people gasp at the news of Beth's illness? No one, I am afraid. They would exclaim *Oh, dear,* and *How terrible,* and offer up sincerest prayers for her recovery. But no one would recoil as they do at the very thought of Beth being taken from us. My own grief were I to lose Amy would be no smaller, but I must own that it would not be stained with the same sense of unfairness. Beth is so good, so selfless, that the very idea of her suffering is an affront to all who know her.

Amy, on the other hand? I do not know how many of the good citizens of Concord have heard of the Buddhist principle of karma, but I am certain that everyone who knows Amy March has entertained a wordless hope, if only for an instant, that her selfishness and snobbery might somehow circle back to nip at her heels. Now twelve years of slights and irritations have sunk their sharp little teeth into her all at once, and though she has earned it, it is pitiful to see. Particularly as I—her own mother—am among those who has wished for this very comeuppance.

The little room at Aunt March's that Amy has fitted up into a chapel with Estelle's help took me quite aback. Amy has always been one to merely recite her prayers. Now it seems she has learned to say them in earnest, asking for things that matter instead of trifling favors like a pointed nose or the notice of a much-admired classmate. Idolatry was my first thought at the sight of the place. Lace and candlesticks, an ebony rosary with a silver cross, and a painting of the Madonna and Child garlanded in evergreens. Thankfully I stifled my distaste, for it is precisely these embellishments that have drawn Amy nearer to God. I could knock my own head for not realizing it before. Of course the trappings of Catholicism appeal to her; what captivates Amy's attention more than beauty?

Her turquoise ring has become something similar. No mere bauble, she intends to wear it as a reminder of the goodness she aspires to. Absurd as such an ornament looks on the hand of a child, I could not refuse her earnestness.

Much to my astonishment, Aunt March has nothing but praise for Amy. That ring Amy so treasures was a reward for exemplary behavior, in fact. Amy has not developed quite the same fondness for the old lady in spite of her handsome prize; nevertheless, it was heartening to hear Aunt March do something besides scold. As we spoke, I could not shake the notion that she had been genuinely glad to help—at least where Amy is concerned. Does she truly not realize that the only barrier between us is of her own making?

After I had returned to Beth's bedside, Jo appeared in the bedroom doorway, twisting a curl so tightly around her finger I don't know why it didn't twist off. For all that Jo can be counted on to speak her mind every day of the year, when something troubles her she always looks like a balloon trying desperately not to burst.

Something about Meg, I guessed immediately. "That Moffat hasn't been here, I hope?" I blurted. It would be just like the Moffat boy to try to come calling in my absence.

To my astonishment, Jo proceeded to tell me all about Meg's lost glove and how it came into John Brooke's possession. It is as if we have all been working over the same jigsaw puzzle without knowing it. Suddenly all the pieces are dropping into place.

Meg herself knows nothing and suspects nothing of this little lost glove that has thrown us into a happy uproar. Jo further reports no signs that her sister is smitten, but Jo expects young women in love to blush and faint and simper like they do in her novels. Our modest Meg is much more subtle. How my heart leapt to hear that Meg read John's reports of Amos's progress more than my letters, and how surprised I was to feel that leap. It has not been a week since I learned of John's affections for my daughter, and already I am in love with the idea.

I saw it for myself, not two minutes later—the soft way Meg smiled when I asked her to append my love to John at the bottom of her letter to her father. And the sweetness in her voice at learning that Amos and I have taken to calling him John. "I'm glad of that," she said, "he is so lonely." She speaks of him with an almost wistful fondness, as if he is someone she used to know and love.

Oh, I must find some way to temper my zeal, lest I thrust Meg into John's arms without meaning to. That choice belongs to Meg, and no other.

My hands will likely be kept full cosseting Jo—something I cannot recall doing since she had windy colic at nine weeks old. All of this intrigue over Meg and John has left her perfectly outraged, as though John's love for her sister were some form of vulgarity. The way she scoffed at the thought of Meg falling in love! Her face wrinkled so her nose nearly touched her eyebrows at the very idea. Where romance is concerned, Jo has the sensibility of a seven-year-old boy. I cannot make heads or tails of it. "I just wish I could marry Meg myself, and keep her in the family," she said. I do believe she meant it, too. Such a queer notion.

Beth nearly succumbed to the fever, Meg may be on the verge of falling in love, and it is thoughts of Jo that keep my mind whirring as I settle in for another night's vigil at Beth's bedside. Jo can see only a hole in our Family at the prospect of Meg marrying. A hole, for heaven's sake. "An end of peace and fun and cozy times together," she called it. As if a family ceases to be so the moment we are no longer under the same roof. What but time could possibly convince her otherwise?

December 7, 1862

Beth's fingernails are falling off. No such thing happened to Meg and Jo, which makes the sight of it doubly unsettling. The nails lift root first, as if plowed up by the new growth beneath. When the loose edges catch on her bedding, the whole nail tears off, leaving her fingertips bleeding. Dr. Bangs says he has heard of such a thing, but never encountered it in thirty-five years of practice. Her toenails are not affected in the least, which I cannot understand, though the soles of her feet are peeling. This I remember from the older girls' bouts with the fever. The thickness of the loosened skin and its dull yellow color turn my stomach; only Jo has the mettle to tend to Beth's poor feet.

For all that she shuns women's work, Jo is as fine a nurse as any I saw in Washington.

December 8, 1862

Birte Hummel has lost her position with the Weddletons. Scarlet fever has taken not only two of her children, but her livelihood as well.

After a week at Beth's bedside, Hannah ordered me out of the room this afternoon. "Better yet, out of the house," she said, insisting that my eyes needed to see something other than the four walls of Beth's bedroom for an hour or two. Beth was napping after a lunch of blanc-mange, so I consented to pay a short call on the Hummels, which was not the sort of respite Hannah had in mind. She was more correct than she could have known. I expected a mournful mood at Birte's house, but what I found there can only be called despair.

The room seemed as dim and disarrayed as the first day I had laid eyes on it. I had not known until today that Karl and Heinrich had had the fever as well. Karl first, likely from the Irish children he shoots marbles with in the alleys. He recovered smoothly enough, but in that one room there was no hope of keeping the little ones from catching it. The week Birte spent tending to Karl cost her the wages that would have paid for a doctor for the others. Worse, Mrs. Weddleton would not allow her back into the house to work, for fear of the contagion spreading to her own children. That was why Greta died in Beth's arms instead of her mother's. Birte had gone out to beg the doctor to come without pay.

I thought Birte must have misunderstood, that surely she could return to work once the children were well and the danger had passed. Scarlet fever is known to be contagious for several weeks; perhaps Mrs. Weddleton only told her to stay away until the new year, I reasoned. My optimism could not have been more foolish. Lottchen had accompanied her mother, to hear the words herself and be certain there was no confusion over the English. The maid would not even let them in, but shooed them from the portico before delivering the ultimatum on her mistress's behalf. I did not wait to hear more. I marched straight to Barretts Mill Road, where I stood on that same portico for a full minute, waiting for the hot cloud of my breath to shrink before I rang the bell. I half expected to be shooed back into the snow myself. But no, into the parlor I was ushered, where I declined to sit.

Mrs. Weddleton came sweeping in as if propelled by her own regret, speaking in that motherly simper that makes me wish I could turn my ears inside out. "Mrs. March, I know you're displeased, and I am, too. Birte really was the most satisfactory employee I've hired in months, but I cannot have people bringing those diseases into my home," she said. "What will be next? Cholera? Typhoid? I have my own daughters to think of. And Mother Weddleton. In her condition, even the mildest of infections is a grave threat."

Those diseases. As if the poor are subject to illnesses the wealthy are too lofty to encounter. As if her wealth grants her immunity to the ills of the world. And yet how could I contradict her, with my own daughter lying at home in bed with the rash still darkening her cheeks, and her fingernails cracking off at the root one by one?

Her next question hit so squarely, I wonder now if she had calculated it beforehand: "Is your Beth much improved?"

I do not know what I said. Something polite and insipid to end the conversation as quickly as possible. It required every shred of my self-possession to leave the Weddleton house without making a scene I would be ashamed of later. Why the snow didn't melt beneath my scorching footsteps as I walked home, I will never know. Of course it did not occur to me to point out to Mrs. Weddleton that she had let me into her house in spite of Beth's fever—not until my hand was on the knob of my own kitchen door. Perhaps she fancies that the disease is somehow cleaner, having been filtered through our home.

I flew past Hannah and straight to my room, slamming the door and latching it for good measure. If anyone comes within range of me, I shall explode like canister shot, and if this fury is to be of any use it must be aimed at a target, not scattered at the first movement that catches my eye.

There are times I think my rages will consume me, and this is one of them. *Touch it to something that will conduct its heat,* my mother would say. But what? If I were a man, this temper would be merely a flaw, not a curse. A man will be forgiven, perhaps even admired, for an angry outburst if the cause is laudable or his honor is at stake, while a woman must never be angry, much less show it.

A tentative tapping at the door. "Marmee?" Meg's voice. I wish it were Jo. Jo would understand without explanation. Meg's feet re-treated before I could think what to say. Now I have added to her worries.

Heavier footsteps followed, and another, firmer knock. Hannah. "Mrs. March? Is everything all right?"

"It shall be, as soon as I've cooled," I told her. I shall make this right. How, I do not know.

December 10, 1862

The Hummels' rent is due in five days, and there is no hope of her paying in time.

"Perhaps it is for the best that we move," Birte said. "It is difficult to imagine being happy in this room where three of my children have died." She thrust her chin toward the corner. "That bed. Greta and Johann were born in it, and now I cannot sleep in it. Minna lay there for eight days . . ." She could not finish. Blitz lay curled where Minna's pillow should have been, his face plunged into the corner. They say not a soul can touch him now that Minna is gone.

The Hummels' circumstances now are—appallingly, unthinkably—worse than what they were a year ago. All of their linens have been burned in hopes of destroying the contagion. Much of it was new, or nearly so. Their clothing ought to be burned as well, but it is Decem-ber, there is not a blanket left in the house, and there is no money for more, despite the fact that Birte has been working steadily for the last six months. Once again she has no work, and not one, but two children are dead.

December 11, 1862

My first day back to the relief rooms, and I was late. I could hardly bear to leave Beth's side, but she insisted I see to the Christmas boxes as usual. By the time I understood that to stay and neglect my duty would cause her greater distress than to go, I was twenty minutes behind my time. Whether that is for good or ill, I cannot yet say. I know only that I have set off a veritable earthquake.

When I rushed in, an apology hopping on the tip of my tongue, Mrs. Weddleton stood with her back to the door, addressing all the volunteers. I do not know what conversation had passed before I arrived. Had I heard more, there is no telling what might have erupted from me.

"Mrs. March can scrub their floors and diapers for them if she likes. I say there are plenty enough ways to help the poor without dirtying our own hands."

Them. Dirty.

White-hot heat blazed up my spine as if it were a line of gunpowder. A sunburst exploded behind my eyes.

I must have been the very picture of outrage. Every pair of eyes in Mrs. Weddleton's audience widened before I had opened my mouth. All I can say for myself is that I did not shout. I spoke so levelly and with such quiet venom that my voice hushed the entire room. "If another of Birte Hummel's children dies because she cannot put food on her table or wood on her fire, your hands will be <u>dirtied</u> with blood."

That single sentence struck like a deftly aimed arrow. Mrs. Weddleton turned, and every speck of color drained from her face. Her expression slackened so, she looked for an instant as if she had had a stroke.

Not a soul flew to her defense. When she realized that fact, she gathered herself up and walked out the door without a word. The tension in the room went with her, the way a draft ceases the moment a window closes. I hardly knew where to look, fearful of the reproachful eyes that would assuredly swarm over me.

When the silence became too thunderous to bear, I chanced a look. The women were turned not to me, but toward Mrs. King. She has always taken the helm here; I knew that whatever example she set, they would follow. Mrs. King gave a nod. Not approval; rather, a signal that it was time to proceed with our work. The room gradually refilled with the sounds of quiet industry, and I heard not a whisper about my outburst.

All day long, I chided myself a thousand different ways. I am her elder. I have just as much breeding as she, and far more learning. I ought to have set an example. If there was something she needed to be told, it could have been said kindly, and privately. What I did was a dreadful breach. Yet I could not make myself feel properly ashamed. Instead I felt as satiated as if I had just eaten an entire Christmas turkey. The feeling faded only when I read of the losses at Prairie Grove, Arkansas. Three thousand men.

December 12, 1862

This afternoon I returned to Barretts Mill Road, determined to humble myself with an apology. The maid rather stiffly informed me that her mistress was not in—stiffly enough to make me wonder if it were true. Just as I was about to step from the portico, I turned and asked if the elder Mrs. Weddleton was perchance well enough for callers today. The young woman's demeanor shifted at that. "No, ma'am," she replied in a kindlier tone, "though I wish I could say she were."

We were quiet for the length of a breath. That is a testament to the character of Adelaide Weddleton—that the mere mention of her name can smooth the air between two people.

I delved into my reticule and with only a wisp of reluctance handed over the very last of my old calling cards, the one with my name embossed in copperplate and underscored with a sprig of blue asters. "Please convey to Mrs. Adelaide my sincerest wishes for her good health," I said. "And tell her that her absence is still felt every day in the relief rooms."

The maid ran an appreciative thumb over the raised lettering. "I shall, ma'am," she replied. We both knew it to be a futile wish. The greatest blessing Adelaide Weddleton may receive now is the mercy of a painless departure.

December 14, 1862

Fighting rages in Fredericksburg, Virginia, for the fourth straight day. I am woefully behind in the news, but the sheer size of the headlines is enough to tell me that Fredericksburg is a name that will pain many a family for decades to come.

One bright spot in all of this: Amy is home again. Even with her lofty new aims and subdued temperament, she brings a splash of much-needed color into our lives.

December 15, 1862

Mrs. King was at the door this morning, with two gray wool blankets draped over her arms like a muff. "For Birte Hummel," she said. "We can't very well send gray to our men in the fields, can we?" Her plump face crinkled at the joke, then sobered a shade. Mrs. Carter had donated them, she explained. They had been her son's. "It's been a year now," she said, since Noah was killed, and she decided it was plain selfish to keep them on her boy's bed while someone else's children were shivering." They were heavy as rugs.

Then, from her pocket came a thick envelope whose contents clinked merrily as she handed it to me. Two dollar bills, and the rest in quarters and dimes, all for Birte. The women of the relief rooms had taken up a collection from their own pocketbooks for the Hummels' rent. There is enough to see her through until February! I was too astonished, too moved to thank Mrs. King properly. Just seeing me speechless seemed to tickle her, though, and off she went.

December 17, 1862

Karl Hummel has taken a job.

When I opened the front door this morning, there he was, so full of glee, he could not keep still. He was so proud—so proud, it hurt me to see. From where he stands, the world is opening up for him; from my vantage, his opportunities are slamming shut with frightful rapidity.

Ten years old, and he will halt his schooling to shovel manure and wash carriages at the livery stable around the corner. Ten hours a day so his family can afford more than flour and lard. A boy who can recite the poetry of Goethe or Shakespeare as easily as he can cipher out long division without the aid of slate or pencil. He might just as well extract his mind from his head and put it into a pickle crock on a pantry shelf, for all that he will use it now.

The effort of not hurting his feelings, of manufacturing a congratulation that did not sound counterfeit, tired me for the rest of the day. Even John's letter containing news of Amos's continued improvement did not cheer me as it should have. Why must it be such a rarity for mind and body both to be well-fed? A boy with Karl Hummel's promise should not have to starve one to feed the other.

December 18, 1862

I nearly stayed home from the relief rooms today. The prospect of having to face Harriet Weddleton again made my breakfast stick in my throat. There was no real question of shirking, though. There is much work to be done this week if the needy families of Concord are to receive their Christmas boxes in time.

Each time the door opened, I steeled myself for a dunking in humility and shame. But Mrs. Weddleton did not arrive. Nor did the Weddletons' December donation, which we sorely need if we are to provision our boxes with more than hand-me-down woolens and gingerbread from our own kitchens.

If only my mind were as quick as my temper. Only now does it occur to me that I may have done the poor of this city a great disservice. The Weddletons' donations constitute a decided majority of our funds. Should they withdraw their support thanks to my outburst, it is I who shall have blood on my hands. Oh, what stupid, useless wrath.

December 19, 1862

Something has got Meg into a state I cannot decipher. Dreamy one minute, jumpy the next. More than once I have asked what troubles her, and she denies that anything is amiss. This is so plainly false that I dare not ask again. I would rather my children spit in my face than lie to it. Neither can Jo wrest any clues from her. The blushing and stammering make me think it is to do with John. Whatever it is pulls Meg in two directions at once.

December 20, 1862

The nearly empty Christmas boxes remain lined up on the tables in the relief rooms. We simply have not the funds yet to fill them. No one reproaches me, though I wish they would. The Weddleton donation has never been late before, and certainly not at Christmas.

I had hoped to use the leavings from Jo's and Aunt March's money to buy gifts for the girls—gifts worthy of each of them—but if these boxes are still empty on Monday, I shall have to forfeit my plan for the good of those whose needs are greater than our own.

By the time I reached home I was thoroughly downcast. All I wanted was a strong cup of tea and a hot fire to melt my stiff, chilled spirits.

But no sooner had Jo handed out the Family post when Meg cried out as if she'd been burned. Up bubbled a torrent of tears, indignation, and accusations. Before I could grasp what had happened Meg rummaged in her pocket and pitched a crumpled paper at Jo. "You wrote it," she cried between sobs, "and that bad boy helped you. How could you be so rude, so mean, and cruel to us both?"

I smoothed out the paper as best I could and read what purported to be a love letter from John Brooke. Little wonder Meg blamed Jo. That letter was the most florid, outlandish confession of ardor I have ever read—outside of the *Spread Eagle*, that is. The idea of John writing of his inability to restrain his passion would have made me snort with laughter under any other circumstances.

Laughter was the furthest thing from my mind, for it turns out that I know Meg's suitor far better than she. Meg answered that silly forgery. Answered it! (There is one thing I can be proud of, and that is Meg's reply. She echoed the very same sentiment Amos and I expressed to John in Washington, demurring at anything but friendship for the time being, that sensible girl!) Nevertheless, this is the cause of her drifting about all week. Beguiled by simpering proclamations of love, she has steeped herself to the eyebrows in honeyed daydreams.

That was only half of the trouble. There had not been one letter, but two. The one that arrived today revealed the first as a sham. This one, also signed "John Brooke" in a suspiciously different hand, expressed nothing but puzzlement over Meg's sudden proclamation of platonic affection, disavowed any knowledge of a love letter, and fingered Jo as the culprit. It, too, is a forgery.

What a commotion then as Jo declared her ignorance of the whole affair and got herself into an indignant lather. It was all Laurie's doing, she insisted. Nothing but a prank, meant to capture Meg's secret as a prize he could use to hector Jo.

All in all, a tangle of absolutely childish nonsense.

Jo would have tongue-lashed Laurie into mincemeat herself; instead I bade her bring him to me without a word about any of it as warning. I wanted to hear what he had to say for himself without any time to scrape together an excuse. While she was gone I tended to Meg. Not since she was a little child has she so adamantly buried her tearful face into my breast. I laid my cheek atop her head and confessed John's true feelings for her, hoping to soothe her broken fantasies with fresh possibility. But this bout of deception had left her feelings so twisted and knotted, she could hardly bear to think about John without cringing. At the first sound of footsteps in the hall she ducked from my arms to secrete herself in Amos's study.

I could hardly have been in a worse state of mind to be confronted with Laurie's chicanery. The state of the relief rooms coupled with Karl Hummel's news had discouraged me so, I had slumped about since yesterday. This new indignation revived me, invigorated me. Here, at last, was something I could rail against.

Until today, Laurie has been a daydream of a son. There is so much I could thank him for, from the trivial kindnesses such as his weekly nosegays to fill my little vase, to the self-assurance he has bolstered in Jo by providing the companionship she has never been able to find in other girls. For ministering to Amy in her quarantine, he deserves a loving cup. The contrast between that Laurie and the one who came to stand before me this afternoon made my head rattle.

Before I could decide what to do with him, he chanced a peek at me with a hopeful look that seemed to beg, *Only a joke, ma'am!* That was a mistake nearly as weighty as the crime itself. A wind rose up in me, fanning the flame I had thus far managed to keep from blazing.

I felt no outward change in my expression; nevertheless, the jollity sank from his face. He has never seen me truly angry before, I realized. There we stood, both seeing a version of the other that we had not known existed. That cowed him, and cautioned me to be mindful of my fury. Despite my disgust, I was determined not to make the same mistake with him that I had made with Harriet Weddleton. Anger need not be wielded like a cannon. But nor must it be buried, lest it resurrect itself at the most inopportune moment.

"Mr. Laurence," I began. The way he blanched at my formality told me I had taken up a powerful weapon. "Up to this day, I have thought of you as a son." He swallowed hard; the muscles of his chin clenched. *Gently,* I cautioned myself. "And I believe you have thought of me as a mother."

He nodded, unable to meet my eyes. We were both silent as we each took our emotions in hand. "You wrote this," I said, handing him the crumpled love note. It was not a question. Laurie accepted it without a word, only a wince.

"You shall answer me, Mr. Lawrence."

He hardly possessed the power to whisper. "Yes, ma'am."

Another long stillness prevailed as I waited for a wave of temper to crest and fall. "My daughters are not figures in a doll's house that you may arrange for your own private amusement," I said very quietly. "It is one thing to inveigle a note out of Meg for the sake of besting Jo. That was plain childish. But to follow it with this?" I proffered the second letter with a flourish that made the paper snap at him.

Laurie started backward, trying to protest that no harm had been done, that John had never seen any of the letters. "After using Meg's emotions as playthings, you have the temerity to tell me that?" I asked, my voice rising dangerously. "What purpose did this letter have but to humiliate her? Harnessing a guileless girl for your prank was not enough—you somehow were not satisfied until you had ridiculed her naivete." That chastened him into silence. "To use deceit as the lever to extract a fellow-being's most tender, secret feelings only to make a mockery of them is not mischief, Mr. Laurence, but cruelty."

The boy's chin was on his chest by then. His shoulders curled forward, as if he hoped to plug his ears with them. When he dared look up his eyes were brimming. "I'll take any punishment," he begged, "and deservedly so. Only <u>please</u> call me Laurie again."

One word more and I would have wounded him, perhaps permanently. For once the furious tide within me receded as quickly as it had come. "I shall," I said, finding room for a hint of kindness. "But not until you have apologized to Meg, and made her understand you are not merely sorry for being caught, but for the anguish you have caused her."

A look of—of what? Resignation and nausea, maybe, settled over him as he prepared to face his penance. But face it he did. All his charm and jokes were set aside, so that Meg could not help but forgive him.

When he returned home he found himself in yet another scrape, so Jo informs me. Mr. Laurence demanded to know what all the trouble had been about and Laurie, sworn to secrecy at Meg's behest, refused to tell his grandfather. It fell to Jo to smooth things out next door. Thank goodness, for I am perfectly exhausted by all this foolishness.

December 22, 1862

To my inexpressible relief, the Weddletons' customary monthly donation arrived today, just in time to fill the Christmas boxes. One of the maids delivered it to Mrs. King first thing this morning. I recognized her—Frieda. We saw to her mother's funeral expenses last spring. She gave me a wink as she bobbed her curtsey and turned to go. I folded my lips tight between my teeth—not in anger, but to keep a laugh from bursting out.

"Mrs. March, are you quite all right?" Mrs. Carter asked. "You look flushed." Only Isobel Carter could ask such a thing in perfect innocence; I spied two other ladies behind her laughing into their sleeves.

The note accompanying the donation sobered us all: Mrs. Adelaide has taken a turn for the worse. From what I saw in July, I know Harriet would not dream of leaving her mother-in-law's side for an instant. And I in my vanity had the audacity to imagine not only that I was the cause of the delay, but that Harriet Weddleton could be so petty as to deprive the neediest citizens of Concord their holiday comforts because of my temper.

Mrs. King gathered all the ladies together for a prayer for Adelaide, then dispatched three of us straight to the grocer for hams, carrots, potatoes, and apples. With my guilt lifted, I fairly sailed through the streets, despite the weight of the crates of provisions.

Before long, I was humming a carol. The tune was infectious, and we filled the boxes to a chorus of *glorias* and *in excelcis Deos*. I felt as buoyant as if I had given the money myself.

Off to the shops I dashed afterward, gleeful at the prospect of giving my girls the Christmas they deserved.

Jo was simple. Books, of course, with *Undine and Sintram* at the top of the stack. For Amy, a framed engraving of the Madonna and Child, like the one she so admired at Aunt March's house. My gratitude for Beth's survival prompted an extravagance in the form of a crimson wrapper knitted of fine merino. And then there was Meg.

In a flight of fancy, I pointed to a bolt of pewter-colored silk and asked Mr. Brown if I could see it. It was the work of an instant to conjure up a picture of Meg bedecked in a dress of such fabric. I could afford no more than the fantasy; what remained in my reticule would have paid for a bodice and sleeve, and little else. Even had I been more sparing with the other girls' gifts, I could not have stretched that far.

Who should step up beside me just then but Mr. Laurence? "Christmas shopping?" he asked.

"Daydreaming, more like," I confessed. "Meg has pined for a silk dress since she was a child. Now that she is of an age for one, I have not the means to fulfill that desire." I signaled for Mr. Brown to put the cloth back up on the shelf again. "Perhaps a silk parasol will make do for now."

"I have an idea," Mr. Laurence said, and then proposed I accompany him to his home. If his suggestion was not to my liking, he promised, he would return me to town before the closing of the shops so that I could seek out the white-handled, black silk parasol Meg had wanted months ago. What could I do but agree?

Upon our arrival he murmured to a valet and the man set off up the curving stairway as Mr. Laurence ushered me into his study. In a few moments the valet returned with a gown draped over his arm, which was laid out carefully before me on the settee. It might have been painted by Winterhalter rather than sewn, so demure and elegant it looked worthy of a Russian grand duchess. And such an exquisite color, a pearly silver that outshone the gray silk I had fingered so covetously in town.

"This was my Tabitha's," Mr. Laurence said. "I nearly always asked her to wear it when we attended the theaters and concert halls." He paused, remembering, then said, "Could it be made over in time? These sleeves, I think, are not the fashion nowadays."

I looked at him dumbly. "Made over?"

"For Meg," he said. "In time for Christmas."

The idea left me too breathless to gasp. I stammered in protest, but Mr. Laurence held up his hands. "It is mine to give," he insisted. "I should rather see it gracing a comely young woman once again than shut up in a wardrobe, and I can think of none more worthy than Meg."

"My Meg?" I asked weakly.

The old gentleman chuckled good-naturedly at that. "Yes, your Meg. This is a dress made for a beautiful woman, rather than a dress intended to render a woman beautiful," he said, "in the same way a frame should not detract from the painting it surrounds. Now, can you think of any young lady in Concord that is more suited to such a thing?"

My own vanity got the best of me and I very nearly choked at the effort of not chuckling back in delight. I bit my lip to tamp down my grin and shook my head.

"Then I insist!" he bellowed, slapping his hands together in a burst of glee. "Do you know a capable needlewoman, or shall I summon one?"

Of course I know a woman capable of this task, and one that would relish two days' work—Birte Hummel.

December 24, 1862

Birte was at my door this afternoon to tell me that Meg's gown is ready. As I counted out her pay, she held out a brown paper bag. "Would you deliver this to Mrs. Adelaide?"

The smell of the spices seeped through the paper. "Pfeffernüsse?"

Birte nodded. "She loves it so. I promised to make it for her. The fever will not travel with the wrapping, will it?"

She is a kinder, more forgiving woman than I.

December 25, 1861

Amos is home.

Amos. My Amos. My husband, my friend, my love.

December 26, 1862

To be held again. I cannot describe it. All these long months I have been the anchor, the one clung to. And all that time, the bedrock I myself was clinging to was invisible to me. Only the fact that we were not capsized assured me that it was there at all.

And then, to lie in bed with my head tucked under Amos's chin and his palm resting in its place upon my hip. I have never known such rapture as this. Every force that has buffeted me since the day he mustered in was calmed.

Before dousing the lamp, he took each of my hands in turn and spread them open, as though he understood how tightly they have been gripped in his absence. "My good, sturdy Peg," he said, and kissed both palms. It did not matter then how much I wished not to cry. Sixteen months of fear and worry melted at those words and drained from me like spring runoff.

But yesterday. I will not rise from this bed until I have recorded the richest Christmas in memory. My mind returns again and again to the moment <u>before</u> the moment, when I sat in my armchair before the fire, steeped in the feeling that at last all was truly well. The girls reveling in the splendor of their gifts. Beth smiling, with hints of color in her cheeks. In my hand, a letter from Amos in his own familiar script, telling me that he would soon be home again. Birte and her children safe from eviction, their holiday plumped by the two days' work Birte had put into tailoring Meg's silk dress. There was not one thing to dread.

The girls had just presented me with their gift—a cluster of five acorns capped in brass and hung from a bar pin, each one woven from hair. One chestnut, one golden, two dark brown, and one gray. All four of my darling girls', and Father's, too. I clapped my hand over my mouth that I would not cry, but it was no use. The tears trickled over my knuckles and seeped into my smile. I could not stop touching it, nor let go of Amos's letter.

And then, the moment. When I revisit the scene in my mind, it has the feel of something out of one of Jo's stories—so perfectly contrived that it seems too flawless for reality.

The parlor door opened just wide enough to admit Laurie's head. His black eyes bobbed all round the room. Counting, I wondered? Satisfied, he drew back, saying, "Here's another Christmas present for the March Family." There was a joyful break in his voice. And I knew. Or I hoped I knew but did not dare believe until there stood Amos, leaning hard on John Brooke's arm.

The whole room seemed to burst. Such a tumult of gasps and tears and shrieks and laughter. I know only that Amos and I were at the center of it, our girls layered around us head to toe. And then came Beth, propelled to her feet by sheer elation at the sight of her father, tottering on legs that have not borne her weight since November.

Seeing Amos in Washington was not the reunion I had longed for, though not for the reason I had supposed. The cause of the hollowness I felt seemed so logical: Danger still loomed over him, closer than it had in my daily worries, so that there was no room for joy. There was only relief at seeing him alive again, tempered with fear that he might yet be snatched away. But that was not it at all. The two of us without our daughters are like the covers of a book without pages.

I have persisted in writing *Family* with a capital *F*, as I always have, but it has been by rote. Without Amos alongside us, that *F* has seemed unfit, looming over the rest of the word as if mocking me. Now, I should like to write the whole word in capital letters.

Later

How could a day, a week, a month as bright as this become brighter still? And yet it has. Meg and John are—are what? Not engaged, exactly, but there can be no doubt now of Meg's feelings for him. She has flung her heart wide open.

Late this afternoon Jo came roaring up the stairs like a fire brigade, shouting, "Oh, do somebody go down quick! John Brooke is acting dreadfully, and Meg likes it!" Writing it now makes me laugh until I quiver. What a thing to say!

Down we all thundered to find John and Meg in the parlor, looking so at home together they might have been the lord and lady of the manor.

And who do we have to thank for this but Aunt March? Of all the people in the world. While the rest of us hoped to nudge our pair of turtledoves gently together, she tried every which way to thrust them apart and failed so spectacularly that I shall have to pay her a visit out of sheer gratitude, though it may be a week or more before I can do so without gloating.

But as to how it happened. Someday I shall have to ask John whether he left his umbrella here on purpose, that he might have an excuse to return, for that is just what happened. Fate winked at him, giving John a moment alone with Meg as well as the courage to act upon it. I do not know just what went on—Meg and John have closed ranks on this point. My impression is that all unfolded very smoothly at first, and then something went badly awry. ("Imagine if Aunt March hadn't come when she did," Meg said, and John, though he laughed, looked as though that were the last thing he ever wished to imagine.)

Just when it seems their emotions teetered at a tipping point from which there might have been no return, in blustered Aunt March. She had meant to surprise Amos with her presence, and instead found herself shocked by the sight of a young man and woman with their hearts laid bare to one another.

Oh, what fury then, what poking and pounding with her cane as she bullied Meg for answers to questions she had no right to ask. Not only that, but threatening to disinherit Meg if she married a poor man. (And where is the sense in that, I'd like to ask?) Little did Aunt March know that the mouse she had backed into a corner was capable of turning into a tiger. Little did any of us know, least of all Meg herself.

Meg, who loves pretty things and remembers our old life better than any of her sisters, defended John's honor and denounced Aunt March's threats to her puckered old face. Oh, I am too much pleased by that. But to think of the sword that woman has dangled over our heads all these long years, parried by the heartfelt devotion of a seventeen-year-old girl, does the pettiest corner of my heart some small good.

The seeds are planted. Not only planted, but already reaching up eagerly toward the sun. Now all we need do is give Meg and John ample room for their love to grow. So long as what Aunt March aroused in Meg were genuine feelings and not the contrariness she so often succeeds in provoking, I believe they shall find that the soil is fertile.

Only Jo is unhappy. Oh, Jo. None of my children are more like me than she is, and still I cannot make sense of her. She remains bedeviled by the notion that John is stealing Meg from her. It is as if she believes there is only one kind of love, and all of us must fight for our fair share of it. How she could have been brought up in this house and come to believe something so contrary, I cannot fathom. Nothing but time and living will prove her wrong.

PART SECOND

January 9, 1865 ∽

Meg has not had a letter from John since before Christmas. Nineteen days of silence, where for the last two years a letter has arrived every week without fail. No one says so, but all of us feel as though we have been yanked backward to the winter Amos lay ill in Washington. My mind performs the same contortions of arithmetic it did then: If John writes every week, then the first seven days do not count. By that logic, his letter is only twelve days late. Perhaps he did not write until the <u>end</u> of the second week. Just five days behind schedule, then. It is no real comfort. The constant whirring of such thoughts is as much a torment as the fear itself.

What could keep John from writing? There has not been a major clash since General Hood's forces were driven from Nashville in mid-December. That leaves illness—the only killer more efficient than bullets. Smallpox rages in Knoxville. Yellow fever ravaged parts of North Carolina last fall. Last we heard, John's regiment was at City Point, Virginia.

January 14, 1865 ∽

Debate over the anti-slavery amendment has raged in the House of Representatives for seven straight days. I do not even want to read the papers. After four years of bloodshed, what arguments can these men possibly be putting forth against abolishing slavery? No doubt they are using the same tired logic that was in circulation when Amos and I joined the cause of abolition twenty-some years ago.

Still no word from John. Tonight as we sewed before the fire, I noticed Meg's lips moving. The same silent words, again and again.

December 21—the date of the last letter she received. Just as I used to do when Amos was at the front. Amos himself is still shut up in his study, trying to finish tomorrow's sermon. "My eyes have been fixed to the mailbox more firmly than my pen this week," he told me. That is what he said, but I know my husband. The mail comes only once a day; what he is truly keeping watching for is a telegram. Should the worst news come, he will see that Meg receives it from his hand rather than that of a stranger.

As for myself, my mind has latched itself to the memory of the day John resolved to volunteer. "You need not prove yourself to us," I told him, recalling his earlier reluctance to fight, "for you have already done so."

Again and again I recall he looked at me then—his face not so much softening as deepening somehow. "I have something worth defending now," he said. "I never felt conscious of my freedom before," he explained. The emphasis he placed on that one word—*before*—touched my heart so that I feel the faint print of it even now. "All my life I have considered myself the hapless prey of circumstance. Another man's freedom is of little consequence when you do not fully value your own."

January 17, 1865

Fort Fisher, North Carolina, is captured, slamming shut access to the South's last open seaport. This war is surely limping to its end. Such news makes me hopeful enough to shout, yet I am afraid that to jostle the world too much in any way might somehow shake John Brooke from its surface.

January 20, 1865

The telegram arrived today.

The sight of that envelope in Amos's hand made my blood feel as if it had turned to stone. The memory of the telegram that bore the news of Amos's illness reared up in my mind, striking me doubly— once with the burn of the memory itself, and again with the knowledge of the pain that awaited Meg. All these months, the thought that she may be widowed before she is a bride has haunted me. I did not want to even touch that paper.

"Should we open it first?" I whispered to Amos. He shook his head. This news belonged to Meg. Our task was only to put it into her hands. We linked arms and mounted the stairs together. My feet moved forward, but my heart shrank back. I don't know how Amos managed to move at all, knowing that he carried the blow that would shatter our daughter.

We had sought to soften the impact, but in reality we only made the dreaded moment worse by stretching it longer. The sound of our matched footsteps on the stairs, and the two of us appearing in her doorway, was enough to turn Meg's face white before we sat down on either side of her and Amos held out the telegram.

Meg's hands shook so that I could not make out the words as she read them. She cried out, a cry like I have never heard before. Anguish and relief together. Then she was bent double, sobbing onto her own lap. "Oh, God, oh, merciful God," she gasped. All I could say was "Meg, Meg." It was not until I extracted the crumpled yellow paper from her hand that I understood.

It is not as bad as we feared. Not yet, at least. John Brooke is not dead, but wounded. The nature of the injury is such that I can scarcely bring myself to think of it without blanching: struck in the eye by a shell fragment during practice maneuvers. Surely at least half his sight is forfeited. Infection is almost a certainty regardless of whether the surgeons attempt to take the eye. His face may well be ruined, too. Despite the sureness that Meg loves more than his face, I worry. Vanity has always been Meg's greatest burden, her love of beautiful things more pronounced than all the others.

"Oh, Marmee, if he should be blinded . . ." She did not need to finish the sentence. All John's prospects would be ruined, and with them, his pledge to wed. I know John. He would never marry Meg without hope of providing for her. Meg has already come to rely on his affection as a kind of sustenance. I think now she could have all the money and fine things in the world, and still feel poor if John were not beside her. How can a price be put upon that?

January 23, 1865

For Meg's sake, we are all pretending resolutely that John will be fine, as if sheer will alone can make it so. All of us are thinking of the worst all day long, the unspoken fear such a constant companion that it seems Hannah should set a place for it at the table. It was not like this when Amos was away. Then, we lived only with the abstract fear that something dreadful might happen. Now it is a question of <u>how</u> dreadful.

January 29, 1865

Yet another day of debate in Congress. The House is set to vote on the anti-slavery amendment next week. All of abolition's hopes and prayers rest on the consciences of those men. One hundred twenty-two of them must vote in favor for the amendment to pass.

Between this and awaiting news of John, my mind is fractured down the center. In praying for one, I fear neglecting the other. If I ask more fervently for one thing, will the other be sacrificed? I know which is the right thing, the unselfish thing. The life of one man cannot balance the freedom of millions.

February 1, 1865

The amendment is passed, praise be to God! Whatever may happen in the South in the months and years to come, slavery in the

Union is no more. The Negro people of Delaware, Kentucky, and West Virginia shall be as free as their brethren from Maine to Minnesota.

For a decade Amos and I devoted every minute and every cent we could spare to the cause of Negro freedom. How many times have I imagined how this day would feel? It is a triumph worthy of trumpets and exaltation. "A new birth of freedom," just as the president said at Gettysburg. Instead, I find myself becalmed. The fury I have harbored over the supreme injustice of slavery simply drained from me as Amos and I sat side by side and wept.

Now that I have washed myself clean of it, I am left wondering what will take its place.

February 3, 1865

In the smallest hours of this morning I bolted out of a dead sleep, taken with an idea so startlingly obvious, I shook Amos awake then and there. "Could John be employed at the Perkins Institution?" I asked him with no preamble. Many of the instructors as well as the students at Perkins are blind, and John is already an accomplished teacher. A sound like a grunt mingled with a sigh rose from the bedclothes as Amos searched for his bearings. "John," I repeated. "A teacher at Perkins."

Some infinitesimal shift of sound told me that Amos was smiling. "My good, sturdy Peg," he drowsed. I waited for more, and received only gentle snoring in return.

I could not return to sleep with such an idea careening from one side of my brain to the other, so here I sit, writing. I'd like to wake Meg, too, but this idea may seem a capitulation to her rather than a comfort. And it is only a notion, after all. A hope with hardly a pebble for a foundation. But it is enough to assure me that prospects for a blind man do indeed exist.

If his sight is lost, there is so much he must learn to do all over again. How to read and to write, to navigate first a room, and then a house, and then the world itself. John is not only a learned man, but an intelligent one. Certainly he is capable of learning such things, so long as his psyche has not been wounded. My spirits are further buoyed by the memory of John improvising yarn and a pair of knitting needles from a shoelace and two pencils as we sat on the train to Washington. He will find a way. If only he survives, I know John Brooke will find a way.

February 6, 1865

Meg has had a letter from John, written in his own hand. The relief was like a rainstorm pelting within me. Meg wept and wept. "I know now, Marmee, what it was like for you when Father was gone," she said. "How did you ever do it? You never once looked frightened."

I pulled her to me and kissed her temple so that she could not see my face. Even through my own jubilant tears I could feel that my smile was an indulgent one. She is a woman now, and should be treated as one, but she does not know, not fully. This is the hardest thing she has done in her short life, and it will surely not be the hardest thing she will be called upon to do. Now is not the moment to terrify her with that. Amos and I had been wed nineteen years when he set off to war. I had a house to manage, and four children. Meg's loss would have been as that of a flower that failed to bloom; mine, a tree axed through its trunk. Without Amos I would have been widowed and destitute, my children orphaned. Still, she has sampled the full flavor, if not the full quantity, of the same fear I bore all those months.

I shall dwell on that no further. Those memories have not yet lost their sharpness, and I have no desire to impale myself upon them. Not when there is good news: John is to be discharged. The doctors judge that he should be well enough to return home by the end of the month.

February 8, 1865

Another letter from John today, this one to Amos and me. He asks if he and Meg may be permitted to marry this summer rather than holding to their three-year pledge. Amos and I both pretended to be grave as we sat in his study to consider the request, but neither of us could maintain the charade. Of course we will consent. What greater evidence of their devotion to one another could we ask them to demonstrate than we have already seen in these last two years?

Our reply was promptly written and posted. Only then, of course, did I begin to wonder if we had acted too hastily. There is always a possibility that war has changed him. That was my most persistent fear upon Amos's return. When the illness faded, he was as quiet and contemplative as he had ever been, but an unfamiliar quality permeated his silences. In place of his tranquility was . . . I have never yet found the proper word to describe it. I know only that this unwelcome substitute enveloped Amos, draping a veil between him and our Family.

There was nothing I could do to help. He could not communicate to me what he had experienced. *Write it,* I remember telling him, for he has always had firmer command of tangible words on paper than the fleeting sounds of speech. But he could not communicate it even to himself. For weeks his diary lay blank upon his desk, leaving me to guess, by the depth of his silence alone, what had lodged itself in his mind and soul. I recall a single unfinished sentence: *My faith in God is unshaken, while my faith in man*

To this day I know almost nothing of what he witnessed.

February 11, 1865

After weeks of practice with pen and ink, Amy has produced the most remarkable portrait of Aunt March, of all people. No one who looks at it can have the slightest doubt of who it is. Amy has captured the pretentious gravity of her presence quite wryly. That is not all, though. There is a genuine benevolence in the inked countenance that has taken nearly all of us by surprise. The woman in the drawing gazes—dare I say it?—affectionately out from the paper.

Jo and I exchanged a startled glance at one another. Is this the Aunt March that Amy has come to know? Here I believed Amy has been politely tolerating Aunt March for the sake of the art lessons the old lady has bestowed upon her for the last two years. But this is more than a fawning homage to a benefactor. For perhaps the first time, Amy has created an image that does not simply replicate something beautiful, but instead <u>expresses</u> something beautiful. For it to be something I myself have never had occasion to observe makes the picture all the more captivating. I am so used to tolerating Aunt March that it is difficult for me to imagine the fondness with which Amy has so clearly drawn her. Put simply, Amy's is an Aunt March that I would like to meet.

Amos sat contemplating the likeness for some time, with an expression I can only call wistful. He alone fully recognizes the woman Amy has drawn. "May I keep this?" he asked. You could see the pride ripple Amy up and down as she answered yes. Amos thanked her, and kissed her, and took the little sheet of paper into his study, where it now sits propped up on the bookshelf alongside the oldest of his diaries.

February 16, 1865

He is home. He fooled us all, that John Brooke, and arrived on our doorstep two weeks earlier than expected. Meg herself answered the door, and how she screamed! I have not moved so quickly in the last ten years as I ran at the sound of that screech. Another telegram, I thought. Infection. Fever. Death.

Instead of collapsed on the floor wailing, there she was, swept up in the arms of a man in Union blue, who sported a patch over one eye as if he were a pirate in one of Jo's stories. Not a pirate at all, of course, but John. *John, John, John.* It was the only syllable any of us could produce for whole minutes.

Meg could not let go of him, would not leave his side all evening even to fetch him a cup of tea. I thought my heart would choke me, it swelled up so at the sight of them together.

He has been remarkably, uncannily fortunate. The shell fragment that pierced his eye did not disfigure the lid, nor damage the bones of the socket—only the eye itself. It is as if that small missile was aimed directly at John's pupil by a master archer. His face bears but one scar, dividing his right eyebrow neatly in half. That narrow white slash lends his expression a roguish look so in contrast with his character, every one of us could not help but grin at the first sight of him. He will not speak of the operation—cannot even think of it without turning faintly gray.

February 23, 1865

Mr. Laurence has made it his duty to procure the finest glass eye money can buy for John. The best come from Germany, Mr. Laurence insists, and he has tasked Amy with making a painting of John's remaining eye, so that the glassblowers cannot fail to replicate the colors. Not only the particular brown of the iris must match, but the white, which, Amy informs us with some regularity, is not truly white at all. John's are the soft yellow of rich cream.

Her devotion to this commission is heartening to see. Never has she been granted such a grave responsibility. As a result, every shade of brown in the house has come under her most intense scrutiny. After what she achieved with her drawing of Aunt March, I have no doubt that if it is possible to capture more than just the colors and shapes within John's iris, Amy will do it.

March 5, 1865

Mr. Lincoln's inaugural address gives much to ponder. Amos and I have each read it more than once and could likely discuss it for days to come.

"Both read the same Bible and pray to the same God, and each invokes His aid against the other," the president said. "The prayers of both could not be answered. That of neither has been answered fully."

"How can men so delude themselves as to the very nature of their God?" Amos asked. He asked it three different ways in the course of the evening. I have no hope of answering him. It is not something he will ever understand, much less believe. Watching him ponder these difficult questions, I wondered yet again at the purity of the world in which his mind dwells. How he bears the daily shock of reality shall remain an eternal mystery to me.

Each time I read the final paragraph, the words resonate as though they are being spoken directly into my own ear: "With malice toward none, with charity for all, with firmness in the right as God gives us to see the right, let us strive on to finish the work we are in, to bind up the nation's wounds, to care for him who shall have borne the battle and for his widow and his orphan, to do all which may achieve and cherish a just and lasting peace among ourselves and with all nations."

To bind up the nation's wounds. Yes. Finally, work I may take an active hand in. <u>My</u> most fervent prayer is that we will take up the president's call for reconciliation as emphatically as the call to arms.

No man who professed to be against enslavement of his fellow-being has moved more ponderously than Lincoln to achieve it, and yet he is among the most merciful of men to walk this earth.

March 12, 1865

Today John came to speak to us regarding his business prospects. (I did not permit my eyes to spin backward into my head at the idea of anyone seeking fiscal advice from my husband.) Mr. Laurence has offered John a generous loan on the most liberal of terms. My heart leapt at the thought, for the old gentleman would be understanding in circumstances where bankers and storekeepers would not.

Amos, of course, counseled against beginning a life of matrimony in debt. "Have no fear of poverty," he said. "The Lord can be trusted to provide for his faithful flock." I suppressed a groan. One need not fear poverty to avoid it, for heaven's sake. What sense is there in capitulating to it when there is another way—a way that leaves the Lord room to provide for the truly needy?

"And you, Mrs. March?" John inquired.

Bless him for asking. His respect for a woman's opinion is one of the qualities that assure me Meg has found a worthy match in him. But how could I say what I wished, with Amos sitting across from me, fingers steepled under his chin, looking the very picture of fatherly wisdom? I could think of no way to speak my mind without also divulging the fact that my husband's perennial indifference to money has burdened me with almost daily anxiety for over twenty years.

"I am of two minds," I replied slowly. "I cannot contradict my husband, for what he says is true. But remember that debts are not only accrued in hundreds and thousands. The butcher, the grocer, and the landlord demand their share each month. If a day should come when expenses outpace earnings, consider to whom you would rather have to beg pardon."

He had the courtesy to weigh both courses, though I could see that my advice did not appeal to him as much as Amos's. No matter how many times I remind him that he has nothing to prove to us, he remains compelled to prove something to himself. For a man of that bent of mind, ideals will always triumph over practicality.

March 16, 1865

Poker-sketching, for heaven's sake. This is Amy's latest artistic preoccupation. Nothing made of wood is safe. The breadboard and the sugar barrel have both been branded with cheerful round faces, and the house smells of burning all day long. The trouble is, she is good at it. Not brilliant, by any means, but good enough that none of us feels we have the right to sway her from it.

Hannah is convinced Amy will burn the house down with her glowing pokers. That does not worry me. This is Amy, not Jo, after all. Rather, we are all so accustomed to the scent of smoke that I fear if the chimney were to burst into flames, we should all sizzle to a crisp before realizing anything is amiss.

March 21, 1865

John has taken a job as a bookkeeper. A bookkeeper! Of course he is amply capable and will earn a steady wage, but a man of his education and ingenuity lining up columns of figures every day? A man who so loves to teach? The thought of him hunched over a stack of ledgers hour after hour is enough to make my own back ache.

Then, who am I to judge? It is steady work that can be relied upon to pay the bills and leave his mind free for other pursuits the moment he shuts the office door behind him. How many times have I silently wished that I could say the same of Amos's vocation? A minister never knows a single minute in which he may not be called to preside over a sickbed or a grave, and his pay is never equal to the duties, entreaties, and demands placed upon him. I count us fortunate indeed when his wages are enough to meet our daily needs.

No matter how modest the income, never having to wonder where the next dollar will come from is a luxury I would wish for all my daughters.

April 3, 1865

Enemy lines outside Richmond broke yesterday. The rebel government, so says the *Evening Transcript*, is "skedaddling" from its capitol. General Lee has yet to surrender, but all the papers predict that federal troops will be in Richmond before the week is out. The evening headlines are already trumpeting "Glorious News!" and "Victory! Victory!" I shall scarcely dare to breathe until it is certain.

April 5, 1865 ∾

The Confederate capitol is evacuated. Yesterday the president sent a dispatch to Mrs. Lincoln dated, "From Jefferson Davis's late residence in Richmond." Over 25,000 rebels have been taken prisoner. Victory is all but assured.

Mr. Lincoln's words have not stopped ringing in my ears. *To bind up the nation's wounds, to care for him who shall have borne the battle and for his widow and his orphan.* How shall we do it? After all these years of scraping lint and rolling bandages, have we any idea of how to heal the wounds that do not bleed? I fear we do not.

April 11, 1865 ∾

The world is aglow with the news of Richmond's fall and Lee's surrender. The war is over—over!—and yet my joy is tempered by that dimness that overtakes me each April since 1843.

The infant who never opened his eyes would be a boy—a man—of twenty-two this month. Had he drawn breath, would he still be alive this day? Or would his blood long ago have soaked the soil of some far-flung battlefield? What futility.

Is it only a quirk of timing that fixates my thoughts on boys like Noah Carter instead of the four million souls that have at long last been unshackled? I should like to know what Isobel Carter feels today, whether her son's death is vindicated by Lee's surrender. To my mind, his demise will ever remain a sterling example of waste.

It does me good to weep freely this day, for all our losses as well as our gains.

April 12, 1865

I remained awake late into the night last night. How many wives are as lucky as I am? I wondered into the darkness. How many women, North and South, now sleep beside a pillow that shall remain forever empty?

Amos woke sometime after midnight to find my palm resting on his cheek, my eyes glossed with a mixture of gratitude, sadness, and joy. "Peg?" he asked.

"Amos," I replied, and the tears fell as softly and unexpectedly as my laughter. He drew me to him, and I unbuttoned his nightshirt, that I might lie my cheek on his bare chest and listen to his lungs billow and his heart thrum. He understood. We lay quietly for a time, touching. Simply touching. Soon there was nothing at all between us.

It is such a rarity for Amos to leave his mind behind and fully enter his body. I relished the opportunity. Our tears mingled as freely as our flesh, and it did not matter that we each cried for different reasons. Before it was over I had let go of my sorrow and given myself over to the joy of it.

The war is ended, and we are all here, under one roof.

April 15, 1865

Laurie burst into the house this morning as we all sat at breakfast. For a moment he stood panting, his face a ghastly white that he looked as if he were made of ink and paper. I stood up at once, ready to go for the medicine box or the undertaker, but Laurie held up his hand. "It is not—not Grandfather," he stammered.

His sorrowful eyes swept over each of us in turn, as if to apologize for what he had to tell us.

"Teddy," Jo demanded, "what _is_ it?"

"Mr. Lincoln is dead," he said at last.

The words pushed me back into my chair. Dead. Shot as he sat watching a comedy at Ford's Theatre. The consequences of this crime are incalculable, and yet my mind has the capacity for only one small thought: a man so weary as he took time to laugh, and was shot through the head for it. The cruelty of that has left me too dazed to recall what happened next. Tears. Prayers.

Unable to understand how time could move ahead, my mind veered backward. Sixteen years ago, Amos and I saw Junius Booth and his son Edwin play in _Richard III_. I was transported. Now, Booth's youngest son, John Wilkes, has enacted a far greater tragedy upon the nation.

And that was not all the news Laurie brought. The secretary of state and two of his sons have also been viciously assaulted by a knife-wielding brute; their wounds may yet prove to be mortal. Rumors that the whole of the cabinet is in peril cannot be quelled.

The rest of the day passed in a haze. I believe the breakfast dishes are still upon the table.

The war is won, Negroes emancipated, and yet an overwhelming sense that all has been for nothing blankets the nation. Amos trembles for the South, which will bear the brunt of the Union's grief. He is right to fear that the president's wish for charity toward all shall not be honored. My own heart and mind are at war over this very question. Such an unparalleled crime demands punishment. "With malice toward none," the president himself said hardly a month ago. Would he have spoken those words if he could have foreseen his own fate?

It was Beth who found the right words this afternoon as we sat numb with shock before the cold hearth. "The quality of mercy is not strained," she recited quietly.

It droppeth as the gentle rain from heaven
Upon the place beneath. It is twice blest:
It blesseth him that gives and him that takes.
'Tis mightiest in the mightiest; it becomes
The thronèd monarch better than his crown.

April 19, 1865

Funeral services for the president were held in Concord today, co-inciding with the hour of the service in Washington. Mr. Emerson spoke most eloquently. Nevertheless, it was the hymn that brought me to tears.

Go to the grave; at noon from labor cease;
Rest on thy sheaves, the harvest task is done;
Come from the heat of battle, and in peace,
Soldier, go home; with thee, the fight is won.

April 22, 1865

John has found the dearest little cottage for Meg, just the color of a mourning dove. There is a bright bay window, and two dormers that peep down over the larches in the front lawn. The backyard is a perfect riot of currant bushes. Best of all, it is so near it could be said to be just around the corner. Somehow I have never taken particular notice of it.

Its charm lies chiefly in the fact that it seems to know precisely what it is, and has no pretensions. Everything inside is small yet per-fectly proportioned, with the happy exceptions of that bay window and the linen closet.

"Just the sort of place where fairy tales begin," Jo declared. "Ra-punzel, and Tom Thumb, and Hansel and Gretel all got their start in a house like this—nestled in a deep, dark wood, of course."

"Perhaps I should take up woodcutting and see what kind of magic happens," John teased back.

Meg said nothing at all. The width of her smile would not permit it. She stood beside me, elbow looped through mine, looking for all the world like a little girl with a brand-new dollhouse.

John shall begin paying rent next month.

April 27, 1865

The president's murderer has been apprehended at a tobacco farm in Virginia. Apprehended and killed. The cavalry regiment that pursued him set fire to the barn where Booth had barricaded himself. His accomplice, a mere boy hardly older than Meg, surrendered, but the assassin refused to yield without a fight. When he appeared to raise a rifle and take aim at the door, a corporal shot him through the neck.

Where now will the nation direct its vengeance?

May 2, 1865

The date is set—one month from tomorrow. Summer felt years away when we all agreed to move Meg and John's nuptials forward, but now, after the tumult of April, it seems that everything is upon us at once.

Even a wedding as simple and modest as Meg desires requires planning. We must see to chairs and tables and garlands and flowers, lemonade and coffee and fruit and cake. And dresses, of course. Meg insists on sewing her gown herself, and Jo and Beth and Amy must all have new dresses for the occasion. I do not see how Hannah and I alone can possibly manage all three with everything else we must do.

Before all that their cottage—now christened the Dovecote by Laurie—must be swept and scrubbed and furnished. The windows must all be measured, and muslin bought and hemmed and hung for curtains. The kitchen cupboards require pots and pans and dishes, the pantry must be filled with flour and sugar and salt and lard. Everything, simply everything, down to brooms and dishpans.

Today I posted a letter to my brother in hopes that he and his wife will attend the wedding. The Kings must also be invited, and I suppose the Moffats as well. The Laurences, of course, and Aunt March and Aunt Carrol and her daughter Florence. But it is Samuel I most wish to see. We have not been together since before the war.

May 5, 1865

I was writing invitations at the kitchen table this morning when Amos called my name. The sound of his raised voice was anomaly enough to jolt the pen from my hand, leaving a splatter across the two I had just finished. I moved so quickly that the sound of that single syllable— "Peg!"—was still reverberating through the hall when I reached him.

There stood Amos in the doorway of his study, an envelope in one hand and a half sheet of paper in the other. Not a telegram, yet my heart insisted on skipping a beat. His face wore an expression that did not match my fear at all, an expression I could not remember having seen before.

"Amos, what is it?" I asked.

He showed the front of the envelope to me. "From my regiment," he said. It was addressed to Chaplain Amos March. My mouth fell open as he tipped it so that I could see its contents. Four ten-dollar bills. *In gratitude for your selfless generosity at the front,* the note said. The soldiers he ministered to had taken up a collection to thank Amos for the boots and blankets he'd bought for them out of his own salary. *It is only a token, but as you gave all that you could spare, so do we.* At least two dozen signatures crowded the bottom half of the paper.

"Amos," I said in wonder.

He did not smile. When he is as pleased as that letter made him, he cannot. Instead, he radiates a contentment so all-encompassing, it warms the room. I put my hand on his forearm, unable to speak. He laid has hand over mine. The way his chin tipped up and his eyes closed, you could feel him wordlessly thanking God for this benediction. After a moment, he tucked the letter into his breast pocket and handed me the envelope of banknotes.

"These are yours," he replied, leaning in to kiss my cheek. "You did without for their sake. Spend it in a way that gives you pleasure." Back to his study he went, leaving me with forty dollars in my hand.

Forty dollars. The sight was enough to make my eyes water anew. There are bills that should be paid. Bills at the greengrocer and the butcher and beyond that could be erased entirely. But Amos had spoken of pleasure—something he rarely does where money is concerned.

All afternoon I pondered on the various delights that could be had for such a sum. Or tried to. What object did I desire? There was nothing. What I desired was not tangible at all. The moment I realized that, I knew just what to do.

I called the girls to me and instructed them to close their eyes and present their hands. "Think back to the first Christmas of the war," I said. "Without Father and without presents." Curiosity and consternation muddled their expressions as those memories rose before them. "Remember all that you wished for, and all that you gave," I said, laying a ten-dollar bill upon each outstretched palm. One by one I looked at my daughters as four years momentarily fell away and they were children of sixteen, fifteen, thirteen, and twelve once more. That image will be forever framed in gold in my memory. "And now open your eyes."

Oh, their faces!

Four silent explosions of delight and disbelief, followed by a chorus of laughter and questions! Not since Amos returned from Washington have I been embraced by so many arms at once. One word again and again: How? I answered only with smiles, making for myself a gift of their enchantment. And then Amos's knowing sidelong glance at supper when they all clamored to tell him "what Marmee gave us"— that was another gift.

Their happiness thrums through me yet. I cannot hope to sleep; nor would I wish to, so long as this feeling persists. The circle of sacrifice and giving that began in December of 1861 is drawn to a close and tied up with a smart bow. At last it feels as if the war—the one fought here as well as on the battlefields—is truly over.

May 7, 1865

Birte Hummel! I ought to have thought of it sooner. What with all of our shopping and cleaning and arranging, it did not cross my mind until today. Birte is the solution to the problem of the girls' dresses. She is a far more capable seamstress than I, and surely swifter, too. If we skimp here and there, I'm sure I can find enough extra to pay Birte to hurry the bridesmaids' dresses along. The dresses will be the better for it; my skills with needle and thread are far more suited to hemming curtains than fitting skirts and bodices.

May 8, 1865

My monthly courses are more than a week behind. What this portends at my age, I cannot be sure. It is either the inevitable end of something, or the beginning of something wholly unexpected. I hardly have time to think of it. Only time will tell.

May 9, 1865

John's false eye has arrived from Lauscha, Germany. He brought it over for Amy to admire up close before putting it to use.

"Look what you have made possible, Little Raphael," he said to her, holding it in his palm.

What a masterful piece of workmanship. It is not round at all, but more reminiscent of the shape of an egg as it lies in a frying pan. The iris and pupil bulge slightly outward, just as the yolk of an egg sits above the white. The depth and interplay of color in the iris caused us all to shake our heads in wonder—coffee- and fawn-colored wisps twine together beneath subtle flecks of gold glimmers like a wheat field in the sun. The white, though, is where the true illusion lies. Amy was entirely correct to devote the time she did to perfecting that crucial shade of barely yellow. Had she not, the eye would look as if it belonged to a puppet or a doll rather than a living human. There are even tiny capillaries, which Amy has determined are neither paint nor glass, but the finest filaments of red silk floss.

When he came back with the new eye in place, every one of our mouths dropped open. Before today I would not have said that his countenance had changed since he went to war, even with the patch covering his right eye, and I would have been quite wrong. Some element of what I can only describe as John-ness has suddenly returned to him. Perhaps it is simply his confidence at feeling physically whole again.

Meg alone had perceived its absence. With a cry of joy she threw her arms around him, then did the same to Amy, pelting her with gratitude. John tried to thank Amy, too, and had to do it without words. But what more eloquent thanks could there be than the sight of happy tears pooling in those matching brown eyes?

May 22, 1865

This morning the taste of cider turned my stomach and sent me dashing for the privy, which has always been the most reliable indication of all. After I had vomited I stood blinking a moment with the sweet burn of the acid still stinging my mouth. Could it truly be? Or is this simply a coincidence? The last time I was troubled with nausea—it has been so long, I cannot recall. But surely since Amy was born.

Fourteen years ago I would not have had this debate with myself.

The signs are plain enough. And still I will say no more than "maybe," or "perhaps." There is no cause for hesitation, and yet I hesitate. From seven pregnancies I have brought forth but four living children.

Joy can be a fearful thing, sometimes.

May 13, 1865

Meg and I began moving some of her things into the Dovecote today. Not the new things—the dusters and teacups and soap and fireplace pokers—but her own things. Her winter dresses and wraps, her boots and quilts and such that she shall have no need of in the next two weeks.

This is not the same as filling the kitchen cupboards and linen closets. This leaves empty places on our own shelves and clothes pegs. I do not like to see those gaps, and busy myself with rearranging the garments that are left, so as to absorb the emptiness.

The trial against those accused of conspiring with John Wilkes Booth to murder the president has commenced. Among the eight accused is a woman. She is my age, a widow with three grown children. The way the papers write of her puts me in mind of the villains in Jo's stories and plays. She may well be guilty, but I find it hard to countenance the notion that such an audaciously wicked person could exist outside the realms of drama and literature.

May 15, 1865

Another week has passed without a spot of blood. Hannah has surely noticed by now that I have added no rags to the laundry. I can no longer abide even the smell of cider. It cannot be denied any longer: Meg's place in our nest will hardly have time to cool before it is filled.

I cannot be certain, but I prefer to imagine this child was conceived the night we learned the war was over—an expression of pure joy after four years of turmoil and bloodshed. Even Amos could not keep his exultation from overflowing his mind and flooding his body after hearing that news. A new birth in our Family to coincide with the rebirth of our nation.

It is far too soon to think of names, yet when I climb into bed after a day filled to the brim with wedding preparations, these are the thoughts that tiptoe across my mind. A child conceived at the end of a war—indeed, because of the cessation of warfare—should have a name that reflects the new era into which it will be born. I cannot help thinking that it is to be a boy. It is a wish, more than a conviction. If it is a girl, I should like to call her, simply, April. The Latin means "to open."

And I have discovered to my great delight that Karl is derived from the low German for "free man." What finer serendipity can there be?

May 19, 1865

John takes the most devilish pleasure in winking at Meg now. She blushes the color of a peony every time. Only Jo continues to be unmoved by their blatant delight in one another.

I confess, the closer the day comes, the more I begin to feel as reluctant as Jo is to see Meg off. Just around the corner, I remind myself at least three times a day. Nearer than the Hummels, near enough that I could stop in every day on my way home from the relief rooms. I hope that it is near enough.

May 20, 1865

I have not been with child since Amy was two years old. Fourteen years. Is there such a thing as a thrill of exhaustion? For that is the sensation that comes over me when I picture myself beginning anew at a task that commenced when I was in my twenties.

Our Family has felt complete for so long that trying to picture who might have been missing all these years stretches the edges of my imagination. I could sooner envision the fourteen-year-old child that might have been than an infant. An infant! Another birth, another newborn at the breast. A year in which I can do no work outside these walls.

Already, the toll on my body is greater this time. Exhaustion plagues me almost from the moment I open my eyes each morning, as though this child consumes each drop of my energy the instant it is manufactured.

A reply from Samuel arrived today. Not only will he attend, but my brother insists on officiating over Meg and John's wedding ceremony—*so that Amos may have no other duty than to be father of the bride and simply enjoy the occasion.* If there is a man alive more considerate than he, I have yet to meet him.

May 22, 1865

Wedding gifts are piling up swifter than snowflakes in January. Yesterday the King family sent a lovely painting for the Dovecote, a watercolor of three little children picnicking with a young lady in a grove of fruit trees. It is pretty enough to make Meg nostalgic for her days as governess.

What a delight to watch the accumulation of these tokens of affection. From the Hummels came a pair of sweet white cups and saucers painted with morning glories of the most vibrant blue. "Those came with Birte from Germany," I told Meg, "I'm sure of it."

Mr. Laurence, who could have bought any number of extravagant gifts worthy to befit a mansion, chose instead to purchase an unpretentious dining room set, perfectly scaled to fit the Dovecote's little dining room, as well as a dainty sofa and armchair for the parlor. "It's like ordering furniture for a doll's house," he said.

The most sumptuous of all arrived today—a bounty of linens

worthy of Queen Victoria herself. Jo read the card and made such a face, then clapped it to her chest. "Guess," she demanded. "Guess who sent it!"

We were all of us mystified. Mr. Laurence seemed the most likely culprit, but he has already exceeded all expectations of generosity.

"Aunt Carrol," Jo said.

No one believed her until we had each read the cards with our own eyes. Mary Carrol, signed in her own hand plain as day. What on earth moved her to such lavishness? Our Family has always been on friendly terms with Aunt March's sister, but these linens are costlier than anything I have seen on the Carrols' own beds and table. A shopkeeper must have assisted; I have never known her to have the taste to select such a well-matched set.

We hardly have time to do it, but such a gift fairly demands that we express our gratitude in person. Tomorrow Meg and I shall steal an hour from our preparations to call on Aunt Carrol.

May 23, 1865

23rd Wedding Anniversary

A four-year-old child could not have fidgeted more than Aunt Carrol did this afternoon as we sat in her parlor with Meg effusing gratitude. Her daughter Florence, who is younger than Meg but much too old to giggle, could not keep her face straight.

"I cannot keep up this charade," Aunt Carrol said. "It was not I who sent the trousseau, but Bess March."

Neither Meg nor I realized who she meant. Both of us thought first of Beth, though we never call her Bess.

"<u>Aunt</u> March," Florence blurted with a look of triumph.

"How?" I said at the same moment Meg asked, "Why?"

Aunt Carrol leaned in, speaking in a conspiratorial tone as if Aunt March herself were in the next room. "You know my sister would rather snip out her tongue than break her word. But two and a half years is enough for even her temper to cool, and she couldn't abide the thought of not giving Meg a wedding gift after all. She selected every last napkin and pillow slip, paid the bill, and bade me sign the card."

We have been sworn to secrecy, a vow we broke within three minutes of facing the expectant faces around the supper table tonight. Jo and Beth were suitably stupefied.

"There is a soft and generous soul under that carapace," Amos said. "Perhaps one day it shall crack after all."

"Perhaps if she is boiled like a lobster," Jo muttered. A look from her father squelched any further observations.

What would it be like, I wonder, to know the Aunt March that Amos and Amy know?

May 27, 1865

Today Amos and John and Laurie took apart Meg's bed and carted it off to the Dovecote. Until the wedding, Meg will share Jo's bed. I imagine Jo will hold to her sister as tenderly as Beth cradles her invalid dolls.

Nearly everything is in its place now. I took inordinate pleasure in filling Meg's linen closet while the men pounded the bed frame together again. There is something so satisfactory in stacks and stacks of white muslin and linen and damask—as fresh and promising as the blank pages of a new diary. The fact that these sheets and tablecloths came from Aunt March only heightens my pleasure.

Small though the house is, John is determined that Meg should have someone to help her keep ahead of the dusting and mopping. A wedding gift of sorts. He told me so today, wondering if I might know a young lady willing to take on light chores a few afternoons a week. "Someone companionable," he said, "to help lessen the absence of her sisters while I am at the office."

"Lotty Hummel," I said without a moment's thought. "She is a good, capable girl, twelve years old now."

He can spare only fifty cents a week, a figure that made him grimace as he said it. It is indeed a paltry sum, even for a child. There was no question in my mind that Birte would accept the wage for her daughter; she is still in no position to turn down any kind of work, no matter how small. Nevertheless, I wanted more for Lottchen. Far be it from me to start her on the road of accepting less than she is worth at such a tender age. And then it came to me.

"Perhaps you might make up the difference with an hour or two a week of lessons?" I suggested. "In the morning or evening?"

John brightened at the word *lessons*. In half a minute, I had explained and he had agreed.

What a felicitous arrangement! Meg shall have company and help, John shall be able to continue teaching, and Lottchen shall be richest of all, filling both her pockets and her mind.

May 29, 1865

The dresses are all finished, thanks to Birte, and all of them fit. She was thrilled at the prospect of Lotty earning two dollars a month, with lessons besides.

There is one thing I have yet to do, and that is to sit down with Meg and make certain that she knows what to expect on the night of her marriage.

Thank heaven for Samuel's wife, who took me in hand before Amos and I exchanged our vows. A bride with no mother or sisters to school her is much to be pitied on her wedding night. Though with a husband as solicitous as Amos, it turned out I had nothing to fear.

I remember how tentatively Amos and I climbed into bed the night of our marriage and lay facing each other with our eyes darting nervously about. Even the small intimacy of joining our gazes suddenly seemed to overwhelm. After an excruciating silence Amos asked, in his fumbling way, if I were ready.

"I don't know," I confessed. My body felt like a horse being whipped forward and reined in all at once.

"Nor I." He held out his palm to me. I pressed mine to it, and we interlaced our fingers. That was all, that first night, and it was enough.

In the morning I found a note from Amos laid into my diary like a bookmark. *Why must we leap the precipice in a single bound,* he had written, *when we might instead lay a bridge together, one board at a time?* And so that is what we did. Slowly, gently, we learned how and when and where to touch one another.

There is between Meg and John a delight I can only call childlike. That is not to demean their affection; it is a measure of how clear and uncomplicated their love is. There is also a glint of mischief—almost naughtiness—in some of their glances that makes me wonder if they have already permitted themselves a few secret indulgences. What affianced couple does not at least entertain the idea? I certainly would have at their age, had Amos been a man of a more adventurous temperament.

May 30, 1865

Today after Meg and I made up the bed in the Dovecote with the finest of the new sheets and pillow slips, I sat down on the bed and patted the quilt beside me.

"There is a talk we should have before Saturday," I began.

Meg put on an expression that was almost indulgent. "Oh, Marmee! I've known those things since Beth and Amy were born. Father explained it all without any silliness."

Of that I have no doubt. Indeed, when Amos tried his hand at teaching primary school, his lessons on conception and birth put most of the county into an uproar.

"Of all the things your aunt Lucretia told me the day before my marriage, there are two that have remained as important as they were that first night: Give nothing that you do not wish to give. Take nothing you would not wish taken from you."

The sheer innocence with which Meg blinked back at me was both reward and remonstrance. That she has attained this age without any concept of the special violence men can do to women gave me pause. Should I be proud of that, or ashamed?

"You talk as if it should be unpleasant," she said, ruffling a bit as though I were impugning John's goodness.

"It may not be wholly pleasant at first," I acknowledged. "You may find after all that it is not so simple as your father made it sound. Be patient with yourselves. Coupling is no different from anything else in that experience is the best of teachers." She colored a little then, heightening my suspicions of clandestine kisses in the garden and the pantry.

"And remember that you have as much right and as much ability to enjoy yourself as John. Perhaps even more. There is no trace of sin in that." I blushed then. Meg tried most nobly to absorb this wisdom with solemnity, and failed. She could hide her mirth or her surprise, but not both at once.

May 31, 1865

Aunt March has summoned Meg and John to Plumfield tomorrow. Never mind all Meg has to do in these last few days—Aunt March, as usual, presumes everyone should drop everything and cater to her desires. You would think she had never been a bride herself.

"Should I thank her for the linens?" Meg wondered at supper. The very idea of facing her great-aunt rendered her too jittery to eat. (As for myself, I found Hannah's good applesauce impossible to swallow after two bites. First cider, now this. Her look as she saw me lay down my half-full spoon told me that she has not only noticed my sudden aversion to apples in all forms, but understands what it means.)

"If she wanted thanks, she ought to have signed her own name to the card," Jo observed.

"Words are not the only way to express gratitude," Amos said after such a long silence that I did not at first know what he was referring to. "Say nothing of it," he advised, "but thank her nonetheless."

Beth understood more readily than all of us. Fluent in the Delphic language of her father's thoughts, she translated the sentiment for the rest of the table. "Remember how you felt when you opened the parcel of linens?" she asked Meg. Her sister nodded, brightening a little in spite of herself at the memory of that lavish surprise. "Wear that smile, and speak in that happy voice when you say hello to Aunt March."

Amos nodded. Those two are so thoroughly in sympathy, sometimes I believe that Beth could have sprung, fully formed, from her father's forehead, just as Athena was begotten from Zeus.

June 1, 1865

Meg came home this evening bearing the pearls Aunt March has promised to the first bride ever since Meg was old enough to toddle. They came with a scolding, of course, though it seems it was a gentler one than most. Aunt March still regards the match with skepticism, but conceded that was no reason to hold back the pearls since her promise had been made without any conditions.

"When she said she never breaks her word, Aunt Carrol's secret banged so hard against the inside of my head, I thought it would burst out of my mouth," Meg said while Amy held the string of pearls up to her own neck in admiration.

I did not fully listen to their chatter, but let my Family's voices and laughter wash over me in the way of waves at the seashore. These cozy evenings shall not cease, I know that. But Jo is right. It will not be the same when Meg puts on her hood and shawl and goes out the front door instead of up the stairs to bed with all of us.

June 3, 1865

Oh, my heart. Standing alongside Amos with our elbows linked and both hands twined together as Samuel joined Meg and John in matrimony, I felt as though the sun was inside my chest, beaming out upon all those I love most. I want always to remember them, all of them, as they looked today. Together my girls are as the four points of a compass to me, with Amos for its needle.

What a joy to watch others see Meg as I have always seen her. Wreathed in flowers and smiles, blushing with pleasure, she was lovelier yet than Raphael's *La donna velata*. The entirety of this day has been one lustrous moment after another, strung together like the pearls Meg wore around her neck. If only I could have each of them printed on a stereoscopic card, to peer into whenever I wish and see the details my mind will not be able to preserve on its own. Here is what I want to remember:

~ Jo, Beth, and Amy clustered around their sister with fistfuls of lily of the valley, curling papers and tongs, laughing about the time Jo burned the ringlets off Meg's forehead.

~ My brother's eyes, so like Marmee's, and his voice, so like Father's, that I nearly cried when I opened the door and heard him say, "Hello, Meg." He is the only person yet alive who remembers me by that name.

~ Jo in her melancholy, which is in essence a measure of her love.

~ Beth, so entangled in her sister's happiness that for once she was not cowed in the least by the presence of so many people in our home.

~ Amy, suddenly a child no more. Many an eye was struck by the first beams of her radiance today.

~ Meg whirling about, calling, "The first kiss for Marmee!" as soon as Samuel pronounced them husband and wife.

And this most of all: sitting with Meg in the last moments before the ceremony began. After weeks of preparation, there was nothing left but to wait for the notes of the processional to sound from Beth's piano. I took her hand in both of mine. "Are you happy, Meg?"

She shook her head in wonderment, making the tiny white lilies in her hair tremble like silent bells. "I don't remember feeling like this ever in my life," she said. "I'd like to grab hold of John with one hand and keep the other just where it is right now." How do I find words to record the tenderness with which her hand squeezed mine then? Perhaps simply writing it down will be enough to let me resurrect that sensation, years hence, when I read these pages.

Amos may be among the least proud men upon this earth, and yet even he had a sheen about him like a freshly polished apple today. He, too, is struggling to capture the enormity of his feelings within the confines of ink and paper tonight. Again and again, his pen stills over the page. Any other day of the year, he can write three lines to every one of mine.

"The right words slip through my fingers," he confessed when he saw that I had noticed his hesitations. "*Success* and *pride* and all the rest are too trite."

"Perhaps we cannot write it until we have finished feeling it," I mused. Amos took to that notion in an instant. Down went the pen, and he settled back into his chair, eyes closed, as he does when we read aloud in the evening.

Me, though? I cannot follow my own advice. There are so many memories forming all at once that I must have another vessel to hold them before my mind spills over. I have hardly mentioned John, after all.

Calling up the image of his face when he saw his bride mists my eyes anew. John had seen Meg but ten minutes before. Her dress had not changed. There were no more flowers tucked into her crown of braids than there had been when she tied his cravat for him. But the way he looked at her as she entered the room on her father's arm snatched the breath from my throat.

John is ours now, in a way he was not before. The tie that binds him to Meg has pulled all of us more tightly into their happy knot.

"Will you call me Margaret at last, Mr. Brooke?" I teased as I congratulated them.

"I should much rather call you Mother," he said with a glint in that newly roguish eye of his. "But if you insist I shall call you Margaret instead." I gave his forearm a playful swat for his insouciance—thanking him in kind for dispensing with that last pinch of formality.

That was gift enough, but it was not all. As we were seeing them off, after the moon had risen and all the merrymakers gone home, John took my hands in his and said with an effort, "The war gave me brothers. You have given me not only a wife, but sisters and parents."

"I have always wanted a son," I told him. How I managed to say those words aloud I shall never know.

June 6, 1865

One hundred dollars. Jo has earned <u>one hundred dollars</u> for a single story! It shall be published in *Frank Leslie's Illustrated Newspaper* three months hence. I am so proud, I feel ten feet tall. No sooner has one of my girls flown from the nest but another sprouts her wings.

She sent it off weeks ago, without a word to anyone. How she withstood the suspense in the midst of all the hustle and bustle of Meg's wedding, I cannot imagine. The manuscript being in possession of the magazine, we shall all have to wait until September to read it. I have not felt such eagerness since I was a child awaiting Christmas.

Best of all, Jo insists upon spending her winnings on a vacation for Beth. "To the seaside with Marmee," she proclaimed, fluttering the check before Beth's pale face in imitation of a stiff ocean breeze.

Beth said yes and no all at once. A little rush of color flew to her cheeks, which had not faded before she tried to protest that it would be too selfish. Oh, my Beth. Somehow she has absorbed the notion that enjoyment for its own sake is a kind of sin.

Thankfully Jo would hear nothing of the sort. For all her immense differences from her sister, Jo knows Beth through and through. The words won't come right when she's thinking only of herself, she said, turning Beth's protests on their head. "So it will help me to work for you, don't you see. Besides," Jo added, "Marmee needs the change, and she won't leave you, so you must go."

My eyes darted to my lap, measuring. Has Jo guessed? Surely not. The symptoms, perhaps, but not the cause. I have not even told Amos yet.

"Grant me one favor, Jo," I said to her after the others had gone upstairs to bed. "Give Amy and Father a token of your winnings, too."

"You're as 'selfish' as Bethy," she teased.

I took her face in my hands. It was like holding the sun, the way she beamed back at me. "And you," I said, but found no words to fill that space. "You," I said again, underlining it with affection. Her eyes watered brightly, and I swiped the tears away with my thumbs. She is fast becoming the kind of woman I wished to be when I was a child—a kind of woman I did not know existed outside of my own imaginings.

She darted forward and kissed my cheek, then put on her jolly voice. "Father's easy enough," she allowed. "Nothing but a book will do for him. But what can I give Amy that Aunt March hasn't already?" she scoffed.

"What you give Amy hardly matters at all," I told her. "You only need show her that she matters to you." We were likely thinking of the same thing, then: Jo's long-ago burned manuscript. Jo half smiled. The wound that had seemed marrow deep at the time has healed into a scar so small, it is barely perceptible. A pert little nod from Jo told me my wish would shortly be granted.

June 7, 1865

First thing this morning Jo bustled off to town and came back with two brown paper bundles tied up in white ribbon.

The thicker of the two she presented to Amos—a newly printed collection of our dear Mr. Thoreau's letters. Amy's parcel was thinner and broader. She tore away the wrappings to expose a sketchbook. On the inner flap, Jo had written, *To Amy, who relishes and fears a blank page as much as I do. Your Jo.*

I don't know who among us was the more pleased.

June 10, 1865

Beth and I leave for Swampscott tomorrow.

There is nowhere else I can confess this: I am a trifle daunted by the prospect of three weeks away. Three weeks without the relief rooms and wards of convalescing soldiers. Three weeks further yet from Meg, whose absence is still so new that it throbs unexpectedly. And the others—Amos and Jo and Amy and Hannah will hardly have become accustomed to the hole Meg has left behind before Beth and I will widen it.

Am I capable of simply sitting at the seaside, with nothing but the waves and the gulls to occupy me? In twenty-three years I have never desired a vacation. Relief from some particular task or vexation, yes, certainly. The chance to see another part of the world entices me as much as it does Jo. But solely for leisure? God has given us one day each week for that, and it has rarely left me wanting.

Of course I will go. Jo must not be disappointed, and Beth must not be denied this opportunity.

June 12, 1865

Swampscott puts me in mind of Duxbury, perched along the coast as it is. I cannot help but enjoy it here. I put more books than dresses into my traveling bag, and thus the specter of idleness does not haunt me as I feared it would. Our lodgings are comfortable, and the proprietress, Mrs. Cox, so warm and welcoming she might well be Hannah's double in all but looks. She offered us everything from a late lunch to an early supper, but our picnic hamper still being half full of Hannah's cold chicken and cheese and pears, we declined.

"Bless you," Mrs. Cox said in a great gust of relief. "Everything is topsy-turvy in the kitchen. The neighbor's cat dropped a litter of kittens under the icebox this morning. Eleven of them, can you imagine?"

What more perfect thing could she have said than that? Beth, who had been keeping herself just behind my elbow, slipped out of my shadow and offered herself to Mrs. Cox as a feline nurse. Before we had unpacked, she was on her hands and knees on the kitchen floor, coaxing the mother and her brood from the dark and damp corner to a warm nest beside the hearth. It required just as much effort for me to lure Beth from the kitchen and out to the shore.

It has been too long since I last saw the sea. The rolling of the waves has the steadiness of a heartbeat. Ostensibly we are here for the air, but I find the sound of the ocean more rejuvenating than anything else. We sleep with the windows wide open so that the rhythm of the waves may caress us all night long.

June 15, 1865

Two of the kittens died in the night. Beth is resolved that no more shall perish. Mrs. Cox has given her exclusive charge over the biggest of the litter, an orange brute who has been bullying his smallest siblings away from the teats. Fergus, Beth has called him. I do not see how he can possibly live without his mother, but as Beth says, that is no reason not to try.

June 18, 1865

Fergus insists upon living. For the first two days Beth kept him tucked into her bodice, cupped against her heart for warmth, feeding him from a twist of cotton soaked in milk. She would not leave the room, but sat reading in the sunny window seat, looking as contented as ever I have seen her. Joanna sits propped on the windowsill.

Nearly seventeen years old, and she packed Joanna as if the doll were as essential as stockings or a toothbrush. And yet it was because of Joanna's implicit companionship that I felt I could leave Beth to her own devices and come down to the shore with nothing but my journal for company.

For the longest time I sat with the wind riffling the blank pages, content to simply <u>be</u>. The only time I can recall experiencing something of this nature is after each of the girls were born. Each time I accomplished that monumental task, there came a comfortable lull of mind and body.

Amos meditates in silence and stillness, a feat I never could master. He closes his eyes and breathes like a man asleep, and somehow this brushes his mind clean. Every attempt I have made at that results in the opposite effect—all my thoughts vying for attention at once. But here, I find that the sounds and movements of the sea and the birds fill my mind with a vast openness that mimics the ocean itself.

This is as near to carefree as I have been in more years than I can count. No tasks tug at me. No one to tend to but myself. My thoughts, when they come, arrive softly, and one at a time. When have I had so much time for pure contemplation? Likely not since childhood.

What profession would I have chosen if not for the impediment of my sex, I find myself wondering today. Had the world lain open before me, which path would I have chosen for my own? No answer is forthcoming. Such fantasies can occur only if I imagine myself a man. Otherwise I must construct an entire world around myself—a world with spaces for women outside of kitchens, schoolrooms, and hospitals.

Man or woman, there is no name for my avocation. Not nurse or teacher. Not even philanthropist, though it combines elements of all three. Advocate is the nearest I can come. Since I was a child, it is what I have done, from waging a campaign for my own education to pledging myself to abolition's cause.

But now? Emancipation is a reality. The war is over. Where am I to direct my energies?

June 19, 1865

Poverty, of course. *For the poor always ye have with you,* Christ said in the Book of John. I believe it is the only matter upon which I disagree with Him, and I disagree most fervently. Poverty is <u>not</u> inevitable.

Yet it is not The Poor I want to aid, as if they are some great mass of misfortune. Relieving hunger and cold only nicks the surface. Ensuring that everyone has what they need to simply survive is not enough for me. A starving child cannot learn, and yet I take more pride in arranging for Lottchen's lessons with John than I do in the milk and firewood we shared with the Hummels on that Christmas morning when Karl came knocking.

Adelaide Weddleton's voice sounds in my memory; what was it she said to me that last time I saw her? I was so intent on preserving her essence in my mind that day that the words themselves have blurred. *A rare affinity for your brothers and sisters in humanity . . . strive to find for them what they most need.* Had I the means, I would do nothing else.

June 21, 1865

Yesterday I insisted that Beth come down to the ocean with me. Kitten or no kitten, we could not very well go home and tell Jo that Beth spent her entire seaside sojourn alone in our room.

Thus, Hannah's hamper has been converted into a nest of toweling and hot flatirons, which accompanies us to the shore so that Beth may feed Fergus at the necessary intervals. With the help of a glass pipette from the local druggist's shop she serves him droplet by droplet. Her patience would awe a saint. Joanna is in the basket as well—for company, Beth says—and indeed when we peek beneath the lid Fergus is curled up against his wooden mother more often than not.

I have not been alone with any of my girls for such a stretch of time since Meg was an infant. For as long as I have been a mother, I have looked on my children as though they are each a single piece of the mosaic that forms our Family. And that is so, but it is also so that each of them is a mosaic unto herself. Away from the glow of her sisters, every facet of Beth shines brighter. She is not different, only more intensely herself. Perhaps we have been wrong to worry ourselves over her health. What if what we have perceived as a shadow falling over her is no such thing? Beth may simply be a steadfast star, visible only when lamps and candles have been doused.

Yesterday evening, Beth played two hymns on the piano in Mrs. Cox's parlor before we retired for the night. In addition to Mrs. Cox and me, there was an elderly gentleman present. Perhaps he reminded Beth of Mr. Laurence. "At home we always have music before bed," she explained to Mrs. Cox. I said nothing of her performance for fear that drawing attention to it would reawaken her self-consciousness.

The more I ponder it, the more I gravitate toward the notion that she is braver here because no one in Swampscott knows Beth March as the shy March sister.

June 25, 1865

Two weeks away and I am not the least bit homesick. All day long, Beth and I read or walk beside the shore. Sometimes we sit, doing no more than watch the peeping sand birds skitter along the water's edge. Twice now I have considered telling Beth of the child to come. It seems very nearly dishonest to let her think these peaceful seaside reveries are shared solely by the two of us. Both times I have resisted. These moments belong to Beth, and they should not be shadowed by another sibling. There is opportunity enough for that at home the other fifty weeks of the year. When I look back upon these days, I want only to remember this little oasis Beth and I formed of ourselves.

Never would I have predicted that so little activity and so few people could be so pleasurable. Always, I have been the one left behind when Amos was called to war, or to lecture on abolition. It is different, being the one who is away. The awareness of the separation is not so sharp.

And Beth, who has never been away from home in her life, shows no sign of distress. Now and then she sees something pretty in a shop window and remarks that Meg would like it. "I wish Amy were here to paint this," she sometimes says of the gulls and the light upon the water. It is not loneliness, only the pleasantly wistful remark of one who is accustomed to sharing her small joys with her sisters.

This morning while Beth was tending to Fergus, I slipped away downtown and bought her some new music. Stephen Foster's last song is chief among them.

June 26, 1865 ∼

Beth's seventeenth birthday.

I whispered the fact to Mrs. Cox last evening and asked her to place the packet I had bought under Beth's breakfast plate. This morning her plate was ringed with a twist of crocheted lace and surmounted by a bowl of plump cherries, strawberries, and raspberries.

Mrs. Cox's other guests applauded softly when Beth sat down, and before my very eyes she blushed and gave a little curtsey instead of shrinking up like a turtle without its shell. They hardly know her, and yet they are already fond of her. She has the gentlest sort of power over people, which she wields without any knowledge of it.

In the evening she sat at the piano with her new songs, silently practicing. I have never seen her do such a thing. Her fingers skimmed the keys without sounding any notes. After half an hour, the tune of "Beautiful Dreamer" began to waft softly through the room.

"Do you think Hannah misses me?" Beth asked tonight as we sat on either corner of the window seat, looking out at the stars.

"I should think so," I answered. "She's never been a day without you."

"I'm glad," Beth said, "for I miss her, too, and that makes it nicer."

I have always been the first to say that Beth is more like her father than anyone, in temperament. There is not a soul who would deny it. The depth of her sense of fairness, though, and her irresistible pull toward those with less than she? Seeing those qualities emerge more and more strongly is like looking in a mirror.

June 28, 1865

An image from Meg's wedding day, one I have not put to paper before, insists upon resurfacing in my mind these last few days: Laurie. Laurie looking at Jo while Meg and John pronounced their vows. She might have been the bride, the way his eyes were fixed upon her.

I cannot make up my mind what to think of it.

That is not true. I know perfectly well what to make of it, and it makes me uneasy, for Laurie is plainly envisioning Jo wreathed in orange blossoms, while Jo cannot even comprehend her sister's marriage, much less entertain the thought of a husband for herself.

I should like to put the whole thing out of my head. Three days of this seaside sojourn remain, and I do not wish to cloud them by brooding on futures that lie outside of my hands. Not when the present is so worthy of savoring.

July 1, 1865

We spent the whole of the day watching the sandpipers. "My birds," Beth calls them. I have thought the very same of them. They are so cheerful and so intent upon their business, so leery of the waves, yet always skittering so near to the surf.

Mrs. Cox has offered Fergus to Beth, to keep. I could not say no. He is still too small to be without a mother, and Beth is the only mother he knows. We have resolved to take him home to Meg, to discourage any mice from taking up residence in the Dovecote.

I shall be sorry to leave tomorrow. This trip has done me nearly as much good as Beth. I feel as if my mind has been washed and rinsed and hung up in the sun to dry.

July 2, 1865

Home has never seemed so fresh and new. Hannah looks as if she has had a vacation, which, I suppose, she has, what with half of us away. Beth hardly knew who to embrace first.

How Hannah yelped when she opened the hamper and found Fergus asleep inside with Joanna! We both had forgotten.

A trace of disappointment clouded Jo's eyes when she loosened her embrace on Beth enough to stand back and look at her. I bit my lip and prayed Beth did not see it, too. The thought of disappointing her sister would be as hazardous to Beth as sickness. Jo had likely hoped that Swampscott would be a sort of magic wand for Beth, and while it certainly put a bit of shine back into her eyes, it has not turned back the clock to 1862.

"I declare, I feel ten years younger," I told Jo. That pleased her.

But even I deflated somewhat to see Beth alongside Amy and Jo. The gains I perceived in Swampscott suddenly receded in comparison. After three weeks in the company of invalids and elderly sightseers, it is almost a shock to see how much vivacity radiates from healthy young people. Though Beth's flame burns brighter than before, the difference between her and her sisters remains like that between a match and a lamp. With the realization a momentary fear, hardly more than a shimmer, passed over me and then retreated as Amy exclaimed, "Oh, Beth, I shall need all new colors to paint you!"

Amy is right. There <u>is</u> more color in Beth's cheeks again, even if it has not the vividness that would put all our minds at ease. Likewise, the heartiness Beth has acquired may be more of spirit than of body. But perhaps the one may help to fuel the other. And perhaps it is too soon to judge. Four hours in the carriage home was enough to leave both Beth and me weary and wincing, after all. Didn't every sign of her fatigue vanish at the sight of our Family gathered at the gate to welcome us back?

As for me, those eager faces and the happy storm they stirred within my breast carried me straight back to Adelaide Weddleton and the last thing she said to me: *If love alone were enough to sustain a life* . . . If that were so, no infirmity could come within an ocean of Beth.

July 3, 1865

Seeing Meg in her own little house is nearly like meeting her for the first time. She and John are quite the pair of turtledoves. The Dovecote is cozier and brighter yet than it was before the wedding, lit as it is with their happiness.

John's hearty "Welcome back, Mother!" warmed me as much as Meg's embrace. I shall never tire of him calling me that.

July 6, 1865

All eight of the accused conspirators have been found guilty in the murder of the president. Four of them are to hang tomorrow, including the woman.

"Thus it is that the murder of one of the most merciful men this world has known will be avenged by the death of four human beings," Amos said with a sigh as he laid the newspaper upon the table, "and the imprisonment of four more. I cannot see the use of it. Men who are willing to perpetrate such crimes have already committed themselves to the possibility of sacrificing their lives for their convictions. No matter their earthly flaws, they will die martyrs to their cause, as Mr. Lincoln himself did."

All five of us regarded him with some surprise. It is rare for Amos to say so much at once, outside of his pulpit.

For near to thirty minutes he argued in his placid way with Jo and Amy and even Meg over the magnitude of the punishment while they countered with the magnitude of the crime. Amy debated most ably of all, firmly entrenching herself in the letter of the law, which leaves no room for doubt. "Every participant in a conspiracy is to be punished as though his finger were upon the trigger," she insisted in eight different ways.

"What do you say, Marmee?" she demanded at last, her question flung out like a desperate little stab. I know what she expected. Justice. Of all my children, she is the one who has inherited in full measure my tendency to be inflamed by unfairness.

"They are so young," I said. All but two of them—Mrs. Surratt and a theater hand—are ten or more years younger than I. "Yet 'justice' consigns them to the rubbish bin. After the bloodshed of these last four years, I would rather give them a chance for redemption than see justice served."

Her brow furrowed. To her credit, she did her best not to scowl. Tomorrow in the Family post she shall find a note which will likely vex her as much as it soothes her:

Dear Amy,
   You are no more wrong than your father. Where he is sage and pensive, you are young and zealous—two qualities that can shake the world, as Mr. Booth and his compatriots have all too vividly proven. In your hands, however, I have no doubt that youth and zeal will make this world a fairer and more beautiful place for us all.
                                        Your loving Marmee

July 10, 1865

Another small triumph for Jo—of the two stories she wrote while Beth and I were away, one has already sold.

"The butcher's bill is paid," she crowed, slapping a gold double eagle onto the kitchen table, "with all of that left over besides!"

Twenty dollars. Aside from ink and paper, she refuses to buy a thing for herself. "It is for Marmee to decide," she says in that tone which brooks no bargaining. There are dozens of trifling expenses I could choose from. A coin like this almost demands something more, something to stand as a trophy for Jo's efforts. The weight of it is like a stone in my palm. Were I to put it in my pocket, I would walk lopsided.

That is it. Oh, that is it! Hannah's apron has but one pocket. When I think of the weeks during the war that she left her wages untouched so that we all might eat more heartily, or add another log to the fire, I am sure there is no better place for Jo's earnings than in Hannah's hands.

July 11, 1865

Jo has consented to my plan, and quite readily. Tonight, after Hannah has retired, I shall slip the double eagle into her apron pocket. Jo and I have resolved to wake before sunrise and sit on the back steps so that we may hear her discovery.

July 12, 1865

What a quiet flurry came up out of the kitchen this morning. First the shuffling of Hannah's feet across the flagstones, then the usual humming and murmuring to herself. The murmuring trailed off, and Jo and I looked at each other and then quickly away before anticipation made us giggle like children. Then came a sharp breath and a little cry, all at the same time.

"Mrs. March, you shouldn't!" That is what she would have said, if I had let her.

"It amounts to less than a dollar a year since you have been with us," I argued before she could locate her voice and remember how to use it. "If I had twenty-two of these coins to give you, it would still not be equal to what you have done for our Family."

"I shan't ever spend it," she declared.

"It is yours," I returned. "Spend it or not, as you see fit, so long as you remember that you are worth infinitely more than we shall ever be able to afford."

July 19, 1865

I have miscarried.

Hannah sits with me, as she has both of the times before this. Until today, she was the only one who knew. This time was more sudden, more painful than the previous two. I am fortunate it did not happen while Beth and I were away.

A tendril of something like guilt encircles my heart. I never truly reveled in the thought of this child's coming. Bewildered, more like, and preoccupied with the preparations for Meg and John's wedding. I know enough of anatomy and physiology to know my heart is not at fault for the workings of my womb. And yet I wonder, did I ever make this small bud of a child welcome? Would its brief existence have been different if I had?

"I thought of it like a parcel instead of a living thing," I told Hannah as I lay weathering the cramps. "One day it would arrive and I would open it up and find an infant inside, like a doll sent through the mail. It might have been a son—" My voice caught. I could say no more. Hannah handed me one of her supply of clean rags for my tears.

"There, now," she said, stroking the back of my hand. "I know that feeling right enough. It's never left me. But in time it's turned transparent, you might say."

"Like looking through a veil instead of at it?" I mused with a wince at a fleeting pain.

"Very like that, indeed."

I motioned for another rag, this time to sop the fresh rivulet of blood that suddenly warmed my thighs. "This shall be the last child I carry," I said. "I am resolved of that."

Hannah's eyebrows lifted a fraction of an inch. I could hear the words she did not say: *And what will Mr. March think about that?*

I have no need for worry on that score. Amos has the self-discipline to join the Shakers; I have always relished the pleasures of the flesh more fully than he.

July 20, 1865

Amos has agreed, as I knew he would. "No man has sovereignty over the body of another, be they male, female, black, or white," he said with one of his sage nods. To hear him say so, to assent without hesitation—it is enough to say that my heart might be made of butter, the way his unfaltering solicitude softens me.

"When my monthly courses have ceased for good, we may be free with our physical affections once more," I told him, settling back into his embrace. "For now, it is blessing enough to simply savor one another's presence." In the almost three years since his safe return to us, my thankfulness has not abated. Amos's time at war has not and never will leave me. Having him here—whether he is shut up in his study pondering the next Sunday's sermon or out philosophizing to the trees and streams—is like being at anchor. No matter how the wind may blow or the seas swell, the vessel that is our Family rocks gently, steadily. I have been to the brink of widowhood and back. It is a territory I pray I shall never set foot on again.

July 21, 1865

The girls bring such sweetness to my bedside. They approached like timid children, so unaccustomed to seeing me prostrated by anything. The times before, we did not tell them. They were too small to understand the loss of a brother or sister who did not yet exist. It is possible that Meg and Jo do not even recall the days I spent in bed in 1847 and 1851.

I might almost have been a stranger, the way they looked at me. No, that is not it. They looked as if they feared not recognizing me. Their apprehension took me back to the doorway of my own marmee's bedroom and how often I used to hesitate there, wondering how much of her the sickness had consumed since I last saw her, even if it had only been hours. I held out my hand the way she used to, beckoning.

Beth came first, tugging Jo along. Then Meg, and last of all, Amy.

As they clustered to my side for kisses and condolences, Jo bumped the work basket dangling from Meg's elbow and a yowl erupted from its flaps. Up popped an orange head. "Fergus!" Beth exclaimed. All self-consciousness vanished in the laughter and scolding that followed. Everyone's but Amy's.

"Let me watch you draw," I told her, patting Amos's side of the bed. She obeyed, and the movement of her pencil quickly soothed us both as she sketched her sisters—Meg darning John's socks, Jo reading aloud, and Beth endlessly smoothing Fergus's whiskers.

For two days I have pondered and grieved over what I have lost. Here before me are four reminders of all that I still have. It does not erase the loss. There shall forever be a notch in my heart where my affection for this child would have taken root. But it shall not be at the center—not as long as my daughters' faces are within my sight.

Our Family is complete. I feel sure of that now.

July 27, 1865

Such a kind welcome back to the relief rooms today. "We can hardly manage without you, Mrs. March," Mrs. King said. Close to a dozen heads bobbed in agreement—even Harriet Weddleton's. I had only to say that I had been unwell for several faces to soften with understanding. Their mute sympathy saturated the air around me.

Some of the people who came seeking help also acknowledged my return with welcoming nods. I, too, come to this place for relief, I realized as I nodded in return. It has become my second home.

August 4, 1865

Meg's currant bushes are picked bare, and there is not a pot of jelly to be seen in her pantry. "Oh," she replied airily when I asked, "I made a mess of it. I'll try again next year." That was all she would consent to say. As Meg shrugged, she and John exchanged a twinkling look like two conspiring schoolchildren.

"What are you two up to?" I asked.

"Not a thing, Mother," John said, the picture of innocence. But I detected a passing crinkle on Lotty's brow that had nothing to do with the geometry exercise on the slate before her.

August 6, 1865

I have gotten the whole story of the currant jelly from Lotty. I ought to have let Meg and John have their secrets, but my curiosity squirmed until I could stand it no longer. After church today I paid a call on the Hummels. And what did I see on Birte's kitchen shelves but four dozen empty jelly pots! Lotty had carted them all home to her mother—"Master's orders," she said, for mistress never wanted to see them again.

Three batches in a row Meg tried, and none of it would jell. When John came home, bringing an unannounced friend for dinner, she and the kitchen both were in a state beyond repair—awash in sobs and trickles of sticky red syrup. And John, hearing what the matter was, laughed. Roared, more like. He might better have thrown water on a grease fire. Lotty did not tell me that, but I know my Meg. When she is vexed, no child can cry more tempestuously. Meg retreated upstairs, the men scraped together some kind of a dinner, and Lotty put the kitchen to rights again.

How the matter was resolved between the master and the mistress of the house no one but Meg and John know, but all is mended.

Oh, how Hannah and I laughed when I told her what had happened! I had not meant to, but once started the image of it became so comical that we could not help ourselves.

"That pitiful kitchen must have looked like a murder scene in one of Jo's stories," I said.

"The poor thing!" Hannah gasped when we had at last begun to get hold of ourselves. "And I might have saved it all with a few table-spoons of lemon juice."

It is a regretful waste. All those berries, and no less than half a barrel of sugar, surely! I am proud of Meg, nonetheless. There is a streak of self-reliance in her, after all.

September 20, 1865

Laurie is off to Harvard—a sophomore now. Between Jo and me, I cannot say who envies him more.

September 15, 1865

At last, Jo's prize-winning story is in our hands. Amos returned from town with an armful of *Frank Leslie's Illustrated*—one apiece for each of us, as well as Mr. Laurence and Aunt March.

A blood and thunder tale, Jo calls it. An apt description, if the pounding of my heart at the conclusion is any indication. She fairly harpoons your attention at the very first sentence and never allows the tension of the line to slacken.

All of us heaped her with praise. And then Jo looked to her father with a question on her face. I half suppose she knew what he was going to say.

"You can do better than this, Jo," Amos told her with a kindly shake of his head. "Aim at the highest, and never mind the money."

Oh, for the love of heaven. Of course he is correct, but as ever, he forgets that a brain needs fuel to work, and that keeping it sufficiently warm and fed to produce such lofty thoughts costs money. Would his sermons be half so eloquent if his mind had to make room for thoughts of groceries, firewood, and shoe leather? I have my doubts.

Any woman with the ability to make her way in the world ought to do so, and with no compunctions. Ideals are a fine thing, but they do not pay rent or put food on the table. At the first opportunity I shall take Jo aside and tell her so. A young woman who so values her independence is better off writing entertainments that will pay her bills than pondering whether her work will one day stand alongside the likes of Shelley and Stowe.

October 16, 1865

Another of Jo's stories has sold at an exorbitant rate. She insists we are to have a new carpet laid in the parlor and hall. To protest would only be to disappoint her. For all that Jo herself eschews luxury, it gives her great satisfaction to dote upon us. "You see to the poor, Marmee," she chirped, "and I'll see to you."

As for myself, I am as proud as I am envious of her ability to earn her own way.

October 27, 1865

My Meg is pregnant. Or so it would seem. Her courses, which have rarely been more than a day late before, are now nearly two weeks behind.

"Could it be?" she asked me. "Already?" she added, her eyes darting bashfully away from mine.

I laughed. "Of course it can," I said. "I have known far more zealous couples." Indeed, Amos and I managed to conceive within the first six weeks of our marriage.

She wondered when to tell John. Having lost three of my own before I had need to loosen my corset laces, I began to advise against it. Meg gasped.

"Marmee!" she exclaimed, grasping my hand. "Three?"

I hadn't meant to frighten her. As it turned out, I had not—her first reaction was wonder rather than fear. "To think, there might have been seven of us," she said. "Seven." She said the number as if it were one hundred. It does make me wonder. My girls are as different as earth, fire, wind, and water. What elements would have been left for another son or daughter to claim as their own?

Meg and I have resolved to keep this secret between us until she feels the quickening. I have told her the signs to be wary of, and to send Lotty for Hannah or me straightaway.

October 30, 1865

The new carpet has come. It is lovely stuff, in shades of navy and wine, and so thick that I must be wary each time I step into the parlor or hall, lest I stumble over the unaccustomed height of it.

"Even if you did," Amy said, "it couldn't hurt you any more than landing in a featherbed."

Amos said nothing of it. He is as oblivious to what is under his feet as he is to the rest of the world outside of whatever book has lately captivated him. Jo's pride, however, was impossible to miss, even for Amos. He walked the length of the hall without ever look-ing down, stopped in front of Jo, who stood surveying the carpet with a look as proprietary as if she had woven it herself, and kissed her forehead. Then he turned right around again and vanished into his study.

November 17, 1865

Meg is looking perfectly dreadful these last few days. Paler yet than Beth, with an inward expression that makes me uneasy. She has come to supper the last two nights in a row—alone. When Amos asked where John was, Meg said only, "Working."

It is not in her nature to lie. Nevertheless, I have the distinct im-pression that a significant portion of the truth was not forthcoming. That and a lackluster appetite have me worried.

November 19, 1865

The trouble is not Meg's health at all. I am nearly sure of that. From the minute John and Meg arrived for our customary Sunday dinner together it was abundantly clear that whatever is the matter is not confined to Meg alone.

The tension between them—no, that is not the right word. It is not tension at all, but a slackening. John is so downcast and Meg so discomfited that the very air around them seems to droop in their presence. Both of them ate little and said less. If I didn't know better I would say they are grieving something.

For the first time, all of us breathed a sigh of relief when they had gone. Jo and Beth and Amy scurried off, eager to busy themselves elsewhere before a word could be said about it. Hannah, too. I followed Amos into his study.

"A spat?" Amos wondered as I closed the door behind me.

"So it would seem," I agreed. "Has John said anything to you?" Amos shook his head. "Nor Meg to me." Having advised them not to "run to Mother" with their every difficulty, I can hardly inquire. We shall simply have to wait and see what comes of this.

November 21, 1865

The great mystery is solved. Of all the things I ought to have guessed, this one had not so much as crossed my mind. The inevitable has at last occurred in the Brooke household. Meg has gone and bought herself twenty yards of violet silk with fifty dollars that does not exist.

Fifty dollars!

Her reasoning is that of a child. With her New Year's gift from Aunt March just around the corner, "only" twenty-five dollars had to come from the household accounts. I refrained from asking her how she will pay back the money Sallie Moffat loaned her to make up the difference if Aunt March fails to wake some morning between now and January.

Oh, how I would like to shake Meg! Thanks to her needless extravagance, John has had to countermand his order for a new greatcoat.

That is what brought her to our doorstep this morning, so distraught that I feared her pregnancy had failed. If that wasn't enough, she has wounded John with a careless remark about how tired she is of being poor. Poor, for heaven's sake.

Meg is more contrite than I have ever seen her, but I must say here, if nowhere else, that I find it something of a chore to scrounge up any real pity for her. After twenty-three years of marriage to a man who considers money as having no more consequence than fieldstones, my sympathies are thoroughly with John. I know precisely how it feels to walk through Concord with Meg as she eyes others' dresses and bonnets. Covetousness emanates from her like too-sweet perfume when she spies some fancy beyond the reach of her pocketbook. Even as she sniffled and whimpered on my sofa, I half wanted to march into town and apologize to John for raising a daughter who could so thoroughly mismatch the value of things.

In retrospect, I think now that it was a mistake, shielding the children from the hardship their father's indifference to money caused me. John tries so hard, and is so conscious of all he cannot give to Meg. What a difference that would have made to me in the leanest of our years. Instead, I was plagued incessantly by a problem that was invisible to Amos. Unlike John Brooke, Amos is a man oblivious not only to the scarcities in our pantry and clothes closets, but the cause of them.

Perhaps if she would spend some time in the relief rooms instead of gadding about in the shops with Sallie Moffatt, Meg would not fancy herself so "poor." She and John lack for nothing of consequence; it is only by comparison that she is able to conjure up this feeling of deprivation. Only the thought of John shivering through the winter for the sake of her vanity has at last opened her eyes to reality.

Between us we worked out a plan to set things back to rights. Meg will ask Sallie to buy the silk from her as a favor, and Meg will put the fifty dollars toward John's coat. Meg's week of distress dissolved in an instant. I wish I could say the same for myself. As always my ire, once roused, cannot be doused but insists instead upon burning every scrap of fuel it can unearth, no matter how old.

Tonight after supper, Amos noticed me brooding before the fire. "My dearest," he asked, "what troubles you?" And I could not tell him. How could I, when my anger toward Meg is tangled together with my age-old frustrations with him? He in his infinite kindness has never meant to cause me distress, and yet he has. He has. For years on end. Our debts are dwindling now, with Meg gone from our household and Jo's stories earning more than Aunt March ever deigned to pay her. And yet that easing of our purse strings only serves to accentuate the tautness with which I have held myself all this time. With each incremental loosening of the knot, the more I resent the old rigidity I thought I had convinced myself not to mind.

Amos came and sat beside me, put his arm around me, eased my cheek to his shoulder. Met with such gentleness, I could not help but cry a little. Hot, silent tears. The tears I least want to shed always burn the most. Amos stroked my cheek, saying nothing. And I calmed, as I always do. How is it that he can absorb my tempests, even when he is the cause of them?

It is not fair to blame Amos for our years of financial strain. It was my temper, after all, that doubled our losses. How it has galled me all these years that no opportunity existed for _me_ to recoup the very losses I was responsible for. With my two strong hands and a stout heart, I would willingly have worked to give our daughters the comforts they lacked, and Hannah the wages she deserved. Instead I was mired in impotence, watching as my girls envied other girls, and Hannah worked harder only to receive less. And through it all Amos lectured and studied and preached with no regard for pay, for he was doing the Lord's work and trusting in Him with the faith of a child to provide for his Family.

A punishment. That is how I have persisted in seeing it, despite all evidence to the contrary. It has only ever been Amos being Amos. If there be any punishment in this it is of my own making, for I am the only one who has not forgiven Margaret March.

December 17, 1865

Meg has felt the quickening. It is unaccountably early, but her description—"as if a goldfish had flicked its fin"—leaves room for no other possibility.

I do believe I saw it happen. We all sat squeezed around the table at the Dovecote after supper, when suddenly Meg blinked and sat up a quarter of an inch straighter. Had I not been seated directly across from her, had I not happened to be reaching for the cream that sat just in front of her, I would have missed it. Her hand dropped to her lap and her expression went completely elsewhere for the count of a breath.

Later, as we wiped and dried the dishes together, she whispered it to me.

December 25, 1865

If any Christmas can come close to rivaling the year Amos came home from war, it is this one. That was a year of riches upon which no price could be placed. This year has its own kind of bounty.

Here we are. All of us together, with the promise of another yet to join us in the year to come.

When Meg and John arrived, I knew at once that Meg had told him. He looked like a man who had just stepped off a carousel. Giddy and dizzied, and perhaps the slightest bit nauseous. We did not even let him get the news out before congratulating him.

"My wife," he said with a look at Meg that told every one of us what he was about to say. "My wife has given me the greatest gift of all," he began again, and such a clamor of hurrahs and exclamations erupted that his words were drowned in good cheer.

Meg wore a sweet string of salmon-colored coral around her neck, her Christmas gift from John. Somehow he managed to find a strand just the shade of pink that colors her cheeks when she blushes, and the effect is infinitely more becoming than Aunt March's pearls. All day long, Meg's fingers stole up to stroke the smooth little beads at her throat and smile to herself.

Jo presented each of the ladies with ten yards of fine merino for a new winter dress—lilac for Meg, a rich burgundy for Beth, and Prussian blue for Amy. Mine is a shade of periwinkle that looks as if it has been spun out of aster petals. And Hannah, too, has yards of sage green.

What a Christmas table we had this year! The fattest of all the turkeys in Concord, and a tower of pears, apples, oranges, and dates, besides. Hannah's fruitcake was so studded with currants, raisins, apricots, cherries, and candied citrus that each slice was bright as a pane of stained glass.

"Three cheers for 'The Curse of the Coventrys,'" Amy proposed with her glass of elderberry cordial held aloft and a grin for Jo. Jo looked nearly as proud as John, for it is thanks to her latest story that we can indulge in such opulence. Her children may be made of India ink and paper, but there is no denying the gratification they bring her. If they feed her heart as well as her pocketbook, perhaps she may one day be as content as I.

January 7, 1866

With the exception of Christmas, we have hardly seen Jo in weeks. She leaves the garret only to eat, sleep, and fetch more paper from downtown. Stacks and stacks of paper. It is not stories, this time, but a novel. She is either crumpling up twice as many pages as she writes, or this book is to be the size of the Old Testament.

This evening I sat paging backward through last year's diary before committing it to its place on the shelf alongside the others. Amidst the earliest pages of spring, I came across a bloodroot blossom pressed between the pages. From one of Laurie's nosegays, of course.

Its slender white petals were nearly translucent. A smudge of pollen yellowed the facing page. How I miss my black-haired crow and his offerings, now that he is at school and preoccupied with the young ladies of Cambridge.

January 10, 1866

Winter is taking its toll on Beth. The cold stiffens her knuckles, and her knees twitch now and again with little bolts of pain. Twinges, she calls them. What color there is in her cheeks this last week is thanks to a fever so diminutive it rarely registers as much as one hundred degrees.

It is not worth consulting Dr. Bangs. Amos and I both agree on that. And yet I feel as if there is a sliver, hardly wider than a hair, lodged in me. Most days I am not aware it is there at all, it is so slight. But if something should happen to brush against it, no matter how gently, the throb is so sharp and so fast, it is all I can do not to gasp aloud.

January 16, 1866

Jo's novel is done. Not only done, but copied out four times over. It is a wonder her hand still functions. Three manuscripts are to be dispatched to publishers in Boston this very afternoon.

January 22, 1866

John has declared that Meg must have a servant now. Not just Lotty, but someone to do all the cooking. In his zeal to spare her physically, she may languish from pure boredom.

Where he will find the money to pay a cook, I cannot imagine, but I suppose that end of it is none of my affair. My task is solely to procure a likely candidate.

A woman I have seen at the relief rooms comes to mind. About thirty or thirty-five, I'd say, with two daughters that look to be younger than Lotty Hummel. Those girls ought to be in school by now; I fear they will soon be pressed into service of some kind or another if their mother does not find work enough to feed them.

Tomorrow I shall inquire of Mrs. King.

January 23, 1866

Mrs. King knew the woman I meant right away.

"Kitty Neal," she said without hesitation. "She is lately arrived from Louisville. Her husband was killed at Jonesborough during the siege of Atlanta. To hear her tell it, his relations turned her out for no reason in the world. The relatives in Boston she had hoped would shelter her here would not take her in. Only the children were welcome, and she refused to leave them."

"What of her husband's pension?"

Mrs. King lowered her voice. "Mr. Neal did not fight on the Union side."

Irish, and a Confederate widow. Two marks against her. I cannot help but be reminded of Hannah, who could not seek refuge with her own family. If I can help bring a woman out of parallel straits, I would rather do that than hire the finest chef in Boston.

January 25, 1866

I cannot make up my mind what to think of Kitty Neal. She eyed me with a good deal of dubiety when answering my knock.

"My name is Margaret March," I said. "Mrs. King at the relief rooms gave me your address."

"Ah," she said. "The inspection."

I hastily explained that was not it at all, that I had come to offer her a job. Her manner changed as if it were on a pendulum. "Please excuse the state of the place," she said. "Leave your rooms too dirty and some'll say you're not deserving of the relief. No self-respect, see? Starch your apron and scrub the dust out from between the floorboards and others'll decide you're not desperate enough for it. I try to keep us smack in the middle."

The room was not terribly different from the Hummels' when I first encountered it. Two beds, a table, a stove. Not so cramped, nor so disheveled, but decidedly untidy. Other people's laundry was strewn about in heaps. One of the girls ironed a petticoat on the kitchen table while the other sat on a bed folding a small mountain of stockings and drawers. They were so close in age, I could not be sure which one was the older.

Something about the place turned me inexplicably formal. "My son-in-law desires a cook for his wife."

She did not quite roll her eyes, nor quite raise her eyebrows, but I detected some hint of derision. "That'd be for your daughter, then?"

"Yes. A new arrival is expected midsummer."

"And what brought you to my door?" she asked. "There's no one in this city's been extolling the virtues of my cooking, that's sure."

I had not considered how to tactfully explain, which left my tongue stumbling over how I thought perhaps certain circumstances might cause her to be overlooked.

"Pity, was it?"

I felt myself bridle. "I prefer to call it compassion," I said with a pinch of heat. "Our late president did not implore us to care only for Union widows and orphans, after all."

That subdued her. "Myself, I had no allegiance to either side," she claimed. "But my husband said there'd be no proper work for Irishmen in this country the minute the Negroes were free to do the same job for half the pay." (She nearly substituted another word for *Negroes* but thankfully caught herself in time.)

"Do any of those circumstances affect your ability to roast a chicken or boil a potato?"

She smirked. "No. And I'd wager a Catholic chicken tastes the same as a Protestant one, though I wouldn't want anyone in County Clare to get wind that I'd said so."

We smiled at one another for the first time. Then I realized—I had not asked her the most pertinent question of all. "You can cook, I presume?"

"If I could afford more than flour and lard, I could cook up a dinner that would make any member of the poor board smack his lips."

I wrote out Meg's address. "Come to Mr. and Mrs. Brooke's house the day after tomorrow, and I shall see that there is plenty in the pantry for you to work with. If the meal is agreeable to them and the kitchen is agreeable to you, Mr. Brooke will likely offer you the position. They are accustomed to supper at six o'clock."

Chicken, potatoes, carrots, and beets will be waiting for her, I think. And I shall add a jar each of Hannah's canned peaches and applesauce to see what she makes of dessert. Nothing will win over John more quickly than a fruit pie.

January 26, 1866

Meg reports that supper did not appear on the table at the Dovecote until almost twenty-five minutes past six. "I can't hold that against her," Meg said. "After all, she'd never worked in this kitchen before."

Hannah looked dubious. "And the food?" she wanted to know. "How was that?"

Meg's eyes shifted from me to Hannah and back again. "John and I could find nothing to complain of," she said.

"That's hardly a compliment a cook would strive for," Hannah replied. "Chicken soup, for heaven's sake! How did she expect to make a proper broth in an hour?"

"And dessert?" I pressed. Kitty Neal opted for warm spiced peaches with cream. Not so impressive as a pie would have been, but a rank higher than applesauce.

When it came time to render a verdict, Meg quailed. "It doesn't seem necessary," she confided. "But John is so set on my having a cook." Again she looked to both of us, as if debating which of our opinions to take up as her own.

"It is up to you and John, Meg, not Hannah or me," I said.

"I can't think of a reason not to."

Hannah threw her eyes heavenward and busied herself with shining the silver. She has taken an unaccountably strong dislike to a woman she has never met. That is of no consequence, however. If Kitty Neal wants it, the job is to be hers.

January 27, 1866

The Brookes' cook is hired, though it was not so simple a matter as I anticipated. When I offered her the figure John had proposed, she scoffed, "That's hardly better than Negro wages."

"Money is but one color, Mrs. Neal," I said evenly.

She had the sense to wince and look contrite. Elsewise I would have been sorely tempted to see myself out on the spot.

"It is what the Brookes can afford," I continued when I could do so without scalding her with my voice. "If you and your daughters prefer to do others' washing, you are free to decline. Or you may accept Mr. Brooke's offer and send these girls to school." Where they belong, I thought, but did not say. I judged I had been crisp enough already.

She considered her daughters, both of whom were dutifully sorting through a bag of soiled laundry to separate red flannel underthings from white muslin underthings. "All right," she said, almost as if she were doing me a favor. How this arrangement is going to work out in practice, only time will reveal.

February 3, 1866

The Senate yesterday approved a civil rights bill with a vote of 33 to 12. If it should pass, all people born in the United States shall be considered citizens, regardless of race, color, or whether they have ever been held in bondage. It is, the *Boston Advertiser* says, the most important piece of legislation since the passage of the Thirteenth Amendment, and I heartily agree. Full property rights, the right to enter into contracts, to give evidence, to sue, and to receive full and equal benefit of all laws shall be granted to all <u>men</u>. (All men but Indians, that is.) Of course the bill has no concern for women of any race. I have not the cogency tonight to record what I think of that omission. Nevertheless, I shall pray for the bill's speedy passage.

Even as I pray, I wish there were something I could <u>do</u> to bring this legislation into being. No matter that it should be enough for God to hear my voice. Will there ever come a day when I am able to see my impact upon the world?

February 10, 1866

What news in the post today—a Mr. Allen of Boston has offered to print Jo's novel! Three hundred dollars, he has proposed as compensation. More than a factory girl can make in a year. Nearly as much as a laborer puts in his pocket after fifty-two weeks of toil. All of that for sitting in the garret with her mind yoked to her pen. And but nineteen years old! I should count myself blessed if I could earn my daily bread in such a way.

The offer comes with a caveat, however. If the book is to be published, she must reduce its size by a third—specifically, by extracting the majority of the narration and leaving it to the characters to convey what she is attempting to say. To do so would effectively erase Jo's voice from her own work. The prospect has left her in a tangle like no other she has faced before.

All of the Family have been called to council. I fear it did Jo no good. Amos, having no concern for commercial prospects, advises her to refuse to sacrifice so much as one word to Mr. Allen's profit-minded wishes. "Let it wait and ripen," he said. Meg, too, cannot give a speck of credence to the idea that any improvements could be made to Jo's work.

Amy and I are the practical pair. As Amy says, a publisher ought to know better than anyone what will sell. All of us are agreed on that point. The one thing we can be sure of is that Mr. Allen has his pocketbook's best interest at heart.

For all that Amos and I consider ourselves connoisseurs of literature, we are too fond of both the author and her work to judge its merits and faults properly. This I know by the way the back of my throat begins to tighten of its own accord at the thought of Mr. Allen consigning this bit or that of Jo's work to the rubbish bin with a mere point of his finger. Just thinking about it makes me feel as if Harriet Weddleton has come sweeping through the house.

To see Jo caught in such a state of inertia puts me thoroughly out of sorts. So often I can tell which way my girls wish to lean when they are caught between two choices. Rarely are their instincts wrong. My job then is to gently assure them it is indeed safe to set foot on the path that tugs at them most strongly. This time, it seems that Jo has come to a dead standstill before her crossroads. Or perhaps it is closer to the truth to say that both options pull at her equally. I myself cannot say what she is most needful of at this moment—commercial success, or the integrity of her vision? Neither one is promised.

What, then, was I to tell her? I settled upon the one thing that seemed self-evident: Jo can <u>learn</u> the most from trying the experiment. The book will sell, or it will not. The critics will praise it or scoff at it. Only then will Jo be able to pinpoint the sources of her successes and failures. Once she has had a fuller taste of the publishing world, she may discover which of its flavors most appeal to her.

I confess, I do not know whether my advice is sound, or is simply the result of my own wish to see Jo's customary momentum reinstated. Something about it has the feel of an evasion. Nevertheless, I don't see how it could hurt to try. If the book should fail, she will have $300 in her pocket and the benefit of some wisdom to apply to her next literary endeavor.

Beth said only that she should like to see it printed <u>soon</u>. The way she said it— Well, I do not like to dwell on that.

March 3, 1866

A welter of weariness and determination—that is Jo, these days. The contract with Mr. Allen is signed, and she has set to the tasks he has appointed her with grim ferocity. She has been at it for three weeks now, and I begin to wonder how much longer she can continue at this pace.

Emerging from one of her writing vortexes often leaves Jo despondent. This is a different sort of despondency. When she is writing, she depletes her own energy so that the characters may live. With this task, both the creator and her creations are being made to suffer as she amputates portions of the story. She has a look about her that puts me in mind of a surgeon in a field hospital, operating with a saw. I can only pray that the sacrifices are for the greater good of them both.

March 18, 1866

Laurie came calling with a little bunch of snowdrops for me this afternoon, and nearly succeeded in hiding his disappointment at learning that Jo is still confining herself to her garret, Sabbath or not.

"I miss her, too," I confessed. "And I've missed you as well." It is not the same, seeing him only occasionally at week's end, now that Harvard commands so much of his time. He flushed, more with pleasure than embarrassment, I think, and accepted my invitation to sit in the parlor with a pot of tea. We discussed the affairs of the day for an hour or better, hoping against hope that Jo might come down sometime before sunset. (She did not appear, even for supper.) Laurie, bless him, let me fulminate to my heart's content about the civil rights bill's tortuous journey through the legislature.

An amended bill passed through the House of Representatives this week, with 111 in favor and 38 against. Thirty-four of them abstained, by courage or cowardice, I am not yet sure. A provision which declared that "there shall be no discrimination in civil rights or immunities" has been omitted, for fear that "civil rights" might be too broadly interpreted in the future. Heaven forbid!

It is all up to President Johnson now. The *Boston Journal* is not optimistic, though the amendment offers some hope that the president will acquiesce and sign the bill.

"I only hope that both the civil rights legislation and Jo's novel will bear some resemblance to their former selves when all is said and done," I told Laurie with a sigh deep enough to ripple the tea in the bottom of my cup.

"Which do you suppose will be completed first?" he asked, a devilish grin playing about his lips. We both voted in favor of Jo. Unlike the government, she knows how to see a task through without dithering.

March 28, 1866

President Johnson is a despicable man! He has vetoed the civil rights bill, despite its passage by substantial majorities in both houses of Congress. Two full columns of his objections appeared in the *Daily Advertiser* today. I did not manage to read beyond the second paragraph. Not only former slaves, but Chinese, Gypsies, and any Indian who pays taxes would become citizens under the provisions of the bill, and this the president of the United States of America cannot abide. The words that come to my mind every time I think of him should not be committed to paper. He is fortunate, indeed, that he lives in Washington and not Boston, lest he should find me upon his doorstep.

April 2, 1866

After two months of work, Jo's task is done at last. The manuscript she dropped onto the kitchen table made a much less imposing thud than the previous iteration. Not even Beth could persuade her to keep it here long enough for any of us to read it.

"I can't bear to think about what anyone else might think of it for one more minute," Jo declared. "I hardly know what I think of it anymore."

Off it shall go to Boston by express, first thing tomorrow. Were it possible, I believe she would have run straight to Mr. Allen's office that very minute. Instead she contented herself with a run through the orchards, her first in weeks.

April 4, 1866

Hannah is ill. The very sentence is so foreign, it sounds like another language.

In all the years I have known her she has been so impervious to sickness, at times I half wondered if she were a member of another species. And now she is not just ill, but laid low enough to take to her bed. Fever, chills, and weakness. Worst of all, she does not protest my ministrations. Hannah has never let me do anything she can do herself. Tonight she shivered too violently to hold a mug of tea without scalding herself, and lay back so that I might spoon it into her mouth.

No one else in the Family is stricken. Nevertheless, we do not dare risk Beth's health. I have sent her to the Dovecote until Hannah recovers. Beth's eyes filled with tears when I told her, until they looked like two deep blue oceans. "Oh, Marmee, can't I help <u>somehow</u>?" she begged. "Hannah is always so good to me when I'm ill." I tasked her with cooking up a pot of good rich broth on Meg's stove. If she makes Hannah enough to fill a washtub, I shall not be surprised.

April 6, 1866

Two days have passed since I was last at the relief rooms. Someone must see that Hannah has cool water, hot broth, and fresh linens.

A day ago, all she could do was stare glassily at me as I rolled her back and forth to change her sweat-drenched sheets every few hours. I cannot say which of us was more disoriented by that circumstance. As for myself, I have not experienced anything similar since Amos was at war. The unsteadiness, the sense of the world having tipped a single degree, leaving everything so slightly off-balance that it seemed only I was aware of it. Today is better. Much better, in fact. Now, when Hannah awakens to find me sitting in the chair beside her bedroom door, a look of calm comes over her before she sinks back to sleep. That alone is unaccountably soothing.

The last time I sat in one place this long, I was at the seaside with Beth. For company here I have a variety of cats and the newspapers. If not for the infuriating news about the civil rights bill, I might find a bit of respite in my hours at Hannah's side.

In Washington all is turmoil, for the Congress is no more pleased with the president than I am. Words like *despot* were thrown about the Senate chamber yesterday in a great heat of debate. Before the senators retired for the day, thirty-three of them had voted to override Mr. Johnson's veto—enough to return the civil rights bill to the House of Representatives for its opinion on the matter. I should like to carry that bill to them myself, on a silver platter, and dare them not to approve it.

April 8, 1866

Yesterday was the seventh of April.

For the first time in twenty-three years, I neglected to mark the birth of my son. The day slipped silently by me, immersed as I was in Hannah's care.

It seems all I can do is sit with my pen poised over an empty line. I cannot write what I feel, for I do not know what I feel. Guilt? Sorrow? Relief? My heart is as blank as the page.

Twenty-three years.

April 9, 1866

A doubly fine day—Hannah is back on her feet, if a trifle wobbly, and the House overturned the president's veto at a vote of nearly three to one. The Civil Rights Act is now law!

I can hardly tell which of these triumphs pleases me more. The two together have me so giddy, I should like to go out in the streets and shout, "Democracy is vindicated!"

Hannah seems not to know what to say to me after this past week. She takes a breath as if to speak, and her face knots up as though she is searching for a word that does not exist. "I was glad to do it," I finally told her. "All of it." As I said so, I felt how true it is. Hannah never seems to need anything. When at last she did, I was there to provide it, whether it was a cool rag on her forehead or a pair of hands to rinse her chamber pot.

I held her gaze tightly as I spoke, thinking of those things. Things you do for those you love, without question or so much as a thought of complaint. Hannah's chin quivered and threatened to buckle. Then she nodded. Accepting it. Just like that. What I have never been able to convince her of in words, I have at long last managed to convey in actions.

April 22, 1866

Kitty Neal may not be the laziest woman in Middlesex County, but she must surely be in the running. That is what Hannah said today, and I am glad someone has finally said it. Give her one small task, and Kitty will make it last the day long. She does what she is paid to do—cook—and not one jot more. The kitchen floor could be ankle deep in mud and she would simply wade through it to put her pots upon the stove. Meals arrive on the table when they are ready, and no clock on earth can implore them to be ready sooner, or even at the same time each day. In between, she sits at the kitchen table and reads her Catholic tracts. Today I had to leave my sewing, march to the kitchen, and inform her that the kettle was wailing—and not for the first time, either. You would think she reads with her ears instead of her eyes. No wonder her relations offered only to take in her daughters.

"I half wish I had foisted her upon Mrs. Weddleton instead of Meg and John," I said to Amos when I returned home from the Dovecote this evening. "Both of them are too kind to let her go. Harriet Weddleton would have had no compunctions."

My own irritation irritates me. How often have I heard myself use my tongue as a lash against those who bleat on and on about the laziness of the poor? Though I must allow, my claim that I have never met a poor man who does not yearn for work has rarely met with anything more than a wall of solid skepticism. Perhaps if I amend my argument to include one exasperatingly useless woman it will lend credence to my claim. It will not justify the wages John is paying Kitty Neal, but it may save me from nailing my tongue to the roof of my mouth to keep from reprimanding her each time I visit Meg.

May 2, 1866

This child Meg is carrying is most active.

"I didn't like it at first," she confided today, likening the movements to the wriggling of a worm. Now she reports that it has become a different sensation altogether, one she struggles to adequately convey. From what I gather, the child shifts in ways that she can make no sense of, as if leaning in two directions at once. Indeed, her belly appears almost to wobble from time to time.

Judging by her size alone, no one would guess that two months still remain. How she will manage not to burst like an overripe grape before midsummer, I do not know. Poor Lotty is overburdened with chores, as Meg can no longer summon the energy to do more than knit or sew. Nor can Meg enter the kitchen before noon, for the scent of coffee, even on someone's breath, is enough to send her racing for the privy.

My gracious, she is young—a year younger than I was when I carried my first child. Had the child I carried when she and John were married lived, I would have a four or five months' infant in my lap today. What a thing to think of. A mother and a grandmother, all in the same year. Two generations, mere months apart. Time is weaving itself into a plait whose pattern I cannot foresee.

May 17, 1866

How often I think of my mother these days, as Meg and I prepare for the little one that is to come. It is nothing new in itself. Always when my girls reach some milestone I think of Marmee and how she would have loved to see it. Now, though, I feel the feelings of a grandmother-to-be and know precisely what she lost by leaving us so soon.

June 8, 1866

This day. Nothing that happened before the front bell rang this afternoon remains in my memory. It was of no consequence anyway.

Sometime after our noon meal the bell rang and I opened the door to a Negro woman. She was a stranger to me, with an unaccountable familiarity about her.

Her name, she said, was Asia Beall. I searched every shelf in my mind, looking for some clue as to why the sense of having met her before was so strong. Before I could lay my hands on a connection, she asked was I Mrs. March. When I said yes, she told me the most extraordinary thing: "You sheltered my boy from the law when he ran north, sixteen years ago."

I don't know how I kept my mouth from falling open. It was "John"'s mother. The cant of her brow, the shape of her jaw, brought his face before me with sudden clarity. I cannot describe the shock. Not only to see her on my threshold, but to hear her voice and know from the way she'd spoken of him that her son was dead.

With my emotions immobilized between astonishment and dejection, I ushered her into the parlor and stammered at Hannah to bring us tea. I ought not have bothered; once Mrs. Beall began to speak about her son, the teapot and everything else in the room retreated from our consciousness.

His name—his true name, for we had known him by an anonymous sobriquet—was Manor Beall. He did escape to freedom, as we have hoped and prayed from the moment his feet left our property, only to be shot by the man who owned him.

His master had come from Baltimore on business in the late fall of 1850, bringing ~~John~~ Manor with him. After weeks of abiding on free soil, Manor deserted his master and found his way to my brother's church, and from there to our back door in December. That much we learned from Samuel long afterward. But until today we have heard nothing of his whereabouts since.

"He worked seven and a half years to buy his freedom, and mine," Mrs. Beall told me. "Eighteen hundred dollars. Took him most of another year to find a safe way back to Maryland to pay Master Beall for the both of us." The pain of what followed is still so hard, it stiffened her as she spoke. "He took Manor's money and drew up papers," she said, biting at the words, "then shot my boy in the back as we walked away. Said he wouldn't have done it if Manor was still a slave."

The man's actual words were, "Property's worth something. But a free n——r?" (I have never yet dignified that word by writing it out in full, and I never shall, no matter who says it or why.) I might have been sick right there. Had I done so, I have no doubt I would have vomited a stream of pure fire.

"I don't know why he didn't shoot me, too. Most days, I wish he had. I nursed that man, and his babies, and he shot my boy. Up to that day, I would have told you he was a good master. Never was the finest of men, you understand, but a good master. Never whipped us any harder than he whipped his own sons. Never broke a family apart to sell.

"Something changed when Manor ran away. Master Beall couldn't understand it, why anyone would run. He prided himself on the fact that no slave had fled before. He and Manor'd been boys together. Almost like friends. That made it worse, I suppose. Manor insulted him by wanting to live somewhere else. For seven and a half years I'd thanked God that Master Beall didn't take it out on me. If I'd known what was coming, I'd have taken the lash every day to prevent it."

My tears seemed so paltry, my own distress so worthless and distracting. Had she stopped to comfort me, I would have been ashamed. This woman has already spent too much of her life tending to others. She did me an honor by ignoring them.

When I finally thought to ask her what she had come for, she said she did not fully know. Asking <u>how</u> she had found her way to us after all this time never occurred to me. The habit of exchanging as little information as possible where the routes of runaways are concerned is still as deeply ingrained in me as it was when lives depended on secrecy.

"Can you read?" I asked her, hating that it was a question that needed asking at all.

"Some," she replied.

"Please wait here a moment," I said, and ran upstairs to retrieve my diaries of 1850 and 1851. I handed them to Mrs. Beall, the first open to the day Manor arrived in December. "Your son was our guest for almost three months. Please read as much as you would like to about his time with our Family," I said. "There will be more here than I will be able to remember to tell you."

I waited as Mrs. Beall slowly made her way through the pages, trying not to watch her finger move steadily across the lines of writing. Now and then she looked up at me with an expression I could not read. Which details prompted her appraisals, I did not ask. She spoke but once in the first hour.

"He ate breakfast at your table?" she asked. I nodded. Of necessity he lived in the cellar, but in the earliest hours of the morning we chanced to give him as generous a ration of fresh air and light and company as safety would permit, so that his long days belowground might be bearable. "With your daughters?"

I nodded again. "He told them stories," I added, the fact returning to my own mind for the first time in years. That was the only time she came close to smiling.

I knew when she reached the passage I most dreaded—the day the bounty hunter arrived. Her face tightened and her lips grayed. As she read, my own thoughts hurtled backward of their own accord.

We never learned how they found us out. Whether we had been careless, or someone had betrayed information. Perhaps someone had noticed the path in the snow that led from the kitchen to the cellar door and wondered why it was so heavily trodden that time of year. Every day I thank God that Hannah happened to be upstairs with the children when the bounty hunter threw open the back door.

I remember hearing the sound and running to the kitchen to see what the commotion was. There he stood, the very image of the villain in an engraving from the masthead of *The Liberator*, taking the measure of the place. The bottom dropped out of my stomach. I backed up to Hannah's bedroom door, not so much frightened yet as overwhelmed by the enormity of what I was about to confront.

The man advanced upon me. "Take your hand off that latch this instant!" I commanded as though I were speaking to a child. "You have no right to search this house."

"Don't you try to tell me you haven't heard of the Fugitive Slave Act, madame."

"That reprehensible 'law' is a flagrant violation of the freedom from unreasonable searches and seizures guaranteed to all citizens by the Fourth Amendment to the United States Constitution, and a stain on the conscience of every God-fearing man and woman," I shot back.

Even now, it gives me one small speck of pleasure to recall the few seconds it took him to absorb the shock of a woman speaking, much less arguing constitutional law with him. In that silence he eyed the row of pegs beside the door, where the girls' four small cloaks hung largest to smallest. When his eyes turned back to me, I felt as though I were looking down the twin barrels of a shotgun. "You don't want to make a fuss over this," he said. "And you can't tell me one n—r is worth more to you than everything in this house."

A fuss. That alone would have lit a fuse within me. But to hear that other word used aloud. Never has my rage reared up so blindingly bright as it did in that instant. "How dare you threaten my Family!"

Outside, cold hinges rasped and the cellar door flapped open onto the snow. The knob of the back door turned. I screamed out, "Don't!" but it was too late. Manor stood in the kitchen, between me and the bounty hunter.

If only he had run instead. That has been my lament ever since. If we had not made every effort to treat him as much a part of our Family as circumstances allowed, would he have thought first of himself and fled?

The white man took the rolling pin from the table and raised his arm toward Manor. As if it were not punishment enough to be returned to bondage, Manor's body had to be made to suffer, too. The glint in the man's eye, the upward curl of his lip, showed a hint of pleasure that sent spirals of disgust corkscrewing through me. That was the part he enjoyed.

Nothing incites me to rage more than injustice. It strikes me like kerosene.

"Don't you dare!" I cried. And I struck him. The only time in my life I have struck another human being. My palm still bears the memory of the stubble of his cheek. I knew, in the instant before the blow collided, that I had altered our lives forever. That sickening sense of time rushing forward all around me, to a conclusion I could suddenly see and had no power to interrupt. Every sharp whisker of that man's face stung, stabbing back at my flesh with a thousand simultaneous reprimands.

He was so utterly stunned that for an instant, everything halted, dizzying the both of us. It was as though I had pulled a rug out from under him, toppling him entirely. Even more so when he shifted his rage toward me and found that I had him matched. I saw his mind fumble with incredulity, saw him contemplate bringing that rolling pin down over my head.

When all is lost, there is nothing to lose. All three of us felt it— the crackle and snap of the rules as they began to break apart. Manor acted upon it. He scrambled under the table and out the door. I ducked under the slave catcher's raised arm, bracing myself in the doorway as Manor mounted his would-be captor's horse. Only then did the man's fury overtake mine. He threw down the rolling pin and grabbed me by both shoulders. The power I had so briefly held over him vanished. All the things he could do to me then flashed across my vision. My only defense was to meet his eye without flinching, to dare him to debase himself by willfully causing me harm.

I was lucky, for he was a man with better mastery over his temper than I have of mine. Lucky, too, that I am a woman, and that the fact of my sex caused him to grapple first with his conscience, rather than with me. Had I been a black man, I would have been bludgeoned to death that day. Instead, his fingers squeezed until I could feel my flesh pressed against my bones. Then, with a jerk, he dislodged me from the doorway and propelled me to the ground.

He stood over me a moment with a hand on the grip of his revolver as we listened to the fading sound of galloping hooves. The feel of his gun seemed to return him to his bearings. "You'll answer to the law for this," he promised.

That promise was kept.

We could have borne the first thousand dollars. The fine for harboring a fugitive was a risk Amos and I had weighed and decided to shoulder. The second thousand, levied for Manor's escape, ruined us entirely. It is the everlasting pride and shame of my life.

Worst of all, I had to tell Amos what had happened. He never once chastised me for that calamitous outburst. After all his years of patiently taming my temper. I remember, though, how dispirited he was.

A stillness in the parlor returned me to my surroundings. I saw that Mrs. Beall had stopped reading. Both our gazes seemed to be fixed on the empty space between us. Silently she closed the two volumes and stacked them one on top of the other.

"Will you permit me to see your kitchen, Mrs. March?" she asked. "And your cellar?"

I took her to the places she wished to see. She stood a moment in each. I imagine that, like me, she was envisioning the events that had unfolded here.

"Thank you, Mrs. March," she said, with a nod toward the front of the house that signaled her intent to go.

I did not know what to say as she stood in the doorway. "If our Family can ever be of the least service to you . . ." I trailed off. It did not sound the way I wanted it to. We looked at each other, muddled in a shared sense of defeat and gratitude.

"Thank you," she said again, and went.

Amos was as stunned as I when I told him of Mrs. Beall's visit. A silence similar to that which prevailed between Mrs. Beall and me settled over the study as he endeavored to absorb what had happened in the intervening years.

"There are days when my faith in mankind feels misplaced," he said at last.

The room ought to have quaked. Such an admission from Amos made it sound as though a stranger inhabited his wingback chair. That was the paradox that made it possible for me to ask the question that has been circling my brain since learning Manor's fate: "Was it worth it?"

Amos did not answer immediately. For a moment I was soothed, knowing that even he needed to weigh the sacrifices of these last fifteen and a half years. But the longer his silence stretched, the more it unnerved me.

"Eight years of freedom," Amos said finally. "And his mother walked free six years sooner than she would have otherwise. Would you trade that for two thousand dollars?"

He did not include his own six months' imprisonment in that measure. Nor the years of financial struggle that plagued us until Jo took up her pen. Nevertheless, the answer was as self-evident as the truths set forth in the Declaration of Independence. "Never," I said.

"Nor I," Amos agreed.

And with that, the room became familiar once more. Amos drew thoughtfully at his pipe while I watched the smoke rise and coil and disappear, rise and coil and disappear, like my thoughts. The words I desired to say were small and simple—so small it seemed I could not catch hold of them.

"Is it time we told the girls?" I asked at last.

He looked long at me. "That has always been yours to decide."

"I would like for them to know," I managed to say before my voice broke. "But I lack the courage to tell it."

"Peg," he said, making of it an endearment. "You must know you have nothing to fear from our children."

I do. And yet I _am_ afraid. Afraid and ashamed of being so. It is an insult to my daughters to harbor such reluctance. We have raised them with the same principles that guided Amos and me to risk our Family's fortunes for the freedom of one man.

It is easy enough to imagine how Jo and Beth might show their pride—one with a hearty *Hurrah for Marmee!* and the other with starry, quiet tears. And Meg, now, is old enough to recognize the value of what was purchased thanks to all the material sacrifices which so vexed her. But Amy. Oh, what will Amy think of me?

June 12, 1866 ✐

It is told. With Amos's help, thank God.

After shedding nearly sixteen years of dread, I would have thought to feel lighter than I do. Then again, the weight being of my own making, I suppose it is up to me to throw it off at last.

Every one of us but Amos was uneasy. The way we had summoned the Family, gathering them with such solemnity around the table, had likely braced them for some terrible revelation.

"What do you remember of John?" Amos began.

Every head turned first to John Brooke in confusion.

"The Negro man," I managed to say. "Who wintered with us."

Understanding dawned and Meg and Jo chorused "His stories," as if they had rehearsed the answer.

How is it that in all this time I have had no occasion to remember those stories? Bible stories, transported to the animal kingdom. Moses became a steadfast camel leading his people through the desert, Ruth a gentle dove, mighty Sampson a lion shorn of his mane, and King Solomon the wisest of owls. Amos had been as enchanted by them as the children, for the way Manor employed the creatures' temperaments to convey human virtues and faults.

All the same, it had been disconcerting to see how quickly Manor fell into the role of entertaining white people, of attending to our contentment before his own. There were no clues to tell me whether he truly enjoyed storytelling, or whether this was just another act in the lifelong performance of docile servility that had allowed him to escape slavery without the physical scars so many Negro men and women bear. I never did think of a way to tell him he did not have to bow to my children's eagerness. Every version of such a conversation that I played out in my mind ended with him answering "Yes, ma'am" and I could not abide that.

"John the Storyman?" Beth said, looking as if she were remembering a long-ago dream. "He was a real man?"

Amy echoed her sister's question with confusion of a different kind. "You were only eighteen months old," I told her.

And then Amos told the story.

How is it that in all my years of cowering from this secret, I never once considered how the events of that day would sound in any voice but my own? Where I would have told it with shame, Amos told it with pride. I sat in awe of myself as he spoke, as if another woman, brave and righteous, had defied the slave catcher in my place. There were tears, as I had expected, but not just from Beth. Jo, Meg, and John, too.

When I chanced a look at Amy, her brow was furrowed, her gaze concentrated on her turquoise ring. I did not look again. She was quiet afterward. All of them were, but her silence was of a different tenor. Amidst the embraces and clasping of hands from all the others, it was easy enough to pretend I did not notice that she seemed almost not to know me.

Later

A note under my pillow:

My own Marmee,
    From now on, whenever I look at my ring I shall think of you and how brave and good and unselfish I should like to be.

                                   Love, from Amy

June 20, 1866

These last few days, I feel as if a garment I have been wearing every day since 1851 has suddenly changed color. Its newfound brightness astounds me. Today I lifted two of my diaries from the bottom of the cedar chest and carried them down to the study. Amos watched from his desk as I placed them on the shelf with the others, filling the interval between 1849 and 1852.

The secrets they contained are no longer a danger to anyone—least of all, me. I did not expect to cry as I stepped back to sweep my eyes along the unbroken length of that shelf, but I did. As if something lodged deep inside me were melting.

I had never allowed myself the luxury of imagining how it would feel to be without this burden. All I permitted was the impossible dream of being a woman who had not committed that one fatal error. That in itself was a punishment of my own making.

What might I accomplish now that I no longer have to carry the weight of shame?

June 24, 1866

Laurie is home from school for the summer. What a treat to hear his halloo, his feet drumming on the garret steps as he trots up to coax Jo from her desk. If not for Laurie, Jo might never see daylight, the way she churns out stories these days. After all her work on her novel there is relief now in her old dollar-a-column "rubbish," moving obedient people about on the page as I so love to move pieces on a chessboard, only with no opponent to thwart her schemes for them.

Laurie is determined to make up for the time he has missed with her, and when she refuses to come down, lounges patiently on the dusty three-legged sofa. The way he gazed at Jo across the table at supper tonight, you would think she had been carved out of marble—as if she is Athena, Hestia, and Artemis all in one. The dear boy neglects to remember that all three goddesses were as renowned for shunning marriage as they were for their extraordinary prowess in wisdom, domesticity, and archery. To hear Mr. Laurence tell it, Laurie has spent most of his time at Harvard falling in love. Perhaps it is only natural that his eye should fall on Jo now that he is among us again.

It was Amy who startled him from his reverie with a pointed, "Will you <u>please</u> pass the potatoes?" How he flushed and stammered! Jo silenced her sister with a kick I pretended not to notice.

"Oh, Josy-phine, you're more beautiful than a whole field of potatoes!" Amy teased after Laurie had gone. In a great whoosh, Jo inflated with fury. Had I not been standing directly behind Amy, Jo might have snipped Amy's head from her neck then and there. Instead Jo caught sight of my grimace. I could feel her temper rising as if it were my own, and could not help but wince at what was surely to come.

In two heartbeats' time Jo overcame herself. "Thank you, Marmee," she said and marched primly up the stairs, leaving Amy bewildered.

"Well, I won't do <u>that</u> again," Amy proclaimed so earnestly that I did not bother to admonish her.

June 30, 1866

Meg's confinement fast approaches. Her belly is the most ridiculous shape, as if the child within rests full length, with its head against her spine and its toes poking at her navel. Each day her excitement and apprehension seem to double. She is full of questions, and being the first of her sisters to bear a child has no one to ask but me.

I hardly know what to tell her when she asks what the first time was like for me. She does not know what she is asking. The first time I held a child of my own he was dead. Warm from my body, slack as a rag doll, and utterly, utterly still. How my heart swelled and crumpled at once. It would have been easier, perhaps, if he had taken even a single breath. Whatever went wrong had gone wrong within me, and I had never felt a thing, never sensed the moment his soul broke free and drifted . . . where? Did it float within me, alongside his empty body, until I began to grunt and strain? Or did it pass silently through my flesh before the first birth pang?

As I look back, it seems to me that we should have told our girls about their brother. Years ago. Now I would have to explain why we kept the knowledge from them, and that I cannot do. I cannot fully understand it, myself. My silence has erased him from our Family. To tell Meg now would only taint the coming days with fear.

"Will it hurt terribly, Marmee?" she wanted to know today.

"It is the deepest pain my body has ever produced," I told her. "Each time its intensity surprised me. But it shall pass over you, and be gone. Remember that your heart, and your mind, are capable of inflicting far greater wounds that are slower to heal." Her eyes asked a question I pretended not to see. "If you are fortunate, you shall endure no greater pain than this."

It frightened her as much as it encouraged her, I think. Better to be a little frightened now than caught by surprise in the thick of it, though.

Then a queer look passed over Meg's face. She put her hand to her belly and quirked her eyebrows. "It felt like . . . like a bubble. A bubble popping. Feel it, Marmee."

I recognized the sensation from her description alone. "A hiccough," I pronounced, and Meg broke into a peal of delighted laughter.

"How can a babe hiccough before it breathes?"

I shook my head. "I wondered that very thing, myself," I said. My boy was taken with hiccoughs nearly every day in the week before he was born. None of the girls hiccoughed in the womb. Only he. The feel of it belonged solely to him, and made me hesitate to feel it again through Meg. Each time I was pregnant, the memory of carrying that first babe blurred as the sensations repeated themselves, until nothing but his hiccoughs and his death distinguished him from the rest.

No, that is not true. That first time, my fears were abstract, my delight as keen as Meg's. Losing him left me wary and fretful, too attuned to disaster to fully enjoy the anticipation of birth again. Four times more, I labored doggedly to bear a child without the slightest assurance that my effort would be rewarded.

Meg snatched up my hand and pressed it to her flank. There it was. A sensation I have not felt since I was twenty-one years old. "Hello, little one," I whispered—aloud to my grandchild, and with my heart, to my son.

July 6, 1866

Amy has finished a conté crayon portrait of Beth for Jo. She has done it all in a soft, warm shade of terra-cotta, which has the effect of rendering Beth's paleness invisible. It is better yet than her portrait of Aunt March. Or perhaps it is only that I am fonder of the subject. I think it is more than that, though. Amy has somehow melded Beth's appearance with the greater truth of how it <u>feels</u> to look at her. The result is something more than a simple likeness, so much so that tears leapt to my eyes without warning when I saw it. If it had not already been promised to Jo, I would not have let that sheet of paper leave my hands.

Jo has put it in a little oval-shaped frame on the shelf atop her desk in the garret, so that each time she lifts her eyes from the paper her muse shall always be smiling down upon her.

July 17, 1866

Meg has been delivered of twins. <u>Twins</u>. Two squalling, squirming babies, red as nestlings. Never have I experienced such delightful bewilderment as this. From the size of her, we ought to have guessed long ago, and yet every one of us managed to be taken entirely by surprise.

It was a long labor, and hard. If I am to be perfectly frank I must admit that by the time the morning sun began to color the window-panes I had begun to doubt my own endurance.

For an hour I had assured her that it was nearly done. Meg was so determined to be brave, but by the time the first child came forth, there was not strength to spare for courage. She cried as she pushed, as unabashed as a little girl in my arms. But though the pain and fear possessed her, it did not stop her, as it does so many women. There was no need to cajole her to keep on; she faced her duty so squarely that it made no difference that her eyes were squeezed shut and tears coursed down her cheeks.

Then Hannah said, "A boy!," and it was my turn to cry. It was as if a bullet of elation had pierced my heart. A boy. A living boy. I sobbed, heaving up grief and exaltation in equal measure.

Hannah understood, and handed the babe first to me, just as Meg had favored me with the first kiss after her wedding vows. Such a plump and tiny thing, with a head round as an orange. Meg's wet cheeks shone as she touched her fingertips to his. I was holding them both, my daughter hugged to one breast and my grandson to the other, when Hannah cried, "Mrs. March!"

Meg winced at the same instant, then gasped. "The afterbirth," I soothed, but Hannah shook her head and beckoned frantically. I pushed myself up with the babe still in my arms and hurried to the end of the bed.

What I saw happening there rendered me temporarily dumb. I passed the boy to Hannah and pressed the heels of both hands into the base of Meg's belly.

"Another?" Hannah said.

I nodded.

That was when the terror took hold of Meg. The thought of doing it all over again snapped her like a twig.

"Not all of it, Meg, darling," I promised. "Only the last." The room filled with wailing, the baby boy and his mother both taking exception to the sudden turn of events. The babe had hardly been toweled off; he ought to have been snug in his mother's arms. Instead we had no choice but to abandon him to the waiting cradle as we tended to Meg. The second child seemed to somersault out, she came so quickly. Meg gave a groan that peaked into a shriek, and there was a perfectly irate little girl raging on the bed.

"Is she all right?" Meg panted.

"Oh, this wee little banshee is as right as anything," Hannah soothed, "only furious with her brother for getting in her way, I'll wager."

What a scream she had! Every inhale expanded her small chest like a bellows, and every exhale rattled her to the very tips of her fingers and toes.

Hannah scooped the child up and laid her next to her brother with their bare skins touching, and the tumult ceased so quickly, the silence seemed to ricochet through the air.

"My youngest brothers were twins," Hannah said simply. "There's no greater comfort to a newborn twin than the other half of the pair. Remember that, Mrs. Brooke, and they'll cry half as much instead of double."

We all three erupted into laughter then for no reason I can name. Shock and relief and exhaustion, all vying at once for sovereignty over us.

"Go tell John, Marmee," Meg begged as Hannah gathered up the birth-soiled newspapers from the bed and fed them to the fire. "He's been waiting so long."

I kissed her, and Hannah, and both of the babies before I would consent to leave.

John Brooke stood up to hear the news and then sat right back down again, so hard that I burst out laughing all over again. The poor man. Later he said that from the look on my face, he half expected me to tell him Meg had brought forth a zebra colt instead of a baby.

In truth, I do believe I frightened him. Happiness had not fully cracked through the shock when I stepped out of the room to tell him. No doubt he had heard the weeping and wailing. "A boy," he repeated. "<u>And</u> a girl."

And. It is a word we shall never tire of saying.

July 19, 1866 ‿∾

These babies. Oh, these babies! The pair of them are a pure and unfettered delight. They have been called Margaret and John Brooke, but already we know them better as Daisy and Demi.

Grandchildren are a revelation. The love for them is so uncomplicated, so much less terrifying, somehow, than what I felt for my own newborn children. I would rather hold them than do anything else in the world.

July 24, 1866 ‿∾

If anyone on this earth can get into a pique more perfectly than Amy, I have yet to make their acquaintance. What in heaven's name possessed her to make Jo promise to go calling with her this afternoon, I shall never know. Of all the things she could have bargained for in exchange for that portrait!

"You might as well put a leash on a lion and expect it not to roar, my dear," Amos said to Amy when she had at last finished enumerating every indignity and embarrassment Jo had inflicted upon her in the space of a single afternoon.

I tried to gulp back a laugh and instead produced a snort. Every eye around the supper table swung to me, round with astonishment. "I <u>am</u> sorry, Amy," I said, "but Father is quite correct." And then Beth began to giggle. Beth!

"Now Amy will roar," she said with a grin both shy and sly.

One by one, Jo, Amos, and Hannah let their decorum topple like dominoes. Amy had no choice then but to join our mirth or go off in a huff. Thankfully, she chose the former.

Oh, I oughtn't admire Jo's disregard for the most inane of social niceties. But I am afraid I do. Perhaps *envy* is the truer word for it. Especially in the relief rooms. So much time is wasted traipsing daintily around what is improper, rather than getting straight to the meat of the matter.

August 2, 1866

Jo's first copies of her novel have arrived. It is a lovely thing, bound in a rich red with her name embossed in a festoon of gold scrollwork on the front cover. I should not be surprised if she takes one upstairs to put under her pillow tonight. I certainly will. Letting it out of my grasp is almost as difficult as relinquishing Daisy or Demi from my arms.

There is something undeniably thrilling about seeing her words bound and printed rather than written out in her own familiar hand. The book seems real now, in a way it did not before.

"To have realized a dream at such an age is truly an accomplishment to be proud of," I told her. The look on her face cannot be captured by a single word. Happy, yes, and satisfied and so proud that you could not stand within three paces of her without feeling it yourself. And something more. She looked as though she'd grown roots—as if she has found her place in the world and is determined never to be dislodged from it. I should like to have that image engraved upon my memory so that I might turn to it again and again, like an ambrotype in an album.

August 4, 1866

This afternoon Amos and I went to the bookshops for the pleasure of seeing Jo's work upon the shelves. Not only was it on the shelves, but

Mr. Simpkins had done Jo the honor of displaying it in a neat stack in the front window. Amos bought a copy, which he promptly delivered to the library, toting it through the streets as proudly as he carries his grandbabies perched upon his arms.

August 8, 1866

Daisy and Demi are proving to be a tonic for Beth. Thank goodness there are two of them, or Beth and I might be tempted to quarrel over who may rock them, cuddle them, swaddle them. Meg is grateful for the help, for a single pair of hands is not nearly enough to manage two babies—not by half.

To my delight, the Dovecote has redoubled the size of Beth's world. She spends such a great deal of time there that I will not be surprised if the babies learn to say "Auntie" before "Mama" or "Papa."

There have been times, looking at her, that Beth has put me in mind of the Ghost of Christmas Past. Bright yet shadowed, at once young and old. One of Mr. Dickens's phrases sticks particularly in my mind: "the appearance of having receded from the view." That is Beth. There is something faraway about her that leaves me ill at ease. The babies are pulling her forward for the first time in months.

August 12, 1866

Kitty Neal is redeeming herself—somewhat, at least. The twins have lit a fire under her.

"My two came eleven months apart, and that was toil enough. Two at once is more than God should ask of any woman. I've no doubt that if my Frank hadn't gone to war, I'd have four extra mouths to feed and another kicking under my apron by now."

August 14, 1866

Amy is more ink-stained than Jo these days, what with Mrs. Chester's charity fair just around the corner. She has given Amy charge of the art table, an honor Amy has every intention of living up to. The windowsills are littered with fans and tiles and seashells she has painted, laid out to dry. Sweet little sketches of kittens and flowers and the like are stacked upon her desk. Most lovely of all is a blank book she is filling with bits of scripture and wisdom, illuminated with scroll-work, flora, and fauna that would earn a smile of recognition from a medieval monk. As she labors over it, she glances now and then at her turquoise ring. In the four years since Aunt March gave it to her, it has never left Amy's hand. It has served as a beacon for her, just as she promised when she asked my permission to wear it. Now it seems that she is channeling all she has learned from that blue stone onto the blank leaves of vellum before her. If I could afford to pay her what that book is worth to me, a family like the Hummels could eat for a year.

Mr. Laurence is poorly with a summer cold. Laurie insists it is nothing to worry over, but that does not banish these wriggling little thoughts. Tomorrow I shall take him a quart of Hannah's good broth.

August 17, 1866

Never again will I look at a book review in the same way. The newspaper notices of Jo's novel have left all of us scratching our heads and grinding our teeth by turns.

The critics will praise it or scorn it, I told Jo months ago, somehow failing to imagine the possibility that they would do both at once. One lauds the story as though it were a masterpiece penned by Nathaniel Hawthorne himself, the next sounds as though they'd just as soon drop it down a latrine pit as read it. No logic governs their reactions, which is the most maddening thing of all. Most infuriating are the reviews that decry the truest bits—the parts drawn from our own life—as the least realistic of all. Just what is it that they find so implausible about how we conduct ourselves, I should like to know!

Poor Jo. I can hardly bear to look her in the eye, for my advice is precisely what snared her in this imbroglio. The criticism I thought would clarify everything has done nothing but the opposite. Would that I could reach backward through time and yank the witless thought from my mind before the words reached my tongue.

Would the critics' reactions be the same if the name on the title page were J. March rather than Josephine March, I wonder? The praise is too high, just as the criticism is too harsh. Coddling or dismissal, that's what women can most reliably count on in a man's profession.

Amos was right, though he is too tactful ever to say it. He may be too tactful to even think it. Nevertheless, had Jo left her work intact, she would at least have the consolation of knowing any mistakes were hers alone. Now there is only a jumble of uncertainty. The three hundred dollars that seemed so enticing when Jo signed Mr. Allen's contract—and is long ago spent—hardly counterbalances this confounding state of affairs.

August 19, 1866

My heart is sore from watching Jo cope with her disappointment and confusion. Where three weeks ago she soared, these days her spirits are simply limp. I should rather have my own diary printed and subjected to the critics of Boston and New York than watch Jo's confidence in her own labors falter this way.

I failed to understand before just how little her blood and thunder tales meant to her. "Rubbish," she calls them, mere trifles. This book was something altogether different. She had put her heart into it, then pulled it back out again at Mr. Allen's insistence. He might as well have asked her to shoot it, stuff it, and mount it on the wall, for something vital has gone from it. Perhaps if the protagonist was not so much like Jo herself, it would not sting so.

If there is one thing she should be unequivocally proud of, though, it is her insistence on bearing this as cheerfully as she can manage. Despite her discouragement her temper has yet to rear up. I would like to be able to say as much of myself in such a situation.

August 22, 1866

It was inevitable that I should overstep my bounds. Today it happened. Another batch of reviews, forwarded by Mr. Allen, arrived this morning. They are every bit as contradictory and confounding as the last bundle. Sort them into two piles—one for praise and another for criticism—and they come within a hair's width of the same height.

Watching Jo sit there with a clipping in each hand and a mask of relentless tenacity upon her face as she tried to make sense of them pitched me over the brink.

Out of my chair I sprang. I snatched the papers from her hands and swept both stacks of reviews from the table and straight into the stove. It was only half as gratifying as I wished, for they made hardly a sound. I would have much preferred them to shatter or crash against the flames instead of shriveling so meekly.

Jo's face—the last time her mouth formed such a perfect *O*, she was an infant. And Amy. Amy looked as though the roof had split open and let in a hailstorm. As well it ought, for didn't I shame her royally for consigning Jo's first manuscript to the flames in just such a fit of indignation?

For a moment, it seemed that I had rendered myself speechless. All those eyes upon me paralyzed my thoughts. And then Amos's finger rose to tap his lips with the gentleness of a kiss. There was no sign of reproach from him or the others or even Jo; only surprise. My mind unclenched itself.

"I'm sorry," I said to Jo. "That was rash of me, and I had no right to do it. Those notices belonged to you." She nodded, wordlessly accepting my apology. "What others think of your work is of but little consequence in comparison to what <u>you</u> think of it," I told her. "That is all I want for you to understand."

"Oh, Marmee," Jo said, "I only wish I knew."

August 24, 1866

The most thoughtful of notes arrived for Jo from Mr. Emerson today. Oh, her face as she read it! Twice more her eyes passed back and forth over the page, gobbling up the words before she was sated enough to pass it round the room. My own heart thumped with renewed vigor as I read his congratulations as well as a frank assessment of her promise as a writer. His praise of her work is as sensible and honest as his criticism—neither too lofty nor too harsh.

After looking as though she was tumbling head over heels, her head spinning like a carriage wheel since the first notices appeared in the papers, it was as if Mr. Emerson's words suddenly scooped Jo up and set her straight back onto her feet again. To receive such encouragement from one whose pen she so admires is worth more to her at this moment in her life than any publisher would have seen fit to pay a fledgling author. Indeed, she pressed the note flat as gently as if it were a flower petal, then tucked it inside the cover over her own copy of her book, which I have not seen her touch in days. When she bid us good night, the stout red volume rode in the crook of her elbow.

Not until after Jo and Beth had gone upstairs did it occur to me that Amos had paid a visit to Ralph Waldo Emerson's residence this week. "Did you speak to Mr. Emerson about Jo?" I asked him.

"He asked after her, as he always does," Amos answered. "And Meg and Beth and Amy as well."

I waited for his smile to unfurl into a signal of collusion. Instead, he returned to his library book. Whole minutes passed in silence before I realized he had no notion of what I was hinting at. "You are not playing coy, are you?" I asked with a pleasant twinge of bewilderment.

"Coy?" he said, as if he did not know what the word meant.

I rose and kissed his forehead. He set aside his book to make a place for me in his lap. "What was that for?" he asked.

"Nothing at all," I replied. Amos picked up his book again and began to read softly aloud. I followed only the cadence, for there was room for but one thought in my mind: If there are finer friends in the state of Massachusetts than ours, I have yet to hear tell of them.

August 27, 1866

The fair does not open until tomorrow and already it is going awry. Today Mrs. Chester summarily demoted Amy to the flower table with an excuse so flimsy I cannot even remember it.

"The way she spoke to me, I thought I must have done something abdominably wrong," Amy said, turning her ring round and round on her finger as she fretted. "And then when I didn't protest, she looked almost sorry."

What on earth has taken hold of Ruby Chester's mind, giving out tables like laurels and then revoking them? How convenient that it is her own daughter, May, who has been given the art table in Amy's stead. This fair cannot end soon enough to suit me. Such a lot of rigamarole over tables and vases. Why it takes a fair to elicit these donations for the betterment of the poor, I do not know. Anyone who can spare a few coins for a trifle can just as well afford to put those same nickels and dimes into their parish poor box. If the money Amy has spent on ink and paint and paper and the time she has devoted to her paintings had been spent at the relief rooms instead, the poor would benefit doubly from her contributions.

But I am straying from the matter at hand. To everyone's silent surprise, Amy has accepted this blow with a meekness that only her father could rival. The child who refused to return to school after the humiliation of the pickled lime affair is now a young woman determined to see tomorrow through without a jab of retaliation or even so much as an audible whimper over her bruised pride.

Had I known what magic that turquoise ring would work upon her character, I might have bought her one for each finger.

August 28, 1866

I don't know what had come to pass by the time we reached the fair this evening. At the art table May Chester cheerfully exhorted passers-by not to miss the chance to own a piece by Miss Amy March. On the far side of the hall Amy sat at the center of a mass of flowers and young men, looking for all the world as if she were the model for a portrait of Demeter among her harvest.

When the story emerged, I learned that Amy had volunteered to display all of her artwork at May's table so that it would not look so forlorn. Meanwhile, thanks to Jo and Laurie, a bounty of blooms and greenery from the Laurence garden had arrived to festoon the flower table. As we watched, the final pieces of Amy's work sold for quite a pretty penny, the flower table was picked bare, and Laurie's chums were dispersed to buy up every pitiful item that had not been purchased. Thanks to the unlikely combination of Ruby Chester's pettiness and Amy's grace, the whole affair turned out more profitable than any of its predecessors.

"I must say, Amy March has grown into a most equitable and magnanimous young lady," Aunt Carrol said as we stood chatting at the sidelines. Pride burst up within me so quickly, I might have been a kernel of popping corn. To hear those words spoken of Amy—Amy! Nor was that the end of it. Aunt Carrol is in need of a companion to accompany her and Florence abroad, and it seems Aunt March has been lobbying firmly in Amy's favor. She will even pay Amy's expenses, should Aunt Carrol choose her. I could have flown to Europe myself, held aloft by such praise.

Then came the pin to burst my bubble. Jo had been Aunt Carrol's initial choice—until the girls came calling last month, that is. Aunt Carrol reconsidered Aunt March's advice after witnessing Jo's "blunt manners" and "too independent spirit." That is what she said. Had she not complimented Amy so lavishly a moment before, I might have combusted right then and there to hear one of Jo's finest qualities disparaged. The two of us are so alike, a dig at her punctures me doubly.

"Did we not fight a war of independence?" I seethed in Amos's study when we returned home. "Do we not celebrate Independence Day?"

"Indeed we do," Amos said.

"Then why should a young woman's independent spirit be deemed regrettable?"

"I have no better answer for that than you, my dear," Amos said, his fingers steepled beneath his chin. "It seems we have a choice: change our daughter, or change the world."

I do not know why or how that derailed my irritation, but it did so. A hot gust of breath hissed past my teeth and I dropped into an armchair. "Then we shall have to change the world," I said with an injured air. I looked up and saw that Amos's long, flat smile had begun to unroll slowly across his face.

"You're as proud of Jo as I am," I said as if it were an accusation.

"Indeed I am," Amos replied. Give my husband a stack of paper and he will fill every sheet, front and back. Ask him to speak his mind, and he will do so in ten words or less.

If Jo has her way, she will change this world faster than Amos and I can, of that I am sure. Whether it will change quickly enough to suit _her_ is another matter entirely.

Postscript: It was something of a relief to see Laurie doting on Amy rather than Jo for a change.

September 4, 1866

Aunt Carrol's invitation arrived today. I ought to have gone off by myself to open it, but curiosity overcame me. Perhaps it would not have been so hard on Jo if she had not witnessed my first flash of pride at seeing Amy's name. I could not help it; reading those words made me glow and there was nothing I could do to dim that pleasure.

"Oh, Marmee, what is it?" Jo and Beth both begged.

"Aunt Carrol is going abroad next month, and wants—"

"Me to go with her!" Jo cried, bursting up like a firecracker.

What followed when she heard the truth was the sort of tantrum I would sooner expect from Amy than Jo. Fairness and entitlement and all the rest. Still, I am sorry for Jo. She blames her "abominable tongue" for thwarting her prospects, and there is no contesting the fact that her offhand remarks about how she hates French and feels burdened by favors counted against her, but there is more behind Aunt Carrol's choice than the hapless visit she and Amy paid at the Carrols' a month ago.

For years Jo spent five days each week sitting in Aunt March's parlor, clenching her jaw and fancying the old woman too deaf to hear her teeth grinding. How Jo has come up with the notion that her frustration is invisible, I shall never know. She can make the air ripple, the way waves rise from a brick path in August. Is it any wonder then that Aunt March persuaded Aunt Carrol to choose her docile pet instead of the most fractious and unruly of the March sisters?

Nevertheless, the thought of Amy being invited abroad has bewildered Jo to utter senselessness. What a mercy that it was Jo and Beth beside me when I opened the envelope. Had it been Jo and Amy, I am sure the combination of sparks and tinder would have been disastrous.

Between us, Beth and I managed to bolster Jo through the first surge of disappointment. By the time Amy returned and heard the news, Jo had fitted herself up with a passable mask of congratulations.

"I am proud of you, Jo," I told her when Amy floated off to pack her dresses and pencils.

I <u>am</u> proud—as proud of Jo as I am sorry for her. I do not dare tell her so, but were I to pick one of my daughters to see the Continent it surely would have been she. Jo has hungered for the world ever since she was tall enough to reach the latch on our front gate. Amy will revel in the sights and especially in the art, but travel will not nourish her in the same way that two years abroad would feed Jo's restless soul.

Then again, Aunt Carrol and Florence would hardly have suited Jo. They are so staid and, if I may be permitted an uncharitable remark, dull. They will visit all the tearooms and museums of Europe at a stately stroll, whereas Jo would prefer to gallop from one spectacle to the next. That will be of no comfort to her now.

September 6, 1866

If this house does not topple over from the push and pull of the opposing emotions it contains, I shall thank my lucky stars. Amy spent the day flitting from shop to shop with Aunt March to outfit herself for her voyage, happy as a butterfly unfolding its wings for the first time.

She had not been gone half an hour when from the garret came the unmistakable sound of sobbing. Up the stairs I crept, trying to gauge from the sound alone if Jo most needed comfort or solitude. As my eyes drew level with the attic floorboards, surprise halted me with one foot still raised.

There on the three-legged sofa was Jo, wrapped in Laurie's arms and crying as if the world had cracked down the middle. It ought to have been a touching scene. But the look on Laurie's face—I have seen it only in church windows and Renaissance sculptures. Blissful suffering. Pained by Jo's pain, and so enveloped in the ecstasy of having his darling in his arms that he did not notice me on the stairs, indeed likely would not have noticed if Judgment's trumpet blared.

The realization struck with such force, my ears rang with it. He loves Jo. So deeply it hurts him.

I felt as though I were plummeting into a hole. Down onto the steps I sank, listening to Laurie's tender murmurings as my thoughts whirled. This is no teasing matter, no schoolboy's crush. And all the worse because Jo loves him, as all of us do. But her affection, sincere though it may be, is of a completely different nature than he desires.

I slunk back down the stairs and shut the door silently behind me, leaning upon the knob as if it would keep my unease locked in the garret with Laurie and Jo. Of course that did no good. All day long the same thought rumbled along behind me, gaining momentum.

If ever Jo did take a notion to contemplate marriage with something besides repulsion, what then? There isn't anyone on this earth she would consider <u>but</u> Laurie. I cannot conceive of them happily paired for life. Playing at husband and wife, as if performing roles in a comedy, certainly. They have done as much already these last four years. But life, <u>real</u> life? They might as well sit in opposite ends of a canoe, paddling, paddling, paddling and getting nowhere. Married or not, Jo will position herself nowhere but in the prow of her own vessel, her oar in her own two hands. Laurie knows Jo so well—how can he not know this?

I cannot think of one thing to do, except hope that should the day come, my Jo knows herself well enough and has strength enough to break her dearest friend's heart.

September 7, 1866

A knock at the back door at breakfast this morning—Laurie. In he burst, with eyes first for Jo. Then, as if he had suddenly remembered why he had come, a hearty "Good morning, March Family!" for the rest of us. How I must have looked at him, to cause him to hesitate even an instant to sit down at the table for the plate Hannah had already begun piling with buckwheat cakes hot from the pan. Poor boy, I have probably never fixed anyone with such a scramble of uneasiness and welcome.

He had come only to tell us that the beginning of Harvard's fall term coincides with Amy's departure, and that he can accompany her to the dock on his way to school. That is a double mercy. Amy will have a familiar hand to cling to up to the very moment she steps from this continent. And the sooner Laurie has something other than Jo to study, the sooner my mind will stop feeling like a beehive.

September 11, 1866

There is not room enough in my head now to fret over imagined futures for Jo and Laurie, not with the certainty of bidding Amy goodbye tomorrow looming before me.

Two years, at least, without her. I confess, there have been days in the last seventeen years when the prospect would have secretly relieved me. But now, just as Amy is finally beginning to grow into herself? To contemplate what I will miss of her maturation is painful. Not so painful that I would deny her this opportunity, but enough to swell my throat nearly shut each time the thought enters my mind.

Amy herself will miss so much, though I do not know if she has weighed the gains against the losses. She did not hesitate for an instant when I handed her the invitation. Were I in Amy's place, the choice to stay or go would have stymied me.

Leave Meg's babies for a year or more, just when they are becoming plump and playful? I could not do it. The sights of Europe have stood largely unchanged for centuries, but Demi and Daisy shall be entirely different people by the time Amy returns. They will not even know her.

September 12, 1866

For all that Amy has tried our patience over the years, every one of us was loathe to see her climb into the carriage beside Laurie today. I myself would have liked to follow her all the way to the edge of Boston

Harbor, waving my handkerchief until the ship traversed the eastern horizon. Instead I looked at her until I felt sure that I had committed the precise shade of blue of her eyes to memory, then tucked one of Birte's lace napkins into her reticule to serve as a handkerchief and held her to me as I have not done since she was an infant.

Through all of that, I managed to contain my tears. And then Amy and Beth said their goodbyes. The way she hugged Beth, the way Beth looked at her—it mirrored a thought I am unwilling to commit to paper.

The house has that strange, bland feeling that pervaded when Amy was quarantined with Aunt March. Now it shall last not days or weeks, but months upon months. I refuse to think in years.

September 17, 1866

A note from Amy. They have reached Halifax. The poor thing is dreadfully homesick already.

Jo's envy burned so bright, we might have lit the parlor without any lamps. She did not say it, but she did not have to. Her disgust with Amy for daring to not enjoy every second of the journey permeated the room like a foul odor. All of us would have been much relieved if Jo had owned up to her antipathy. Instead we feigned ignorance, sparing Jo the indignity of admitting her foibles—probably to no one's benefit.

And me? I pitied both of my daughters at once. Amy has never been further from home than Plumfield. Part of me is trying to stretch across the ocean, to protect Amy as I always have. It would be easier, I think, if she were not both the youngest and the furthest away.

This is the last we shall hear from her until the ship docks in Southampton. Until her next letter arrives I shall live in suspense. Never have I felt it so literally—as if I am indeed suspended within the empty space of time it shall take for the steamer to cross the sea and the news of Amy's safe arrival to return to us. Days in which the only thing I can be assured of is that the only news that might come is news of disaster.

September 23, 1866

Every night Amos sits at his desk with six notebooks open before him, setting down Daisy's and Demi's development and charting their individual milestones alongside the painstaking chronicles he kept of our own daughters' babyhood.

"How fascinating it would be if I also had a record of John's infancy," he said to me this evening as he leafed through the record of Meg's first months.

Two decades ago, there were days when I should have liked to pitch every one of those notebooks out the window. You might have thought the children were specimens, the way he entered every ounce and quarter inch of growth, every half syllable of babble. While I was mired in nursing and soothing and diapering, tending to colic and teething, he labored over his hand-drawn charts and graphs with the single-mindedness of an ant.

Now, his delight in his records is contagious. He can tell me all manner of facts, such as who smiled earliest (Beth) and who mastered the art of lifting their head to peer at the world before all the others (Demi).

Tonight I paged through Amy's notebook, surprised by how many long-forgotten memories those simple facts and figures could revive. The day she discovered her hands. When we first noticed her hair was inclined to curl. Her love affair with the ragbag, and all the colors and textures it contained.

September 24, 1866

"Can you imagine who I saw at the greengrocer today?" That is what Hannah said to me when she returned with her basket full of fresh cranberries and parsnips. Half a dozen names I offered before she announced, "Mrs. Beall."

Hannah might have snapped her fingers before my nose, I was so startled. "Manor's mother?" Hannah's lifted eyebrows asked me if I knew any other woman by that name.

"Did she— What did she say?"

"Not a word. She nodded at me, and I at her. That was all."

Such a little thing, but oh, how it has pleased me to think that Mrs. Beall has remained in Concord. When we sheltered her son it was without any expectation of future connection. To know that she is here—I cannot explain, even to myself, why it should give me such a—such a settled feeling.

"I knew you'd be pleased," Hannah said with one of her satisfied smiles.

"Did you?" I asked. How remarkable.

"A reminder," Amos said when I told him, "that our efforts were not futile." How like Amos to speak of efforts rather than risks or sacrifices. Before today I might have felt compelled to correct him, if only in my own mind.

"That is close to it," I said. For so many years, I carried an image in my mind: Manor galloping away on the slave catcher's horse. A straight line toward freedom, I thought, I hoped, I prayed. Now that line has looped back around to touch us again, what can I do but marvel?

One day, I hope to see Mrs. Beall on the streets of Concord myself, to see that the journey her son began the day he left Maryland has ended. Here, among us.

September 27, 1866 ❧

Jo has moved into Beth and Amy's room. More than a year without Meg has not accustomed her to sleeping alone. I wonder now why we paired their bedrooms the way we did—oldest and youngest—when Meg has always had an affinity for Amy, and Jo for Beth.

October 8, 1866

What more marvelous gift could I have received this day than a letter from Amy! She is safely arrived in Southampton, after an uneventful crossing. My spine tingled with relief when I saw her handwriting on the envelope.

October 11, 1866

Stopping in at Meg's on the way home from the relief rooms today, I found Beth crying over the babies as they napped in their cradle.

"Oh, Marmee," she said, "aren't they just too beautiful?" They are. Of course they are. So much so that it sometimes hurts to look at them. "To imagine all the places they might go, all the things they might do," Beth mused. "They don't even know how big the world is yet." Beth shook her head at the wonderment of it. But the way she swiped the tears from her cheeks and kept her eyes averted from mine as she said it has lodged itself in my mind. I cannot dispel the notion that Beth envies Daisy and Demi. It makes no sense to me. Beth is but eighteen years old. The world is before her, too, if only she would step out into it.

October 15, 1866

A letter from Olive Kirke, the first in many a month. Running the boardinghouse demands so much of her time that she finds herself in need of a governess for Minnie and Kitty, and hopes I might know a likely young lady. Kitty turns five this December, and Minnie is seven.

I'd wager she is unconsciously wishing Meg were still sixteen years old. If any of the Hummel girls were old enough, I'd suggest one of them in a heartbeat. This is just the sort of position I would love for Beth to occupy, amidst a warm and welcoming home with a hospitable family. But I must learn to accept that her temperament will not permit such experiences. Besides, even if she were the bravest girl alive, her devotion to Daisy and Demi renders the question moot.

October 17, 1866

An odd remark from Amos today. I do not recall just how he phrased it, as he did it in such a gentle and oblique way. In effect, he feels that the babies have usurped him in Beth's affections. She has hardly been in to talk to her father this last month.

If anyone else had told me this I would have laughed at the very idea. It is as unlike Amos to be jealous as it is for Beth to play favorites. She cannot even bear the thought of bestowing unequal attention upon her dolls. But as I watched my husband puzzling over his unaccustomed discontent, a memory scratched its way to the front of my mind.

"The way she cried over Daisy and Demi's cradle as they napped last week—" I began, but Amos interrupted.

"Cried?"

Beth had not told him. He let out the smallest sigh and his lips drooped almost imperceptibly. I felt a pinch in my own heart for Amos, and another, down deep in my belly, for Beth. The idea of Beth keeping an experience of such depth and beauty from her father defies explanation. That is the very plane in which Amos dwells. Something is indeed amiss.

October 23, 1866

Beth is keeping something from me as well as Amos. That would not trouble me if it did not seem to trouble her. In all her life, I have never seen her discontent within these walls—only at the prospect of leaving them.

It cannot be her health. She has gone weeks without a fever or twinges in her knuckles and knees.

A strange reluctance keeps me from asking her if anything is wrong. "Is there anything you want to tell me, Beth?" I ask instead.

"No, Marmee" is all she says. Eddies of affection and sadness swirl across her face each time she answers. Something is wrong, and neither of us are willing to say so.

October 29, 1866

I have asked Jo to suss out Beth's trouble.

It hardly seems fair to burden one daughter with the care and keeping of another, but if Beth will not confide in me, I do not know what else to do. Jo and Beth balance one another in the same way Amos and I do. If Beth will speak to anyone, it is Jo.

November 4, 1866

I am awash in bewilderment tonight. Jo has taken a notion to leave Concord for the winter—to take a place as governess to Olive Kirke's children, in New York City. "To hop a little way and try my wings," as Jo tried to put it in the breezy tone she uses to belie the gravity of a situation.

That alone signaled to me that something was amiss. And Jo a governess, for heaven's sake? Even Meg, in all her docility, came to loathe her job with the King children and they were not the least bit troublesome. My mind refused to contain the idea of Jo finding happiness in such a job, even as she tried to rhapsodize over the prospect of gathering up new sights and sounds to transfigure into fresh plots and characters.

How I managed to find the presence of mind to make my tongue ask the right questions instead of the ones ricocheting from one side of my head to the other, I hardly know. Holding very still, I said, "Are these the only reasons for this sudden fancy?"

And then out it all tumbled, like a spool of thread skittering and spinning across the floor.

Laurie is at the heart of it. Or rather, Laurie's heart. His affection has finally reached a height Jo can no longer pretend to ignore. Her relief when I confessed my own doubts about their compatibility could have filled a bushel basket. She agreed with me wholeheartedly about the strength of their wills and the likelihood of their tempers clashing. Their friendship has been one long and amiable fencing match. That is all well enough when each is assured of going home to their own separate beds at night, and another thing entirely if your opponent is under your nose every moment of the day.

That is muddle enough, and it is only the half of it. The other half—the half that makes my head swim—is Beth. Of all the things in the world that might have troubled Beth, what Jo told me is something I could not have foreseen had I peered into a crystal ball through a set of field glasses. Jo is convinced that Beth is in love with Laurie.

Could it be so? Always it has seemed to me that Beth is in love with the world. Just the world itself, and her small slice of it. Could she have kept something so monumental from me—from all the Family—with no hint seeping out until now? Of course she could; she is a grown woman, for all that we treat her as a beloved pet. Likely there are whole universes contained within the quietude of her heart and mind. Still, no matter how I try, I fail to make myself believe this is the root of Beth's discontent. The feeling I have come to trust, a sensation like that of a key turning inside a lock in my mind when the haze of a question lifts and everything becomes clear, is absent.

But Jo is adamant. And I admit I can find no other explanation for why the sight of Laurie passing beneath her windowsill would bring Beth to tears. Jo watched it happen—saw Beth gaze longingly out the window at him and then spied the tears falling so quietly that Beth believed them unnoticed.

Jo is nearly frantic, knowing how much Laurie cares for <u>her</u> rather than Beth. Even if Jo harbored the least bit of ardor for Laurie, the last thing she would permit herself to do is deprive Beth of her heart's desire. And so Jo's solution is to flee—to remove herself entirely from Laurie's gaze, let alone his reach.

However genuine Jo's concern for her sister, I am certain it is far from her only motive. There is a sort of panic that flashes up in her eyes at the notion of Laurie's desire for her. It leaves me with the sense that any reason I had given for their incompatibility would have un-creased the furrows on Jo's brow, so long as my feelings affirmed her own instinctual aversion to the match.

In all her life, I cannot recall one instance of Jo wanting what other girls and young women want, unless perhaps it was a book. There are times she has put me in mind of the actress Charlotte Cushman, and how she could make an audience's blood run hot and cold whether she was playing the role of Hamlet, Romeo, or Lady Macbeth. I have heard the rumors about Miss Cushman and her affairs, of course. But outside of her own sisters, Jo has never had any use for the company of girls or women.

Jo's capacity for love is deeper and fiercer than anyone's I know, yet I cannot say with certainty that I have ever known her to <u>desire</u> another. The fire she possesses burns a different fuel—a fuel I am thus far unable to name. I suspect it may be a fuel Jo herself has yet to identify.

"You I leave to enjoy your liberty till you tire of it," I told her as if quoting from a mother's manual, "for only then will you find that there is something sweeter."

Already, I regret saying that. Jo gave me that look I have come to know so well, the one I have yet to fully decipher. There is sadness in it, though I cannot say whether it is directed inward or outward. Perhaps both. She seems to be pleading for something. Something I cannot give her? Or is it something she cannot give me?

For all love's sweetness, I begin to wonder if my Jo has the taste for a honeyed life. She takes so much pleasure from the world's savories that now and then I half fancy that I am missing just as much as she. Jo goes for the meat of life, stripping the bones bare and cracking them open for the marrow.

Perhaps it is not romance I truly want for her, but the fulfillment that being loved by Amos and my girls gives to me. I do not know what else could provide that for her, but if it exists, I pray she finds it. New York City may well be as good a place as any to search for it.

November 6, 1866

A letter is posted to Olive Kirke. And now we wait. If in the meantime the position has been filled we shall have to come up with a new plan.

As it stands, I do not feel entirely easy with this one. With Jo gone, Laurie may well pine for her all the more. But what other way is there to thwart his affections? Besides, Jo's discontent here is not to be denied. Watching her these last days, it is evident that she is every bit as restless and anxious as she professes to be. Holding back from Laurie, ensuring that she does not feed his hopes, is exhausting her. A separation will benefit her at least as much as him, if not more.

"Olive Kirke is as fine a woman as I know," I said to Amos as we sat across the chessboard from one another this evening. He nodded, unperturbed by my sudden declaration. "And it will do Jo good to see how another family lives, as well as to experience the city." Another nod. I waited as long as I could tolerate, then counted to fifty for good measure. "Have you nothing to say?"

His eyes fixed me with a mixture of admiration and bemusement. "It seems you have summed it all up quite succinctly."

"Then you agree?"

"Would my opinion, if it differed, change yours, or Jo's?" Oh, that sly smile. No one on this earth can grin as slyly as Amos can without employing even a hint of antagonism. He knew the answer to that question, just as well as I had known the answer to mine.

"The similarity between Jo's situation and that which you faced with Mr. Frothingham is striking," Amos remarked.

I sat staring at him. How had that not occurred to me? There are times when I wonder if I have lived my life with my eyes shut. When Father pressed me to marry my cousin, I demurred, fleeing to Duxbury and Miss Allyn instead, hoping, as Jo hopes, that passions would fade in my absence. The experience was among the most valuable of my life. I can only pray that Jo will fare as well as I did.

November 12, 1866

Olive Kirke is delighted at the prospect of hiring Jo. "Positively de-lighted," she wrote, her emphasis such that I could not fail to hear her gusto. Her reply returned so quickly, she must have written and posted it within minutes of receiving mine.

Jo took the news with the resolution of a soldier. One curt nod, and an about-face up the stairs to pack. The fact that she is leaving not only Laurie but all of the Family has begun to set in. Abandoning Laurie is chore enough for her heart, for she does love him, just as she loves books and apples and running through the woods.

If only we could know in advance that this is the right course of action. The task of stymieing a romance is ticklish enough, but to do it while also preserving a treasured friendship? That could well be a futile endeavor. Both of them are bound to change in the coming months. I should hate to see their natural affinity sacrificed if they were to grow apart, or if Laurie were to become resentful of the separation. So, too, would Beth, if she knew the full truth.

"Why must love change when it could simply grow stronger instead?" Jo demanded today. What answer could I give? The question itself flummoxed me, for I had never contemplated the difference. Within the realm of my own love for Amos, the change from friendship to romance represented a deepening. For Jo it is plainly not so.

November 15, 1866

Off she went, her face a smear of tears and smiles. Whatever Jo whispered as she hugged Beth sent an indecipherable look across Beth's face.

I had promised myself I would not cry—a promise I broke within half a minute of seeing her satchel lifted up into the carriage. Jo herself could not keep her cheeks dry. What a shame that on this, her first adventure, sadness must outweigh her excitement.

As for myself, I felt almost ashamed to look at Laurie. That young man is no fool. The way he cast his eye toward me told me he knew that I have had a hand in this. To his credit, he seems determined to be resigned instead of resentful, though it is achieved only with an effort.

November 17, 1866

Jo is arrived safely in New York City. Olive Kirke was kind enough to send a telegram upon her arrival, though the sight of the messenger at the front door frightened the life out of me. Will it ever occur to me that a telegram might contain <u>good</u> news?

November 23, 1866

The sofa is so terribly empty now, with the sausage pillow lying alone in Jo's customary corner. How can a pillow seem lonely? And yet it does. Without Jo to animate it, it is simply an old horsehair bolster.

When Amos was at war I longed for nothing more than tranquility. Now, with Jo gone, I find that the house is once again out of balance, in the opposite direction this time. Tranquility taken too far, it seems, leans near to apathy. A pinch of chaos would be a welcome antidote, for the current that runs through her has such vitality that I cannot help drawing strength from it.

Beth, too, shows an uncharacteristic lack of interest in her usual duties and pleasures. After all the care Jo has insisted upon taking over Beth's heart, I hope her absence will not be a detriment to her sister's health. But that is irrational. If anything Beth's constitution has strengthened since Daisy and Demi arrived.

December 6, 1866

Daisy and Demi. We say their names as if they are a single word—Daisy-and-Demi—but in fact they are already becoming quite different little creatures. Daisy will let you sing and read to her all the day long, so beguiled is she by the sounds of voices. Demi shows little interest in that which he cannot touch. We are forever extracting all sorts of mysterious objects from his fists. Feathers, flower buds, buttons. Once, a darning needle. Anything that moves pulls his attention like a magnet.

December 25, 1866

Our first Christmas with the babies. They have been our greatest gift this year. Despite all we have to rejoice in, it was impossible not to miss Jo and Amy. It is odd to say, but I missed Jo more. We have had months to accustom ourselves to Amy's blank place at the table. Jo's still throbs. Laurie called, as he always does, staying but a few minutes. His single, furtive glance toward Jo's chair told me how much he blames himself for her absence.

January 7, 1867

Another overdue visit to Aunt March today. I owe her a great many thanks for all she has done for Amy.

She was in a mildly volcanic mood, her groundskeeper having had the audacity to announce his plans to retire. "First Josephine, then Amy, and now this!" she huffed.

To hear her talk, you might be persuaded that no one on earth suffers as she does. Although I must grant that old Addison has been part of Aunt March's household for longer than anyone living or dead, including Uncle March. Likely it is because so much of Addison's time was spent outdoors rather than under her close scrutiny. So long as the roses, lilies, and violets are seen to be thriving, he was free to smoke his pipe in peace.

January 10, 1867

"Wonders never cease," Amos said as he finished reading Jo's latest letter aloud to Beth and me. She has already made the acquaintance of a lady—a lady!—in Olive Kirke's boardinghouse. A Miss Norton, "rich, cultivated, and kind," Jo says. If Amy were here, she would fall over in a dead faint from surprise.

How soothing it is to imagine Jo in her "sky-parlor," as she puts it, gazing out the window over the rooftops and church steeples of the city with her pen poised over a stack of paper. Even Beth gave a little sigh of contentment at that.

There is much to be contented with outside our walls as well. Suffrage has at last been expanded to Negro men in Washington, D.C., thanks to the votes of the radical Republican senators. President Johnson has once again been bested by the legislature, much to my gratification.

If I were forced to choose which of these two pieces of news gives me more pleasure, I would simply spin like a weathervane in a spring gale.

January 12, 1867

The babies shall begin crawling any minute now, and then will Meg ever have her hands full! Both of them are able to poise themselves on hands and knees. Then they huff like little locomotives as they rock forward and back. John entices them with rattles and balls placed just out of reach.

"Not one of our girls crawled so soon," Amos informs me, as if Daisy and Demi have already begun.

January 17, 1867

Twice this week, there has been a young woman standing across the street from the relief rooms. Dark-haired, with a face pretty enough to turn heads and an expression that announces that she does not wish to be noticed. Her clothes are neither patched nor ragged, but the garments are not nearly warm enough to stand up to a Massachusetts winter. She watches people going in and out, some with grocery orders, and eyes their bundles with an intensity so covetous I half expect her to pounce.

This morning she crossed the street as if on the verge of approaching the door, then abruptly shrank away when Mrs. Carter and Mrs. King arrived. What holds her back, I do not know.

Next time she appears, I shall speak to her.

January 19, 1867

No matter how closely I observe Beth and Laurie, I cannot see what Jo saw. If Beth is in love, she shows no trace of it. True, Laurie is different with Beth. All his brash jocularity is gone, rendering him so attentive and courtly, you would think Beth had newly been crowned Queen of Concord.

Nor can I loosen the impression that each of them is treating their time together as a favor for Jo. There is something almost like formality between Beth and Laurie as they read and talk before the fire. Their enjoyment is somehow both authentic and vicarious, with the latter prevailing. This afternoon they sat upon the sofa with the sausage between them. Each of them unconsciously rested a hand upon it, as if Jo herself were there. Indeed, she is the topic of conversation more often than not.

But the Jo that each envisions sitting between them is not the same person. Laurie's eyes drift upward each time he speaks of her, as if he were painting a likeness of Jo onto the air before him. I can only imagine that the portrait becomes more ornate each time. The longer she is away, the greater opportunity he has to create an ideal Jo in his mind, the Jo he longs for. No doubt he has already christened her Josephine Laurence.

"What will he do when the real Jo returns," I asked Amos, "and stands shoulder to shoulder with his vision?" My husband has spent his life reconciling ideals with reality, after all.

"You assume that Laurie will recognize the two as distinct from one another," Amos replied with remarkable placidity.

His words sank through me, settling somewhere near the soles of my slippers. If that is so, this separation may indeed do more harm than good. Laurie's poor heart. Jo's will bleed, but his will shatter. What a bleak prospect, and not one thing we can do to avert it.

January 23, 1867

The young woman returned to her post across the street late this afternoon, after an absence of four days. I hung the skein of yarn I was winding over a nail and went outside. She was younger than I had guessed from a distance. Certainly under twenty, if not less than eighteen. "Would you like to step in out of the cold?" I offered, gesturing toward the door.

She shook her head. "Your clothing does not look equal to the weather," I observed. "If you should find yourself chilled, please know you are welcome in the relief rooms." She said nothing, and I returned to my work.

At the close of day, she was still standing in the same spot. I approached again. "You look hungry," I said.

"I was born that way," she retorted.

"If you need a meal, you're welcome to come home with me and share mine."

That disarmed her for an instant. Her face lost its hardness, and she eyed me differently. "What I need is a job," she said.

"Very well," I replied. "Come with me and we'll see about it. My name is Margaret March," I added, offering my hand to shake.

She extended her hand with some suspicion, as if she expected me to change my mind and jerk mine back at her touch. "Mary Ann," she replied.

At supper she had eyes for nothing but her plate. The relief on her face at the size of the servings Hannah spooned out for her spoke volumes. Despite her hunger, she managed to observe all the manners of the table. I had given her Amy's place, across from Beth. She is about Amy's age, and every bit as pretty, if not more so, and buxom as a storybook milkmaid.

We had a private talk afterward, for she would say nothing of herself in Amos's presence.

"My ma followed General Hooker's troops from camp to camp. To keep up the men's morale," she added. Her look was a test. Using the majority of my self-possession to hold my face impassive, I nodded understanding and she continued. "I was eleven when the war started. Too young. By the time it ended I was fifteen. That was old enough for some of them. Ma wouldn't let me take any man over twenty-five. It's the only trade I've worked since."

That makes her but seventeen years old. Hardly more than a child. "And what of your ma?" I asked.

"Dead. Camp fever. Thought I'd say something else, didn't you?"

"Strike before you're struck," I said, trying not to betray my irritation. "That's your motto."

"If you'd been struck as often as I have, you'd do the same," she countered.

I closed my mouth, nodded my concession, and began again. "How did you come to be in Concord?"

"Why do people always ask questions that don't matter?" she asked wearily.

She was right. It was irrelevant, and none of my business besides. "You said you need a job. What other kind of work can you do?"

"I might learn to do anything, if anyone would bother to teach me. But they won't. Women look at me like trash. You'd think they could smell it on me, as if I never washed. Well, I do wash. I wash every time."

Thankfully I managed not to blanch at that. No doubt she would have dismissed me as one of those prim ladies who won't give her the time of day. But what she said is true—it does show. Her utter lack of modesty gives away her history at a glance. That is not to say that her dress and manner are lewd. It is more the absence of any . . . oh, there is no proper word for it. The invisible veil of virtue that shields most women does not shield her. Her gaze conceals nothing from men, and challenges women.

"Let me ponder this, and we will discuss possibilities in the morning," I said.

I led her to Meg and Jo's room, where I took a set of fresh sheets from the dresser drawer and began to make up the bed. Mary Ann stood in the center of the room, eyeing it and me with equal suspicion. "Aren't you afraid I'll make off with something in the night?" she asked.

Her insistence on refusing to be trusted irked me so that I marched to my room and took from its satin cushion the five-acorn pin the girls gave to me the Christmas Amos returned from the war. "Here is the article I value most in this house," I said, holding it out to her. "If your object is to hurt me, take it now. If money is what you need, you will find it in the lower drawer of my husband's desk."

From her expression I could not judge whether she thought this pronouncement kind or cruel. In truth, I myself was not certain. "What I most fear losing cannot be taken by any thief but God," I said more softly. This confession quieted both of us.

"Whose hair is that?" she asked after a moment's silence, stretching a tentative finger toward the gray acorn. "Your ma's?"

"My father's. My mother left this world long before her hair had time to turn gray. The rest are my daughters'."

She nodded. "May I . . . may I lock that door?"

Her voice was that of a child. Despite all she has seen, I realized, she is younger yet than Amy. "I'm afraid the keys to these doors have all been misplaced from lack of use." A gesture, a slight hugging of herself with her crossed arms, betrayed her unease. "You have nothing to fear from my husband," I assured her. "But if it will help you to rest easier, I will bring you a kitchen chair to wedge beneath the knob." She nodded, showing a hint of shame for the first time. Ashamed of being afraid, of all things.

I fetched the chair, and listened from the hallway as the legs scraped the floor and the doorknob rattled gently.

"What use may we be to her?" Amos asked when I returned downstairs for the evening.

"I declare, I don't know yet," I said. There was almost nothing I could tell him without breaking her confidence. Any solution to this quandary is solely up to me.

January 24, 1867

A night and a day of pondering, and still I remain at a loss for how to help Mary Ann find employment, knowing what I do. It is no one's business, and yet if Mrs. King were to take her on as a maid and then learn of Mary Ann's past? Some form of scandal would surely ensue. And it is more than probable that the truth would indeed leak out. A "likely girl" can always find a gentleman in need of a favor or two, Mary Ann told me today, even in the most reputable of neighborhoods. Though she did not say so outright, I was given to understand that some few residents of Concord have already purchased certain favors of her, thereby tarnishing her prospects for reputable employment in this vicinity.

It is enough to make my stomach turn and my head ache, wondering who in this town has the abundance of funds and lack of morality to indulge in such offenses. But that is beside the point. The relevant matter is that Mary Ann must seek a situation somewhere else—somewhere large enough that she may go unrecognized. A fresh start in New York or Boston, perhaps. Surely there must be organizations in the cities devoted to the cause of such women. If anyone will know, it is Olive Kirke.

With Mary Ann's permission, I shall write to Olive first thing in the morning.

January 25, 1867

The letter is posted to Olive, leaving us little to do but wait. To my immense gratification, Mary Ann is not content to sit idle. Assisting in the relief rooms is tantamount to anathema for her, however. ("All those women looking at me? Never," she vowed.) I suggested lessons, seeing as there can be no question that her schooling has been neglected.

"How well can you read?" I asked her.

"I got partway through the second reader before the war broke out. And I learned to cipher well enough to know if I've been cheated in my pay." Amos was off paying calls on his congregants, so I led her into the study. The sight of our bookshelves stopped her cold. "Do you have any . . . any books about animals? With pictures?" she asked shyly. "My favorite thing in school was to look at the drawings of fish and birds in the teacher's big books."

I pulled a stack of zoology and ornithology texts from the shelves and piled them up on the table beside my armchair. You'd think I had put a pot of gold there. All afternoon she sat contentedly poring over diagrams of everything from whales to finches while Beth practiced her piano. For the first time since Jo left for the city, the house did not feel so lopsided.

January 29, 1867

Today was spent in cutting up one of Amos's old wool army blankets to make a suitable cloak and hood for Mary Ann. Between the four of us—Hannah, Beth, Mary Ann, and I—we managed to get it pieced together and hemmed by suppertime. "It's worn a bit thin in spots," I acknowledged, "but wool will keep out more of the cold than your old flannel, at least."

"The color reminds me of the camps," she said, "and Ma. Her favorite color was blue." It was the first she has spoken of her past in anyone's presence but my own.

Mary Ann has taken an especial liking to Hannah, I've noticed. Is it coincidence, or do the parallel aspects of their lives somehow speak to one another? Beth she insists upon calling "Miss Beth," as if she were a servant and Beth her mistress.

Tonight as we sang around the piano before bed, Mary Ann joined us in a tentative alto. Though the notes sometimes wavered off tune, they were a welcome addition to our diminished Family choir.

Tomorrow I shall look through my notions and see if I can't find a bit of trimming for her hood. I believe I have a length of black braid that would do well.

February 2, 1867

Miss Mary Ann Donnelly is a keen observer. Too keen, perhaps. Noticing I was out of sorts after breakfast today, she inquired what was the matter.

"I'm afraid I have promised to pay a call on my husband's aunt this afternoon," I confessed. "It is a duty I dread, no matter how many times I perform it."

"Only you? Not Mr. March?"

I had to admit that though Amos calls on Aunt March almost once a week, I have not been in close to a month. Mary Ann studied me long enough to make me want to fidget, then asked if she might accompany me. "Why on earth?" I asked.

"I want to see the woman who can fluster <u>you</u>," she said with a grin that rivals Amos's for slyness. Beth gulped back a laugh. Hannah, too, made some sound of surprise. Amos sipped his tea with irksome placidity.

Of course it was a dreadful idea. After all the uproar over our hiring Hannah those years ago, what kind of commotion would Aunt March make if she suspected me of bringing a teenaged prostitute into her home for a social call?

Yet with Amos sitting there, blissfully unaware of the stains upon Mary Ann's virtue, I could offer no sound reason for refusing her request. Mary Ann has not been in the least ill-mannered or indiscreet during her time under our roof, after all. The more I thought of it, the more the idea tickled the most mischievous part of my brain. Reprisal is not something I ordinarily hunger for, but the notion of pulling the wool over Aunt March's eyes presented an undeniable appeal.

So we went, and Mary Ann charmed Aunt March as effortlessly as Beth wins over stray kittens. I sat there and watched every instant, and still I don't know how she achieved it. Chameleon-like, she become demure and deferential to every member of the household. First the poodle took a liking to her, and then the parrot, for heaven's sake. Once the animals had deemed her worthy of their attention and affection, Aunt March had no chance of resisting.

Never once did Mary Ann lie, or even bend the truth. She presented herself as an orphan, displaced by the war. "I called at the relief rooms and Mrs. March kindly took me in until I can find a proper place for myself," she explained.

"Margaret has a decided propensity for such things," Aunt March replied, "some more successful than others. I am gratified to see that she has at last taken an interest in someone with bright prospects."

"That is the most pleasant visit Aunt March and I have had in— well, I don't know how long. Years, certainly," I marveled as we walked back home. "As far as she was concerned you were far more agreeable a guest than I."

"The maid knew better," Mary Ann said. "The French lady. I don't suppose she figured out the particulars, but I could see her trying. People who've seen a . . . a girl like me, they remember it the way a hound remembers a scent."

We walked awhile, each cloaked in our own thoughts before she said, "Mr. March and Miss Beth and Hannah, they wouldn't like me so well if they knew."

I put my hand to her shoulder. "I believe they may have already guessed," I said gently, "simply by virtue of the fact that I have taken such care to divulge nothing about your prior circumstances."

That troubled her. "But why are they so kind to me?"

"Why shouldn't they be?" I countered.

She had no answer to that.

February 5, 1867

Reading Jo's letters is very much like reading one of her stories. Even Mary Ann sits rapt with attention when Amos and I read them aloud, for the characters are so bright, you can fairly hear their voices. One in particular, a German boarder by the name of Bhaer, has been prominent in her correspondence for the last few weeks. He is a bachelor, some thirty-five or forty years old, with two orphaned nephews to whom he is utterly devoted. Her anecdotes of how he frolics with them on Saturdays are charming in the extreme. It sounds as though he is a most considerate man, lending Jo books and bringing up her mail. She is taking German lessons from him now, and doing his mending, which he calls "good fairy work." What an immense pleasure, to know that Jo is learning. And what a treat it will be to have someone to practice my own German with when she returns.

It is a fine thing, too, to know that she is enjoying the society of others outside of our Family and the Laurences. Her life thus far has been more insular than I ever intended it to be.

February 12, 1867

Olive Kirke writes of the Magdalen Society in New York, which has erected a reform house at Eighty-sixth Street and Fifth Avenue dedicated to the purpose of rehabilitating girls and women like Mary Ann. "Send the young lady to me this Thursday, and I will see to it that she is safely delivered to the asylum the very next morning," Olive promised.

We shall just have time to sew the trim onto Mary Ann's cloak before she departs.

"Asylum?" she said when I read Olive's letter to her. "Reform? What will they do to me there?"

"They will provide you with a bed that is warm, safe, and clean;

resume your education; and help you find employment you need not be ashamed of."

"There were reformers outside the camps sometimes," she said, her tone dubious. "The way some of them talked, they could just as well have thrown mud at us and saved their breath."

"Do you trust me?" I asked. Her head bobbed up and down, quick and a trifle grudgingly. "And I trust Olive Kirke's judgment. My own daughter is boarding with her, after all. Olive and I are of one mind when it comes to serving those whose needs exceed their means. She would not approve of any establishment that lacks in dignity or compassion, no matter how well-meaning their aims." Mary Ann did not reply. Nor did she protest, so I continued. "You'll take the train to the city and a cab to this address," I said, handing her a note with the street and number of the boardinghouse. "Mrs. Kirke will put you up for the night with my daughter, Jo, and then see you to the Magdalen Asylum in the morning."

"Jo?" she interjected. "That's the one Miss Beth misses so much, isn't it?"

That seemed to make the difference. A look of forbearance settled over her face from top to bottom, like a shade being pulled. "If you cannot abide the conditions with the Magdalens, send word," I told her. "You will always be welcome with the March Family."

"I don't like to go. I've . . . I've got fond of you," she admitted. "You've been as good to me as my own ma. Better, sometimes."

I had not expected that. All this time she has been so reserved. "It has been good for all of us to have you here," I said. "This house does not fully feel like home with so many of my girls away." The impulse to embrace her crossed my mind then, but I refrained. That child has had enough hands upon her body.

February 14, 1867

All of us are sobered tonight with Mary Ann gone.

She looked so smart at the train station in her blue cloak and hood with the black braid making a frame around her dark hair. A small basket Hannah had filled with bread and cheese and two piping-hot baked potatoes hung at the crook of her elbow.

Beth presented her with a scarf and mittens, knitted in rich blue wool with white tassels and cuffs. "I was making them for Jo, but I'd rather you have them," Beth said. To prove it so, she had embroidered "Mary" on the left cuff and "Ann" on the right. Mary Ann put them on, and kissed Beth's cheek with utmost tenderness.

From Amos's pocket came a small volume bound in green, the cover embellished with a gilt thrush. *The Book of Birds: Intended for the Amusement and Instruction of Young People,* the spine said. Mary Ann's mouth fell open as he held it out to her. Amos said not a word, only gave her a small nod to encourage her to take it.

Last of all I handed her a packet of paper and stamps and envelopes. "I took the liberty of addressing several of the envelopes to me," I said. "I hope you'll write from the city, and from wherever life takes you afterward. If ever I hear of a job in Concord that suits you, I shall send for you," I promised, "for I have become fond of you, too."

Tears spilled down her cheeks then, though her expression did not change. I reached into my own reticule and pulled out a handkerchief—one of Birte's fine napkins. When her face was dry, I tucked the lacy square of linen into her basket, praying that I would not need it myself before she departed. I managed it then, but now I find I must dab at my eyes after every paragraph. I shall be almost as eager for news from her as I am from Jo and Amy.

February 18, 1867

Demi is taken ill with croup. Meg has taken Daisy to our house, in hopes of sparing her the infection, while Hannah and I tend to Demi at the Dovecote.

We have turned Meg's kitchen into a combination nursery-infirmary. Kettles simmer on the stove at all hours to keep the air moist enough to soothe Demi's constricted throat. When he breathes, the sound is like something from underwater.

Poor Meg is run ragged, between the worry and running back and forth to deliver the jelly jars she manages to fill with her milk every few hours. Each time Demi hears her voice, he cries, which only worsens the cough. It is a dreadful thing to hear emanating from such a small body, like nothing so much as the barking of a seal.

February 20, 1867

The cough is no better or worse. Demi's temperature has been slowly climbing all day. It is not yet cause for alarm, but John is poised to run for Dr. Bangs at any moment. He will sleep on the sofa tonight, with his boots and coat within reach. Hannah and I will not sleep, but take turns watching and listening for any signs of distress from Demi.

February 21, 1867

I woke in a state of terror in the middle of the night, startled by silence. Hannah sat beside the cradle, a bundle in her arms and a thin shine of tears upon her cheeks. I felt the world go still, and then Hannah saw me and smiled. Demi was sleeping peacefully. The fever has all but vanished. John nearly fainted with relief when we told him, then put on his boots and hat and ran out to tell Meg the news without stopping to put on his coat.

February 22, 1867

Nothing can be so trying as keeping these babies separated until the danger of Daisy catching the croup has passed. Demi frets in his sleep, throwing his arms over the space his sister usually occupies in the cradle, and cries each time he wakes to find her missing. Meg reports that Daisy is no happier, despite Beth's best efforts with music, dolls, and every kind of plaything she can improvise.

February 25, 1867

It was nearly worth the worry and tribulation of the past week to see Daisy and Demi reunited. How he crowed, and how she cooed! Nothing of the coddling and remedies we have plied Demi with since his breath began to whistle has done him half the good that seeing his sister did today. We put them in the cradle together and they promptly cuddled down to sleep, so close that the eyelashes of one could tickle the cheeks of the other. As dear as my husband and my girls are to me, I envy those two babies. The bond between them has a depth I can never truly fathom.

March 2, 1867

Jo's letters these days are filled with concerts, plays, lectures, even visits to Barnum's New American Museum. A place brimming with marvels and humbugs, she writes. How like Jo to set her sights across the ocean before exploring the wonders of our own backyard, as it were.

As much as I savor the adventures contained in her letters, it puts me in a strange muddle of gratitude and resentment to know that thanks to Miss Norton's generosity, Jo's horizons are finally expanding in ways we have never been able to afford. She ought to have had these opportunities so much sooner. If not for the bounty hunter who came to our door, she surely would have.

I may have forgiven myself, but I do not find it possible to forgive those who forced me to choose whether my daughters had more right to an education than a Negro had a right to be free.

Of course, that was not the choice we believed we were making at the time. Always, Amos and I have given what we could spare, and we believed we could spare the fines. But had I known what the price would be to the girls, the decision would have given me greater pause. It is not a just comparison. Their psyches do not bear the scars of bondage, but there are fetters—however weak by comparison—on their minds.

How I have hated the very thought of those fetters all these years! Hated them. I cannot write it boldly enough, or repeatedly enough to express it. Before Asia Beall called upon us, I could not even allow myself to acknowledge it. How could I dare resent the price my daughters paid without diminishing what it purchased for Asia's son? But now I shall say it once again: There is nothing I have hated more than the limits placed upon my children by my worst fit of fury.

Only within these pages will I admit that there are still nights when I dream of alternate pasts and futures, of how life might have been if we had not defied the Fugitive Slave Act. Of the assurance of money in the bank, a dinner table filled with the best the market can bear, clothes that don't render my daughters objects of mute pity, and, greatest luxury of all, tutors worthy of my four girls. Music lessons for Beth, and drawing instruction for Amy. The hardest thing of all was to see Meg and Jo tramp off to work each day instead of school. Especially Jo. Unfair though it may be, her lack of learning has always troubled me more than her sisters', for she hungered for it most. Her mind has certainly never been starved, but neither has it fully flourished. Perhaps now it may receive the nourishment it has craved for all these years.

March 7, 1867

Jo's and Amy's letters are as different as the sun and the moon. Where Jo writes about everyone and everything but herself, Amy is ever at the center of her own universe, seeing the sights of Europe as if they were erected solely for her own delight. We hear all about how everyone looks, and what they buy in the shops, and in what style their whiskers are trimmed. Laurie's friends, the Vaughn twins, squired her about London as if she were a duchess, and then turned up in France for more "parley-vooing," as Amy puts it. Their paths may cross yet again in Rome this winter. She exists in a perpetual whirlwind of pleasure, so bright and gay that I can all but hear her laughter punctuating each paragraph.

Beneath her gaiety, there is a deep and abiding love of the world's beauty that makes me proud. I hear it in her descriptions of the countryside as seen through the train windows, and even in her inability to describe Westminster Abbey in words. Colors and shapes beguile her just as thoroughly now as they did when she was an infant. I simply ache to see her sketchbook already.

March 12, 1867

Olive Kirke writes to inform me that Jo is spending a good deal of time with another of the boarders, one Professor Friedrich Bhaer—as if we have not heard all about him already from Jo. You can practically hear her conspiratorial wink as you read the words. She does not yet know my Jo as I do. Still, it is good to know that Olive holds this professor in high regard.

March 17, 1867

Demi is walking—walking!—at just eight months old. Perhaps it is more correct to say that he is stepping. He takes one step, and then another, and then stands still and crows with ecstasy until every face in the room has turned to congratulate him. Demi's glee can only be rivaled by Amos's as he scribbles down his grandson's exceptional progress. It would not surprise me to see Amos on his hands and knees, gauging the length of Demi's steps with my measuring tape.

Daisy will not tolerate this for long, I sense. She glowers darkly each time her brother is showered with applause.

March 24, 1867

What began as a mere coincidence this afternoon has turned into serendipity.

As I stood awaiting my turn at the counter at the butcher, I could not help but hear the conversation Mr. Derby conducted with the man in front of me as he weighed and wrapped the man's bacon and chops.

"I'm afraid I have miscounted," the customer said when it came time to pay. "I shall have to come back for the chops another day." The back of his neck turned pink before my eyes as he fumbled with his coins. The voice sounded a faint note of recognition, and I stepped closer. Just then he turned around, nearly colliding with me.

We looked at each other as if struck by lightning. Here was the very same man I had encountered in the relief rooms years ago, on that day when I was so consumed by worries for Amos that I could see no one's troubles but my own—the father who had so proudly given four sons to the army.

From his pocket he pulled what served him as a handkerchief—a faded blue-and-white-striped square of cloth which I recognized as the napkin I had used to bundle up my lunch and a few dollar bills that day in January of 1862.

"You're her," he said, speaking to me as if I were the Queen of England. "Aren't you?"

"I am the very same," I answered, "and so pleased to see you again, sir. Your words that day have given me much to ponder over the years."

"Have they?" he said, nonplussed at the idea.

"Indeed. I have often remembered you and your boys in my prayers. May I ask how they fared?"

His name is Silas Ward. Out of four sons sent to war, one returned. One died fighting, two of dysentery (one in an army hospital and the other in a Confederate prison). His remaining son, the one he was setting out to visit in Washington when our paths crossed, recovered from malaria only to return to battle and be wounded beyond repair. Both limbs on one side of his body claimed by cannon fire, and yet the boy lived.

I would so have liked to introduce him to Amos and Beth and Meg, but Mr. Ward declined my invitation to accompany me home to dine with our Family, explaining that his son could not be left alone for so long as that.

"May I . . . may I be permitted to stop in and see him?" I asked. It was an impulse—a desire to see the face of this young man I had so often imagined, and to thank him for all that he has given in service to the cause of freedom.

Mr. Ward considered, taking the measure of me. "You're sure?" I nodded, which was almost a lie, for the way he asked had caused a sudden sprig of doubt to shoot up like a weed within me. "All right." He conducted me through the streets to a part of town I have spent little time in. Not so poor as the alleys where Birte and Kitty Neal live, nor so comfortable as the homes of the shopkeepers and schoolmasters of Amos's congregation.

I do not know now what I expected to see when the door opened, for the sight that greeted me swept away any visions my mind had conjured. Succulents in everything from jelly jars to teacups lined the windowsills. Ferns filled every corner. Not the Boston ferns of highbrow conservatories, but those you'd find in any common woods. A cactus plant with dark red berries stood in a pail of sand beside the stove. But it was the violets that took my breath away. Dozens upon dozens of dainty white- and purple-faced blooms smiling up at me from crates and coal hods.

"Spent my life hoeing other men's fields," Mr. Ward said. "I'd hoped by now to have saved enough to tend a little garden of my own. But seeing as my wages won't stretch so far as a cottage requires, I bring the outdoors in instead."

My surprise was so all-encompassing, it came almost as an

afterthought when he introduced me to his son, Aaron. In a room so crowded with color and greenery, Aaron Ward hardly stood out from the planks of the walls. None of the faces I had pictured in my prayers matched the young man's before me. Two sunken eyes looked out from a pale and poorly shaven countenance. Two wide bands of linen held him tied to a ladderback chair for balance.

My right hand had begun to lift before I realized he had no right hand with which to shake. Quickly I substituted my left and received an expressionless squeeze in reply. He is not the sort of cheerful invalid you meet in books. It is quite possible that I have never encountered a man so morose. To my greetings and inquiries, he answered in a monotone that fell somewhere between a murmur and a grumble. The only flicker of interest came at the sight of the scars on my right hand. I turned my head slightly so that those on my neck and jaw became visible, too, but he said nothing of them.

My innate compulsion to try to gladden his spirits left me tongue-tied. What on earth had I imagined that I could say to this man that he would be glad to hear? When the president implored us "to care for him who shall have borne the battle," I failed to realize all that he was asking.

My visit did Silas Ward some good, at least; I cannot imagine he has much opportunity to enjoy the society of others.

It was not until I was walking past the unpruned hedges of Plumfield that it occurred to me—Aunt March is still without a groundskeeper! If there is a reason in the world why Silas Ward should not replace Addison in Plumfield's gardens and conservatory, I cannot think of it.

March 25, 1867

Twenty-five years of acquaintance has still not taught me that Aunt March's enthusiasm for extending a helping hand to her fellow-beings will never match my own.

"I need a capable groundskeeper, not a charity case," she replied when I told her of Silas Ward's circumstances.

"And if he is both?" I countered.

"If he fulfills the former, the latter is no business of mine," she conceded. "The lawns and shrubs are one thing, but how do you expect a man who has spent his life hoeing potatoes to tend to my roses and lilies?"

"For sheer concentration of blooms, the inside of his rooms might be said to rival your conservatory," I said, extolling the lushness of the ferns and violets.

"Violets?" she interrupted, her voice like that of another woman entirely.

Oh, what happy chance! I had plunged my arrow without even taking aim. Bunches of white violets lie upon her daughter's grave more often than any other flower.

"Enough to fill a bathtub," I said.

All resistance broke then. She did not admit it, but the atmosphere of the room had altered so fully, the paint on the walls might have changed color.

"I shall give him a month's trial," she announced with her unrivaled imperiousness. "If my conservatory does not suffer any losses in that time, he and his son may move into the groundskeeper's quarters."

I left Plumfield feeling as if I had eaten a feast. Nothing satiates my spirits like this kind of triumph. For a triumph it is—not just in besting Aunt March, but in finding a space that seems perfectly carved out for one person and fitting them into it.

March 31, 1867

Daisy has bested her brother. Today after our Sunday dinner she stood for a long time at John's knee as he sat on the sofa, seemingly entranced by Beth's music. Then suddenly Daisy let go of her father's pant leg and plodded solemnly across the room to the piano bench. Such a roar of cheers went up that Daisy sat down and cried. For her reward, she was given a seat beside Beth and full reign over the keyboard, while Hannah consoled Demi with sweets from her apron pocket.

What an unexpected joy it is to be able to savor each and every instant of these moments as they unfold. I had thought that I'd reveled in my own children's progress; not until Daisy and Demi arrived did I realize how fragmented my attention had been during those childhood years. Now the delight is doubled in so many ways—first by virtue of <u>twin</u> grandbabies, of course, but also by watching Meg and John's joy and wonder at the two little souls they have begotten.

April 13, 1867

A letter from Mary Ann! Everything is so much the same at the asylum, she writes, that it took weeks to accumulate enough news to warrant a sheet of paper.

She does not sound quite like herself, a circumstance I hope is due to the simple fact that her stunted education forces her to write in the voice of a schoolgirl.

"The assilum is the cleanest place I have ever lived," she said. "It has to be, for every thing is white." The matrons are kind enough, she assures me, adding that they would be kinder if some of the other girls and women would let them. "Some of the girls are almost as sweet as Beth. Some are sourer than Mr. March's aunt."

I let out one bark of laughter so sudden and short, it sounded as if I had choked on my tea.

"Are you all right, Marmee?" Beth asked. Amos was half out of his chair, looking alarmed.

"Very much so," I replied.

April 24, 1867 ⚬

A squib in the *Herald* this morning regarding a most interesting situation on the streetcars of Richmond, Virginia. It seems that a Negro man insisted on being permitted to ride, even daring to enter the car itself. When the conductor put him off, a crowd of hundreds gathered, echoing the man's demand. "Much excitement was caused at the time," the *Herald* blandly reports. I would imagine so, culminating as it did in the man's arrest.

Such a sense of gleeful spite rose up in me as I read those few lines that Beth said, "Why, Marmee, you're grinning like a naughty cat." She was right. I could feel the tight curl at one corner of my lips, the narrowing of my eyes as I imagined the shock of those white men and women watching Negroes "disobey." I can only hope this is just the beginning of such so-called excitement. The Civil Rights Act has been federal law for more than a year and yet there has been very little in the way of equality to show for it.

May 3, 1867 ⚬

Jo has resolved to come home for Laurie's graduation next month, she writes. In June it will have been six months since they last saw one another. I hope it has been long enough. If it has not, I fear there will be no remedy for Laurie's affection but an unequivocal refusal. All these months will have been for naught if that is the case.

No, that is neither true, nor fair. Jo has reaped benefits from her time in the city that cannot be measured, regardless of whether the separation works on Laurie as we had hoped. The people she has met, the sights she has seen are all food for her hungry intellect.

May 8, 1867

Another streetcar incident, this time in New Orleans. Those formerly held in bondage are not willing to submit to the invisible chains the South would use to shackle them, it seems. What a shock to those who insisted for generations that the Negroes were docile and content to be cared for by their white masters.

These incidents are taking a peculiar hold in my mind. For over half my life I have lamented my inability to impact the injustices that so rankle me. But these black men and women have turned the most everyday action—stepping onto a streetcar—into something so revolutionary it cannot be ignored. All this time I have wished to play a role in a cataclysm, never fully appreciating the tiny fissures that must first crack the surface.

May 18, 1867

Meg took the babies to Plumfield for the first time this afternoon.

"The parrot sang to them. Actually sang," Meg told me. "Aunt March seemed quite overcome."

"Overcome?" I asked. "Whatever do you mean?"

According to Meg, there were tears in her eyes. She lavished Daisy in particular with the kind of affection that is usually reserved strictly for her poodle. How I wish I had seen it. Whatever humanity that woman contains never appears in my presence. Perhaps if I were permitted to witness it, I might cease behaving toward her as if she were a villain in a play.

May 28, 1867

On this ordinary day, an ordinary occurrence that has left me feeling anything <u>but</u> ordinary.

I was on my way home from the relief rooms, half lost in calculations of the yardage of today's donations of flannel and calico, when a voice said, "Good afternoon, Mrs. March."

I glanced up to find myself looking into a brown face framed in a navy-blue bonnet.

"Mrs. Beall!" I exclaimed. "Good afternoon." I stopped, and so did she. And then I proceeded to stand there, saying nothing, feeling as if I had at last reached the final page of a book I have been reading for sixteen years. Her bemused gaze told me I was on the verge of making a fool of myself. "You are . . . you are comfortably situated in Concord?" I asked, groping for small talk.

"I am."

I burned to know more—Where is she living, working? How did she come to settle here?—and had not the boldness to press for details.

She shifted her shopping basket a little further up her arm, and I realized I was holding her there. Even in Massachusetts it fell to me, as the white woman, to release her from our conversation. And then in the midst of clumsily bidding her goodbye, a different kind of boldness overtook me. "Should you ever find yourself in need of employment, Mrs. Beall, it would be my pleasure to recommend a situation to you," I said. The words leapt straight from my tongue without passing through my brain; I had not taken the time to consider whether such an offer would be welcome, or an intrusion.

Her face flickered with a reaction I could not parse. "Thank you, Mrs. March," she replied, and with a cordial nod was on her way.

There I stood until I could no longer distinguish her figure from those of the other passers-by. What would it be like to know Asia Beall, to be privy to more about her than the facts that make up her tragedies and former servitude, I wondered. I have never had the opportunity to count a Negro among my friends. In a just world, I can imagine working alongside her in the relief rooms. In this world, however, the most likely fantasy I can conjure is seeing her replace

Kitty Neal in the Dovecote. I cannot help but hope our paths may intersect again, if only to pass the time of day.

June 13, 1867

My Jo is home. Home!

The city has done her such good, more than I had anticipated. Her vitality is back, if somewhat altered. A new steadiness pervades her. The Jo that stands before us now is more refined, though not in the sense that Amy would hope for. It is as if she has been distilled somehow, filtered and skimmed of extraneous dross. *Fortitude* is the only word for it, and the depth of it all but takes my breath away.

Her astonishment over Daisy and Demi can hardly be expressed. To the rest of us they are still babies, but to Jo, they have transformed into walking, babbling wonders.

She embraced Beth with such fervor, as if she hoped to transfer all of her newfound strength into her sister. The way Beth held fast to her, I half believed it was happening. Beth closed her eyes and inhaled deeply enough to reach her toes, just the way she did each morning at the seashore last summer, as if the air itself might fortify her. I hope, for Beth's sake, that Jo will make this visit a long one.

June 15, 1867

Mr. Theodore Laurence—our Laurie, Jo's Teddy, my Herz-Junge—graduated from Harvard University with honors this afternoon. All of us accompanied Mr. Laurence to the commencement exercises in Cambridge. Hearing Laurie give the Latin oration I was proud enough to fly; how John and Mr. Laurence managed not to burst I do not know. (I was proud, too, to understand every word of it.

Languages so easily fade without use.) In my hand fluttered a white banner of elation—his mother's handkerchief.

Daisy and Demi had run Hannah nearly ragged by the time we returned, poor thing. Not a word of complaint from her, though. Two generations of March babies have found refuge in her arms, a fact for which I am at least as thankful as she.

June 16, 1867

The clash with Laurie which Jo had so hoped to sidestep cannot be avoided, I am afraid. Where he is concerned, this separation has been of little consequence. The looks he stole at Jo yesterday made me grimace. You might as well try to press together two magnets of the same pole; the greater Laurie's attraction, the more forcibly Jo recoils. He simply refuses to see it.

Oh, I dread to think how this will all turn out. What a joy it has been all these years to watch Jo and Laurie romp together like a pair of pups from the same litter. Have I indulged in daydreams of what sort of children they might produce? Of course I have. Babies quick and bright as fireflies have flitted through my imagination on more than one occasion, with no regard for the sheer impossibility.

There is no way around the fact that some aspects of their pairing would make for an appealing fantasy. The two of them together might form one ideal human being, but whether male or female, I could not say. His refinement and her rough-and-tumble, his romantic bent of mind and her practicality. If they were statues instead of human beings, poised together in an eternal marble pose, they might have a chance of existing side by side.

The reality is that he wants something Jo cannot give, indeed, something she may not possess. I half fancy sometimes that Laurie loves the boy in her, rather than the woman. Likewise, Jo has no need of what he offers—like a fish presented with a fine pair of wings.

June 19, 1867

It has happened. Jo is practically ill with regret. She is crying still, as if determined to empty herself of every tear and be done with it.

"Why does everyone think I don't mean what I say unless I smash them over the head with it?" she demanded when she came in, exhausted by the ordeal. I had no answer. I, too, am guilty as charged, secretly harboring hopes that she may one day change her mind, settle down, find contentment—only not with Theodore Laurence.

It is not that I want to change her. There is not one aspect of Jo that I would dilute. I simply want her to have everything I have, as well as everything I do not.

That is what I tell myself, at any rate. It cannot be the truth, for although Jo is not now discontent at the prospect of remaining unmarried, I persist in imagining that she will be someday, only because I cannot conceive of my own life without Amos and our children. What will be her anchor, if she has no family of her own?

I hardly know who to be sorrier for. All evening, the sounds of Beethoven's Pathétique tumbled out the window of the Laurence house. There are few more aptly named sonatas. What a mixture of anger and anguish! The way he struck the keys made me pity not only Laurie, but the piano itself.

June 20, 1867

Mr. Laurence and I had a long talk today. Or rather, we sat long together in his library. There was not much left to say about it. Jo had been there already yesterday, to explain. There was little need. He knew as well as we did—as well as everyone but Laurie himself—that this day could not be avoided.

"I am sorry the boy is so blind," he said.

I had no consolation to offer in return. There is no quality of Jo that I am sorry for. Her behavior in all of this has given me occasion for nothing but pride.

Mr. Laurence has resolved to take Laurie to Europe. It seems to me the only sensible thing. Here, every sight will remind him of that which he cannot have. What dreams he must have built, with Jo as the centerpiece.

"Would you—" Mr. Laurence began, half scoffing at himself. "Would you like to play chess, Mrs. March?"

To my surprise, I did. Three matches ensued, with Mr. Laurence ultimately prevailing. It seemed somehow to put everything back in order between the two of us. How long will it be, I wonder, before Jo and Laurie can enjoy themselves together again?

June 21, 1867

This has taken so much out of Jo. She drifts from room to room, depleted and discouraged. The courage it took to speak, and to do so gently, wore her out completely. The friendship we had all hoped to preserve may now be forfeited, and that has left her in a veritable state of mourning.

Watching her makes me ever more thankful that I was spared the task of refusing my suitor face-to-face, by none other than the hand of God. Before I completed my studies in Duxbury, my cousin Frothingham had died. To this day, the thought of his death brings on a strange dizziness. I would not, could not, rejoice over it and call myself a Christian, but the way my heart lifted when I heard the news cannot be denied. I can feel it hovering there still, as if it never fully dropped back into place. To think of what my life might have been had I capitulated, and had my cousin lived, is beyond the scope of my imagination.

My refusal would have been doubly difficult, for my father was set upon the match. My cousin's financial prospects were considerable, and I knew how much Father wished me to have the best of all the world had to offer. The promise of his disappointment, far more than my suitor's, weighed upon me.

I am thankful at least that we were able to spare Jo that. No one but Laurie shall cast any doubt upon her decision.

June 24, 1867

Each time I glance at the Laurence house, there is Laurie, sitting in his window as if it is a frame and he is a portrait titled "Sorrow."

He will take comfort from no one. Yesterday I happened upon him in the garden, stripping petals from daisies with mechanical precision. "Please don't. Please," he insisted before I had spoken a word of sympathy.

His words struck so deeply, so unexpectedly, that I could not hide my hurt from him. He looked away, looked inward, and his pain seemed to twist down upon itself like a screw tightening. My own sorrow bloomed up to see him hating himself for hurting me. What could we do but stand before one another, each helpless in our own suffering?

My hand lifted, my impulse always to outstretch, to soothe, but not quite daring to reach toward him lest he refuse again. Right then and there I would have told Laurie all that he has meant to me, if only it might have made a difference. But it is not my love he craves. Without words, without touch, I could only hope that the urgency of my sympathy would somehow permeate his misery. But the longer I lingered, the more he seemed to curl in upon himself. Slowly, gently, I crept away.

I have not been able to write about it before tonight. I expected Jo and Laurie to be hurt. But the grief I feel now? That jolt has knocked my feet from under me. If I bring Laurie's memories of Jo too near, if he is unable to bear my presence without pain, what then? Must I give up my Herz-Junge?

July 10, 1867 ∽

Laurie and Mr. Laurence departed for the continent today. For much of the night I pondered what to say to Laurie—if he would even hear me. Telling him to be cheerful would only be cruel. A wound is determined to hurt until it heals, after all.

The mask of jollity he put on to bid us farewell was almost grotesque in its brightness. He nearly bounded from Amos to Meg to John to Beth and the babies, like a wind-up toy whose key has been turned too far.

"Take fine care of your grandfather," I said when my turn came. "It will be lonely here until you both return, for you have become more family than friends." Laurie latched his arms around me. A tremor ran through him as he fought not to cry. I battled just as hard to keep my own composure. The thin stream of relief that trickled over me at his embrace threatened to turn into a flood of tears.

What he said to Jo at the very last, I do not know. I only saw her shake her head the instant before he turned and marched smartly away.

I had devoted so much thought to seeing Laurie off that our parting with Mr. Laurence caught me almost by surprise. Beth reached out both hands to him. Into one he placed a key. "Play the big piano as often as you please," he said. "Too much silence hurts an instrument. And a house, even if it is empty." He looked for such a long time at her that I was reminded of the day they met. It seemed to me that he was bidding two people farewell—Beth, and the granddaughter whose eyes so resemble hers. How will the sights of Europe possibly compare?

All my hopes are pinned on Laurie's farewell embrace. With time, I pray that his affection for the March Family will someday outweigh his heartache.

July 17, 1867

Daisy and Demi are one year old today—a year of absolute delights.

Hannah made them a pair of honey-soaked applesauce cakes the size of muffins, which they devoured with great ceremony while we all watched with attention so rapt, you would think their high chairs had been placed on the stage of the Boston Music Hall.

Thanks to God's mercy, they have not been sick a day in their lives with the exception of Demi's bout with croup. If He will grant us the grace of another year of hearty growth before the babies must face mumps, measles, scarlet fever, and the like, I shall be thankful to my last breath.

July 19, 1867

With all the distractions now swept away, I can ignore Beth's condition no longer. All the gains she made in Swampscott last summer have faded.

The aches in her joints are more pronounced, the joints sometimes swelling with a heat that can be felt through her clothing. Her color is better, but that is thanks to a recurring fever that visits so often, it ought to have a calling card.

If I only knew what is lacking. Carbonate of potash with lemon has no effect on her temperature, nor does sumac tea. A rubbing of cajuput oil brings only temporary relief to her pain. Cayenne pills have no effect whatever. She has no shortage of rest. Indeed, she does not even desire rest, but has no choice other than to capitulate to it.

Whatever it is, it is not like infection, which overpowers a body. Something is draining from her, bit by bit. If I fed her solely on beefsteak and ice cream, it would not replenish her. No matter how much I encourage her to save her strength, it cannot be conserved. What she does not use is simply lost, like a penny dropped down a grate.

Yet life is no less delicious to Beth; if anything it is suddenly sweeter, richer, for only the smallest bites satiate her.

It is Jo who has forced us to confront our fears. Ever since she arrived, she has looked from Beth to me with her brows canted as if to ask, *Do you see? Are we looking at the same Beth?* Perhaps we are not. I cannot clearly picture the Beth of six months ago, as I can Daisy and Demi.

"Let me take her away," Jo proposed tonight. "To the mountains, this time." Amos and I have no objections. Pure air and rest cannot possibly do Beth any harm.

July 21, 1867

Beth has demurred. The Adirondacks are too far from home, she pleads. That is Beth through and through, and yet the nature of her pleading strikes me as different this time.

A return to the seaside was deemed amenable, however, to which Jo has readily agreed. Jo would take her to Africa, or to the moon, if Beth asked. Perhaps another few weeks of the Swampscott shore and Mrs. Cox's good cooking will revive her.

July 24, 1867

Beth looked almost uneasy as we saw them off today. It put me somewhat in mind of the first time I asked her to meet Mr. Laurence. This is how Beth looks when she fears she cannot do what is expected of her.

Be well. That is what I wanted to say as I hugged her goodbye, but a quick flash of intuition stopped me. "Enjoy yourself," I told her instead. "Let Jo spoil you, and come back to us with stories to tell." She brightened at that, and leaned in for one more squeeze.

And then I went inside and cried.

July 27, 1867

This house has never been so muted. Amos and Hannah and I cannot even fill four sides of the table. What a difference Beth makes, despite her quiet. Her empty chair, the closed lid of her piano, her unused bed unsettle me to the core. This has the feel of a rehearsal for a play none of us hopes to perform.

At night I read aloud from the collected stories and sketches of Mark Twain. They are of little consequence, but we cannot keep from chuckling in spite of our preoccupation. Even Amos must give himself over to mirth most evenings. Mr. Twain's expressions are most singular, and his humor has a wiliness about it that proves impossible to evade. It does us good to surrender to these bursts of laughter, lest our tensions erupt in less felicitous ways. As for myself, as long as my lips and tongue are forming words, my mind cannot entangle itself in the worries that are tethered to it.

July 30, 1867

The knock at the door this morning was unmistakable. No one uses the same lopsided cadence as Karl Hummel: ba-BUMP, ba-BUMP, ba-BUMP. And yet the sight that greeted me when I swung the door open left me too surprised to say hello.

On the step stood Karl in a suit of clothes so crisp, they had to be new. Cap, shoes, and all. "Guten Tag, Frau March," he said, doffing the cap with a gallant sweep. I opened the door wider to beckon him inside. "Thank you, but I can't," he said, "or I'll be late for work. I only wanted to leave this for Mr. March." He dug into his pocket and pulled out a stack of quarters—three dollars in all.

"For Mr. March?" I said dumbly as the warm line of coins clinked into my palm.

"For the shoes," Karl replied. "He said I could pay him back from the bottom up." With a flash of a grin and a tip of his cap he was off, trotting down the street toward town. Questions battered my brain as I stared at that money and Karl's retreating form.

Amos was ensconced in his study composing his sermon, but my bafflement could not be contained. In I went without a knock to find him so immersed in his own thoughts, he would not have heard a fire brigade. He did not appear to notice me standing before his desk at all until I spoke.

"Karl Hummel brought this for you," I announced.

Amos surfaced, blinked twice at my outstretched hand, and smiled. "Three dollars already!" he said. "He must be getting on well at the *Concord Freeman*."

"What on earth has Karl Hummel to do with the newspaper?" I asked in utter exasperation. Ten more seconds and my confusion would have flooded the room to Amos's neck. Even when he explained, I could hardly absorb the words quickly enough to make sense of them.

Weeks ago—weeks!—Amos was at Whitcomb's buying paper when he overheard the stationer talking with the printer. Some of the businesses in town have taken a notion to advertise in German, and the *Freeman* was in need of someone to proof the foreign copy and set the type. "I thought of Karl," Amos said. So he walked straight to the livery stable to confer with Karl.

"I asked him if he could read German backward," Amos said. "After a moment's thought he recited the alphabet in reverse without hesitation. He is as bright as you've always said."

Not only did Amos procure the boy a job, but the next day he took Karl to Brown's for new clothes—"his old ones smelling rather horsey," Amos confided. The coins Karl brought today are the first payment on a loan of $8.75.

I simply stood there, gaping at my husband while he opened his desk drawer and deposited the quarters into the money box in a silver waterfall. I could do nothing, nothing at all but look at him.

"You are pleased?" he asked at last.

"Pleased?" I said, still so stunned that my tongue could hardly remember how to articulate. "I am delighted beyond comprehension." He has lifted that boy out of nearly six years of dung and straw to a printing press. A trade. It is the kind of situation I have hoped for Karl almost as long as I have known him.

Amos nodded, as if to himself. "I knew you would be," he said, bending back over his composition. He wrote two more lines and scratched them out again before I managed to speak.

"You never said a word to me."

"As Matthew 6:3 instructs," he said with a simplicity that left me half dizzy with amazement. The Sermon on the Mount. *But when thou doest alms, let not thy left hand know what thy right hand doeth.* Trust my husband to follow Christ to the very essence of the letter. "Though I would say you are more often the right hand and I the left," he added. "What better example could God have given me to follow than my wife?"

Again, I could not speak. I could hardly breathe for the emotion that came over me. Such a wave, as strong as my temper but its opposite in every way. Soft, caressing. It caresses me still.

Always I have set myself as an example for my daughters. But my husband? We have been equals in everything but temperament; I would not have married him otherwise. To know that he admires me in this way—that he has done this for Karl because of me—it overwhelms me in such a way that I cannot properly express it.

From a faraway place in my mind comes the echo of Adelaide Weddleton's voice: *Strive to find for them what they most need.* I did just that for Birte, Lottchen, Kitty Neal, Mary Ann, and Silas. Hannah, too. And now Amos has done so for Karl. Links in a chain—a chain I should like nothing more than to lengthen.

August 2, 1867

A postcard from Swampscott. It is maddeningly vague—lovely air, hearty food, glorious sunsets. Not a hint about Beth. Surely if Jo had good news to report, she would not hesitate to do so? Everything implies a lovely seaside holiday, but I cannot shake the suspicion that Jo is lying by omission.

August 6, 1867

Beth and Jo are due back tomorrow. How much do I dare allow myself to hope for?

August 7, 1867

They are home. The moment I saw Jo's face, I knew, without even a glance at Beth. Jo met our eager smiles with such a look of dread and despair that her pain registered before my own.

Up she went to help Beth into bed. Amos and I looked at each other. That was all. What could we say? His face had gone as slack as mine. He turned to the mantel and put his head in his hands. I simply sat, waiting for something to penetrate my mind, my heart, my senses. The worst of all fears had materialized before me, beckoning, and I could not feel it.

When Jo appeared in the doorway of the study, nerved to break the bad news to us, I held my arms out to her. All her strength and fortitude fell away, and mine with it.

After Jo and I had swum through the first wave of sadness, I crept upstairs and drew a chair to Beth's bedside. Her strength has faded in such tiny increments, it was possible not to see it from one day to the next. Now, after weeks apart, it cannot be denied. How I wish Amy were here to draw Beth, to capture her as she is now, before she dims further. As her strength diminishes, her outline seems to sharpen.

August 9, 1867

"I think the tide will go out easily, if you help me." That is what Beth said to Jo as they sat at the seashore.

"Cannot the tide be turned?" I asked Amos as we sat, benumbed, before the empty hearth. "Remember how Daisy and Demi reinvigorated her?"

"I have no doubt Meg would bear a set of twins annually if it would keep Beth on this earth," Amos said. The words could have been a joke, but his tone was one of utmost futility.

August 15, 1867

I feel nothing but my physical senses, and even they are too dulled to register anything but extremes. Heat takes the place of anger. Instead of fear, there is only cold.

Beth consented to a thorough examination with Dr. Bangs today. It took him only minutes to diagnose rheumatic fever. The damage has settled in her heart. Her precious, golden heart. Within months it shall no longer have the strength to beat.

I would rather sever my hand than write this, but it is a fact: Beth's illness is the result of the scarlet fever. Without the one, the other would never have occurred.

Don't forget the Hummels. That is what I said to my four daughters as I left for Washington, D.C., when Amos was struck with pneumonia. Had I been home, I would have been the one to attend to the Hummels. Beth would have been safely quarantined with Amy. Greta and Minna might yet be alive as well.

I could blame Meg or Jo for not obeying sooner and letting the responsibility fall to Beth. I could blame Amos's illness for calling me away, or the slave owners for the war that put his life in peril. Or I can own up to what I have done. The price of my concern for others is to be my daughter's life.

Dr. Bangs assures us that even had the true severity of Beth's condition come to light sooner, a reversal would still be impossible. I cannot make myself find comfort in that. All this time, the ailment has been sinking its roots deeper and deeper.

We did not have to tell her. Beth is no longer living, but dying, and she has known it far longer than we. The details matter not to her. I wish I could say the same.

August 17, 1867

I posted letters to Amy and Mr. Laurence today. A dozen times I sat down at my desk, only to find myself attending to some trifling task moments later, virtually unaware of having stood up. I did not want to see the words myself, much less imagine Amy and Mr. Laurence reading them.

August 28, 1867

Mr. Laurence cables with instructions to summon any doctor we desire. He would pay Beth's expenses at any hospital, any sanatorium. Mountain air, sea air, anything that might cure her is at our disposal. Everything is to be billed to him. Dr. Bangs says there is nothing to be done, but he is not the only doctor in the world. He is not the only doctor in Concord, for that matter. Do we not owe it to Beth to try?

August 30, 1867

A small crate of medicines has arrived from New York City, via express. Tinctures, decoctions, liniments and tonics, tablets and liquids—all thanks to Mr. Laurence. I hardly know where to start. The three witches of Macbeth had fewer ingredients for their bubbling cauldron than I now possess.

September 4, 1867

"I'm not sorry anymore that Aunt Carrol didn't choose me to go to Europe," Jo confided today. "I could not bear to have an ocean between me and Beth now." I am every bit as thankful. Jo is as good as a medicine for Beth, and the only one thus far that works reliably. You might think some alchemy is at work between them, the way energy seems to trickle from Jo to Beth.

Another way I am grateful for Amy's absence: Each time I finish reading one of her letters, I am surprised to find that I am still sitting in an armchair in Massachusetts instead of an English countryside or a Paris balcony. As much as I love to read them to Beth and watch her imagine the scenes, I prefer most of all to read them over to myself, so that the words sound in Amy's voice within my mind.

To think of our Little Raphael, looking at the lines and colors of a true Raphael! Such images pry me from the worn-out corners of my own thoughts.

Amy's life seems to be filled with color. Indeed, sometimes pressed leaves and flower petals fall from the envelopes. Amos marvels over them. "A pattern, a shape, a color we have never seen!" he exclaimed over a deep purple stem of *Fagus sylvatica*. "And yet we all know it to be a leaf. That is the wonder of God's work."

September 23, 1867

I have lost count of how many doctors have been to this house in the last month. All they can be relied upon to do is contradict one another. One from New York sees a vial of tablets upon her bureau and says, "Oh, yes indeed, best thing for her!" The next that comes from Boston scowls at the selfsame tablets and pronounces them flimflam.

The only thing these medical men agree upon is that they must be paid for their expertise, regardless of whether their knowledge has offered any solutions. If women were allowed into the hallowed halls of medicine, would they be every bit as exasperating?

Thankfully, Beth will submit to nearly anything for Mr. Laurence's sake. I am another matter, however. Frustration makes me more waspish by the day. And however petty it may be of me to complain in the face of Beth's trials, I must have an outlet for my own discontent if I am to greet each day with the warmth and steadiness Beth's circumstances demand from me.

October 11, 1867

Yet another doctor, this one from Providence. He, too, says there is nothing he can do. Like the rest, he left a bottle of something that smells as if it was milked from the bile ducts of some unfortunate beast.

October 24, 1867

An envelope from overseas today, addressed to me in Laurie's hand. No note, only a half dozen crimson maple leaves, carefully pressed and tied with blue ribbon.

Such a feeling came over me when I saw that little red nosegay. Like a pair of hands smoothing down every ruffled thought I have had of Laurie since Jo refused him. My crow, my Herz-Junge. I had feared that the distance between him and Jo might expand to swallow me as well, but it is not so. Four thousand miles between us, and yet none at all.

November 1, 1867

Amy has decided that should Fred Vaughn make a proposal of marriage, she will accept.

I shall be ill.

Did she write that letter in a singsong tone, or am I injecting it with my own revulsion at such false sweetness? To be raised as she was, and to persist in conflating happiness with affluence! Pages and pages she went on, and never once did the word *love* appear.

The Vaughns are "ever so much richer than the Laurences," she writes. As if the Laurences' worth could be measured in dollars and cents! Amos and I never entertained the thought of spanking the children when they were small. Today, however, I would have very much liked to turn Amy over my knee.

Oh, but the Vaughns are so generous, so kind, she insists, almost as if she hears my protests from across the sea. Kind? There isn't a Vaughn alive who has been as kind to anyone as Mr. Laurence has been to Beth.

I am not angry. I am furious.

"Send as much advice as you like," Amy said. She would do well to get down on her two knees and thank God that I have trained myself to commit my thoughts first to my diary before communicating them to another human being. Slashing and stabbing at the letters so that the pages beneath this one will bear the permanent imprint of my fury brings me some small satisfaction, at least.

"Peg," Amos said, distressed by my distress. "It is not our ship to sail."

"Nevertheless, if she should strike the shoals, it is we who shall have the privilege of watching helplessly from shore as she founders," I shot back.

"So we shall." That is what he said, but the sangfroid of his words did not match his expression.

"You <u>are</u> worried, Amos," I insisted.

He took his time answering, sizing up and measuring all the words at his disposal. "Concerned," he allowed. After another long silence he added, "'Love and trust me.' That is all she asks for." I looked again at the perfumed sheets of stationery in my hands. Those were indeed Amy's final words, just above her signature.

"She asked for my advice," I countered, pointing.

"Amy is as trusting as she is courageous."

I opened my mouth and closed it again. Amos's knack for saying more than the words he speaks is unparalleled. "How are we to dissuade her from this foolishness?"

Amos shrugged, saying, "The only thoughts I can ever hope to govern are my own."

When my daughters come to me with a dilemma, their tone and manner more often than not tell me that they have already made a tentative choice. All they truly wish is for me to affirm the wisdom of their decision. Rarely have I had to redirect their inner compass. But Amy is across the ocean. For all that I have been able to conjure her voice from her letters, the words on the paper before me defy certainty; I can hear them equally well in a vainglorious tenor as a dubious one.

My hopes lie solely in Amy's assurance that she has made Fred no promises. And Fred has been called off to his brother's sickbed. I do not recall ever rejoicing at the illness of another, but I am thankful that something has intervened to separate Amy from her paramour. Perhaps enough time remains for her to come to her senses.

November 2, 1867

I awoke this morning feeling sheepish and groggy, as I imagine I would feel after a night of drunkenness. Anger can be intoxicating, it seems.

Here is the true root of my dilemma: I cannot cure Beth. I should not presume to "cure" Amy. At my core, I wish the situation were reversed. If rheumatic fever were vulnerable to reason, if I could lecture it away, Beth would be restored to health in mere minutes.

The fact is that if this is a mistake Amy is determined to make, nothing I say will deter her. It is entirely possible that trying to do so will only strengthen her resolve. And it is further possible that in the time it has taken her letter to reach me, coupled with the time it will take mine to return to her, Frank will have proposed and Amy will have accepted.

"Trust your heart," I wrote to her. After sealing the envelope I tore it open again to underline the last word, trying to press all of my hopes for her into that single stroke.

If I have fulfilled my task as a mother, that is the best and only advice I can offer.

November 29, 1867

Beth is out of sorts. It is not her health. Or rather, it is not only her health.

Today she shouted at me. Shouted. I did not know Beth knew how to shout.

The tincture Dr. Chitren (or was it Dr. Sanborn?) recommended has sat unopened on her bed table for four days. All I said was "Beth," but she had seen me look at it.

"Oh, leave me be," she cried.

Out the door I scurried, nearly slamming it behind me in my agitation. My tone had betrayed me, I suppose. Somehow I have learned how to plead in a single syllable.

Why she will not even try, I cannot understand.

December 17, 1867

One small bright spot of news arrived today: Amy has refused Fred Vaughn's proposal. I am too relieved to properly express it.

December 25, 1867

Christmas.

Only the babies truly enjoyed themselves. They have no fear of the future, no real concept of its existence beyond tomorrow or the next day. All that matters to them is what is before them. Perhaps that is the best way to live.

For the rest of us, it felt almost as though there might never be another Christmas. It was next to impossible to look at Beth without also imagining her empty chair next year. The gifts we gave her seemed so paltry, though every one of us indulged her with some extravagance. How much of the great stack of music she received will she have time to learn? Where will she wear the exquisite gloves and sweetly painted fan Amy sent from Europe?

Beth is not oblivious to the way we look at her now. No doubt she can feel us trying to commit every facet of her to memory—she who so hates to be looked at, much less scrutinized. I do not know how to keep myself from doing it. I would like to set every detail of her in amber.

January 6, 1868

A frank talk with Dr. Bangs today. Beth's case is hopeless. He said this as if it were news. I protested that we have known that for months.

"You know it, but you have not accepted it," he returned. "Allow me to be candid. The medicines I have prescribed these last weeks were not so much for Beth as for you. They could do her no harm, and I thought they could do you no harm as well. In that, I was wrong."

He counsels us to embrace death. Embrace it! "Make it welcome," he said, "for it shall come regardless of your wishes. If you lock the doors and bar the windows, it shall only arrive more forcefully."

"For the first time in my life I have not the energy to be angry," I told Amos this evening, long after the last log in the hearth had burned to embers. My own voice sounded flat enough as to be almost unrecognizable.

Something passed over his face as he studied mine. Then his gaze turned inward, translating his thoughts into words. "I can only take that as a sign that Dr. Bangs is correct," he replied softly.

That is when I cried. Once begun, I did not want to stop. Amos laid his hand over mine. I leaned forward, touching my forehead to his. The thread of our hope had spun itself out so fine and thin, it had become all but impossible to balance upon without breaking. Now that it has snapped, I feel . . . I am not certain what I feel.

Lighter. Heavier. Saturated. Rinsed clean.

January 9, 1868

Make it welcome. Very well. If Death is determined to call upon Beth, we shall treat it as an honored guest. After all that I have done poorly where Beth's health is concerned, I am intent upon doing this properly.

John and Amos moved her piano upstairs today with help from Karl Hummel. Fifteen years old, he is now, and sturdy enough to carry my armchair to the second floor without assistance. I should have guessed on that Christmas morning years ago that he would find a way to thrive despite all that was stacked against him. I suppose I shall never cease to be baffled by the fact that Beth will not be able to do the same, despite all that was stacked in her favor.

But I must train my focus on the practical. I shall have the rest of my life to ponder the peculiar imbalances of the universe when this is over. The rest of Beth's life shall not be squandered on such things.

Dr. Bangs advises we be prepared for the eventuality of her physical suffering. A supply of good wine will be necessary for the pain, and then brandy. Mr. Laurence can surely be relied upon for that. When alcohol is not enough, we are to turn to ether. Hannah is eager to know what to cook for her. The answer is simple: There are no restrictions, no recommendations. No food will harm her, any more than it will cure her. Nothing will. Anything Beth possesses the desire and energy to do is to be encouraged.

"No more doctors," I promised Beth this afternoon. My God, the way her face lifted. I have not seen Beth express more than a dram of happiness in . . . how long? A sunbeam finding its way past a cloud could not have personified her relief more clearly. "Only Dr. Bangs," I hastened to add, "and only to ward off whatever pain we can."

She flung her arms around me and squeezed—squeezed!—with a newfound strength. Only then did I finally understand why we ought not to have set so many doctors upon her. The time we spent hoping for a nonexistent cure would have been better spent enjoying Beth's presence, just as the energy it stole from her could have been devoted to living.

January 15, 1868

Jo's desk is in Beth's room now. In many ways, those two are a more unlikely pair than Jo and Laurie ever were. And yet if they loved each other more, the room would not be large enough to contain it.

Hour after hour, Jo writes while Beth knits and sews. Their silence is so companionable, it trickles down the stairs and touches Amos in his study, Hannah in the kitchen.

"How beautiful this is," Beth said as she surveyed her snug and restful kingdom this evening. And how right she is. A picture painted correctly down to the smallest detail could not capture its beauty, for it must be felt rather than seen. This room has been made a sanctuary, in every sense of its meaning.

We all leave something behind each time we walk through the door, determined that this sacred space should not be sullied with any detritus from outside these walls.

January 20, 1868

Concord shall be littered with small mementos of Beth for years to come. The appetite of her hands for work far exceeds that of her stomach for food. Every day there is a new pair of mittens or a scarf. Sometimes a drawstring sack to hold marbles. When she wearies of yarn, she pastes together bits of scrap into pretty pictures and puts them in cardboard frames.

In the afternoon when school has let out, she sits in her windowsill and tosses her handiwork down for passing children, who wave and blow kisses.

The following morning I sometimes see those same children pause as they walk by, pointing out Beth's widow to disbelieving companions. She is working magic on this town.

January 23, 1868

She is so content. In some ways, this is the kind of life she has always craved—sheltered in her room with her family, her sewing basket, and her cats. No one pushing or pulling her here or there.

A shift has taken place in all of us. After so much straining toward something that exists only in our hopes, we can be still. It is new to me, this relishing of stillness. As long as Beth is here, as long as this lull persists, I shall endeavor to rejoice in it.

January 26, 1868

Three of the Hummel children—Ada, Monika, and Heinrich—came to see Beth today, bringing Blitz for a visit, too. Age has not improved his temperament. "He scratched me, Marmee," she reported with an incongruous smile, "just as he used to." The thin red line runs clear across the back of her left hand. Beth regards it as some kind of trophy. "He begged pardon," she said, stroking the shallow wound with fondness, "and licked it clean."

More likely Blitz recollected the scent of her blood and wanted another taste, but I reserved that observation for myself.

She sent each of them off with a pair of new mittens, and a promise to make more for all their siblings.

January 29, 1868

If I thought I had come to a true acceptance of what awaits us, I had fooled myself. Indeed, I fool myself still. Even in lamenting this failure, I dodge the necessity of stringing five particular letters together: *d-e-a-t-h*. As if keeping those letters apart from one another will keep my daughter upon this earth.

Today Beth told Amos that she could best be spared of the four.

Those words stilled me as I have never been stilled before.

Spared by whom, I wonder? I cannot contradict her; it comforts her to think her going will cause less pain than it does. But who will be our hearth cricket, our tranquility?

Such a little patch of earth has ever felt Beth's footfalls. I console myself with the knowledge that the prints she leaves on the soil of our hearts are deep. In her own way, she has been as fiercely herself as Jo.

Hers is not a giving up, but a willing surrender, and the strength of it humbles me.

February 3, 1868

The axis of the world has tilted. Always for me it has run through the center of our home, but now it is tipped sideways so that everything seems to revolve around Beth's room.

February 6, 1868

Jo has taken up *Alice's Adventures in Wonderland* to read to the Family in the evenings. The story delights Daisy and Demi, who squeal with laughter over the animals' antics, while the ladies and gentlemen in the audience smile knowingly at the parodies of humankind. Beth fits snugly in between. There is enough youth about her that she laughs right along with the children, and enough wisdom to nod sagely at Mr. Carroll's allusions.

A glance at the books piled on the night table tells me that Jo is giving her sister as much of the world as she can before Beth leaves it. *Five Weeks in a Balloon* by Jules Verne. Mr. Dickens's *American Notes,* and *Pictures from Italy. Les Misérables.*

It is a sentiment we have universally adopted without discussion. Picture postcards from Mr. Laurence arrive for Beth two and three times a week, most of them famous concert halls of Europe. Today it was a portrait of Bach, looking a great deal like Cotton Mather, as Amos pointed out with a hearty chuckle.

Tucked inside Amy's letters are sketches of the cats of Europe. One napping on the steps of St. Paul's Cathedral. Another licking its paws on the banks of the Seine. The most recent was lapping from the Trevi fountain in Rome. "None of them seemed to like me," Amy reported last week, "until I realized that they do not speak English." Now she includes the proper way to befriend a cat in each country she visits. Minou-minou in French, micio-micio in Italian. Even the British do not coax their felines with puss-puss or kitty-kitty, but chh-chh-chh.

Grapefruits, pears, oranges, and dates find their way to our table at least twice a month, thanks to John. I do not know what he and Meg and the babies are doing without to afford this luxury.

Even the grocer and the butcher add small delectables to our orders, wrapped in brown paper with *for Beth* scribbled in pencil.

With every kindness, my heart enlarges. By the time it breaks, it shall be the size of the sun.

February 8, 1868

Aunt March came to see Beth today, for the first time. She stayed only a few minutes. The way she fidgeted and stammered, you would have thought the room had not enough air to go around.

"You will tell me if there is anything she lacks," Aunt March instructed me at the front door as she gathered herself to leave. "Anything at all. I shall see that she has it." That she means it, I have no doubt. Were I to ask for a symphony orchestra to play the complete works of Beethoven outside Beth's window, she would certainly send it. But even after all these years of living mere steps apart, she does not know our Beth—her own namesake—well enough to send the merest trinket.

February 17, 1868

There are small grimaces now and then. Sometimes Beth's breath escapes her, leaving her panting. If I take her hand during these spells, I can feel the irregular rushing and retreating of her heart. Hannah has brought a bottle of port up to Beth's dresser, so that she may have a glass close at hand when the pain strikes.

It took some coaxing before Beth would accept a dose without reluctance, for Amos has preached for decades that men who indulge in strong drink lose their ability to see the world as it is. Those who surrender to it daily lose themselves entirely, he says.

"But everything is so lovely here, I can't bear the thought of blurring it," Beth protested when I poured a glass.

"You cannot perceive the world properly if you are overtaken by pain," Amos countered. A wry look on Beth's face is a rarity, but there it was, telling us that she is far more accustomed to seeing the world through a veil of pain than we had yet realized.

"A glass of port never makes anything <u>less</u> lovely, Beth," Meg assured her. "If I learned nothing else from the Moffats, I learned that." Everyone, right down to Amos, chuckled and Beth was won over.

Perhaps twenty minutes after the glass was drained Beth said, "Oh!" All eyes turned to her and she blushed—blushed almost as if being looked at were a pleasure. "Meg is right," she confessed with a smile that uncurled just the way Amos's does.

Struck by a whim, I ran downstairs and called to Hannah for more glasses. "Enough for everyone over the age of two," I said. "And count yourself, too," I told her.

I poured out a glass for everyone—even Amos—and lifted mine in a toast. "To loveliness," I said, looking to Beth, enshrined upon her pillows like the Madonna herself. Five more glasses rose to meet mine and a chorus of voices proclaimed, "To loveliness!"

Beth watched in awe as her father drained his glass and then with a wink, lifted it toward her like a man tipping his hat to a lady in the street. Again her cheeks flashed pink for an instant and she made a little half bow, which was greeted with applause.

Feeling left out of the jollity, Demi demanded a taste, so John dipped his smallest finger into his glass and offered it to Demi to suck. The child's eyes bugged like a bullfrog's and his tongue flapped in and out, trying to rid itself of the flavor. Undaunted by her brother's disgust, Daisy demanded her share and the performance was repeated to much applause.

There must be few such lucky women as I in this world.

February 19, 1868

A note in our mailbox today, addressed to The Mitten Lady. Oh, Beth's face as she read it. When she is gone, I pray that the image of her joy will outshine all the darker days that surely await us.

February 22, 1868

The guest we have so carefully and reluctantly prepared for makes its way ever nearer. Beth's knitting needles have stilled. They have grown too heavy, she says.

February 23, 1868

Harriet Weddleton. There is a name that has not crossed my mind in weeks. But as Beth's condition begins to worsen more swiftly, I find myself thinking of her, and how she cared for Adelaide. Tenderly. Loyally. Completely. After all my private denigration of her work in the relief rooms, what an irony that I should look to her example now, when I am most in need of strength.

February 25, 1868

Though Beth's needles have stilled, the current of notes and drawings to our mailbox shows no sign of abating. There is no more room on her dresser for them. The four that came today Jo pinned to the curtains like banners. Daisy and Demi so delighted in making them flutter that we pinned them all up. "Beth's laurels," John dubbed them.

February 29, 1868

Port is no longer enough. Only the brandy will soothe the aches that shoot through Beth's joints so swiftly it makes them twitch. The stronger liquor dulls her senses, makes her groggy. She no longer resists it, though. The pain has become more demanding, muting the small enjoyments she has thus far been able to eke out of her waking hours.

Jo and I have begun taking turns at her bedside. The days are mine, the nights, Jo's.

Thank God for Hannah, who somehow manages to keep the rest of the house in order. Beth never wants for a clean nightdress or pillowcase. The chamber pot is always spic and span before it is needed again. And for none of these tasks do I ever have to leave Beth's side. Hannah deserves a rest. More than that, she deserves time with Beth. But I cannot make myself give up any of the minutes that are left to us. I am treating her like a servant, and it shames me.

March 3, 1868

"Marmee," Beth asked me today, when the pain had retreated enough for her to speak, "will you bury me with old Joanna? I'm much too old, but I should like to have something I've loved all my life beside me, to keep me from being so homesick." I could not answer in words. I nodded.

She speaks of her own end so much more easily than I am able to do so. Somehow I have permitted myself to forget that Beth is the only one of my girls who has seen death—indeed, the only one who has felt with her own arms the life departing from another human being. Perhaps it is the familiarity that makes her so unafraid.

March 5, 1868

A restless day. Every comfort I offered, she refused. "Nothing hurts," she insisted. Still, she could not find ease. She lay half within and half without herself, it seemed to me—eyes open, then closed, flinching now and again. It was as if her mind and her body, though both still present, had somehow disconnected from one another. Jo would have known what to do; she withstands Beth's distress far better than I. She is better for Beth, too, for I think Beth knows that her pain causes me pain, and tries to subdue it in my presence. But I could not summon Jo. She needs her rest to endure the long nights.

"Did you know, Beth," I said, the words arriving unbidden, "that you had a brother?" Everything stilled. My heart, Beth's juddering. The very air between us opened, beckoning me to fill the space I had made. "A baby boy, born before Meg, who died before he could breathe. He never opened his eyes in this world. You will be the first of us he sees. It is a comfort to me, to imagine you taking him into your arms."

A light flickered in her great blue eyes, like stars in a twilight sky. "What is his name, Marmee?"

A current ran through me, just under my skin, from my scalp to the soles of my feet. Never in twenty-five years has anyone asked me my son's name. Amos and I had tailored it so carefully for the kind of man we would raise him to be. Suddenly I felt fragile as an egg. I could only whisper, "Samuel. Samuel Garrison March."

"Samuel," she repeated. "How will I recognize him?"

I could have told her how beautiful he was, how the point of his chin and his dark widow's peak shaped his face into a perfect heart. Instead, I told her, "Just as you know each of us, Beth. Your hearts will recognize one another, for they were fashioned in the same place, out of the same love that made you and Amy and Jo and Meg."

A shadow of a smile flitted across her face. When Jo came in at midnight, Beth was asleep.

March 8, 1868

It is far too easy to forget the person when ministering to the body. In the last few days Beth's pain has become an entity all its own, a monster we must subdue. I would so much rather put my mind toward comforting my daughter than placating the beast that is intent upon consuming her. But it is so much louder and more demanding.

March 10, 1868

Today, for a moment, she returned to us. Lying in Amos's arms, placid for the first time in days, Beth asked for each of us by name.

"All here," she said, taking every hand in turn.

The feel of Beth's lips on mine as she kissed me produced the sweetest pain of my life. I have no doubt she has bid us goodbye this day.

Were this a play, the curtain would sweep closed to the sounds of muffled sobs, cloaking the true end in merciful darkness. There shall be no such clemencies here; we must live what is to come.

March 11, 1868

Beth has not spoken since yesterday. Three days ago I would have torn the lungs from my chest to hear her small cries of pain subdued, and now I would do the same to hear her voice again.

Four more notes came for her today. We pinned them to the curtains, as we always have.

March 12, 1868

Her body suffers, but her mind, I pray, is at ease. The paroxysms are a horror to see. She, who never fought, never shouted, bridling against the pain while her throat flings out unintelligible sounds. Only ether brings her peace. For the rest of us there is no relief, for muting her pain blots out the last fragments that are recognizable as Beth.

Each time I moisten a handkerchief with ether, I hold the cloth to the bottle a little longer. Will she die of her own volition, or will one of the ever-strengthening doses coax her into a sleep she does not have the strength to wake from? I wonder if we would even know the difference.

March 13, 1868

Death would be a kindness now. Even Jo cannot deny it any longer. How long must Beth wait, and we with her? Her body, which for so long has seemed so frail, now evinces the cruelest tenacity. I hate to think that it is holding her captive, preferring to imagine she has already fled. All we can do is care for this body, this vessel that held our Beth.

March 14, 1868

It has ended.

I do not know what called to me to leave my bed and settle onto hers. Whether Beth needed me, or I needed her, I could not say.

All we have done is wait, at once stretched forward and drawing back from the inevitable moment when her pain would cease and ours would surge. Perhaps neither of us could endure balancing on that precipice any longer. I wanted only to be with her again, without gauging her every breath. Slipping my arm beneath her shoulders, I drew her to me so that her head laid on my breast. Her eyes opened and she recognized where she was.

If all my other memories fade, I pray that I may be allowed to keep that one. The look in her eyes then—I cannot describe it. It was wordless, and deserves to remain so. To think of it now, it is much more a feeling suspended within my whole self than a picture confined to my brain. Somehow her entire essence was communicated in that single gaze.

Beth sighed, and that was all. Soon afterward, she was gone. I do not know just when. Jo, who had memorized every cadence of her sister's inhales and exhales, knew it before I did. My eyes never left Beth's; I realized it only when she did not blink. Somehow I failed to hear her breaths cease.

When I broke my gaze to look to Jo for confirmation, I saw that her attention was not on Beth at all, but just above her. The air there seemed to have softened. Even in the darkness the change was apparent. I can only compare it to the difference between satin and velvet. As we watched it blurred like a passing mist. Then all was clear. Gone. She entered this world through me, and through me she left it.

All that remained in the room was the sound of Jo's grief. For many long minutes Beth's empty eyes held me transfixed. Despite the knowledge that Jo needed me more than her sister did, I could not bring myself to end my last true moment of communion with Beth.

When the first spasm of her sorrow had passed, Jo eased Beth's eyes closed with the tips of her fingers and lay herself down beside us. For a time we held her, cradled between those who loved her best. Neither Jo nor I could bear to let her go long enough to summon Amos or Hannah. They came with the dawn and joined our circle. Amos at my side, Hannah at Jo's. The tranquility of it—all of us together, loving her.

With every new daughter I marveled at the love my heart could contain. Now I wonder at how much pain I must make room for. It is an ache that seems to thrust me aside, pouring in and radiating out all at once. My heart will not shatter; I fear it may burst open instead, and hang in my chest like a tattered banner.

I wanted her to venture out into the world, and that she could not do. Perhaps all along she was mustering her courage to lead us into the next world. When we arrive, I have no doubt that Beth will have heaven all swept and tidied for us, looking like home.

Later

The body is strangely heavy without the lightness of the soul. That was my one thought as Jo and I prepared Beth for her coffin. All this time she spent wasting away, and now she feels dense and leaden. It has been so long since I have seen her in a dress instead of a night-gown, her hair done up in curls. Meg did that for her, curled her hair into perfect ringlets to frame her face.

My greatest ache as we stood around her bier was not for Beth's absence, but for Amy's. Our Family has not been together in eighteen months, and now we shall never be again.

March 15, 1868

We have left Beth's coffin closed all day, while friends and Amos's congregants come with their condolences. She did so hate to be looked at, and she had changed so much in the last days, that it did not seem right to do otherwise. In the evening, when all but the Family had gone, I lifted the lid so that we might take our separate turns with her. Mr. Laurence has sent an ocean of flowers—roses, lilies, and orchids fit for a society bride. I have not the heart to tell him that none of his hothouse beauties are right for our modest Beth.

Birte Hummel brought my greatest comfort. When I saw her, my grief seemed to cry out.

"I wanted to bring you something you love," she said, "so I have brought you two words. *Mütter*, you know already. In German, we say we are *verwaiste Mütter*. It means orphaned mothers." She had written it down in her beautiful handwriting.

Liebe Margaret,
  Wir sind jetzt verwaiste Mütter.

In Sympathie,
Birte

My heart did not break or shatter. It crumbled.

Among the sea of mourners only Aunt March looked right, all in black as usual. It was the oddest kind of reassurance; for a moment, one inconsequential thing felt exactly as it should. It was like a breath of air. The way Aunt March took my hand, I can only call it an embrace. She did not speak. Reflecting on it now, I do not think she could. She, too, is a verwaiste Mütter. I have always known it, without ever realizing that holding her grief at bay is what has rendered her so impermeable. There was nothing pinched about her today. Her chin, though it could not be said to tremble, gave two small lurches in quick succession, and I understood how difficult it had been for her to come, and how necessary. I clapped my hand around hers and brought it to my lips. Her eyes filled as I put a single kiss to her knuckles, then closed. How her cheeks remained dry, I cannot comprehend. That woman has learned to weep without shedding tears. There was a surge in her grip, a little rattle of strength passing from her to me, and then she broke away. I could not have endured the rest of the day without her.

March 16, 1868

The hardest thing I have done is to lay Joanna beside Beth and close the coffin lid over them both. I would rather bury Beth's piano than the most beloved of her brood of invalids. Had I asked, had I told her what that doll would mean to me after she was gone, Beth would have told me to keep her. Of that I have no doubt. But Beth asked for so little, I would not deny her this.

Last night I brought Joanna into bed with me, like a child. Her face is scratched and smudged, her left leg held on precariously with a bit of twine, the right missing entirely. Beth loved her most because she needed it most. That was what Beth did, her whole life long. Her dolls, her kittens, her Jo. Mr. Laurence. Even her battered old piano, for all it frustrated her, she could not bring herself to hate.

For almost twenty-five years, I have envied women who lost children later than I. I had not fully realized how much more they buried than I did when we laid Samuel into the ground. Hopes and dreams are weightless things, compared to two decades of memories. Samuel I knew only as an abstraction of a child; his name has come to signify absence. *Beth* means so many things. Tranquility. Contentment. Selflessness. Patience. And now, to my great surprise, courage.

March 17, 1868

This morning I awoke and lay in bed, absolutely emptied of . . . what? Everything. Thoughts, emotions. Nothing spurred me to move. Beth did not need me. Jo did not need me to relieve her after a long night at Beth's side. Amos had already risen.

I don't know how long I lay there. Long enough for the shape of the shadows thrown by the curtains to alter. My eyes were not capable of focusing on anything but the air between myself and the ceiling. From below I heard the sounds of plates on the table and pots on the stove.

Some time afterward came a gentle tapping at the door, and Amos's voice. "Margaret?" he said. Then, more softly, "Peg?"

"I'm here," I answered, not knowing what else to say.

"Hannah has breakfast ready."

With an effort I rose, put on the black dress I must wear for the next six months, and descended to the kitchen. The faces assembled around the table looked like facsimiles of my Family. Almost void of expression. They in turn looked back at me as though I were not fully recognizable. My presence brought them no comfort, I realized. Instead I had done just the opposite, frightening them with my inertia. Today I am not the Margaret, the Marmee, the Peg they know. I hardly recognize myself.

March 19, 1868

For weeks, my every thought and movement has been filtered through the prism of Beth's needs. Now what am I to do?

Emptiness is not what I feel at all, I have realized. Rather, it is as if I have been crammed full of cotton, packed so tightly with blankness that it leaves me immobile.

March 22, 1868

These last three nights, Jo has wakened herself crying. She thinks it is Beth's cries.

Each time I hear her, a feeling very much like relief washes over me. Here is something I can <u>do</u>. If I hurry, I can be beside her before she fully awakens, bracing her against the first wave of disbelief as she remembers, yet again, that Beth is gone. She burrows against me like a child. Head buried in my neck, or diving into my lap to clasp her arms about my waist.

I cannot by any means call this a joy, but each time I see the solace in her eyes, my heart is lifted upward for a moment. In that fleeting instant, I can remember how it felt to be free of this weight of sadness, and I am reassured by the thought that though joy eludes me, it exists.

We say little. There is little to say. It is enough to link our sorrow. Doing so balances one against the other. My grief may be fathoms deeper, but I have been immersed in this ocean before. Jo's tides are so new and tumultuous, and she is so inclined to flail against them. Together we empty ourselves of tears and rage, so that we may sleep peacefully again.

"Promise me, Jo, that you will close my eyes at the end, as you closed Beth's," I told her last night. She made no sound. I felt only the movement of her chin against my belly as she nodded assent. "There is no one in the world more like me than you, Jo," I said fiercely. "I thank God you are here with me."

The two of us are so different from Amos, who seems quite at home in his sorrow. He bears it meekly, without any sign of struggle. I cannot wish his grief were heavier. But I do. I <u>do</u>. I want him to need me the way Jo does. For the first time in memory his calm presence infuriates me. How can he surrender Beth without a fight, without resistance?

I know the answer as well as I know my husband. Amos's is the gift of turning his gaze forward without the encumbrance of the past. Never have I known him to dwell on what should have been. Every day he is in his study before I rise, and every night he is asleep before I put aside my sewing and climb the stairs.

I am not angry with him, only at his ability to accept Beth's death as if it is all in the natural order of things. Amos will grow in spirit and in faith, while I feel myself shrinking.

March 23, 1868

A child wearing a pair of Beth's mittens passed by the house today. I cannot say that I recognized the mittens, nor the child, but the look of sadness that overtook the boy's face as he saw and understood the crepe draped over the front door spoke for itself. How strangely comforting it is to know that people I have never met nevertheless share my grief.

March 24, 1868

When Samuel died, it seemed so natural to lay his small casket into the ground beside his grandmother in Boston. Though I knew I would not be able to visit their graves as often as I'd wish, the thought of my son forever resting next to Marmee gave me greater comfort. Now that Beth is gone, I wish Samuel were here in Concord. Marmee has Father beside her now. Beth has no one.

March 28, 1868

Sometimes I think I could bear it if I could only have Amy here. My baby, my pretty little pet. My arms ache for her more than Beth, for I know she is still in this world, only out of my reach. The house is so hollow with three of my four girls away. One just down the lane, one across the sea, and one on the other side of eternity.

In Amy's place I cling to Daisy, smothering her so that she squirms free to romp with Demi. The love between those sweetlings is so deeply rooted that watching them together hurts as much as it heals. They are not quite two years old and suddenly I cannot evade the thought that on some far-off day, one of them will have to grieve the other.

Only Amos has the equanimity to answer their questions about where Auntie Beth has gone without succumbing to tears.

March 29, 1868

A postcard of La Scala arrived today for Beth from Mr. Laurence. Amos took it to the cemetery, to lay upon her grave.

I worry for Mr. Laurence. Beth was a kind of bandage to his sorest wounds. With her gone, they may bleed again. I wish I had thought to clip a lock of her hair for him.

April 3, 1868

This morning I found Jo seated at Beth's piano, stroking the edges of the keys with the tips of her fingers. It made me think of the way I touched Amos's things while he was at war—wanting to feel his presence but fearful of rubbing it away forever. All of us feel it. Hannah has not even washed Beth's bed linens and nightdresses. Now that the scent of ether has left the room, the fabric smells of her again. I wish there was some way to preserve it. That, and the sound of her voice.

My poor Jo. She has lost her darling and has no one to provide the kind of solace that John and the babies bring to Meg. Amy, thank heaven, has Laurie to console her. But here on this side of the Atlantic, Jo is left alone in the world.

"Write," I told her, not knowing what else to say. It would do her good to melt into one of her vortexes and leave this world behind.

She shook her head with a far-off look, saying she had no heart for it. I ought to have remembered that Beth was always her muse. Jo never could write only for herself. Nevertheless, I think she is wrong. Jo is nothing <u>but</u> heart, these days. It is her fire that she lacks— something I have never seen her without.

"Write something for us," I told her, "and never mind the rest of the world."

April 14, 1868

A month without Beth.

A month, and still I feel like a tree with a wedge hacked out of its trunk. Sliced to the core and ready to fall at the slightest breeze. And yet I find that I am stronger than I want to be just now. I should like to fall, to give way entirely and let nothing but the bare ground hold me, and I cannot. No matter how I sway in the gusts of my grief, I do no more than creak and splinter.

I think of Aunt March often now. It has never before come into my consciousness that everything she has objected to in our lives has been something she feared would cause us harm. Hannah, the Fugitive Slave Act, Amos going to war. All these years, her fear has disguised and disfigured her love for us.

April 29, 1868

I cannot stay at home. Four and a half more months of sitting quietly within these walls in my mourning dress and they will have to put me into the ground beside Beth.

Amos finds his way through meditation. Stillness has never suited me, least of all in times like this. When Samuel died and I was confined to bed for the two weeks that followed his birth, I thought I might die of it. Not the grief alone, but the inertia that accompanied it. I could not mark his birth as a birth, nor his death as a death. All the rituals of welcome and farewell were skewed by the simultaneity of his arrival and departure.

When I am still, I am submerged in sorrow. Especially in this house. So much of what I knew as home was infused with Beth's presence. Now that she is gone, the house feels like a stage set for a play, with props and pasteboard backdrops standing in for all that has been left wooden and lifeless without her warm touch.

Hope, and keep busy, I have always said. But what am I to hope for now? The thing I have pinned my hopes to all those long months is lost. In its absence there is nothing else for me but work. I cannot put my grief aside, but I would rather strap it to my back and carry it with me than be swept away by its currents. Tomorrow, I shall return to the relief rooms.

April 30, 1868

It was a mistake. Safe in the sanctuary of our home, I did not realize how fragile I am yet.

I was overwhelmed the moment I stepped through the door. The people and the activity swarmed my senses so that my mind, my very skin, seemed to buzz. Thankfully, my eyes alighted almost immediately on Isobel Carter. Our gazes met, and the way her face changed at the sight of me told me that she recognized my distress. I went to her, feeling as if I were swimming toward a little patch of shore.

"May I work with you today, Mrs. Carter?"

She answered as though we were reading from an old script, this time with the roles reversed.

"Certainly, Mrs. March. I shall be glad for another pair of hands."

She was a refuge, placing herself between me and the bustle of the place. My mind would not stay fixed to any but the simplest of tasks. She read off the grocery orders, and I placed the items, one by one, into the crates and baskets that were put before me. Even that I could manage for only two hours.

I am lost. If I cannot hope and I cannot work, what am I to do?

May 2, 1868

All I seem to be capable of anymore is holding Daisy.

Meg hardly knows what to say to me. The way she looks at me when I arrive on her doorstep in my thinly disguised desperation almost makes it worse. Now that she has children of her own she understands my grief almost as well as Birte does, and it frightens her, I think. Nothing but the grace of God stands between her and this pain.

Daisy, too, is troubled by my sadness. I hold her too tightly, dribbling salty tears onto her curls instead of rocking her merrily to the rhythm of the nursery rhymes and songs she has come to expect from me. Nor does Demi know what to make of me. He regards my smothering of his sister with a mixture of envy and wariness.

May 3, 1868

I found myself knocking on Birte Hummel's door early this morning. I wanted the solace I had not been able to find in the relief rooms.

Ada answered the door. A big girl of twelve now—older than Karl was that Christmas morning when he came begging for milk.

I tried to tell Birte what it had been like when Beth died. I did not have the English words, much less the German ones. Yet she understood nearly at once.

"Geborgenheit," she said. The term defies translation, she insists, even for one with a full command of both our languages. It is a jigsaw puzzle of a word, an amalgam of deeply experienced feelings: love and comfort, warmth and peace, honesty and trust. Tenderness. Calm. One by one she gave me these pieces of its meaning until there were enough for me to fit together into an image.

I had to close my eyes as it swept over me again. "Geborgenheit," I whispered. And I wept as I had not wept before. Birte laid her hand over mine. When my tears did not abate, she moved to crouch beside me, placing her palm in the center of my back. Her hand had the soothing warmth of a candle flame. The new word flickered softly in my mind: *Geborgenheit.*

"I'm sorry," I said when the tide finally passed, worried my outburst might have upset the children. I ought to have known better—they have seen as much grief in a single year as I have in the last decade.

"Nein," Birte said. "Wir sind jetzt verwaiste Mütter. We understand each other's pain."

It is true. She gives me something Amos cannot, something I lacked when Samuel died. It was as though we had each lost a limb, but for me it was my right arm, for Amos, his left. He had never experienced Samuel as a living thing, never felt him flutter and squirm, grow and hiccough, and so Amos's grief was more abstract than mine. He could carry on despite the brutality of the pain, while I was left not only wounded, but struggling to accomplish the most basic undertakings. Once I was finally permitted to leave my bed I found that I could hardly follow a recipe or compose a letter.

Without Hannah, I don't know what I would have done. She saw how much I craved something to do yet lacked the concentration to do it. That was when she sat me down and taught me to make broomstick lace. The task was so small and the stitches so simple that I learned them in fifteen minutes' time and had the comfort of work again. During the final days of every one of my confinements that followed, I busied myself with lacemaking. It has been years since I indulged in fancywork.

I wish now that I had been a greater support to Birte when Minna and Greta died. I was so wrapped up in my fury with Harriet Weddleton, so determined to cure the practical ills that plagued the family, that I lost sight of the fact that she was mourning. We only fix what can be repaired, after all. I could not resurrect her children, but I could find her a job, and rent.

May 11, 1868

Last night as I came in to bed, I found Amos lying facing the ceiling, eyes shut, moving only to lift his handkerchief to his cheeks. "Amos?" I asked.

He shook his head. Unable to speak, or unwilling, I could not tell. Another tear seeped from the corners of his eyes to trickle onto the pillowcase. A feeble throb of anger tried to pulse to life within me and just as quickly fell back defeated. Let him have his grief in whatever form it takes, I counseled myself. There is no sense in forcing his sorrow into a shape to match my own, after all.

Not until I doused the lamp and climbed into bed beside him did he make a sound. What had been a silent lament became a low wail.

"Amos," I said again, feeling in the dark for his hand. "Please. Tell me."

"The music has gone from this house," he said. "We have not sung together at night since Beth died."

Quicksand seemed to fill my chest, a watery sensation leaving me with no footing even as I lay in bed. For he was right. It is so. "I have not wanted to hear our voices without hers," I confessed. The thought of only three voices—mine, Amos's, and Jo's—where there should be four if not six is more than I have allowed myself to imagine. "Next time Meg and John come," I promised.

May 14, 1868

We sang this evening, with Meg and John, and Hannah, too. I had half hoped that some transformation would occur, that the sound of Beth's piano and the words of Beth's favorite songs would become the magical thread to knit our wounds. No such fairy tale played out in the parlor tonight.

Though it did not hurt as deeply as I feared, there was no real pleasure in it for me. I shall do it to honor Beth, and to comfort Amos.

May 17, 1868

Today I asked Hannah to sit with me in the parlor and make broomstick lace. I feel nearer to Beth in her fireplace corner than I do in the cemetery. The ground may hold her body, but this house holds her spirit.

How Hannah goes on with her daily tasks, I cannot fathom. Every day since Beth left school, her work has been accompanied by Beth's music, Beth's voice, Beth's presence. Were I to do the arithmetic, I suspect I would find that Hannah spent more hours in Beth's company than I did.

I understand, now, what Beth's piano playing meant to Mr.

Laurence. There are tunes enough that I could play for myself, but it is not the same. The way Beth played a song, the way her fingers touched the keys, was as unique to her as her handwriting.

I have been wrong all these years to equate Beth's contentment with surrender. Contentment need not be a gentle form of giving up. That is what I learned from Beth. It has not made me crave less of the world, but more accepting of those, like Beth, who find all they need within a small sphere. What I saw as narrowness and stricture was, in reality, depth. She loved few things, and loved them deeply: her dolls, her kittens, her music, and her Family.

Everyone does not need what I need.

May 29, 1868

It is better for a time if I do not write. Sitting at my desk each night and measuring the weight of my grief, to see whether it has grown or diminished, does me no good. To think of this as a battle for territory that can be measured at all is foolish.

Always I have savored this time to reflect upon myself. But it is possible to peer too deeply for too long. The reflection before me now feels distorted. For now I must only live, without examination.

June 26, 1868

Beth's birthday. She ought to have been twenty years old today.

June 30, 1868

A new story from Jo. She said she had no heart to write, and yet this story is nothing but heart. The restraint of it is astonishing, coming from Jo. Before, her tales were all flash and dash—blood and thunder, she called them. This is permeated with softness. More happens within these characters than happens to them, and yet the emotion is drawn in a few delicate strokes.

She has left room for her readers' hearts to enter the story, to bring their own feelings into this warm and gentle world she has made.

Beth's world. That is what Jo has done. It is the world as seen through the prism of Beth. Each time I read this story—and I have read it three times already—I immerse myself in a tiny sphere that feels familiar and undisturbed, a place suffused with Beth's presence, though she is not among its characters.

Write something for us, I told Jo. Nothing like this had entered my mind when I said it, and nothing could be more perfect. Until today, I had not been conscious of any abating of my grief. But now it seems as though I can feel the thinnest of needles pulling closed one single stitch in my heart. The first in three and a half months. There must be no fewer than ten thousand more to bind the wound, but I am comforted to know at least that such a thing as a stitch is possible.

July 9, 1868

Amy and Laurie. I must say it again and again. Amy and Laurie. After all these years of Jo and Laurie, Amy and Laurie are engaged! The way I feel, it is as if someone has picked up the world and given it the gentlest of shakes. Amy and Laurie have collided, just as my own emotions collided upon reading the news. This is the happiest I have felt in the better part of a year, and still I cannot summon all the joy this felicitous turn of events deserves.

Jo is not the least bit perturbed by Amy's announcement, only as pleasantly dazed by this revelation as the rest of us. The whole lot of us keep looking up from our newspapers and knitting to exchange half smiles and incredulous shakes of the head.

How I wish I could have been there to see Amy and Laurie rediscover each other.

He could have anyone or anything he wants, and all he wants is me, Amy writes. What am I to make of that, I wonder?

"I should hope she thinks of herself as more than a prize," I said to Amos.

"She is a prize," he replied. "For any man, rich or poor." Amos is not prone to mischief, and yet now and then he teases so slyly that I am fooled every time.

"Of course she is," I said a little hotly. "And so is Laurie, for that matter. But that is not all they are." Out crept Amos's smile, and I knew I had been hoodwinked. Only a man with the cool serenity of a millpond would dare to play with the fire of my temper and come away unscathed. I lowered my brow and pursed my lips in a mockery of the expression I so often used to subdue the children when they were naughty. He only chuckled softly and settled his head back into the crook of his wingback. "Amy and Laurie," he mused.

"What would Beth think of this, do you suppose?" I asked.

"Beth was always one to rejoice at anyone's happiness."

I nodded, determined not to reach for my handkerchief yet again. For most of my life, *was* has been such an innocuous word. Now its power over me is untrammeled. I am so tired of crying. It seems a dreadful thing to say, for Beth is worthy of every tear. Even when this reservoir of sorrow has emptied, I shall mourn her until my dying day. I wish only that I could live my life without grief's intrusions. How long will it take to remember simply how it felt to have Beth among us, without the pain of loss trespassing upon the dearest of my thoughts and memories?

July 17, 1868

Daisy and Demi are two years old today. What a mercy that God has granted them a year of near-perfect health. There is no greater gift than that upon this earth.

August 9, 1868

A note from Aunt March:

Dear Margaret,

I confess, I have learned to miss seeing you hurry right past my parlor window each morning, bustling off to repair the world.

Grief takes time. It cannot be rushed. This I know. I also know that given the scantest opportunity, grief will steal time. I pray that it will not take from you what it has taken from me.

Yours in Christ,
Bess March

September 14, 1868

Six months to the day after Beth's death, I have returned to the relief rooms. The welcome I received was most heartening. Mrs. King, Mrs. Carter, and all the rest—I have missed them. Beth's absence has been so all-encompassing, I did not know how much I also missed the society of others.

The work I found more tiring than invigorating, like an exercise to long-neglected muscles, though it is not so much my body that is fatigued. When I returned home, Amos and Jo and Hannah all seemed brighter. My first thought was that the weight of my grief has been pinning them down these last months, that my absence brought them some long-overdue relief. For an hour I lost myself in a stew of regret, not understanding that I was only half correct.

When I lifted my eyes after Amos finished blessing our supper, I found my husband gazing at me. "It does me good to see you out doing good again," he said, and smiled. From every side of the table came a nod of agreement.

Tomorrow, I shall go back again.

November 28, 1868 ✑

Amy. Oh, my Amy. To hold her again set me to weeping as I have not wept since Beth died.

Thank goodness I did not have Daisy or Demi in my lap when she came gliding up Meg's front walk. I sprang up so fast my grandbabies would have tumbled to the floor as soon as I heard her call out, "Marmee!" Her voice plucked a string in my heart that has been silent for two years. Something deep in my depths recognized that vibration before my mind could register her voice, and I had flung open the door faster than Meg could rise from her armchair.

Amy has changed completely, and not at all. The beauty and charm that has been part and parcel of her since the moment she opened her eyes remains almost untouched. It has only deepened. No more does she put on airs. The dignity and refinement she has always craved come not from her fashionable clothes and coiffure, but from her carriage and poise. She has become the Amy she always wanted to be.

There we stood in Meg's little foyer, locked in one another's arms, laughing and sobbing so that we could hardly breathe. It has been far too long since any of my handkerchiefs have been soaked with joy.

Demi demanded to know why everyone was crying, which necessitated explanations and introductions to Auntie Amy.

"Did you come from where Auntie Beth went?" Daisy asked. Meg and I were stricken, but Amy answered with as little hesitation as if Daisy had asked for a drink of milk.

"No, darling," she said, kneeling down before the child. Her voice was as tender as it was direct. "Auntie Beth went up into the clouds, to be with God. I came from across the sea."

And just like that, my own baby girl became a woman in my eyes. Perfectly satisfied, Daisy and Demi both began pelting her with questions about her dress, her hat, her rings. Her rings, indeed!

On her right hand is her beloved turquoise. The left now bears an elegant gold band engraved with asters and ivy—love and fidelity twined together. (It was Laurie, not Amy, who told me that she had drawn the design for the jeweler to copy.) And that is how we learned that Amy and Laurie are not only engaged, but married. Married!

To see the two of them together is a revelation. They might have been carved from the same piece of wood, they suit each other so well. Has it always been there, right before our eyes? *He could have anyone or anything he wants, and all he wants is me,* Amy wrote of him. Until she stood before me with her husband on her arm, I did not understand. There has never been a shortage of love in Amy's life, but always it was an equal portion, carefully shared between her sisters. Now, she is not only cherished, but <u>chosen</u>. That has made all the difference.

Laurie is as much changed and unchanged as Amy—himself, but more fully so. There used to be a sort of breathlessness about him as he shadowed Jo, like a dog begging for scraps. That puppyish quality is gone now. In its place is a self-assuredness that runs from his shoulders straight to the soles of his feet. Has this man always been hidden inside the boy we all thought we knew so well? Or is it only the boy after all, having finally sated himself with the love he, too, has craved for so long? With Amy at his side he is radiant with happiness, perfectly radiant. I have never used that word in regard to a man before, but there is no better one for him.

He and I grasped each other by the forearms, the better to stand back and appraise the alterations these two years have wrought. His eyes passed over all the places my sorrow has lodged. A twitch of his jaw betrayed his failed effort to speak of Beth.

"I shall always be grateful you were there for Amy when . . ." I had thought I could say it, but my throat snuffed out my voice.

"So shall I, Mother," he said. "I have always wanted to call you that," he added, his smile gone watery.

"And I have wished I could call you son from the moment you came through the back door with two armloads of flowers for our Christmas table," I returned. "I've never forgotten how hungry you looked."

"I was. And I have never been since."

Oh, what an afternoon we had! For the first time in months, the house felt full again. Seeing my girls together at last pulls my heart in two directions at once. No matter how tightly they embrace, I shall always see the empty space between Jo and Amy. The place where Beth should be.

I saw Mr. Laurence's glance falling upon Beth's places, too—the hearth corner, the piano keys. In seven years, he has managed to love her nearly as much as our Family did in nineteen.

For a long while I have considered him family without ever saying so. Now it is official, tied with the bond of Amy and Laurie's marriage. There is no word for our relationship—grandfather-in-law, perhaps? I shall have to ask Birte if the Germans have invented a term for it.

"Margaret!" he said in a tone of utmost gladness when he arrived, and held his arms wide as if he were my own father.

I felt as though I'd been christened. "James," I returned. And then with a little gasp, I ran to the kitchen and plucked an item from the windowsill that I had hitherto been unable to move. Just a jelly jar half filled with murky water. A few green leaves draped over the lip, and a pale and spidery root dangled in the water.

"What is this?" James asked when I held it out to him. He had the look of a father whose child has just presented him with an indecipherable drawing.

"Beth always kept a pansy slip in the house over the winter," I explained, almost breathless from the suddenness with which the idea had come to me. "I thought you would like to have it in your conservatory."

His hands tightened gently around it, cradling it as if it were a newborn kitten. "Heart's-ease," he said in a whisper.

"Beth never knew either of her own grandfathers—" I began, and could not finish. He closed his eyes, took a breath. Then another. When he opened them again, he said no more. A thin smile and a squeeze of my hand conveyed it all.

He and Jo clicked together like a key in a lock, though who was the latter and who the former, I am not entirely sure. Perhaps they may anchor each other, as Beth anchored each of them.

Lost in my reveries as I was, I did not hear the knock at the door. Next thing I knew, there stood Jo with a stranger. Or should I say, there stood the <u>old</u> Jo, the one with a spark in place of sadness. "Father, Mother, this is my friend, Professor Bhaer," she said. Such simple words, but said with a flourish in her voice that has been too long absent. If not for the transformation he had so suddenly wrought in Jo, I might have been tempted to resent his intrusion into our reunion.

"Guten Tag, Herr Bhaer," I said, "und willkommen."

At the sound of his native tongue his face metamorphosed from an almost apologetic apprehension to childlike delight. "Sie sprechen Deutsch?"

I explained to him—or attempted to, my German being woefully underused—that I have been an informal student of the language for six years. The way he leaned forward, anticipating every word and nodding a silent congratulations with each one, revealed him to be a most enthusiastic teacher.

Scarcely have I known a kinder man. He radiates warmth and cheer, so that sitting beside him I feel as though I am toasting myself before a hearth fire. His age melts away when he speaks of his nephews; the thought of them lights him up as though they are his boon playmates rather than his wards. No wonder Jo has grown so fond of him, he is so boyish. Daisy and Demi climbed all over him and picked his pockets, which turned out to be filled with chocolate drops.

It seems Jo has finally found a mind equal to hers outside of these walls, for Herr Bhaer conversed most ably with Amos and John on one topic after another. Laurie could hardly decide who to gaze at, his bride or his childhood darling. The same dilemma took hold of me, for as much as I have longed for Amy in the months since Beth's passing, watching Jo's faltering spirits suddenly illuminate lifted my own heart high enough to bump my collarbone.

I suspect only a German portmanteau would suffice to describe

Herr Bhaer's reaction when I handed him a volume of Goethe and asked him to read a few poems aloud in his own language, it was such an amalgamation of pride, happiness, surprise, and eagerness.

"But will the others not be left out?" he asked.

"We are content in one another's company," I said, looking at all the faces around me, which shone in agreement, "and a kind voice transcends language."

"It does one good from time to time, to float upon rhythm and rhyme without pondering the depths of meaning," Amos added.

Herr Bhaer was moved. You could see it, how his chest expanded as he absorbed this sentiment, and how his smile seemed to deepen. We did just as Amos said, following the curving cadence of the professor's voice as he imbued the words with pride and adoration of his country's great man of letters.

And then we sang, as we always used to do. With Amy and Laurie and James and the professor added to our chorus, the silence where Beth's voice ought to have been no longer seemed big enough to fill the room. Amy sang "Come, Ye Disconsolate" for Beth, and her voice touched every surface of the hollowed-out places within me.

Each minute of this day has been a pleasure, I thought to myself as I wound up the clock. How very long it has been since I was able to say that.

November 29, 1868

I cannot get enough of the feel of Amy in my arms. This morning I took her onto my lap as though she were no older than Daisy and Demi. What balm, to wrap my arms around her waist and lean my head upon her shoulder. She is not Beth. There will never be another Beth in this world. But she is Amy, and she is <u>here</u>.

We went to the cemetery this morning, Amy and I. A bouquet of white roses—no less than three dozen—lay upon Beth's grave, tied with a lavender ribbon. From James, of course. Before we turned to go, I pulled one stem loose and laid it upon the marker of Aunt March's little girl.

Later

Today was Amos and Jo's shared birthday. For the first time since March, we truly felt like celebrating. To feel happiness and sadness together is something for which I have a newfound gratitude. The wistfulness that comes over me when thoughts of Beth drift by, this is something I can acquiesce to, something I can imagine permeating my life.

My only regret is that I did not think last night to invite Professor Bhaer to the festivities before he returned to his lodgings. I have an inkling that his presence around the table and at the fireside might have been as much a gift to Jo as anything we gave to her wrapped up in tissue and ribbons.

December 2, 1868

Laurie and Amy came to me today, bubbling over with plans—plans for which they intend to enlist my help.

They looked so exuberant, so bursting with news when they asked to speak to me, that before they had spoken I had already indulged in a vision of what my next grandchild might look like.

"Mother," Laurie began, and my heart gave a little twirl in my chest to hear him call me by that name again. What came next was so outside of my expectations that he and Amy had spoken for half a minute before the words began to organize themselves into a shape I could grasp.

All of it amounted to three simple words: *Charity. Benevolence. Philanthropy.*

They propose to use Laurie's wealth not for themselves, but for the benefit of others—and not out-and-out beggars, Laurie insisted, but those who manage to quietly scrape along, subjugating their talents and education for the sake of food and shelter when they could be doing greater good in the world.

"People like our Family," I interrupted as soon as I understood. "And John Brooke."

He looked a mite abashed to have it put so plainly, as if I would be embarrassed or ashamed to have myself counted among his intended beneficiaries.

And Amy! "Ambitious girls" are to be her special protégées, most especially those with a talent for drawing. Amy, who has reached toward luxury since the moment her fat little fists could perceive the difference between linen and satin, and who before the age of seventeen hardly spent more than a few minutes each week thinking of anyone but herself.

"Marmee," she said, "I have not seen you so stupefied since the Christmas Father was at war." I opened my mouth and shook my head, for she was entirely correct.

That alone would have been sufficient to make my pride swell up big as the moon and bright as the sun. And then, to my unending gratitude, Laurie asked, "Mother, will you join our endeavor?"

Join them! The invitation lifted me from my chair to grasp their hands. I felt as if I were made of an entirely different substance, something bright and shining. I did not answer—I simply beamed at them.

As they explained, my mind and body thrummed in concert as if each word were a tuning fork. For all who suffer for lack of necessities, there are very few willing to stretch out an empty hand and ask that it be filled. My task shall be twofold: to ferret out those who are secretly in need, and to contrive ways to meet those needs without sacrificing their self-respect and dignity.

"No one in Concord has a keener eye for what people are lacking than you, Marmee," Amy said.

"And none gives more fully," Laurie added, "whether that need be tangible or intangible." Oh, his smile—a smile that stretched back across seven years to the boy he used to be.

What could I do but embrace them again and again? To have a role in this myself, to be given work to do that equals the heights of my own aspirations is a prospect I had all but given up hope of ever attaining.

The possibilities—the opportunities! When have I ever felt so rich? I shall tell you: never.

December 8, 1868

The professor has been here nearly every day thus far this month. It is not only Jo who looks forward to his visits. Indeed, Jo has him to herself only when they go out walking, for the whole Family relishes his company. A more cynical mind than mine might suspect him of trying to woo us all to get to Jo, but only a person who has never met the man could conceive of such a thought.

The sheer improbability of Jo, Laurie, and the professor chatting congenially around the dining table long after dessert has been served and the tea gone cold cannot be calculated. Nevertheless, that is just what happened this evening. (Laurie looked as though he wanted to beg Amos to crack his Bible open and unite the two in marriage right then and there. Laurie, for heaven's sake!)

If I am not mistaken, Professor Bhaer is as kindly disposed toward all of us as we are to him. He has generously given over whole hours to demystifying some of the finer points of German grammar which have thus far eluded my grasp. Amos engages him in lengthy discussions of philosophy. Even Daisy and Demi, who at first regarded him as little more than a candy dispenser, have come to enjoy the Bearman, as they call him, as much as his chocolate drops.

And Jo, of course. She is different with him, and yet so very much herself that it makes me wonder if we have ever seen the true Jo before.

I don't believe I have seen her so purely happy—fairly twittering about like a bird—since before the war.

There are moments, though, that give me pause. Jo has a way of looking at the professor with such a sweet yearning that it puts me in mind of how Beth gazed at all of us when we gathered round her bed in those last weeks. *Here is something I love, yet cannot have,* Jo's face seems to say. Jo and her father have little in common, but these last few days as I watch her glide about the house I am somehow reminded of Amos, who, smitten though he was, could not persuade his mouth to form the words to ask for my hand in marriage.

Whatever can it be that holds Jo back? It is perfectly apparent that Professor Bhaer would love nothing more than permission to openly adore her. The rising warmth in his voice betrays it every time he speaks to her, or even <u>of</u> her. The light in his eyes shines all the more softly when they fall upon her.

Jo and the professor are somehow more than friends and less than lovers, neither of them sure where to let their affection settle. Whether there is some obstacle in the way, or a gap that has yet to be bridged, I cannot say for certain.

Whatever it is, if it is within my power to open the way for them, I shall do so.

December 12, 1868

This afternoon after Jo and Hannah had excused themselves from lunch, Amos reached into his waistcoat pocket and drew out a small white envelope. "This also arrived in the post today," he said, handing it to me.

The note contained just one line—*May I request the honor of a private interview with you and Mrs. March tomorrow after Sunday services?*—over a signature that read *Prof. Friedrich Bhaer.* I felt a flutter of excitement such as I have not felt since Meg confessed to me that she was pregnant. "You told him yes, I hope?" I asked.

"Of course," Amos said, placid as ever.

"And you will tell him yes tomorrow?"

"Has my wife become clairvoyant?" he asked with a lift of an eye-brow.

"No more than you, Amos March," I returned. "Surely you won't pretend to wonder what this is about?"

"I will not pretend to be certain. Only hopeful," he conceded.

Who is capable of greater understatement than my husband? I shall hardly sleep tonight for wondering what might transpire tomorrow. Professor Bhaer may be a treasure, but I know my Jo. All her life she has stoutly refused to entertain the idea of hitching herself to a man's yoke like a beast of burden. But if the burden were to be equally and amiably shared between husband and wife, what then?

December 13, 1868

My heart is so full tonight, it does not know whether to sink or float. Amos may be content to surrender all to Providence, but after our meeting with Professor Bhaer I find myself left with much to ponder.

I expected the professor to be nervous, but the solemnity with which he greeted us took me by surprise. His expression was more suited to an undertaker than a man in love.

"For a long time I have thought about what to say this afternoon," he began. He paused to look at his clasped hands as if they held his courage, then took a great breath and continued. "There is a question I would like to have your permission to ask Miss Josephine."

A hummingbird's wings could not have beat faster than my pulse just then as delight and foreboding warred for possession of my emotions.

"But first it seems to me that I should find out whether this question ought to be posed to her at all," he continued. "That is, if it is a question she would like to hear. And so please allow me to ask this first." For all it seemed that he had pondered in advance what to say, he hesitated, perhaps still unsure that he had in fact chosen the correct words. "Does your daughter . . . has she ever expressed . . . a desire for matrimony?"

The hope and anxiety with which he asked this question wrung my heart. For what could I tell him but the truth? "I have never known her to," I said, sorry for every word.

A mournful nod. "I have been much concerned that perhaps this was the case. Even as a child I could not bear to keep a Glüwürmchen—a firefly—trapped inside a jar for my own pleasure. So it is with Miss Josephine. I would not like to ask her to be my wife if doing so would mean that I must sacrifice the gift of her friendship," the professor explained. "My wish is to spend my life alongside her, in whatever capacity she will permit. Her companionship is worth far more to me than—than ardor or passion," he added with a faint coloring of his cheeks. That is when I knew Friedrich Bhaer to be the perfect match for Jo, if such a thing can be said to exist. His kindness, his intelligence, his depth of feeling. And most of all, his complete understanding not only of Jo's quicksilver nature, but of her deepest merits as a human being.

The room felt so heavy, it would not have surprised me if our mutual disappointment had caved in the floor. And then Amos spoke.

"My dear?" he asked, turning to me as if he had uttered not a single sentence, but delivered a monograph on the dilemma before us. He might well have done so. In twenty-six years I have learned to read the lines and contours of his countenance as clearly as his handwriting. A wisp of hope dared to tantalize me.

"Of course," I answered, baffling the poor professor, who looked from one to the other of us as if we were speaking in Portuguese instead of scraps of English.

"Some feelings change with time. Others do not," Amos told him. "Only time will reveal the map of Jo's heart. But should you ever find yourself moved to risk asking Jo for her hand, you shall be doing so with our blessing."

The veil of formality dropped, and Professor Bhaer's face seemed to burst open like a firecracker. "Danke schoen," he exclaimed, reaching out to shake both of Amos's hands, and then mine, and then Amos's again. "Oh, I thank you so very much!"

The prospect of the professor remaining at Jo's side whether or not she will consent to marry is one I had not considered, and it consoles me. I only pray we have not given him false hope.

December 15, 1868

For two days, there has been no sign of Professor Bhaer. I am as confounded as Jo. He floated away on a tide of optimism after our conference, and has not been seen in all of Concord since. His room at the lodging house has been vacated. Nothing could be more unlike him. Surely he knows how hurtful a sudden disappearance would be not only to Jo, but to all of us. That very fact alone gives me hope that he will return.

Last night in bed I cried, thinking of Jo and her kind professor. I could not help it. They are so marvelously suited for each other. The puzzle of what keeps them from pledging their hearts to each other gives me no rest. Even Jo's lifelong allegiance to her freedom seems a paltry excuse in light of her evident affinity for the professor.

This is not as it was with Laurie. Every one of us can see that Jo is happier in Professor Bhaer's presence than she is anywhere else in the world, with the possible exception of her garret.

Later

I have the answer, if only it is not too late. It came to me when I remembered Jo's lament about Laurie, and how his love for her had changed instead of deepening.

That is the root of it—the inevitable shift from friendship to ardor. All her life long, everything from flirtation to lust has baffled Jo, as if it is a flavor she cannot taste.

There is a look that passes between a husband and wife that speaks of their most intimate pleasures. Even Meg, in all her modesty, cannot always keep it from straying across her cheeks at some invisible signal from John. It is a look I have never seen so much as hinted at between Jo and Friedrich. There has been none of the blushing and averting of gazes that accompanied Meg and John's courtship and engagement. It is simply absent from Jo and Friedrich's affection toward one another. I choose that word—*absent*—after much deliberation, for it seems to me that neither of them suffers from this want of passion. In its place they have the seeds of something so strong and deeply rooted that I do not believe Amos and I began to cultivate it for ourselves until the second decade of our union.

Devotion. That is the unwavering core of Jo's love. Her heart is not ruled nor even swayed by fire, but by great depths and currents only the ocean itself can equal. In that she is like Amos, only more so. Intimacy of the heart and mind has always eclipsed that of the body.

The task before me now is to guide Jo toward understanding that the love she and Friedrich share need not match that of any other couple on earth, so long as it serves and nourishes <u>their</u> partnership.

At my disposal I have a single sentence. Something, whether instinct or the hand of Providence, I shall never know, sent me to page through Jo's ill-fated novel. And there before me lay the gentlest weapon I could hope to wield. The words are Jo's own: *Friendship is love's twin.* In the story, she bent the meaning to fit what everyone expects from a love triangle: that to marry for friendship rather than passion is a recipe for woe and regret. But lifted from their fictional backdrop the words themselves ring so true to Jo, I do not know how I missed their significance before. Reading them tonight, my mind began to vibrate with understanding. I tore a page straight from my diary and wrote a note, which I then slipped under Jo's bedroom door:

Dearest Jo,

Tonight as I paged through your novel, my eyes lingered long upon one line in particular: "Friendship is love's twin." However did you grasp such a fine truth at such a tender age, and express it so succinctly?

Ofttimes I have mused that the happiest and most enduring of human pairings are rooted in friendship rather than in ardor. Such has surely been the case for your father and me, for we fell in love first with each other's minds; everything else we needed followed in its own time.

We have spoken over the years of my "plans" and wishes for my daughters. Here is the final iteration of mine for you: If ever you find a friendship such as I have found with your father, I pray that you will clasp it with both hands and never let go.

Ever your loving Marmee

December 16, 1868

Not a word about my note passed between us this morning, but there was a new quality to Jo's dejection, a contradictory mixture of hope and despair that hurt my heart even as it lifted. She has realized that she wants Professor Bhaer at her side, that much I was sure of.

How I wanted to tell her all that he had laid bare to Amos and me on Sunday! But he had done so in confidence, and I had no right to break that trust. Besides, his unannounced departure has left me as confused as Jo. My mind has insisted on concocting stories to explain his absence these last three days, none of them with happy endings.

All I want for Jo now is to have what <u>she</u> most wants, in whatever form it may take, I thought to myself as I watched her trudge down the garden path toward town.

Not an hour later Jo was back, drenched and grinning, with her dear, dear professor on her arm.

The minute they came through the door, I knew. There was no

mistaking it. The very glow of their happiness made the raindrops sparkle on their faces.

He has asked, and Jo has consented to marry him. After a lifetime of refusing to entertain the thought of marriage. In all honesty, I do not know that she desires it now—at least not in the way most women do. What I do know is that she loves Friedrich Bhaer. Plainly. Simply. Whether she is <u>in</u> love with him, I cannot say. There is a giddiness about her, though. If I were to guess, I would wager that it comes from realizing that everything she loves most in the world is hers for the asking.

If there are more contented souls than I upon this earth tonight, I cannot envy them. As I sit recording all that has happened, it feels at last as though every one of us has found their proper place in the world. Even Beth, in a way. I shall never resign myself to the shortness of her life, but the knowledge that we steeped her in all the love she could contain in those final weeks is a consolation I shall hold close to my heart until its last beat.

Every one of my girls shall live out her days as Beth did—in households rich with love.

December 25, 1868

Looking from one face to the other around the table tonight, I felt like a queen upon her throne. What a bounteous kingdom Amos and I have been given charge over. Even Beth's empty chair, with all of the memories it signifies, has come to betoken a peculiar kind of richness.

As I sat reveling in the sight of my Family, an absurd question burrowed into the folds of my mind and lodged stubbornly there: Which of my girls am I most proud of? It is rather like asking which of my four limbs is most essential. Each of them has blossomed into a woman that embodies one of my fondest aspirations.

Meg, who has fashioned a nest for her own dear little Family that is every bit as warm and happy as ours.

Jo, for being all that she is, for allowing every facet of herself to shine in its own way.

Beth. Oh, my darling Beth. For her invisible, invincible courage.

And Amy. Generous, generous Amy, who has cleaved to her heart the lessons I had all but given up teaching her.

The four of them together form a kaleidoscope of womanhood in all its various colors and patterns. Truly, Amos and I have raised a matchless crop of daughters. Not only that, but their capacity for love has more than doubled the breadth of our Family circle. First Laurie and James. Then John, and with him and Daisy and Demi. And now Friedrich. Each time we open our arms to embrace another into our fold, I wonder how we were ever satisfied with a smaller circle. Life without any of them would be incomplete.

Am I not the richest woman alive? All that I desire has settled comfortably within the sphere of my existence. And now, thanks to Laurie and Amy's abundance, I once again have the luxury of helping to spread the material blessings of this world more equally among my fellow-beings.

And yet . . . It is audacious of me to even write, but if I could ask God to grant me but one more wish, it would be for the ability to share the gift of our Family's warmth and gladness with all whose hearts hunger for such vital sustenance. Then would my happiness be truly boundless.

AUTHOR'S NOTE

In the autumn of 1868, Louisa May Alcott put into her mother's hands a copy of *Little Women*, the book that would immerse generations to come in the singular warmth and affection of the March family.

Abigail May Alcott, the inspiration for Marmee, was the unequivocal core of both the Alcott and March families. There was no one Louisa May Alcott cherished more; indeed, many of her stories and novels were written with the express hope of providing her mother with the financial security, leisure, and luxury which had been sorely lacking in the Alcott household during Louisa's childhood.

Louisa was not alone in her adoration. Abigail's husband wrote of his wife as "a heroine in her ways, and with a deep experience, all tested and awaiting her daughter's pen." But even Louisa May Alcott's usually dauntless pen did not do full justice to her mother in the guise of Margaret March. At least two motives, one personal and the other practical, likely affected her portrayal of Marmee:

- Both of Louisa's parents' faults and eccentricities would be minimized during their metamorphosis into Mr. and Mrs. March—so much so that her famously unconventional father became barely more than an off-stage presence.

• Although *Little Women* was praised for its lively and lifelike por-
trayals of the March sisters, nineteenth-century parents still expected to find a good deal of old-fashioned propriety between the
covers of children's novels. (Under the guise of her alter ego, Jo
March, Louisa May Alcott once expressed her frustration with being relegated to a position as "a literary nursery-maid who provides
moral pap for the young.") The character of Marmee thus bears the
brunt of those expectations, cloaking Abigail May Alcott's foibles
and her radically progressive views alike behind a façade of spotless
rectitude and self-control.

The real Marmee, on the other hand, was a volatile and outspoken
woman with a temper whose heat was second only to the warmth of
her love for her Family—which she did, in fact, spell with a capital *F*.
She was a staunch abolitionist, a zealous advocate for the poor, and
an early proponent of women's suffrage. And so as biographer Harriet
Reisen put it, the character of Marmee is Abigail May Alcott "but
with the edges smoothed." My task as I have seen it is to gently re-
store the sharpness to at least some of those edges so that the woman
behind Marmee may shine through more brightly than before.

As most fans of *Little Women* are well aware, Louisa May Alcott borrowed freely from her own family history to create the beloved Marches, often altering circumstances to suit her fiction as she
pleased. (For instance, it was Louisa herself who fell dangerously ill
in a Washington, D.C., hospital during the Civil War, prompting her
father to rush to her bedside.) What remained constant despite her
alterations were the family's emotions—the shared joys and sorrows,
but most of all the unbreakable bonds between sisters, parents, and
children that have nourished generations of readers. I have endeavored to follow her lead, adopting and sometimes adapting incidents
from the history of the real-life Alcotts without ever sacrificing the
emotional integrity at the center of the March family.

Here are the most prominent of the loans I have taken from the
Alcotts' history:

- Like my fictional Marmee, Abigail May Alcott suffered a still-birth. Born on April 7, 1839, the "fine boy, full grown, perfectly formed" was her fourth child, placing his birth between that of Beth's and Amy's real-life counterparts. However, the timeline of the March sisters' births is too tight to fit a full-term pregnancy between any of the fictional sisters. Therefore, Samuel Garrison March became Marmee's firstborn.

- Louisa May Alcott's single vague reference to the cause of the Marches' poverty had the ring of coded language to me: "Mr. March lost his property in trying to help an unfortunate friend." That "unfortunate friend," I decided, would be a runaway slave. In fact, the Alcotts did indeed harbor a fugitive slave, known to history only as John, in the winter of 1846–47. Two things led me to alter the date of the fictional John's sojourn with the March family to the winter of 1850–51. First, the recurring reminders in *Little Women* that Meg and Jo remembered their family's former prosperity. According to the story's timeline, Meg would have been two and a half, and Jo only a few weeks old in December of 1846. Second, the Fugitive Slave Act, which levied hefty fines as well as jail time against anyone found guilty of harboring a runaway, seemed to me the perfect backstory for the reversal of the Marches' fortunes. Conveniently for my purposes, this infamous legislation was passed by Congress on September 18, 1850, when Meg and Jo would have been five and four years old, respectively.

- Last of all, the most scrupulous readers of *Little Women* will no doubt notice that I've had the audacity to alter Mr. March's name. In the four March family novels, there is only one fleeting reference to his Christian name—the fact that Jo's eldest son, Rob, is "named for grandpa." My choice of Amos is a nod to Louisa May Alcott's father, Amos Bronson Alcott.

Selected Bibliography

PRIMARY SOURCES

Alcott, Amos Bronson. "Memoir of Abigail [May] Alcott," 1878, *Amos Bronson Alcott papers,* Harvard University, Houghton Library.

BOOKS

Alcott, Louisa May. *Hospital Sketches.* Boston: James Redpath, 1863.

Alcott, Louisa May. *Moods.* Boston: Loring, 1864.

Barton, Cynthia H. *Transcendental Wife: The Life of Abigail May Alcott.* Lanham, MD: University Press of America, 1996.

Bedell, Madelon. *The Alcotts: Biography of a Family.* New York: Clarkson N. Potter, Inc., 1980.

Gowing, Clara. *The Alcotts as I Knew Them.* Boston: C.M. Clark Publishing Company, 1909.

LaPlante, Eve. *Marmee and Louisa: The Untold Story of Louisa May Alcott and Her Mother.* New York: Free Press, 2012.

LaPlante, Eve, ed. *My Heart Is Boundless: Writings of Abigail May Alcott, Louisa's Mother.* New York: Free Press, 2012.

Matteson, John. *Eden's Outcasts: The Story of Louisa May Alcott and Her Father.* New York: W.W. Norton and Company, 2007.

Matteson, John. *The Annotated Little Women.* New York: W.W. Norton and Company, 2016.

Myerson, Joel, Daniel Shealy, and Madeleine B. Stern, eds. *The Journals of Louisa May Alcott.* Boston: Little, Brown, 1989.

Reisen, Harriet, and Nancy Porter. *Louisa May Alcott: The Woman Behind Little Women.* New York: Henry Holt and Company, 2009.

Rioux, Anne Boyd. *Meg, Jo, Beth, Amy: The Story of Little Women and Why It Still Matters.* New York: W.W. Norton and Company, 2018.

Salyer, Sandford Meddick. *Marmee, The Mother of Little Women.* Norman: University of Oklahoma Press, 1949.

Stern, Madeleine B. *Louisa May Alcott.* Norman: University of Oklahoma Press, 1950.

Willis, Frederick L. H. *Alcott Memoirs.* Boston: Richard G. Badger, 1915.

ACKNOWLEDGMENTS

Many thanks to:

Barb Mayes Boustead, for tracking down Washington, D.C., weather reports for November and December 1862.

Christopher Czajka, Kate Heilman, and Belinda Chu, who formed a virtual human chain to Harvard's Houghton Library and photographed Abigail May Alcott's memoir on lunch hours and days off when COVID-19 restrictions thwarted all my best efforts to access it in time.

And my editor, Tessa Woodward, who thought first of Marmee, and then of *me*. If not for her, this book would not have been written.